LEGEND OF THE FIVE RINGS

The realm of Rokugan is a land of samurai, courtiers, and mystics, dragons, magic, and divine beings – a world where honor is stronger than steel.

The Seven Great Clans have defended and served the Emperor of the Emerald Empire for a thousand years, in battle and at the imperial court. While conflict and political intrigue divide the clans, the true threat awaits in the darkness of the Shadowlands, behind the vast Kaiu Wall. There, in the twisted wastelands, an evil corruption endlessly seeks the downfall of the empire.

The rules of Rokugani society are strict. Uphold your honor, lest you lose everything in pursuit of glory.

T0023267

THREE
OATHS

A Daidoji Shin Mystery

JOSH REYNOLDS

First published by Aconyte Books in 2023

ISBN 978 1 83908 231 3

Ebook ISBN 978 1 83908 232 0

Cover art by Shen Fei

Rokugan map by Francesca Baerald

Distributed in North America by Simon & Schuster Inc, New York, USA

Printed in the United States of America

9 8 7 6 5 4 3 2 1

ACONYTE BOOKS

An imprint of Asmodee Entertainment Ltd

Mercury House, Shipstones Business Centre

North Gate, Nottingham NG7 7FN, UK

aconytebooks.com // twitter.com/aconytebooks

Dragon Lands

Unicorn Lands

CITY OF THE
RICH FROG

Lion Lands

Rokugan

CHAPTER ONE
Golden Frog Dojo

Daidoji Shin sighed and snapped open his fan. The humidity was stultifying this late in the day, and the smell of the river was pervasive. The heat made it worse; everything on this side of the river stank of fish and mud.

Shin was slim, handsome, and white-haired, the epitome of a Crane courtier in his finest azure robes. Silk, of course; it made the heat bearable, if only just. His bench creaked beneath him as he tried to find a more comfortable sitting position. Around him, the small crowd gave a subdued cheer as two new contestants entered the sumai circle and fell into the traditional preparatory squat.

The circle, made from partially buried rice-straw bales, sat in front of the dojo proper at the center of the proving ground. The circle was surrounded by students acting as attendants and sumai wrestlers sitting on stools, awaiting their turn.

Hard, wooden benches had been arranged at irregular intervals around the circle, for the exclusive use of the few observers present. Normally, the crowd for a sumai tournament was quite substantial. In this case, however, the tournament was an informal one, and attendance was by special invitation only.

As such the audience was small; barely thirty people in total, counting Shin. Most of them were local merchants, but there were a few higher-ranking individuals scattered throughout. Their servants and bodyguards lounged behind the benches or stood off to the side, talking quietly amongst themselves.

Inside the circle, two large individuals met with a slap of flesh and a crash of bone. Shin winced at the impact. Sumai was, at its heart, a duel of skill and strength – flesh against flesh, rather than steel against steel. He gave his fan a forceful flutter, causing the metal tines to rattle. It did little to help and he folded it shut with another sigh. "Any sign of her?" he murmured to his companion.

Hiramori Kasami grunted. "No." She stood at attention beside his seat, her arms crossed over her chest. She'd forgone full armor – under protest – and wore only robes emblazoned with the Daidoji sigil. But she'd brought her weapons, obviously. Few things short of the kami themselves could part Kasami from the tools of her trade.

A child of the Uebe Marshes, she'd been born a vassal of the Daidoji and trained to serve them in all things. At the moment, that service consisted solely of keeping Shin from suffering the consequences of his own actions. It was not a service she particularly enjoyed, as she was often at pains to remind him, but she performed it admirably. She grunted again and shifted her weight slightly. "We should leave."

"That would be rude, after all the trouble Lady Minami went to in order to invite me." Lady Akodo Minami was the current commander of the Lion garrison that controlled one-third of the City of the Rich Frog. The note she'd sent had been written in a battlefield cipher commonly used by the Akodo. He felt a flutter of satisfaction as he thought of it; Minami had obviously assumed he was clever enough to decipher her message. She was definitely thawing toward him.

"It might be an ambush," Kasami said, watching the match. Shin couldn't tell whether she was enjoying herself, but given that it involved violence, he suspected she was.

"Yes, the Lion are traditionally known for their ambushes."

"They are soldiers," Kasami said, glancing at him. "Soldiers do what they must."

"Yes. And as Lady Minami is a soldier, she must have a very good reason for inviting me to this gathering." He tapped his robes, where the folded note lay concealed. "I don't know about you, but I'm very curious to find out what it is."

"It will mean trouble," Kasami persisted stubbornly.

"Quite possibly. But things were getting a trifle boring, don't you think?"

"No." Kasami paused. "Boring is good."

"So you do agree," Shin said, smiling slightly.

Kasami growled wordlessly and looked away. Shin let his smile fade. Scoring points against Kasami was of limited entertainment value these days. Especially when she was right. It might well be an ambush. A clever ruse, devised by an unknown foe to draw him out.

It was an invigorating thought. He'd never imagined he might have enemies one day; angry husbands, yes... angry wives, also yes, but real enemies? He shivered slightly, delighted. His grandfather had a saying – a man measures his worth in the curses of his enemies. If so, Shin's worth had increased quite a lot in recent days.

Of late, he'd begun to make a name for himself as a solver of puzzles, discreet or otherwise. Thefts, disappearances… even the odd murder. That sort of thing got around. People talked. Other people listened. Then they came to him. It was to be expected.

A wiser man would have stopped. But Shin had come to realize that he quite enjoyed investigating the conundrums that crossed his path. They provided him with an outlet, a way of using his mind for something other than the tedious travails of a courtier's life. The mysteries he investigated had become his whetstone, for the sharpening of his wits. Much as dojos like this one were for the sharpening of a warrior's skills.

There were quite a few dojos in the city. He knew only a few of them by name. Rich Frog Dojo, located on the eastern bank of the river in the Lion district, was the best-known dojo in the city, with an emphasis on the martial teachings of Ikoma. There was also the Silk Frog Dojo, run by the Badger clan, which sat in the Lion District as well.

This one – the Golden Frog, so named because of the gold paint that covered the gates and roof of the dojo – occupied an innocuous side street near the Unicorn district. Despite that, it wasn't run by the Unicorn, but the Kaeru ronin clan.

The Kaeru technically owed no allegiance to anyone save the Imperial Miya family – and that only because the Miya were willing to pay the Kaeru's quite frankly exorbitant asking price. Given the city's tripartite nature – ostensibly split between the Unicorn, the Lion and the Dragon – the Kaeru's position as enforcers of the imperial will made them all the stronger. The other clans jockeyed for the favor of the ronin in a variety of matters; everything from shipping schedules to warehouse expansion.

The Kaeru, for their part, were careful not to abuse this privilege overmuch. Shin found them a pragmatic bunch on the whole. By and large, they were mainly interested in maintaining the status quo and keeping the port open for trade, which suited both he and the Daidoji Trading Council just fine.

He couldn't help but wonder why Minami had chosen this dojo for their meeting, rather than one in the Lion district. Was she trying to avoid prying eyes? If so, why meet in the open at all? The more he thought about it, the more curious he became. Whatever Minami's reasons, they were bound to be interesting, if nothing else.

A bead of sweat rolled down beneath the collar of his robe. He snapped his fan open again as one of the contestants stumbled from the circle in a most ungraceful fashion. The winner raised his arms in victory, and Shin applauded politely. "Luck," Kasami muttered.

Shin glanced at her. "Was it?"

"Obviously. His opponent slipped. They were evenly matched until then." She sneered. "As I said, luck."

"But is luck not a part of any fight?" a rough voice interjected. Kasami stiffened, her expression turning sour. Shin turned to see a louche Ujik, dressed in rough, dark robes bearing the insignia of the Badger, standing nearby. The man's hair was bound up in an informal topknot, and he was unshaven. Like Kasami, he was armed, albeit with one of the curved blades favored by the steppe riders.

"Then," he continued, "I am but a simple nomad, and see these things differently than civilized persons." The nomad smiled and sketched a bow just shy of disrespectful in Shin's direction. "Lord Shin, Gota bid me bring you his greetings. So... greetings."

"Hello, Arban. As always, it is a delight to see you." Shin

gave his fan a desultory twitch, warding off the smell of milk and meat that emanated from the Ujik. He half-suspected that Arban bathed in horse milk, if he bothered to bathe at all.

He rose from his bench, searching for the Ujik's master and caught sight of the broad, sturdy form of Ichiro Gota standing near the ring. Gota caught Shin's gaze and waved a weighty paw in invitation. Shin returned the gesture with his fan and looked at Kasami. "Gota looks like he wants to chat. Keep your eyes peeled for our tardy lioness while I go be social."

Arban looked at Kasami, who was doing her best to ignore him. "Don't worry. I'll keep her company."

Kasami pointed to the other side of the bench without looking at the nomad. "Go sit over there and don't talk to me."

Arban grinned and sat in Shin's vacated spot. "Here'll do me, thank you."

Shin left them to it and ambled toward Gota. The Badger was easily upset and if he'd gone to the trouble of making an official greeting, he might take offense if Shin chose not to reciprocate. As he walked, his eyes strayed to the circle, and the match taking place. Once, his first impulse would have been to see if there were any wagers going. These days, the urge was still there but not the boredom that had been its impetus. He had new vices to indulge in. What were games of chance next to the risk of running a theater? What was reading the faces of your opponents next to matching wits with thieves and murderers?

"I thought that was you, Gota," Shin said as he joined the Badger. "You look well."

"Thinking of becoming a patron of one of the local stables, Crane?" Gota rumbled without preamble. The Badger's stubborn refusal to bend to propriety was one of the reasons Shin liked him. "Gods know some of them need it. Between them, the Lion and the Unicorn gobble up all the decent wrestlers in the city." A nearby wrestler grunted at this and Gota gave him a friendly thump on the shoulder. "No offense."

"It's a tempting thought, but I'm afraid my plate is rather full these days, what with the theater and all." Shin knew that while most sumai stables were attached to a dojo, they were expensive to maintain, even for dojos with clan backing. Private patrons were necessary to keeping a stable well fed and fit for action.

Gota waved this aside. "Nonsense! It's not like you have to do anything really. Just provide a bit of money, and we both know you have plenty of that." The Badger paused. "That said, I am hearing stories that a certain auditor is still prowling about."

Shin frowned. "Lord Kenzō you mean?" Junichi Kenzō was ostensibly an auditor sent by the Daidoji Trading Council to inspect his finances; he was also a spy, looking to report on any shameful activity on Shin's part, presumably to the council, though Shin had a suspicion that the auditor was reporting to his grandfather as well.

Shin had managed to distract Kenzō for a time by unleashing him on the Foxfire Theater's account books, which had been in a less than optimal state when he'd purchased the business. But that hadn't occupied him for long.

"That's the bird," Gota said.

"When you say prowling about, what do you mean exactly?" Shin asked. That Kenzō was still here, months after the fact, was somewhat alarming and he was doing his best not to think about it. If he just ignored the man, the whole mess might blow over. Unless it didn't, in which case he was definitely going to be in trouble.

Gota sniffed. "Word is, he's been talking to anyone and everyone who's had any sort of financial dealings with you.

Threatening them with repercussions from that blasted Trading Council of yours if they refuse to discuss matters with him." He eyed Shin with amused suspicion. "Any idea why that might be?"

"No, though rest assured I will certainly ask him next time I see him."

Gota chuckled and thumped him on the back. "Say no more, Crane. I'm a merchant myself. I know how these things go. You'll get no judgement from me."

Shin cleared his throat. "Yes, well… are you here acting as a patron?" he asked, quickly changing the subject. "Or, you were a wrestler in your youth, as I recall – planning a return to the circle?"

Gota laughed harshly and slapped his ample stomach. It sounded like a drum. "No. My best years are behind me. I'm here for my niece." He indicated a young woman sitting nearby, her full concentration directed toward the match taking place. She was tall and broad, built for battle or the sumai circle. "Fureheshu Reo. Trained her myself. Got a grip like iron and better balance than a cat. She'll go far, if she gets the opportunity."

"Fureheshu," Shin repeated. "Brewers, aren't they?"

Gota glanced at him. "Yes, though most don't know that." Shin smiled. What he meant was that most didn't know that the Badger had more than one family.

"Well, she looks quite imposing, if I do say so. I… ah." He paused as he caught sight of Kasami signaling him. "My apologies, Gota, but I've just remembered why I'm here. Tell your niece I wish her luck."

He strode away quickly, and, following his bodyguard's gestures, saw Lady Minami walking across the proving ground toward the benches, trailed as ever by her own bodyguard,

Yoku. Shin hurried to intercept her. "Lady Minami, you do me a great honor by inviting me here," he called out, even as Yoku stepped between them.

"Lord Shin," Minami replied, in strained greeting. "You came."

"I did. How could I not?" He sketched a low bow, deeper than was strictly warranted, and highly visible given their surroundings. Minami gestured sharply.

"Stop it, Shin," she hissed. "I am trying to be subtle." She gestured to a nearby bench, and he followed her over. In the circle, two wrestlers strained against one another.

"And failing miserably," he said, cheerfully, as they sat. "But do not let it worry you unduly. We all have our weaknesses. Oh look, that fellow has fallen out of the circle. How embarrassing for him." He paused, as a thought occurred to him. "You used my name. No honorific."

"I did," Minami admitted. She grimaced and looked away. "We know each other well enough now, I suppose, that titles are simply a conversational encumbrance."

Shin studied her for a moment, bemused. "Are you saying we're friends?"

"No!"

"Then we're not friends?"

"No," Minami repeated. A gong sounded, signaling the beginning of a new match.

"No, we're not, or…?" he continued, in a teasing tone. Minami glared at him. Shin looked away, snapping open his fan. In the circle, the two wrestlers moved toward one another warily. "Never mind," he said. "Why sully what we have by defining it?"

"I am starting to regret inviting you."

"Speaking of which, why did you?" Out of the corner of his

eye, he saw Kasami take up a position nearby. Yoku shadowed her. The two bodyguards glared at one another. No love lost there, he knew.

Minami was silent for a moment. Then, "What are your thoughts on marriage, Shin?"

Shin affected a look of sadness. "We would be very unhappy, I fear."

Minami pinched the bridge of her nose. "No doubt," she said, in a frosty tone.

Shin pretended not to notice. "Forgive me, but it is something of an odd question. Perhaps if you came to the point?"

"I have a problem."

Shin smiled at her. "There now. Was that so hard?"

Minami looked at him. "You are not making this easy, Shin."

"You're the one avoiding the subject," Shin countered. Conversations with Minami were, at times, akin to a sparring match. "Whose marriage are you talking about? Not yours, I think. Certainly not mine – unless you know something I don't. So, whose?"

Minami sighed. "My cousin's."

Shin frowned. There'd been some gossip of late about a wedding in the Lion quarter, but he'd paid it little attention, given that it wasn't likely that he would be invited. "Your cousin… that would be Akodo Moriko, yes?"

"Yes."

Shin hesitated, attempting to recall what he'd heard about the matter. Something about a delay due to the indisposition of the groom, one Itagawa Mosu. No, not indisposition – death. He looked at Minami. "I'd heard there was some… difficulty with the groom. Something about a shipwreck, I believe."

"Pirates," she said. "Or so he claims."

"He's alive?"

"So he claims," she repeated.

Shin peered at her. "Either he is or is not."

"That is the problem," Minami said, softly. "We do not know which it is."

CHAPTER TWO
Dead Man

Shin stared at Minami. "How can there be any question as to such a thing?" he asked after a moment. "You've met him before, presumably."

"Yes, once," she said, as if admitting to a breach of propriety. "A most unpleasant evening for all concerned." She hesitated. "I came close to killing him."

Shin blinked at the bluntness of the admission. Minami wasn't prone to hyperbole. If she claimed she had been close to murder, then her intended victim was very lucky to still be breathing. "I won't ask why you didn't, as it is obvious. But if you've met this... Mosu, wasn't it? Itagawa Mosu?" At her nod, he continued, "If you've met him, and been driven almost to murder by him, how can you be uncertain as to his identity now?"

Minami hesitated. Then, "His face – it's impossible to recognize him. He claims to have been badly injured during his captivity. His family swear it is him, and my family are eager to believe them. But if we cannot identify him – if there is no proof, beyond his word…" She bowed her head and gripped her knees. "I must be certain."

Shin felt a twinge of pity. Minami was not built for uncertainty. Much like Kasami, she looked at the world through a warrior's eyes. He cleared his throat. "And why do you doubt him? Has he said or done something to arouse concern?"

"No," Minami admitted. "He has been beyond reproach in all things."

"Then why suspect him?"

"Because he has been beyond reproach. Before his… disappearance, he was a worm. A galling, insufferable creature. Always complaining, always pouting. Obnoxious."

Shin was momentarily taken aback by the vehemence of her tone. "Like me, you mean?" he asked. Minami blinked and looked at him.

"No," she said, after a moment. "No, Shin. You are obnoxious, yes. But you are not a worm." She gave a brief smile. "I rather fancy you would have made a quick meal of him then, after the fashion of a Crane. You would have counted him among your favored prey."

Shin grasped her meaning immediately. "He's a courtier, then." That explained some of her dislike. Courtiers were not well respected among the Lion; they were regarded as a distasteful necessity, rather than a useful tool in the clan arsenal. "Do the Lion even have those?" he asked, in a teasing tone. "I thought you people only went to court under protest."

Minami sniffed. "We are as cultured as any great clan, Shin. That we do not flaunt that culture is no reason to doubt its existence." She frowned. "He was a bad match, but both families approved nonetheless. They thought Moriko, my cousin, could… temper him, as befitting an Akodo."

"Change him for the better," Shin supplied. Minami nodded. "Was she up to the challenge?" he asked. Another hesitation – a telling one. It wasn't often he saw Minami uncertain. Normally she was sure-footed, even when making the wrong moves. But she was clearly on unfamiliar ground here. It was no wonder she'd contacted him.

"She was willing to try," Minami said. "It was her duty, as a daughter of the Akodo."

Shin snapped open his fan and gave it a flutter. "And now? Is she still willing to try?"

Minami looked at him. "Why would she not be?"

"Feelings change. People change. For instance, according to you, captivity has done wonders for the would-be groom's personality."

Minami grunted. "No. She is overjoyed to see him. More so, in fact, than she was when they were first introduced."

"Oh?"

"As I said, he is… different. Respectful. Mild of voice and bearing. Courteous, even." She shook her head. "If the Itagawa hadn't spoken for him, I would have sworn it was a different man."

"Have you mentioned these doubts to anyone else?" She looked away. Shin sighed. "Of course. Silly of me to ask. I take it that your suspicions were not welcomed."

"The Itagawa were insulted. They claimed I was trying to prevent the marriage."

"So, you decided to come to me instead. A neutral party." A sensible strategy. And an interesting puzzle. The gong sounded again, signaling a new match and startling him in the process. He saw that one of the contestants was Gota's niece, Reo. The other was a heavyset young man wearing Golden Frog colors.

Both he and Minami paused to watch as the contestants made ready, Minami with evident interest.

Shin studied her from behind his fan, watching her lips part, the slight intake of breath, the widening of the eyes. All familiar signs to a trained observer. He followed her gaze, and saw that it was fixed on Reo. That was interesting. He cleared his throat. "The reason for your invitation has become clear."

Minami didn't reply, seemingly entranced as the young woman rolled her shoulders and cracked her neck before falling into the traditional squat. Shin coughed. Minami appeared to have forgotten his presence entirely. He prodded her with his fan, causing her to jump. "What?" she snapped guiltily.

"Friend of yours?" he teased, indicating Reo.

Minami flushed. "I don't know what you're talking about."

"Of course, how silly of me. Never mind." He fluttered his fan and studied her over its top. "What exactly do you want of me?"

"You like mysteries," Minami said. "This is a mystery. Solve it." Her eyes strayed again to the circle, where the young woman had begun to once more shove her opponent toward the edge of the circle. Unlike the fellow she was grappling with, her face showed little sign of strain or tension. It was as if she were shoving a bale of hay, rather than a living, struggling wrestler.

"And why should I do that?" Shin asked lazily. Carefully. There had to be a reason Minami wanted him involved besides the obvious, and he wanted to know what it was before he made any promises.

"Because I am asking you to," she said. The words sounded as if they pained her.

Shin was silent for a moment, considering. She hadn't

answered his question, but they could come back to that. "Very well. Answer some questions, if you would."

Minami gestured impatiently for him to continue. "Ask," she said, her eyes on the circle once more. Reo had nearly forced her opponent all the way to the edge. He watched them push against one another for a moment, before turning back to Minami.

"First, some context. This marriage... presumably it was meant to strengthen familial bonds between the Akodo and the Itagawa?"

"Yes," Minami said, tearing her gaze from the circle with visible reluctance. "A daughter of our family was to be married to a son of theirs."

Shin nodded. Such marriages were common among the clans. Families like the Itagawa might be vassals, but they had certain rights and privileges which must be upheld. One of those rights was to a dynastic marriage.

From the perspective of the Akodo – or any of the great families – such an arrangement only made sense. The more blood ties there were between vassal and lord, the harder it would be for a rift to develop between the two families.

"You said *was,*" Shin pointed out. "The marriage was called off, then?"

"In all but name," Minami said. Her eyes strayed to the circle once again. "When word reached us last year about the attack on the vessel Mosu was traveling aboard, many gave him up for dead."

"Were you one of them?"

She grimaced, as if embarrassed. "Yes."

"I see. And how did you learn of his survival?"

"The Itagawa informed us, prior to his arrival in the city some days ago." She frowned. "Apparently, they had known of his survival for some months. Why they chose to keep it a secret, I do not know."

"Perhaps they shared your doubts as to his identity," Shin ventured.

"If so, he managed to convince them he was who he claimed to be," Minami said. "As I said, they fully support proceeding with the wedding."

Shin nodded. "Did he happen to explain to them how he managed to escape? Given your description of him, presumably he wasn't actually on the vessel that was attacked by these pirates you mentioned."

Minami shook her head. "He claims that he was taken captive, and that they meant to ransom him."

"He escaped, then?"

Minami nodded. "That is what he says."

Something in her tone caught Shin's attention. "You doubt his account of the affair?"

"I do."

"Why?"

A faint sneer danced across her features. "He was no fighter."

Shin frowned. "One doesn't have to fight to escape. Greed can be as keen as any blade, and bribery is generally approved of in piratical circles. Or so I'm told."

She paused. "He does claim to have secreted coins in the lining of his robes." Her expression made it clear that she thought this preposterous. Shin coughed lightly and her eyes narrowed. "What? What is it?"

Shin proffered his sleeve. Minami stared at him for a moment, and then touched the material. Her eyes widened, and Shin knew that she'd felt the money sewn into the lining of his sleeve. She grunted in surprise and Shin pulled his sleeve back. "It's a common precaution among courtiers of a certain… predisposition, you might say."

"Ones prone to vice and foolishness, you mean."

Shin inclined his head. "Only to be used for emergencies, of course. And depending on the thickness of the robes and their general quality, all but undetectable to the naked eye. Of course, one wonders why the pirates didn't steal his robes as well as everything else."

"He didn't say," Minami growled softly.

Shin peered at her. "Did you ask?"

"Yes."

"And?" Shin pressed, though gently. Minami shook her head and looked away. It was clear she didn't want to discuss it, yet she had invited him along to do that very thing. He was impressed, though he was careful not to let it show on his face.

"He claims to have escaped during a brawl," she said. "He says the pirates turned on one another when they realized his true worth. Some wanted to kill him then and there, while others wanted to ransom him."

"An improbable occurrence, but not impossible," Shin allowed, though privately he doubted that such things occurred outside of pillow books. From what he'd been told about the life of a pirate, it was rather more sedate than that. Threats and extortion? Yes. But unnecessary carnage was frowned upon. "So he escapes, and returns to his family. They presumably verified his identity before informing the Akodo, who decided that the word of the Itagawa was unimpeachable."

"Yes," Minami grunted. "To question them would be to imply that we doubted their competence. Or so they insisted, when I mentioned needing proof of Mosu's identity."

"I see," Shin said. "And the Akodo accepted this... why?" Minami fell silent. Shin waited, but no answer was forthcoming. He decided to change tactics. "A moment ago, I asked you what you expected of me. You didn't answer me."

"I told you I wanted you to solve the mystery," Minami protested.

"And then what?" Shin murmured. "The decision has been made. All parties seem satisfied. What will discovery of fraud do, save make a lot of very important people unhappy?" He snapped his fan shut. "What does it matter to me if your cousin marries an impostor? What does it matter to anyone, really? Both families seem satisfied and Moriko, by your own admission, prefers the new Mosu. So why interfere?"

Minami was silent for long moments. Then, "It matters to me," she said softly. "If he is a fraud, she must know. It is not for anyone else to decide her fate. But she cannot make that decision without the truth."

Shin looked away from her bright gaze. Minami armored herself in the regalia of duty and disdain, and it was rare that he got a glimpse of what lay beneath. That she'd allowed him to see such vulnerability convinced him she was honest in her desire for his help. He took a breath and nodded. "Let me think on it."

"But–" she began. Shin interrupted her with a flick of his fan.

"It is no little thing you ask, Minami. There is much rough water between the Crane and the Lion, and to cross it will be dangerous. For both you and me. If your clan were to learn you'd employed someone to investigate this matter – a Crane, no less – your position might become untenable. And if I were found to be interfering in the business of the Lion, well... I shudder to think what might result. No. Give me time to consider the matter."

Minami frowned, but nodded. "You are right, of course. I wasn't thinking."

Shin chuckled and stood. "You should know by now, dear Minami, that I am always right. Expect a response tonight." He looked down at her, and then at the circle, where Reo had spread her arms in victory. "She is quite pretty, you know."

Minami jolted in her seat and scowled up at him. "Shut up."

"My apologies. But, one last question, if I might..."

Minami gave him a suspicious look. "Go ahead..."

"Why here?"

She blinked in surprise. "I have been tasked with organizing the... festivities, for the wedding. I am supposed to be looking for wrestlers for a tournament to be held at the Rich Frog Dojo, in honor of the newlyweds. Moriko is quite the fan of sumai. I have never seen the appeal myself." But she was watching Reo as she said it.

"Ah, that explains it," Shin said. Such a role was a high honor in most clans, though he didn't say as much. Doubtless Minami didn't regard it that way. She probably thought of it as a form of punishment. Then, given the way she was looking at Reo, maybe not.

Minami turned away. "Go away now, Shin."

Shin smiled and bowed. "Of course. I shall let you know my answer tonight."

CHAPTER THREE
Gossip

"Tonight? You're not giving yourself much time, Shin." Iuchi Konomi put her book aside and smiled. "A matter such as this requires some thought, I believe."

"I don't know what you mean." Shin closed his own book with a sigh and turned to his guest. "Have you ever read Hida Chiyo's *A Year on the Wall*?"

The two were in Shin's private box in the newly refurbished Foxfire Theater. It was early in the day and the theater was all but empty. On stage, members of the Three Flower Troupe practiced for their next performance, moving through a dizzying array of routines. Practice swords cracked and red-dyed ribbon flurried as the villain collapsed in a heap.

Shin found observing such practices remarkably calming, especially on days like this. His box had become something of a refuge for him in recent days. It was the easiest place from which to conduct his day-to-day business without fear of interruption. It was also much cooler than his home, with the stone foundations of the theater drawing up the chill of the river and dispersing it throughout the building.

"Not that I can recall," Konomi replied. She was, he noted, looking as pleased with herself as ever. Even seated, she was taller than he was, with the sort of figure that inspired awe and dread in equal measure. She reminded him somewhat of Reo in that regard, and he idly wondered whether Konomi had ever given any thought to stepping into a sumai circle.

"You should. Fascinating work. There's a certain blunt poetry to her writing, like a tiger on a leash. Or rather, a crab." He tapped the book against his chest in time to the music rising up from the stage as he took a seat opposite Konomi. He set the book down on his writing desk and smiled. "Thank you for being patient. I've been trying to finish reading it for a week now. It was starting to gnaw at me."

Konomi waved his apology aside with a languid gesture. "Anytime, Shin. I know what it's like. A life of constant interruptions is the burden we must bear as nobles."

"And thank you for meeting me here," Shin added. Like himself, Konomi wasn't one for propriety, or boundaries for that matter. But of late, it seemed as if she'd been at his home more than her own. People were beginning to talk, and in a city like this one, gossip was its own form of currency. Then, perhaps that was her goal. One could never tell with Konomi. Either way, he didn't mind. Gossip was good for his reputation.

"Well, anything to get out and about." Konomi paused, and her expression became calculating. "But we were speaking of your encounter with the Lion. And this ridiculous task you've given yourself."

"Hardly ridiculous. And I haven't agreed to anything yet." He was about to elaborate when one of his servants entered the box, carrying a tray with tea and millet cakes. "Ah, Niko. Punctual as ever."

Niko was the youngest of his household's three servants. She was also a spy, though not a very good one, perchance due to her relative youth. Or the fact she was covering for one of the others – a possibility Shin had considered more than once. She scurried forward, deposited her burden, and hurried out. Shin watched her go and then checked the temperature of the tea. It was warm, but not as much as it ought to have been. "I wonder how long she was listening at the door before she decided to come in?" he murmured idly.

Konomi studied the millet cakes hungrily. "Oh, not long enough to hear anything of value, I should think. Why?"

"I'm fairly certain she's a spy."

"Not one of mine, I assure you," Konomi said, with obvious humor. "From your tone, she must be quite bad at it. Perhaps I should ask one of my people to speak with her."

"And make her better at spying on me, you mean?"

"I hate to see talent go to waste, is all."

Shin tapped the pot. "Niko can barely make tea."

"But she moves well. She is polite and pretty. With some proper training she would be quite the little sneak. Or do you prefer her to be terrible at her job?" Konomi waved aside his reply. "No, no. I understand. It must be exhausting to live in your head, Shin. A spy who is not very good at spying must come as something of a relief to you."

Shin stared at her for a moment, then sighed. "It does, yes. But I see no reason you can't help her, if you wish. I'm sure the Daidoji Trading Council would be grateful to you. Perhaps they'd even send you a gift."

"In the form of money, one hopes."

Shin laughed. "Not likely."

Konomi looked around. "Where's the other one, by the way?

The shifty one with the missing finger. He's usually close to hand."

"Kitano? On an errand," Shin said without elaborating. After speaking with Minami, he'd sent Kitano to look for a woman named Lun – a ship's captain of his acquaintance who owed him a favor or three. If anyone knew anything about the pirate attack Minami had mentioned, it would be Lun. Especially as she was a former pirate herself.

Konomi was not to be deterred. "What sort of errand?"

"Looking for someone," Shin said, with a sigh.

"Or something? A game of dice, perhaps?" The question sounded innocent enough, but the look on Konomi's face was anything but.

Shin paused, his cup of tea halfway to his lips. "Now why would I be looking for a game of dice? I am entirely too busy these days to partake in such vulgar activities."

Konomi snorted. "But you like to know when and where they're taking place, don't you? I heard that your shiftless servant was seen slinking about a certain house of ill repute a few weeks ago, looking to hire the services of a–"

"That was for an investigation," Shin said quickly.

"Was it? And what were you looking for there, I wonder?" Konomi selected a millet cake and took a nibble. "Delicious."

"I'll let Kitano know," Shin said primly. The former gambler had many hidden talents. Making millet cakes was apparently one of them. Konomi raised an eyebrow, but continued to eat. "As to the rest, I was looking for a name, which Kitano found." He paused. "Why are you concerned about such things? You sound like Kasami."

"She and I share a most burdensome task – keeping you alive. She protects your body, but someone must safeguard your reputation."

Shin laughed lightly. "And you've taken that responsibility on yourself, have you?" The thought wasn't an unpleasant one. Konomi had become a friend in the time that he'd known her, and her counsel was always appreciated – if not necessarily heeded. It was why he sought her advice.

Konomi inclined her head. "I am nothing if not generous." She paused. "But you were saying something about not having agreed to anything."

"I haven't decided whether to help her yet," Shin said as he reached for his tea. "I wanted to talk to you first, before I made any plans."

Konomi smiled widely. "Oh Shin, it's wonderful to hear you say that. You've finally realized that I know what's best for you."

Shin nearly choked on a swallow of tea. "Not quite," he wheezed. "I wanted to ask you about the wedding; specifically, about the groom, Itagawa Mosu."

"You mean you wanted to gossip," Konomi said teasingly.

Shin coughed. "Yes, please."

Konomi sighed and arranged her sleeves. "You know, if you paid more attention to what went on around you, you'd be better informed."

"I only pay attention to things that interest me," Shin said.

She batted her eyes in a most unsettling manner. "Does that include me?"

"So far. Itagawa Mosu."

Konomi frowned. "He was dead. Now he's not." She hesitated. "It's quite the story, really. The wedding was originally set for last year, but was delayed when the ship carrying Mosu was attacked by pirates. A fishing boat from a nearby village witnessed the whole thing, apparently. They reported it to the city, but by the time the Kaeru and the Lion got there the ship had been burnt to the water line, and there was no sign of the passengers."

"Passengers – as in more than one?" Minami hadn't mentioned that.

Konomi nodded. "Mosu had servants. A lot of them, by all accounts."

"The pirates took them all for ransom?"

"It happens more than anyone cares to admit," Konomi said.

"But Mosu is the only one who escaped," Shin said.

"Yes." Konomi paused. "Minami suspects something, doesn't she?"

"Whatever gave you that idea?"

"Besides the fact she wanted to speak to you in private? Mosu wears a mempo now, on account of a disfiguring injury. Or so it is claimed." Konomi gestured to her face. "Rumor has it the pirates cut pieces off to send to the Akodo as proof of life."

"What sort of pieces?"

Konomi gave an elegant shrug. "Lips, ears, nose, it depends on who's telling the story really. The only constant is that he was quite handsome, and now, he is not." She leaned forward. "Minami thinks he's a fake."

"Yes," Shin admitted. "Though she seems to be the only one."

Konomi snorted. "I met him once. Briefly. If he is actually dead, well, it's no real loss. He was a vile little man. All poison and innuendo."

"A courtier, you mean."

"No, Shin. Mosu was no Lion, but rather a viper. He caused trouble wherever he went. He was careless of others' secrets, or maybe he simply delighted in making things difficult for his peers."

Shin shook his head in puzzlement. "Knowing the Lion as I

do, I find it hard to believe that no one ever challenged him to a duel."

Konomi's smile was brittle. "From what I've heard, he was an expert at pushing things just far enough to make people unhappy but not far enough to warrant a formal challenge."

Shin flinched inwardly. That sounded unpleasantly familiar. He pushed the thought aside and asked, "What about informal?"

"Ah, well. There are rumors about that as well. Mosu's manservant figures in most of those. An odious creature named Jiro. Your man Kitano probably knows more about him than I do, given that they likely traveled in the same circles."

Shin sat back, a speculative look on his face. He made a note to talk to Kitano later. "Is that so? How intriguing. What else can you tell me about this fellow – or fellows, rather?"

"Not much. Most of what I know about Mosu is secondhand. I know even less about Jiro, other than that he supposedly wasn't unfamiliar with a sword. Though he reportedly preferred knives."

Shin was silent for a time. Then, "Why would the Akodo think a man like Mosu was a good match for one of their daughters?"

Konomi chuckled. "You'd have to ask them. Frankly, I'd love to be a fly on the wall if you do." She paused. "When you do, I mean."

"You assume I'm going to help Minami."

"Of course you are. It would be ridiculous to pretend otherwise, Shin. You are bored, and here is a pretty little mystery for you." Konomi gestured. "It is obvious." She paused. "Dangerous, though. Minami must be desperate to ask you to involve yourself."

"Yes."

"Which is why you're going to help her." Konomi paused.

"I can't imagine how you're going to conduct one of your little investigations. Lion weddings are notorious for being insular affairs. No one outside the clan is invited to the accompanying festivities."

"I've already got a plan in mind."

"Oh? Do tell."

"Not just yet," Shin said. Konomi pouted, but didn't argue the point. Shin paused and studied her. "Tell me what you think. Not facts, but feelings. Why that match?"

Konomi leaned back. "Ah. I can only guess, you know. The Lion is not the Unicorn. We do such things differently."

Shin gestured, accepting this qualification. "Even so."

She selected another cake and broke it in half, offering him a piece. He took it and she said, "Money is the simplest explanation."

Shin raised an eyebrow. "Are the Akodo in need of funds?"

"Not in any way that a layman might notice. But to someone like myself, or your friend Kenzō, it would be obvious." She paused, then smiled slyly. "How is he, by the way? Flown back to the nest yet?"

"You know very well he hasn't," Shin said testily.

"I did warn you."

"Stop changing the subject. The Akodo are in financial difficulties?"

"Minor ones. The boat is not sinking; it merely has a leak. Easily patched by the application of funds. Thus, a marriage is arranged." She gestured with her cake. "As to why Mosu, presumably because the Itagawa offered the best price. They did so because Mosu is a wastrel, and his only value is in the potential heirs lurking in his loins."

"That sounds familiar," Shin muttered. Konomi snorted. Shin

ignored her and continued, "You say the Akodo's difficulties aren't apparent to outsiders... what about those within the clan?"

"You mean the other vassal families?"

"Yes, but not just them. The Matsu, the Kitsu, the Ikoma – they all might have reason to see the Akodo humbled, however slightly."

"Possibly," Konomi said, her tone doubtful. "But to suspect them of attempting to sabotage a wedding in such a manner... that is dangerous thinking, Shin." She looked at him. "You must be careful in this; the way of the courtier is not that of the Lion."

"I have met Lion courtiers," Shin protested.

"But were they truly courtiers, or merely at court?" Konomi shook her head. "Besides which, this is a different field of battle entirely."

"I know." Shin nibbled on his piece of cake and smiled. "I'm rather looking forward to it."

CHAPTER FOUR
Arrangements

Shin leaned over his writing desk and studied the missive before him. Konomi had departed earlier, though not without a final warning. Shin appreciated her concern, but thought it was a trifle overblown. There was danger, true, and her worries weren't completely unfounded. The Lion and Crane had been at each other's throats since the beginnings of the empire. Their repeated clashes, often as bloody as they were unnecessary, had inspired plays, books, songs – puppet shows, even.

But he hadn't been alone in his box for long; only moments ago, Kasami had shown in Ito, one of the trio of merchants whose activities Shin had initially been dispatched to the City of the Rich Frog to oversee. The merchants were the sole interest the Daidoji Trading Council maintained in the city, finding it overcrowded with factions.

Of the three, Ito was the only one whose name he'd bothered to learn and for good reason. Ito had a mind as keen as a well-honed blade hidden behind his guileless smile and eyes and ears that saw and heard everything in the city. Like Konomi, he was a collector of gossip and innuendo; unlike her, he was more than happy to share it free of charge.

Ito waited patiently for Shin to finish what he was working on. He was a short man, stout and as bald as an egg. His merchant's robes were well-made, but lacking utterly in the ostentation that usually marked the servants of the Crane.

At last, Shin set his quill aside. "Thank you for waiting, Ito. I'm finished for the moment, though. We may resume our conversation."

"A letter of some importance then, my lord?"

"Just an invitation. Nothing special." Shin paused. "Ito, have you ever read Hida Chiyo's *A Year on the Wall*?" He tapped the book, where it sat beside him. "You'd find it interesting, I think."

"I am not familiar with that particular work, my lord. What is it about?"

"The Crab, mostly. Never mind. You're not here to talk about my tastes in literature. You are here to tell me how much money I've lost the Crane."

Ito smiled thinly. "I am pleased to say none, my lord. In fact, you have increased revenue substantially with your recent efforts on our behalf." He indicated a small stack of ledgers beside him. Ito wisely kept his own set of books. Shin's own attempts at bookkeeping were lackadaisical at best. While he found the cut and thrust of financial dealings invigorating, the paperwork it inevitably required was stultifying.

"And my investments?" Shin asked.

Ito paused. "The theater eats money like a starving wolf, obviously. But the soy sauce brewery and Captain Lun's shipping venture are both doing better than expected. The brewery in particular is coming along nicely. Nozomi is an artist. Taking care of his money woes has freed him to perfect his recipe." Ito smiled slyly. "I am also given to understand a certain prominent soy merchant is quite unhappy with how well his rival is doing, in fact."

Shin hid a smile. "Is he? How sad. It was not my intention to undercut Master Odoma's business." He slid his metal-tined fan out of his sleeve and snapped it open with a brief flutter. "Be sure to remind me to send him a bottle of Nozomi's finest sauce by way of apology."

Ito bit back a laugh. Odoma had been the previous owner of the theater, and had become quite vociferous in his belief that Shin had somehow cheated him. Shin suspected that Odoma was the reason that Kenzō was investigating his activities. However, of late, the soy merchant had been thankfully quiet. Perhaps he was waiting to see what came of Kenzō's efforts. Shin cleared his throat.

"Onto a different matter. Lady Konomi tells me that representatives of the Crab have been scuttling about, looking for a ready source of paper."

Ito gave a small smile. "Ah. The cloud lifts."

"Eh?"

"The book. I wondered what had provoked your interest in such things."

Shin gave an embarrassed smile. Ito was correct of course, as always. "Yes, well, perhaps we should extend an invitation to them… discreetly, of course. The bad blood between the Crab and the Crane might prevent them from immediately seeing the sense of such a proposal."

Ito grimaced – a brief flicker of expression, quickly banished by the bald man. But Shin saw it, and took note. It was rare that Ito's composure was shaken. "You think that a mistake?" Shin asked thoughtfully.

"No, my lord. It is sensible, as you said." Ito hesitated. Again, unusual. Ito might occasionally make a show of prevarication, but this was real, and thus curious. "But I am not the best person to initiate such contact," he went on. "Though I can find another to do so on your behalf, if you wish."

Shin peered at him. He tapped the book he'd just finished. "You really must read this book, Ito. I desperately wish to discuss it with someone."

"I'm afraid such a work is not to my taste, my lord." Ito paused, and again, something like a shadow passed across his normally placid features. Shin studied him, wondering what the other man wasn't saying. He'd never known Ito to display any prejudice against anyone, regardless of clan or station. But before he could discreetly pry further, he heard the door to his box slide open.

His manservant, Kitano, slunk in. Shin raised his fan, indicating that Kitano was to wait. He looked at Ito. "I'm afraid we must cut this short, Master Ito. But before you go, I'd ask a favor of you."

Ito bowed his head. "Anything, my lord."

"It has come to my attention that the Akodo recently suffered a small financial setback. I would like to know more about that, if possible. Do you think you could...?" Shin left the request hanging. Ito glanced at Kitano and then back at Shin.

"I will keep my ears open, my lord. Word of such matters often carries quickly through the commercial districts." He bowed again and departed, leaving Shin alone with Kitano. Shin gestured to the seat Ito had vacated.

"Sit." A bowl containing spiced rice balls sat by Shin's elbow, and he nudged it toward Kitano as the latter sat. Ito hadn't touched them, having eaten earlier or so he insisted. "So, did you find her?"

"I did, my lord. She's staying at a gambling house just north of the Unicorn wharfs. Do you want me to fetch her?"

"Not just yet." Shin paused. "Have you ever heard the name Itagawa Mosu before?"

Kitano smirked. "Oh yes. He was a fine one."

"Why do you say that?"

"Mosu was in debt up to his ears," Kitano said, scratching his cheek with his prosthetic finger as he eyed the rice balls. "That lunatic Jiro was the only thing standing between him and an army of creditors." He paused. "Worse guard dogs to have, I suppose."

Shin recalled what Konomi had said about Jiro, and asked, "Was this Jiro particularly fearsome, then? I was under the impression he was a servant."

"His parents were wave-people," Kitano said. He speculatively nudged a rice ball with his false finger. "Ronin, both of them. At least that's what I've heard. Jiro knew how to fight, and he wasn't particular about how he won." He paused and looked at Shin. "He sunk more than a few bodies in the river."

"Something you'd know nothing about, of course," Shin said, in a mild tone. He tapped the rim of the bowl. "Niko made them for you."

Kitano had the good grace to look embarrassed, but Shin wasn't sure which comment had elicited the reaction. He coughed and said, "Jiro held off the collectors while Mosu racked up debt. Anyone they couldn't bully... had an accident. Or went missing. Or both, if they were stubborn." He grunted. "You mark me, my lord – the only reason Mosu was never challenged was because it was all too likely that Jiro was the one who'd show up." He hesitated. "Most dangerous person I ever met."

"What about Kasami?" Shin asked, with a smile.

Kitano didn't return the smile. "Begging your pardon, my lord, but I'd be hard-pressed to choose between them, if it came to a fight. I once saw Jiro kill three men in as much time as it took me to draw breath. And with a knife, no less."

Shin sat back. "Not the sort of man I'd imagine pirates would be able to take alive."

Kitano snorted. "I'm surprised he wasn't one of them."

"What do you mean?"

Kitano hesitated. Shin snapped his fingers. "Now is not the time to get reticent, Kitano. Out with it."

Kitano sighed. "Pirates are opportunists, my lord. But they can't just... sit and wait for a ship to come by. They need to know schedules, cargoes, passenger lists. So, every few weeks, someone will slip into the city and pass along some coin in return for information. And not just pirates. Smugglers, too."

"And were you one of those sources of information?"

Kitano looked away. Shin sighed. "The past is the past, Kitano. You have a new life now. And that life belongs to me." He paused. "Leave aside your own sordid doings; was Jiro a participant in this scheme?"

"He was," Kitano said, in something like relief. "It's how he – well, Mosu – paid down some of the debts they'd accrued."

"Mosu," Shin said. He felt something shift, but wasn't sure what it was just yet. "Mosu was involved as well?"

Kitano shrugged again. "That's the rumor."

Shin frowned. It made sense. Jiro wouldn't have had easy access to the sort of information pirates and smugglers might need. But Mosu would've. He wouldn't have been the first nobleman to turn to larcenous means to pay down his debts. It wasn't banditry at least, but it was close. It also added a new wrinkle to things.

Had Mosu really been taken captive? Or was there something else afoot? He considered the question and said, "Could Jiro have orchestrated the attack on the vessel transporting Mosu?"

Kitano frowned. "Why would he do that, my lord?"

"I don't know. But could he have done it is my question."

Kitano nodded slowly. "He was in thick with a few of them. Can't trust those river folk, though. They'll gut you like a fish as soon as pay you, if they think they can get away with it." He tapped his chin. "Though Jiro was likely to think he could handle that sort of thing, if it occurred." He glanced at the rice balls. "Are you sure Niko made them, my lord? Only you told me that last time, and… well."

Shin drew himself up, mildly insulted. "Of course!" Of late, he'd begun to experiment with the culinary arts, learning how to make the perfect millet cakes and rice balls. Only Kitano's palate had failed him, and Shin still wasn't sure how his creations measured up to those of more experienced cooks. He couldn't taste them himself, after all. It wasn't appropriate for an artist to judge their own art.

Fears assuaged, Kitano tucked in greedily. Shin sniffed in annoyance and looked back at the missive he'd been composing. Judging it complete, he sprinkled sand on it to dry the ink and carefully folded it into the shape of a small crane. "When you've finished stuffing your face, I need you to deliver this to Lord Gota's residence. You remember where that is, I expect?" Gota lived in the same part of the city as Shin, closer to the merchant quarter than the noble district. Kitano, mouth full of rice, nodded and reached for the crane. Shin jerked it out of reach. "Finish eating first!"

Shamefaced, Kitano completed his meal and wiped his hands

on his robes. Then and only then did Shin allow him to take the crane. "Thank you. Send in Kasami on your way out, please." He dismissed Kitano with a gesture. A moment later, Kasami entered.

"What?" she asked without preamble. Hardly respectful, but then, she rarely was when it came to him. She knew him too well for that.

"I've just sent an invitation for Lord Gota to meet us on Blue Feather Wharf at dusk," Shin said, referring to his private wharf. It was only a small space, meant for small vessels; he'd purchased it recently, after Konomi had pointed out how much he was spending in docking fees to use the Unicorn wharfs. He'd rationalized it as a cost-cutting measure, but in truth, he just wanted the right to come and go as he pleased.

"Why are we meeting him at the wharf?"

"Because he and his niece will be accompanying us to the Lion district this evening."

Kasami paused. "And why are we going to the Lion district?"

Shin couldn't resist a grin. "We're going to help with a wedding. Isn't that exciting?"

Kasami stared at him. Then, bluntly said, "This is a bad idea. Then, of late, you have had a surfeit of bad ideas."

"Hardly a surfeit," Shin protested.

She indicated their surroundings. "You bought a theater."

"It's turning a profit," Shin said. "Mostly."

"You got involved in Unicorn clan business."

"That was a favor for a friend!"

"You started investigating murders," Kasami continued relentlessly.

"A handful of murders. A sprinkling of murders."

She stared at him, her expression a mask of disappointment.

"And now, now you wish to involve yourself in Lion business. What would your grandfather say?"

"Something hurtful, I'd guess," Shin replied, in an offhand manner. He looked away, his hands clasped behind his back. She'd struck a nerve. He hadn't spoken to his grandfather – to any member of his family – since his arrival in the city. He'd written to them, of course, as was the done thing. Instead of a reply, they'd sent an auditor. "It doesn't matter what he would say. He is not here."

"No. That means the responsibility is mine." Kasami sighed. "Lady Konomi wasn't your only visitor today. Lord Kenzō came by as well. He was most adamant about needing to speak with you. I told him you were otherwise occupied discussing business with Ito."

"How sad that I missed him." Shin turned and looked at her. "Did he mention what he wanted, by chance?"

"No. But whatever it was, it seemed to be of great importance."

"He didn't elaborate, then?"

"No."

"No, of course not. To him, you're nothing more than a bodyguard." Shin pinched the bridge of his nose, annoyed on her behalf. "Never mind. I've sent Kitano to deliver an invitation to Lord Gota and his niece, Reo. They will accompany us to the Lion district."

"I still say that this is a bad idea."

Shin smiled and snapped open his fan. "Yes, well, when has that ever stopped me?"

CHAPTER FIVE
Blue Feather Wharf

Blue Feather Wharf barely qualified for the name. It was more like an overgrown jetty – a forgotten protrusion into the river. A brief stretch of white-washed stone and newly replaced wood, now marked by an ornate arch wrought in the shape of a crane taking flight. Blue flags emblazoned with the Daidoji mon hung sadly in the humid air. It occupied a small tributary of the river, off the beaten path, which suited Shin just fine.

Shin had, through Ito, managed to track down the owner and buy it for a song. Literally. The woman, an elderly widow, hadn't wanted money. She had plenty of that, thanks to her husband's estate. Instead, she'd demanded season tickets to the Foxfire Theater, and use of Shin's private box. Shin had eagerly obliged. It was only later that Konomi had pointed out that Shin had significantly overpaid.

But that was no matter. The Widow Ueno was a convivial guest, with many amusing stories about her husband and their time in the city. She was also somewhat feisty, but that was really Kitano's problem more so than Shin's.

Shin and Kasami arrived discreetly. They'd come on foot,

allowing Shin to enjoy the cooler temperatures of the late afternoon. A few crafts were anchored along the length of the wharf. The vessels were small; local merchants, bringing in wood pulp or charcoal, for the most part. Shin had gladly provided the use of the wharf to those merchants whom Ito had spoken for. In return, they paid a small fee, and were allowed some relief from the higher docking tariffs of the larger wharfs. Shin had even hired guards of a sort, to ensure there was no trouble.

"Good evening, Chobei," Shin said to the older man sitting at the end of the wharf. Chobei looked up and smiled in welcome. He was carefully weaving a fishing net, and, by the look of it, had been for some time.

"Lord Shin. A good evening to you as well." At first glance, Chobei was a short man; stooped and bent by age and a lifetime spent on a fishing boat. In reality, he was quite tall and broad. Indeed, he cut quite the formidable figure, even taking into account his missing hand and eye. Kasami eyed him warily, her hands near her swords, but not on them.

A curious tool was attached to Chobei's ruined forearm – a cross between a hook and a needle. Given how dexterously he was weaving with it, Shin wondered if he missed the hand at all. Part of him hoped not, especially given that Shin had been the one who'd cut it off in the first place.

Shin cleared his throat. "How are Yui and her son?"

"The boy is growing like a reed. He will make a fine fisherman, one day." Chobei smiled slightly as he said it, and Shin felt a flicker of unease. He knew better than anyone that Chobei's family were more than simple fishermen. Beneath their humble exterior lurked the skills of shinobi. They'd nearly killed Shin on several occasions, before Shin had decided the most expedient method of ensuring peace was to hire them himself.

"Is that all he will be?"

Chobei chuckled. "Are we any of us just one thing, my lord?"

"Perhaps not. I'll be heading to the Lion district tonight, with some guests." Shin paused and turned. "Ah, there they are now." Gota approached the wharf, his niece beside him and Arban trailing in their wake. The Ujik paused upon sighting Chobei, but said nothing. Gota threw out his hands in greeting as he drew near.

"When I got your letter, Crane, I thought it was a joke at first," he said, clapping Shin on the shoulders. Shin winced.

"No joke, I assure you. You're doing me a favor, in fact." Shin turned to Reo and Gota extended his hand. The young woman smiled widely as she approached them.

"Lord Shin, may I introduce my niece, Reo," Gota said. "She is still learning the art of the circle, but I expect she will outshine my accomplishments in time."

Reo bowed. "A pleasure to meet you, Lord Shin." She had a breathy voice all at odds with her size. Shin thought it an attractive contrast, and up close he could see why Minami was so obviously taken with the wrestler. She was stocky with muscle, but her features were softly rounded – almost gentle. She and Minami were of an age as well.

"She's been trained by the best," Gota said proudly, as he enveloped Reo in a rib-cracking hug that made Shin wince again, in sympathy this time. "She's even been invited to join a local stable – though I think she should hold out for an offer from Rich Frog Dojo." He directed this last comment at Reo, who flushed pink in embarrassment and pried herself free of her uncle's grip.

"I keep telling you, Uncle, they only invite wrestlers from the Lion to join."

Gota waved this aside. "Nonsense! You just have to impress them. Show them your mettle, girl. That's why we go to competitions, after all."

"Informal competitions, Uncle," Reo said pointedly. "They don't count, especially when it comes to rising through the divisions." She flexed her hands. "All I'm doing is marking time and making bruises."

"Sometimes the informal is more meaningful than the formal," Shin said. "Opportunities are like weeds in a garden. No matter how many you pluck, there are always more the next day."

"Wise words," Gota said in approval. He clapped Shin on the arm, nearly knocking him off his feet. "He is a clever one, Lord Shin. You would do well to take his words to heart, girl." He paused and peered up at Shin. "Speaking of which, this invitation of yours... what's it all about then?" He paused, and added, "I saw you talking to the Lion at the dojo. Did you manage to finagle an invitation to the wedding?"

"In a sense," Shin said. While it was tradition to invite guests from outside the clan for the festivities, the wedding itself would be a private affair. Add to that the Lion's insular nature, and you had less a party and more a formal clan gathering. "Lady Minami is looking for wrestlers for the wedding festivities. That's why she was at the dojo."

"I know. That's why we were there. I was hoping Reo might catch her eye, but... well. No such luck." Gota glanced at his niece, and Shin felt a pang of sympathy as he noted the crestfallen look on the young woman's face. Gota leaned close and murmured, "Reo idolizes Minami. Don't know why, can't see it myself."

"Ah," Shin said noncommittally. Inwardly, he was pleased. Minami had too much integrity to choose someone simply because she was attracted to them. But if that same person were brought by an outside party, she'd have no reason to turn them away. "Well, we'll simply have to rectify matters this evening. I know for a fact that Minami was quite taken with Reo's performance. Rendered speechless, in fact."

Gota frowned. Shin looked at him meaningfully, and Gota grunted as he realized what Shin was getting at. "Oh. That's interesting." He looked at his niece, who was happily chatting with Chobei, watching him weave his net with every sign of interest. "Not married, is she? Minami, I mean."

"No. Reo?"

"No. Been too focused on her training." Gota hesitated. "Why would you do this for her? For us?"

"As I said, you're doing me a favor. I need an excuse to speak to Minami, and if I can do you a good turn in the process, well…" Shin shrugged. "Besides, the look on Minami's face alone will be worth it."

Gota frowned. "A nice story, but you're up to something, aren't you?" he growled, raising a hand to forestall Shin's protest. "Never mind. You are, of course. But I'm not so much a fool as to turn down a good deed."

Pleased, Shin nodded. "I… ah. There we are." He turned as a bell mounted atop one of the mooring posts sounded, interrupting him and indicating the approach of one of the flat-bottomed skiffs that prowled the river. The skiffs were the quickest means of transport across the river, if one didn't want to bother with the bridges, which were invariably crowded, even this late in the day.

The vessel was barely more than a raft, but its pilot – a stringy, rawboned youth dressed like a fisherman – guided it steadily across the choppy waters. He balanced the pole across his shoulders as the skiff bumped against the jetty. "How many today, my lord?" he called up cheerfully. Shin laughed.

"Five, Yoshi. I trust your craft can handle our weight?" Yoshi was young; barely past his fifteenth year, but with the musculature of one born to hard work. The river was a difficult taskmaster, and only the quickest or most durable survived their apprenticeship. Shin had employed his services on several occasions.

Yoshi pursed his lips and gave Gota a speculative look. "That depends on whether the big one has eaten today or not, I think."

Gota flushed at this show of disrespect, but Shin laughed again. "I can always summon one of your competitors…" he began. Yoshi's eyes widened.

"No need for that, my lord," he said quickly. "We'll see you safely across."

"Excellent." Shin gestured for Yoshi to help the others aboard his skiff. "Gota, Reo – if you would." He turned to Kasami. In a low voice, he said, "When we cross the river, keep your eyes and ears open. I don't think anything untoward will occur, but one can never tell."

Kasami frowned. "Where was this common sense earlier?"

"I am always sensible." Shin hesitated. "After my own fashion." He stiffened as he heard someone call his name. Kasami did so as well, and her face settled into a scowl as she saw who it was. "I warned you," she muttered.

Shin ignored her. "Lord Kenzō," he said, in greeting, as the newcomer made his way along the jetty.

Junichi Kenzō was a slim needle of a courtier, with a face like a hatchet and the expression of one who saw life only as a series of disappointments. "Ah, Lord Shin – how lucky that I caught you before you departed," he said.

"For which of us?" Shin asked, not bothering to hide his annoyance. He wondered how Kenzō had known where they were going. Then, the man had been in the city for months; perhaps he'd used some of that time to establish his own spy network. It wouldn't have surprised him. It did bother him, however. Kenzō was too clever by half.

If Kenzō was taken aback by Shin's rudeness, he didn't show it. The auditor merely smiled pleasantly and said, "Myself, of course. I went by your home earlier, but you were not in. Though, I must say, your bodyguard was quite discourteous." He gave Kasami a sidelong glance. "I think you should have a talk with her. It is not done for the bodyguard of a Daidoji to speak so to a representative of the Crane."

"I'll bear that in mind. Now, if you'll excuse me, I have to get across the river and the tide waits for no man, as they say." Shin turned away. More rudeness, but still Kenzō didn't take the hint. He trotted after Shin, hurrying to keep up.

"That is the Lion district, is it not? What business could you have over there?"

Shin quickened his pace. "The private kind, Lord Kenzō." He didn't want to talk to the man; not here, not ever. There would be consequences, of course. But there would be consequences regardless. Kenzō's very presence ensured that.

"Of course, my lord, but we simply must discuss several discrepancies I've discovered in your finances of late," Kenzō said quickly.

Shin stopped, sighed and turned. Kenzō was determined to have it out here and now. He pointed his fan at Kenzō as if it were a blade. "Talk quickly, my lord. Lord Gota isn't the patient sort, and today, neither am I."

Kenzō blinked, as if startled. Perhaps he was. Until now,

Shin had done his best to be polite to the auditor. Or mostly polite. But that time was past. Kenzō had tarried in the city overlong. Shin was beginning to feel as if he were under siege. Kenzō bowed his head. "Perhaps it can wait, at that. For a more appropriate time."

Shin stifled a growl of irritation. Kenzō knew all the courtier's tricks; the tactic of push and delay among them. But two could play that game. Shin took a deep breath and said, "Yes. That would be for the best. I suspect I will be engaged for two or three days, at most. After that, I will happily discuss my finances with you."

Kenzō's face fell. "Two or three...?" He recovered quickly. "That will be fine, my lord. I look forward to speaking with you at your earliest convenience." He folded his hands and stepped back. Shin studied him for a moment. Kenzō normally protested more. That bothered him. But he was careful not to show it. Instead, he gave the auditor a polite nod and turned away. Kasami fell into step beside him.

"He's up to something," she whispered.

Shin smacked his fan into his palm. "I know. The question is – what?"

CHAPTER SIX
Lion's Den

At night, on the river, the city looked as if it were lit by foxfire. For Shin, the soft glow of a thousand lanterns washing across colored stone was a breathtaking sight and one he wouldn't trade for anything. The sounds, too, were unique. The slap of the river against the hulls of boats and mooring posts. The cry of nightbirds, on the hunt for insects. And above it and within it all, the soft susurrus of croaking frogs.

Such was the eternal murmuration of Saibanshoki, the oldest and largest willow tree in Rokugan. Legend had it that an impish frog spirit – the little god of the river junction – made the roots of the great tree its home. Further, some said that the evening song of the frogs was the frog spirit's love song for the spirit said to be contained within the tree. Shin couldn't say whether there was any truth to such a claim, but he hoped it was so. He felt that spirits ought to be able to proclaim their love as openly as mortals did.

As he listened to the chirruping of the frogs, Shin felt a sudden urge to accompany them. His fingers twitched, as if plucking at the strings of his biwa. Annoyed with himself, he reached into his sleeve and drew out his fan, snapping it open. The humidity had lessened somewhat, but the air was still sluggish, with pockets of heat drifting above the water.

"On another case, my lord?" Yoshi asked as he plied his pole, pushing them through the water. He stood at the rear of the craft, nearest to Shin. "Did another rich merchant get stuffed into a barrel of his own rice wine?"

"No, Yoshi," Shin said. "Just a friendly visit."

Yoshi deflated slightly. Then his face took on a sly expression. "That's what you said last time, my lord." Yoshi had an avid interest in Shin's investigations. He wasn't the only one, either. They'd formed something of a club, to hear Yoshi tell it. An informal gathering of youthful rapscallions – ferrymen, fishermen and dockworkers – who pored over the stories of his investigations as if he were a character in a pillow book.

Shin still wasn't quite sure what to make of it. The thought that his comings and goings were being pored over by Yoshi and his fellows was somewhat disconcerting. On the other hand, their devotion had proven useful on a number of recent occasions – especially when he needed someone followed or watched.

Kasami snorted, eliciting a glance from Shin. "You have something to contribute?" he murmured. She looked away without replying. Shin shook his head. Kasami, needless to say, didn't approve of Yoshi and his lot. Or rather, she didn't approve of Shin's encouragement of them. He suspected that to her, it was yet another sign of his eroded morals. Shin sighed and continued to fan himself. He glanced at the others and noted Reo's pensive expression. Recalling what Gota had said, he eased himself toward her. "You look nervous," he said softly. Even so, she jolted in surprise.

"I... yes. A bit, my lord."

"Shin, please." He unfolded his fan and gave it a desultory flick. "Formality is so stifling, don't you think? An artificial barrier, imposed by dullards who want to keep us all as boring as they are."

Reo goggled at him slightly. Then she giggled. An odd sound, coming from a young woman who looked as if she could snap Shin in half like a twig. "I don't know. Being in the circle – it is all formality and ritual," she said softly. "It gives structure to what is otherwise structureless." Her hands clenched and relaxed as she spoke.

"Something to hold onto, in the current of life's river," Shin said.

Reo blinked. "Very poetic, my lord – I mean, Shin."

"Yes. I wish I could claim it, but it came from a book I just finished. By Hida Chiyo. Have you ever read her work?" he asked hopefully. But to his disappointment, Reo shook her head. He sighed. It seemed he was never going to get to discuss Chiyo's work. "Your uncle says you are a great admirer of Lady Minami."

Reo nodded. "She is the youngest person to ever reach the rank of general in the armies of the Lion. She is a swordswoman and an archer without peer." Her voice went soft as she recited a list of Minami's accomplishments, mostly martial. Shin tuned them out, only focusing when it was time to ask a question or when Reo mentioned poetry. He'd been aware that Minami could turn her hand to poetry when she wished, but he hadn't been aware that she made a habit of it – especially given how it had gotten her in trouble the last time.

Nonetheless, the conversation made for a quick trip. Yoshi was an expert at piloting across the rough surface of the river with a minimum of fuss. Shin studied the approach with a critical eye as he listened to Reo. As in so many things, what the Lion lacked in panache they more than made up for in scale.

The Lion district wasn't fronted by wharfs; rather, a defensive wall towered over the entirety of the eastern bank. It dated from a more violent period in the city's history, and the scars it bore – as well as the sunken remnants of blackened wrecks that littered the nearby shallows – were a testament to the ferocity of the fighting between the clans in those days.

The heavy palisade of stone and wood was inset with half a dozen gates, each of which led into a network of canals that extended far inland, past the city limits and to the riverside storage facilities of the Lion. He'd visited one of those facilities, during an earlier investigation, but had seen little of the Lion district itself. He assumed it was much like that of the Unicorn or the Dragonfly, but even so, was curious to see it for himself.

Kasami whistled softly, and Shin looked up. There were archers on the wall, overlooking the water. The Lion took no chances, even in a theoretical time of peace. A bell began to ring somewhere atop the wall, signaling for the nearest gate to open. "The lion's jaws open," Shin murmured as Yoshi poled the skiff toward the rising gate.

"They are expecting us," Gota said. Shin nodded.

"I took the liberty of sending a messenger ahead. Just in case."

A clatter of levers and pulleys sounded as the gate rose from the water, and Yoshi sent his skiff sliding through. The Lion didn't allow any vessel larger than a skiff into the canal network. Merchant vessels were forced to offload their goods onto rafts to make the final leg of their journey downriver.

Past the gate, quays of smooth, pale stone lined the walls of the canal. Beyond them were several large forecourts, where soldiers performed evening exercises. Shin watched the torchlit drills with interest. Though the city had been ostensibly at peace for some time, the Lion maintained a substantial military presence in the city, as did the Unicorn and the Dragonfly. Three armies, staring at one another across the river.

They were met at the quay by a delegation of spearmen. Unlike the first time Shin had visited, their spears weren't leveled. Even so, he didn't immediately step off onto the quay. Instead, he waited until he caught sight of Minami hurrying toward them. She looked anticipatory and annoyed in equal measure. "You came," she said as she motioned for the guards to disperse.

"I told you I would have your answer for you this evening, and so I am here to deliver it." Shin stepped lightly onto the quay, and gestured to Gota and Reo with his fan. "Lord Gota you know already," he said, and Minami frowned. She and Gota had been part of a blackmail case he'd investigated earlier in the year; of course, neither of them liked being reminded of that. "But allow me to introduce his niece, Fureheshu Reo. She is a wrestler of some skill, and I thought she might be a valued addition to the festivities you are planning."

Minami paused, her eyes widening slightly. "L-Lady Reo," she said, bowing her head slightly to the young woman. "I had the privilege of watching your match earlier today. You are indeed quite skilled."

Reo flushed and seemed tongue-tied. Gota cleared his throat. "She is, yes. And she will make a fine addition to the sumai stable at the Rich Frog Dojo."

Minami paused. "I... am certain she will, but I have no say in that."

Shin smoothly interjected himself, hooking Minami's arm like a parochial aunt, and turning her away from the group with a final warning glance at Gota and the others. "I have, of course, decided to lend you my expertise in the matter we discussed. But there are conditions…"

"Of course," Minami growled, eyeing him suspiciously. "Why did you bring them?"

"Mainly as cover – I've decided to become a patron of the martial arts, Reo, specifically, at least for the moment. As a favor to me, you will let her try her skills during the festivities against those of the Ikoma and Akodo. If they think her worthy, you will speak on her behalf to the master of the Rich Frog Dojo."

"What?"

"Further, in return for such a favor you have engaged my services as coordinator of the festivities. I'll see to the decorations, the activities – even the food. I have several recipes I'm dying to try out on the… cultured palates of the Lion."

"What?" Minami hissed again.

Shin gave his fan a flutter. "You heard me. I want to take your burden for myself. You're welcome, by the way."

"You want to organize the wedding? Why?"

Shin snapped his fan shut and tapped his lips. "Oh, several reasons. Bragging rights, boredom, the opportunity to annoy a great many Lions with little fear of repercussion. But mostly because it is the only way I can have complete access to the guests and the happy couple."

"Why do you need access to any of them?" Minami snarled, albeit quietly.

"If you want me to find out what, if anything, the groom is hiding, I have to be in a position to ask questions. More, people must not think it odd that I am asking questions. Thus, I will plan and organize the festivities. Your family will not think it strange; after all, who better to organize a party than a Crane?"

"But it is my responsibility," Minami protested.

"And what does a general do, when they have too many responsibilities?" Shin tapped her chest with his fan. "They delegate, Minami. So, delegate. You have an entire garrison to oversee, after all – and so many worthies attending. Their safety should be your first priority, don't you think?"

Minami swatted his fan away and glared at him. "Are you certain this is the only way?" she demanded.

"If it wasn't, would I suggest it?"

"Yes!"

Shin inclined his head. "Possibly. But really, it solves our problems nicely."

Minami glanced at Gota and his niece. "And you brought… them to – what? Sweeten the poison before I ingested it?"

"In a sense. You can send them away, if you wish…"

Minami stared at Reo for a moment and then released a long, slow breath. "No. It would look odd." She looked at Shin. "Are you absolutely certain that this is the only way?"

"Yes," Shin said, softly. He touched his hand to his chest. "I will not humiliate you, Minami. You can trust me with this." He needed to be close, to better investigate. He also wanted to see more of the Lion district, but that was beside the point.

"I hope so." Minami took another long breath, clearly centering herself for the trials to come. "Fine. I'll make arrangements for your stay. I presume you'll send for your belongings?"

Shin nodded, pleased. "Kitano will be along shortly. And only Reo and I will be staying. I don't imagine Gota will stay longer than it takes to see to the comfort of his niece. And Kasami will be leaving as well. I have an errand for her." He paused. "Though you will need to make sure that she can return without being stopped by overzealous Lion warriors."

Minami nodded slowly. "What sort of errand?"

Shin smiled. "One of utmost importance, I assure you."

CHAPTER SEVEN
Further Arrangements

"Absolutely not," Kasami said, bluntly, when Shin informed her of his plan. Anger thrummed through her at the very suggestion that she would abandon him. Especially here, in the very den of the Crane's foes.

"I will be perfectly fine," Shin said. "I will be protected by an entire garrison of Lion soldiers. What could happen to me?"

"It's the Lion I'm worried about," Kasami said, casting a suspicious glance about her. She was too tense, she knew. She was making the nearby guards nervous. She forced herself to calm down. "They cannot be trusted."

Lady Minami frowned at her words, and her own bodyguard, Yoku, flushed with anger. "He will be safe," Minami said. "I swear it."

Kasami paused, torn between further insulting Minami and making her feelings known. "How?" she asked, her tone skirting the edge of rudeness. She didn't doubt Minami's intentions. Indeed, she respected the other woman, at least insofar as she could respect a member of the Lion. But Yoku was a different matter. She'd had her share of run-ins with the surly bodyguard, and her opinion of him was low.

Minami hesitated. Then, she gestured to Yoku. "Yoku will look after him. I would not assign my own bodyguard to watch a man I wanted dead."

Kasami, who thought that was exactly what one would do in such a situation, refrained from pointing this out. Instead, she watched Yoku's expression as the latter realized what his mistress was proposing. He didn't look happy about the idea. Then, Yoku rarely looked happy at all. "My lady," he began, shooting a glare at Kasami. "I do not think–"

Minami raised her hand, silencing him. "Yoku will guard Lord Shin with his life. This I swear to you. If you cannot take my word for it–"

"I don't want your word for it." Kasami glanced at Yoku. "I want his." Admittedly, she also wanted to see him squirm a little. It wasn't a worthy impulse, but she was angry enough to yield to it regardless. Yoku was everything she despised about the Lion, and anything that caused him discomfort was a pleasing diversion.

Yoku bared his teeth. "You dare question me?" he began, his hand hovering far too close to the hilt of his sword. Yoku made rudeness an artform; the Lion bodyguard had never met a situation he couldn't make worse with a sneer or the wrong words. Social graces seemed to be a foreign concept to him. Or maybe he was simply trying to provoke a confrontation. If so, she was more than happy to respond in kind.

"I dare," she shot back.

Shin intervened before matters could escalate. He tapped Yoku's forearm with his fan. "Of course Yoku will give you his word. Won't you, Yoku?"

Yoku looked down at his arm, and then up at Shin. "Yes," he said grudgingly.

Shin smiled and looked at Kasami. "See? He is quite fierce, after all. No footpad would dare interfere with me, so long as Yoku is my escort."

Kasami hesitated, but finally nodded reluctantly. "Fine. But don't come crying to me if they murder you." Shin looked surprised by her agreement. "Of course, rest assured that when they do, they will answer to me."

"He will not be harmed," Yoku snapped. "I have sworn it."

"And so?" Kasami snarled back. The two of them glared at one another once more, the air between them practically writhing with the promise of violence. Shin snapped his fan open and gave it a flourish, puncturing the tension. They both looked at him, somewhat shamefaced. Kasami felt annoyance at her own behavior.

"Enough," Shin said firmly. "I am growing bored of this. I arranged earlier for Kitano to meet you at the wharf. He'll show you where Lun is. Make sure to send him to me when he's done so. I will require his services while I'm here."

Kasami made as if to protest further, but instead closed her mouth with a snap and turned on her heel, heading back to the skiff. Shin followed after her, to make his goodbyes to Gota, and his assurances that he would look after Reo. She waited impatiently for Gota and Arban to board the skiff, watching as the heavyset man spoke quietly to his niece.

Shin sidled up to her. "You understand, of course, why I need you to find Lun." It wasn't a question. She glanced at him in annoyance. Obviously she knew, otherwise she would have asked.

"Yes."

Shin nodded, pleased, and went on, "Once you find these pirates – if they can be found – you are to question them…"

"I know," she said, through gritted teeth.

"And by question them, I mean talk to them," he finished. He indicated her sword with his fan. "Only talk."

"What if they refuse?"

"Pay them," he said.

She grimaced. "They are probably already dead."

"But if they are not, Lun will almost certainly know where they are." Shin sighed. "I understand your anger, but this is necessary, I assure you. And the quicker you accomplish it, the better." He smiled. "Besides, you would be bored sitting here with me."

"I am supposed to be bored. Boredom is good. It means I am doing my job." She took a deep breath. "I should be used to it by now, I suppose."

Shin tapped her shoulder with his fan. "I will be fine. If I'm not, feel free to take it out of Yoku's hide."

"I will." She looked at him. Then her eyes slid to Yoku, who stiffened at her look. "And not even an army of Lions will stop me."

When they finally departed, she didn't look back. She didn't fear for Shin, not really. It was more a matter of propriety. To send her away showed that he didn't value her presence. Or at least, that was how it felt at times.

She knew it wasn't so; she knew that Shin did value her counsel, as well as the strength of her sword arm. But sometimes it didn't feel that way. She wished she could tell him that, but propriety prevented it. A good bodyguard didn't have feelings.

She settled back on her bench, content to ignore the others until they reached the wharf. Unfortunately, they didn't share her need for silence.

"So," Arban began. Gota's bodyguard shifted toward her on the bench.

"Quiet," Kasami said flatly. She gave the Ujik a warning look. He raised his hands and sat back. She turned away, knowing that he wouldn't take the hint. She was right; a moment later, Arban cleared his throat.

"He'll be fine, you know. He's a clever one, your master."

"Too clever for his own good," she muttered.

Gota laughed. "Yes, that he is." He turned toward her. "But Arban is right. He is clever. If he sent you away, Crane, it's because he knows you're more useful out doing whatever he wants you to be doing than lurking in his shadow." He paused. "Speaking of which… Arban?"

Arban glanced lazily at his master. "Yes, Gota?"

"You will accompany the Crane on her task."

Kasami stiffened. "There is no need for that."

Gota glowered at her. "There is every need. The sooner you are done, the sooner you will be back with Lord Shin. He may not fear for his life, but I worry that his scheme – whatever it is – might endanger my niece. You will look out for her." He indicated Arban. "And Arban will make sure you survive to do it."

Kasami frowned. "Why not just leave him if you're that worried about her?"

"Reo doesn't like me," Arban said with a shrug.

"She is a smart woman," Kasami said. She looked at Gota and inclined her head. "I appreciate the offer, but it isn't necessary."

"I say it is," Gota insisted. "And since I am the lord here, it is settled. Arban will go with you to do… whatever it is you are doing."

"Hunting pirates," Kasami said bluntly. Gota's eyes widened, but after a moment, he laughed and slapped his knee.

"Of course. That makes as much sense as anything that tricky Crane does. Well, I wish you luck." He looked at Arban. "Try not to die."

Arban snorted. "As if any mere pirate could get the best of me." He paused, and craned his neck, looking toward the wharf. "Someone is waiting for us."

Kasami turned, expecting to see Kitano. Instead, she saw the angular form of Lord Kenzō standing on the edge of the jetty, his hands clasped behind his back. He frowned as they docked. "Where is your master?" he demanded, looking down at them.

Kasami ignored him and looked at Chobei as she climbed up. "Why is he still here?"

Chobei shrugged, his attentions on his net. It was coming along nicely, she noted. For a ruthless killer, he was quite adept at making fishing nets. Kasami turned back to Kenzō, who was still glaring at her. "How dare you turn your back on me, woman?" he spluttered. "And where is Lord Shin? Why have you abandoned him?"

Kasami glanced at the auditor, and he retreated quickly. They were both servants of the Crane and vassals of the Daidoji; of equivalent rank, though Kenzō might argue the point. He was an official, after all, and she was but a bodyguard. But in matters relating to Shin, she was the authority. She spotted Kitano sitting nearby, watching the confrontation with undisguised interest. "You," she said, pointing at him.

Kitano hopped to his feet and sauntered over. She spoke first. "Tell me where she is," she demanded, ignoring Kenzō for the moment.

Kitano jerked a thumb over his shoulder. "Close. Two

streets over, in fact. A gambling house called the Yellow Chrysanthemum."

"I know where it is," Arban said, with a nod to Kitano. "I've lost money there a time or two myself." He tapped the hilt of his sword, an unconscious gesture that infuriated Kasami. A samurai knew that a sword was not to be touched, save when violence was implied or imminent. Arban, on the other hand, touched his so often it might as well have been a pet.

Kitano paused. "It's a dive. Lots of unsavory sorts."

Kasami snorted. "You must have felt right at home." She looked at Arban. "You, too." She paused, and then turned her attention back to Kitano. "Arban will show me the way. You are to report to Lord Shin in the Lion district." She gestured to Yoshi and his skiff, waiting. "He claims to have need of your services, though I cannot imagine why."

Kitano nodded, with a sly smile. "Have fun on the boat." He made to move past her, and she caught his arm. He froze, eyes wide.

"Keep your knife close, gambler," she murmured. "Keep him safe. Or I will take the rest of your fingers."

Kitano nodded, and she let him go. He headed for the skiff without a word. She turned to Arban, but before she could speak, Kenzō cleared his throat. "If you're finished, we have much to discuss, I think."

Kasami gave him a cursory look. "Such as?"

Kenzō frowned. "Watch your tone, Hiramori. I am an official representative of the Trading Council."

She let her hand rest atop the hilt of her sword; not gripping it, but a threat nonetheless. "And I am the bodyguard of Daidoji Shin, whose business I am about. Now, you can get out of my way, or accompany me. But I will do as he has charged me."

"Accompany…?" Kenzō began.

"Oh, this is going to be fun," Arban muttered. Kenzō gave him a stern look.

"Is he allowed to talk?"

"No," Kasami said.

"Yes," Arban said. He leaned toward the other man. "You, on the other hand…"

Kasami extended her arm, separating them. "Enough. I have said all I will say. You may come with us, if you wish answers. Or leave. It does not matter to me." She made the offer, hoping – knowing – he would retreat.

Kenzō stared at her, a muscle in his cheek jumping. Restrained anger, or maybe simply frustration. It was hard to tell. Shin would have known. But Kasami lacked his skill at reading faces. She knew when a man was going to draw his sword, or when he was going to run, but not what he was thinking or feeling.

Abruptly, Kenzō nodded. "Yes. I wish to see what is so important that Lord Shin has seen fit to dispatch his bodyguard." His smile was needle thin and sharp as he took in her expression of surprise. "Yes, I will accompany you."

CHAPTER EIGHT
River Keep

Shin found his first real glimpse of the Lion district to be an interesting one. On his previous and sole visit, he'd only been allowed to see the storehouses at the farthest edge of the city limits. Past the high stone walls that segregated the canals from the rest of the district, however, was something wholly different and not a little unexpected.

If he was being honest with himself, he'd assumed that the district would be arranged like a military camp. Instead, it was no different from that of the Unicorn or Dragonfly. A little tidier, perhaps, with regular patrols of soldiers. Lanterns lit every doorway, and the streets were full of sound. He and Reo walked amid an escort column, led by a spearman holding aloft a lantern hooked to the end of his spear. The soft glow illuminated orderly streets and well-maintained buildings.

"You look surprised," Minami said as she noted his expression.

"Forgive me, I am a victim of my own expectations," Shin admitted.

"Yes, that is often the way with you Crane," she said, in a

teasing fashion. Shin looked at her, startled by the flash of humor.

"You seem to be in a better mood."

Minami hastily wiped the smile from her face. "I was merely trying to be friendly."

"Oh, by all means do go on," Shin said. "It's rare I hear anything resembling a joke escape from your lips." He smiled as he said it, and Minami snorted.

"If you must know, I am relieved." She hesitated. "You have… taken a great burden from me, Shin. I will not forget it."

"I hope not. But let us save the thanks for afterwards."

"You know you only have two days before the ceremony is set to take place," she said after a moment. She clearly wished to change the subject.

"I'm aware," Shin said, as he folded his hands into his sleeves. "I do so love a tight schedule. I positively thrive under pressure." He paused. "How much of the preparations had you already finished, by the by?"

Minami's smile was almost cruel. "Very little."

Shin kept smiling. "Then I arrived just in time."

Minami snorted. "You do know what an Akodo wedding entails, I hope."

"Obviously. I spent the afternoon reading up on it. Several days of festivities, as the guests arrive in ascending order of rank, followed by the ceremony–"

"Which you are not invited to," Minami interjected.

Shin pouted in displeasure, but didn't argue the point. "And after the ceremony, a banquet, followed by more festivities as the happy couple takes their leave, followed by the guests, in descending order of rank." He glanced at her. "I'm thinking three days, all told. Two prior, one following. Does that sound right to you?"

Minami frowned. "Yes, though the departures always take a bit longer than estimated, in my experience. And there will be late arrivals, obviously."

"Obviously," Shin agreed. While the guests of lower status would arrive on time, those of higher status would show up aggressively late, in order to discomfit their rivals. At one wedding he'd been to, two boatloads of guests had dropped anchor in the river, each refusing to disembark before the other. The ceremony had been delayed for nearly two days, until his grandfather had stepped in and politely intimated that he would burn both boats to the waterline rather than let the embarrassment continue.

"This is to be expected," Minami went on. "You shouldn't have to worry about it. There are ceremonies in places when such issues arise, and all Akodo know them."

"And who is on the guest list? Who will I be entertaining?"

Minami hesitated. "Everyone."

"Oh, not as many as that, I think."

Minami swallowed nervously. "Representatives of the Itagawa, the Ichime and the Seizuka. And... Akodo Arasou and his betrothed, Matsu Tsuko."

"The Akodo Daimyō?" Shin blurted in surprise. No wonder she'd been nervous – and so eager to hand her responsibilities over. "You could have mentioned that earlier, Minami."

"Would it have made a difference?"

Shin paused. "No. No, it wouldn't have. But still, that is a great weight on my shoulders." He straightened. "Thankfully, I'm told they're quite broad."

Minami glanced at him. "Whoever told you that was possibly being diplomatic."

Shin snorted. "Just as well. But speaking of muscles..." He

glanced back meaningfully at Reo, who was too busy gawping at their surroundings to hear them.

Minami grunted. "No."

"You will let her take part, of course."

Minami growled wordlessly. Shin smiled. "She is a great admirer of yours, by the way. Bit of hero worship there, I imagine."

Minami's growl stuttered to silence. She side-eyed Shin, wordlessly encouraging him to continue. His smile widened and he said, "Oh yes. She has heard all the stories about the city's youngest garrison commander. Granted, I told her a few of them myself, but still… she enjoyed them. She's a fine young woman, from a noble family, if you were concerned."

"I wasn't," she said quickly.

"While I understand the Badger are not, perhaps, considered of suitable status to attract the eye of the Akodo, they are a respected clan." He produced his fan and used it to count off points on his fingers. "She enjoys the obvious physical pursuits, of course – not just wrestling, mind. According to her, archery is a passion of hers. Apparently, her drawing power is such that she can put a single arrow through a pair of wooden posts."

"Can she?" Minami murmured weakly.

"Oh goodness, yes. She likes to paint, as well. And play music." He'd learned all of this on the boat ride over. Reo had been all too willing to share. He had the impression that she was somewhat lacking in positive reinforcement, at least in regards to anything taking place outside of the sumai circle.

"Music?"

"Mm. The biwa, interestingly enough. I play that myself. Though I fancy she's far more proficient with the instrument." He gestured. "Strong fingers, you know."

Minami swallowed. "You learned all of this today?"

"It's a wonder what you can learn when you talk to people." Shin paused. "You could do worse, you know."

Minami silenced him with a gesture. "We are not that close," she said simply. Shin nodded, accepting her words. She was correct. They weren't close, and he'd been pushing the boundaries of civil conversation. But boundaries were meant to be pushed; limits, nudged. He'd spent most of his adult life doing so, mostly for his own amusement but also because he simply couldn't bring himself to acknowledge the restrictions of polite society.

But this wasn't a matter of principle. Minami had made the first overtures of friendship, and he had no intention of risking that for a bit of point scoring. He decided to move on to a different subject. "Where will we be staying?"

"With the rest of the guests at the River Keep."

"That name rings a bell."

Minami smiled. "It was established when we made to take the city. It sits on a natural island and commands a view of a bend in the river, as well as the opposite shore. Not so important these days, but it is a fine castle nonetheless." She paused. "By the way, who's Lun?"

"Remember the affair of the poison rice last year?" Shin asked, bemused by the question. Minami's eyes widened in recognition.

"Her?"

"Oh yes. I decided to employ her. She's quite the captain."

Minami glared at him. "That one-eyed pirate delivered a load of poison rice to us! By rights, I should take her head!"

Shin waved this aside, even as he winced internally at his slip of the tongue. He'd forgotten that Minami wasn't privy to all the details of that affair. "Oh please. You've had a year to hunt her down if you were that concerned about it. Besides, she wasn't aware of what she was carrying. And she's under my protection."

From behind him, Yoku gave a harsh laugh. "What does it matter to a lion if its prey takes shelter beneath a crane's wing?"

Shin nodded agreeably. "Nothing at all, I expect." He peered at Yoku. "Then, surely the lion can find more agreeable prey if it so wishes. Lun isn't the sort to go easily, and I won't stand idly by. In fact, I might even take offense." Shin tapped Yoku in the chest with his fan. The samurai looked down and then up at Shin, a frown on his face. He made to speak, but Minami cut him off.

"I'm willing to overlook the matter for the moment. Why send your bodyguard to look for her?"

"You wanted me to investigate Mosu."

"That's why you're here," Minami said.

"Yes, but I can't be in two places at once." Shin snapped open his fan. "Don't worry, I'm not inviting her to the festivities. I just need her to find the site of the alleged pirate attack. And perhaps the pirates themselves."

Minami looked at him in bewilderment. "Why?"

Shin smiled thinly. "Because the best people to ask if Mosu is dead are the ones alleged to have killed him."

Minami shook her head and looked away. "We're approaching the bridge," she said, changing the subject. "Try not to provoke any of my people into putting an arrow in you." Shin looked ahead and saw the curve of a wooden bridge, lit by paper lanterns hung along its length. At the opposite end rose the blunt mountain of River Keep.

"It's quite tall," Shin said. The keep towered over the surrounding district, despite its isolation. From where they were, he could see several bridges curving from its base, to connect it with the mainland at different points.

Minami nodded. "The island isn't very big. We had to build up, rather than out." She signaled to the guards on duty and they stepped aside, allowing the party onto the bridge. Orange lantern light washed across the wooden confines, and Shin could feel the reverberation of the churning waters below.

Each of the bridges that jutted from the island was composed of three levels: the largest was the one Shin and the others were currently crossing; above them was a web of enclosed, narrow walkways, dotted with murder holes, that crisscrossed the bridge's span; and above that, a wide platform roof. The latter could undoubtedly be made into a temporary redoubt, in the event of an attack. It was impressive in its way, if betraying that peculiar paranoia that seemed to afflict the military mind.

Shin cast his eye over the castle as they drew near the gate. He noted gently sloping gables, meticulously tiled and decorated. The high stone walls, built without the use of mortar and each stone in harmony with its fellows. The outer gates, snug against the edge of the island, were open; the walls of the gatehouse patrolled by yet more archers. The gatehouse opened onto a small, enclosed square, and a second, primary gate rested within the left wall of the square.

Past the primary gate was another enclosed square, this one richly decorated with statuary, clan banners and green, growing things – an outdoor reception room. Willow trees sprouted from stone bases, designed expressly to allow their growth through the keep's foundations, and wooden troughs carried water from hidden wellheads nestled within the walls. It was from here that one entered the heart of the keep complex proper.

As Minami had mentioned, space was clearly at a premium,

so the builders had gone upwards where possible. Looking at it from below, Shin was struck by its resemblance to Saibanshoki. When he mentioned this to Minami, she looked smug. "Say, rather, Saibanshoki resembles River Keep. The complex was designed as a willow tree – a central core of stone, with branches of wood."

"And the roots?"

"More stone. We dug down, knowing that we would have to build up. The foundations of the keep are reinforced with equal parts clay and sand. I myself have overseen the digging of new drainage tunnels and sapper blinds." She saw the look on Shin's face and shrugged. "It keeps the men busy."

"It reminds me of something I read recently. Tell me, have you ever read *A Year on the Wall*, by Hida Chiyo? If not, you might find it interesting."

Before she could reply, Yoku sniffed. "What does a Crab know of war?"

Shin glanced at him, and Yoku had the good grace to look embarrassed. "Besides the obvious, I mean. Proper war, not… the other kind," he added, lamely. Shin rolled his eyes but didn't reply. Instead, he watched as a flock of servants suddenly spilled into the square and hurried toward them. Lion servants always struck him as living contradictions; simultaneously servile and arrogant. These were no different.

Minami turned to him. "Rooms have already been prepared, thanks to the imminent arrival of our guests. You and… Reo will, of course, have those set aside for late arrivals." She glanced at the young woman, but Reo was still looking about herself in awe.

"Small, in other words," Shin said, with a knowing smile. Minami flushed.

"Yes. And largely isolated from the main complex. I trust you understand."

"Oh, certainly. It wasn't a complaint, Minami, merely an observation. Now, as to tomorrow, I assume you will introduce me to the bride and groom, as well as their families? That would be the best place to start, I think."

Minami nodded reluctantly. "I suppose."

Shin smiled widely. "Oh, cheer up, Minami. I'll be on my absolute best behavior, I promise." He paused. "I expect my manservant will be allowed to attend to me, when he arrives later this evening."

"The sneaky one," Minami said doubtfully.

"Yes, that's him. He'll keep his hands to himself, I assure you."

She sighed. "Of course." She paused. "And when will you begin your... investigation?"

"I have already begun," Shin said. He noted her look of surprise with some satisfaction. "But I will keep you appraised of my findings, never fear. Now, if you would have a servant show us to our rooms...?"

Minami nodded and motioned the servants forward. Shin and Reo were escorted into the complex and taken along a circuitous route through lantern-lit paper corridors decorated with scenes of battle and stalking lions. Their rooms proved to be on the third floor of the keep, overlooking the stretch of river between the keep and the Lion district.

Reo was fairly brimming with excitement as she said her goodnights. Shin had seen to it that all her needs for a stay of several days were met. "Do you think Lady Minami will really allow me to compete?" she asked. Shin nodded.

"I do. But that is for tomorrow. Tonight, you should rest. But if you have any need of me, I am at your disposal." He waited until

Reo was safely in her room before allowing Yoku to see him to
his own. The bodyguard was silent as Shin inspected his quarters.

The guest room was sparsely decorated, and not to his taste
at all. He said nothing of that, however, and instead turned his
attentions to Yoku. "Tell me, Yoku... you are not an Akodo, I
think."

Yoku didn't look at him. "No."

Shin waited expectantly, but Yoku didn't appear to be inclined
to elaborate. Shin sighed. "Are you an Itagawa, by chance?"

Yoku's gaze hardened but remained fixed on the opposite
wall. "What of it?"

"What do you make of this affair?"

"It is not my place to say."

"I give you permission," Shin said. Yoku snorted.

"You are not my lord, Crane. You can neither give me
permission, nor remove it."

"A good point. But I feel I must mention that you have been
placed under my authority by your lord. Ergo, your assumption
is somewhat erroneous." Shin gave his fan a flick. "So, I ask
again: what do you make of it?"

Yoku gave a disgruntled sigh. "It is... highly unusual."

"Which bit?"

Yoku's eyes flicked toward him, and then away. "All of it."

"Even the initial engagement?"

Yoku fell silent, but Shin thought that was answer enough.
"Did you know Mosu at all?" he asked.

"He was – is – my cousin."

"Then you were close?"

"No."

Shin paused, parsing Yoku's terse reply for hidden meaning.
"But you knew of him?"

"I knew enough."

"Which means?" Shin pressed.

Yoku made a guttural sound and shifted his position, as if readying himself for attack. "He had many vices. Gambling, drinking... shameful."

"Had? Or has?"

Yoku bent his head. "They say he has changed."

"But you don't believe it."

"I did not say that."

"You have said very little, in fact. But we will leave it for now." Shin opened his fan and gave it a swipe, stirring the air. "What about Lady Moriko? How well do you know her?"

Yoku stared at him for long moments. "Are you accusing me of impropriety, Crane?"

"No, of course not." Shin sighed. "I'm trying to help, you know."

"We do not need your help."

Shin let some steel creep into his voice. "Speaking for your mistress now, are you?"

Yoku blanched. Upon closer examination, Shin realized the other man was older than he'd first thought. There was silver in his hair, and lines on his face. Then, age in a bodyguard often implied skill. Shin filed the thought away. "Never mind. Thank you, Yoku. That will be all until the morning, I think. Good night." He dismissed Yoku with a wave of his fan and turned back to his room. It didn't look any better upon second examination. Kitano would bring changes of clothes and other necessaries when he arrived.

He went to the balcony and looked out over the river. Reflections of the city lights danced on the surface like fireflies, and the croaking of the frogs seemed to grow in volume. "Well," he murmured. "Here we are. In the lion's den."

He tapped his fan against his palm and smiled. "Now to make sure I'm not devoured."

CHAPTER NINE
Lun

According to Arban, the Yellow Chrysanthemum crouched near the most rundown of the Unicorn wharfs – those used almost exclusively by fisherfolk, and for cargoes of little importance. As such, the area had become inundated with unlicensed sake houses, gambling establishments and the like. The crooked streets were the preserve of smugglers, touts and criminals of all stripes.

"I can see why you enjoy it here. So many criminals, all in one place," Kasami said to Arban. Lanterns burnt in the doorways around them, and the sound of drunken laughter spilled out of open windows. At the far end of the street, a richly appointed litter hove briefly into view and sailed past, borne atop the shoulders of its bearers. Peasants carrying heavy baskets hurried in the direction of the wharf, and the vessels leaving with the evening tide. The aroma of spicy noodles drifted out of a shop across the street, reminding Kasami that she'd skipped her evening meal.

Arban laughed. "I am a tiger among sheep."

"You mean you're a bigger criminal than the rest of them?"

"I mean I am a different beast entirely." Arban glanced back at Kenzō and Kasami followed his gaze. The auditor followed them closely, but seemed to be paying more attention to avoiding the

occasional mess on the street than to them. "Speaking of which...
want him to have an accident?" he asked, in a low voice. "Ask me
nicely, and your clever lord need never fear this one again."

"Lord Shin doesn't fear him. He is merely an aggravation."

"I'm just saying he goes to a lot of effort to avoid the man."

"How would you know?"

Arban scratched his cheek. "It's the talk of the city – at least
the part where the merchants are." He sniffed. "They say your
Lord Shin has attracted the ire of the Trading Council, whatever
that is. Gota seems worried about it."

"Is he now?"

"Mostly in regards to himself," Arban admitted. "He thinks
whatever befalls the Crane may well befall anyone associated
with him. Myself, I don't see why anyone would fear merchants.
Even Crane ones."

"Then you are a fool," Kenzō interjected, suddenly. Clearly,
he'd been paying more attention than Kasami had realized. "The
Daidoji treat trade as they would war: a cold thing of strategy,
utterly lacking in honor or mercy. And your master is right. If
Lord Shin is found to have committed some infraction, we will
turn our eyes upon those who have dealings with him. In fact,
we already have–"

Arban stopped so suddenly that Kenzō almost ran into him.
"Was that a threat?" he asked, in a mild tone. "Because while
she might not wish me to kill you on behalf of her lord, I will
cheerfully do so on behalf of mine."

Kasami expected Kenzō to retreat. Instead, he sneered. "You
will not touch me. You know better. I am under the protection
of the Council, and their reach is long."

"Is that why you travel with no bodyguard?" Kasami asked
lightly. Kenzō blinked. Kasami gestured to his robes. "You carry

no sword, you have no guard. Your servants are borrowed, and do not accompany you. Do you think their authority will protect you from an assassin's blade?"

Kenzō straightened his robes. "What I think is of no importance. I am here to find the truth, nothing more. You would do well to aid me in this. Both for your master's sake, and your own."

"That was definitely a threat," Arban said helpfully.

"Yes," Kasami said, studying Kenzō. To his credit, he met her gaze squarely. She was having difficulty figuring him out. One moment he seemed nothing more than a functionary, one more irksome courtier in a clan full of them. But in other moments she detected a steel in him that was at odds with his way of presenting himself. Perhaps she was simply confusing his overinflated sense of self-importance for courage. But maybe not. It was something to ponder, at least.

"It was not a threat," Kenzō said swiftly. "Merely an observation. Contrary to what some might believe, audits are not duels – merely the cost of doing business." Again, the convulsive straightening of his robes.

Kasami shook her head and glanced at Arban. "Where is this gambling house of yours? I want to find Lun and be gone from here."

Arban gestured to a nondescript building lurking among a nest of unlicensed bathhouses. A faded sigil depicting a golden flower hung from the doorway, and two men were on guard. Rough-looking, unshaven – but armed. Kasami paused and let her eyes roam the street. She spotted three more potential guards within spitting distance of the two on duty. Arban caught her glance and nodded. "They take their security seriously here."

She started toward the door. "Then it is just as well that we do not intend to cause trouble. Come."

The guards almost immediately moved to intercept her. Perhaps it was the fact she was wearing armor. Or maybe she didn't look like a gambler. The first, a lean man with an eyepatch and a flamboyant topknot of hair, said, "We're full." His hands were inside his robes, away from the hilt of either sword. His companion, shorter and heavier, with a permanent scowl stamped on his face courtesy of a scar that bisected one cheek, added, "Come back tomorrow."

"I am here now," Kasami said.

"Not our problem," eyepatch said flatly.

"I think it might be, Manabu," Arban said, with a friendly wave. Eyepatch – Manabu – grunted and glowered at Arban. His companion swallowed audibly.

"Ujik," Manabu said, making the word sound like a curse. "If she's with you, she's definitely not getting in." He rolled his shoulders, loosening up to no doubt attempt something foolish. Kasami studied him. He was a ronin, or doing a very good impression. His companion, on the other hand, was nervous – a thug, nothing more.

"And if they are both with me?" Kenzō said, in a haughty tone. He kept his hands folded, the very picture of the courtier at ease. "Or am I, too, barred from this establishment?"

Manabu grunted again and looked him over. Then his remaining eye flicked to Kasami. "You his bodyguard?"

"I–" she began.

"She is," Arban said. "And I'm their tour guide." He indicated the entrance. "Should we go in?"

"I said no," Manabu began. Kasami's hand fell to her sword.

"I am on my lord's business. Step aside, or there will be consequences."

Manabu paused, visibly weighing his options. Then, with

a sigh, he stepped back. "Let them in," he called out. Kasami glanced around and saw the other guards she'd noted earlier edging toward them. Manabu waved them back and stepped aside. "Good luck, my lord," he said as Kenzō stepped past him.

Inside, the Yellow Chrysanthemum was much like any other gambling den she'd been forced to enter in order to keep Shin from suffering the consequences of his vices. A large open space, a few tables in the corners. At the far end of the room was a small, square stage. A musician – an old woman in robes decorated with chrysanthemums – sat upon it, playing a shamisen with more diligence than skill.

Several games of chance were ongoing, with small crowds of onlookers hovering over each, throwing up a cheer as dice rattled and curses flew. Kasami spotted Lun easily enough, sitting near the door. She strode over, shoving a path through the onlookers with no regard for their complaints. Lun dressed like a common sailor, bar the blue silk jacket she wore. Her hair was cropped short, and scars marked the cheek below her missing eye like cracks in porcelain. "Pirate," Kasami said.

"Bodyguard," Lun said, her good eye on the dice. "What brings you to this establishment? If you've come for a game, you'll have to wait until Kano and I finish up." She indicated the man sitting opposite her. He was a big man, unshaven and stinking of fish. A sailor, maybe. He had an ugly gleam in his eye as he studied the board.

"Your game is finished," Kasami said.

Kano glanced at her. "Not yet. She's won every toss so far and I'm not letting her leave until I win one."

"I'd listen to her," Lun said. "She's not the type to take no for an answer."

"I don't care who she is, I want my money," the big man

growled as he heaved himself to his feet. His stool clattered to the floor as he reached for a knife. Kasami took a single step back and drew her sword in the same instant. She wasn't sure which of them the threat was meant for, but it didn't really matter. A blade was a blade, and her training took over. Nonetheless she pulled her blow, and the edge of the blade bumped teasingly against the man's throat. He froze.

"I do not care about you or your money," she said, in a firm tone. "But you reached for a weapon in my presence. Normally, I would remove your head for that, but my master is a gentle soul, and he frowns upon such things. So, I leave it to you – head or hand?"

There was a murmur from the crowd at that. The big man swallowed thickly but made no move to speak. Kasami frowned. "Shall I choose for you then?" she asked, her voice laced with menace.

"You can let him go, bodyguard," Lun said, in a mild tone. She thrust a finger beneath her eyepatch and scratched at the empty socket beneath. "He's three sheets to the wind and not responsible for his choices. That's why I was dicing with him in the first place."

Kasami looked at her. "You were cheating, you mean." She pulled the edge of her blade away from the heavyset man's throat, but didn't sheathe the weapon. Lun snorted.

"I wasn't cheating. Taking advantage of him, perhaps... but not cheating." She tapped the hilt of the knife thrust through the wide leather belt encircling her waist. "You can go now, Kano. We'll finish the game another time."

The big man stepped back and, with a parting glare at the two women, turned and shoved his way through the crowd. Kasami forgot about him as soon as he vanished from sight and turned her attentions to Lun. "Lord Shin has a job for you."

Lun picked up the overturned bottle of sake and poured the remnants into her cup. "Does he now? And what if I don't feel like doing it?"

Kasami tilted her head. "He is your patron," she said simply.

Lun emptied her cup. "That's not really an answer, now is it?"

Kasami smiled thinly and sheathed her sword. "It is, actually," she said. "Are you going to hear me out or not?" She looked around, but all eyes in the gambling house studiously avoided hers. She sniffed, satisfied that the correct impression had been made.

Lun tossed the empty cup over her shoulder. "Might as well, since you ruined my game." She turned and scooped up her winnings, sliding them into a pouch. "What does he want now?"

Kasami scowled at the other woman, but Lun was one of the few people on whom her scowls had no effect. It irritated her, but also pleased her. It meant Lun was truly a worthy servant for Shin. Lun simply bounced the pouch of money on her palm insouciantly. Finally, Kasami said, "Pirates."

"What about them?"

"He wants you to find some."

Lun's good eye narrowed. "I never took him for that sort."

Kasami's temper flared. "Not to hire, fool. It is part of one of his… puzzles." She bit down on the last word. "Can you help or not?"

Lun sat back. "Of course. It'll cost him, though."

Kasami nodded. She'd expected no less from the pirate. "Obviously."

Lun smiled. "Excellent. We'll depart with the morning tide."

CHAPTER TEN
Bride and Groom

Shin tried to hide a yawn behind his fan as he breakfasted the next morning. Reo smiled at him. "A late night, my lord?" she asked with equal parts politeness and amusement. Reo looked bright and perky, despite the early hour. Shin, habitually a late riser, found it hard not to resent her a little. Even so, he smiled and closed his fan.

"Shin, please. And yes. Unfamiliar surroundings, you know." He looked around the room as he spoke. It was a small space, adjoining their rooms. A central area for eating and socializing, with a small balcony that overlooked the keep gardens. Beautiful, in its way, but utterly utilitarian and in keeping with the Akodo ethos. He wondered if he'd be allowed to decorate it while he was here.

Reo shook her head. "I know what you mean, my lord." She picked at her food without enthusiasm; Shin didn't blame her. It was by no means meager provender, but it was bland. He was beginning to fear that the Lion palate was singularly uncultured. Something would have to be done.

He thought of the box of spices he'd procured from an Ide

trader some months back. He'd been waiting for a special occasion to put its contents to use. Perhaps now was the time to roll up his sleeves and put his mind to the culinary grindstone. He resolved to send Kitano to retrieve it at the first opportunity.

Thinking of his servant, he wondered how Kitano was getting on with the other servants. He'd arrived in the night, bringing Shin's luggage with him. If things were going well, the former gambler would already be insinuating himself in the kitchens. Making friends, hopefully; at the very least, learning names.

Servants knew more about what went on than their masters realized. Any courtier worth his silk learned that the best source of gossip was inevitably the servants and took pains to cultivate them. Money was the easiest way, but Shin had come to learn that there were many routes to learning what others knew, and that sometimes the easiest way gave the worst results. Flattery, challenge, insinuation – each of them had their uses.

That said, servants hesitated to talk to one of his rank; but Kitano had no such difficulties. He would winnow through the staff of River Keep and find the ones who knew something of value. That would take time, of course. In the meantime, Shin would direct his attentions to other sources of information. He glanced at Reo, watching as she ate. "How are you feeling?" he asked softly.

She paused. "I will admit I am nervous. Do you truly think you can help me?"

"I will do my best." Seeing her crestfallen expression, he added, "I think they will give you a chance. But it will be up to you to make the most of it."

"I just hope I don't disappoint you or my uncle."

Shin rapped her knuckles with his fan, causing her to yelp. "Disappointing either of us is the last thing you should worry about. I'm told focus is key in these matters. So, stay focused on your goal and success will surely follow. To consider otherwise is a waste of imagination."

Reo rubbed her knuckles and nodded. She made as if to speak, but was interrupted by Yoku, who stepped into the room. "Lady Minami wonders if you are awake," he said stiffly. He looked around the room, as if checking for anything untoward.

Shin nodded and stifled another yawn. "Awake and eager to start the day."

Reo pushed herself to her feet. "I-I must take my exercise. Will I see you for lunch, Lord Shin?" She looked so anxious that Shin nodded.

"Of course. I look forward to it. Hopefully I will have better news for you then."

Reo hurried out, by way of her own room, leaving Shin alone until Minami entered, accompanied by a handful of servants. One of them bore an armful of paper. Shin had an unsettling premonition as he gazed at it. "Is that...?" he began as Minami sat.

Minami gestured, and the servant brought forward her burden. "As you requested, the guest list. Every invitee and their entourage, as well as the seating charts for previous weddings."

Shin blinked. "Seating charts."

Minami smiled. "Yes. You know all about seating charts, don't you? I expect the Crane learn of them in the womb."

"Yes, well..." Shin looked at the papers in mild consternation. He'd known that such things were necessary, of course. But knowing and understanding were two different things apparently. He unrolled the first one, giving it a quick once-over – and paused. "You've segregated the families. No mingling."

"No. Do the Crane… mingle?"

"Such occasions among the Crane are designed to facilitate the flow of conversation. We arrange our seating accordingly, so that there are no weak strands in the social web."

Minami shook her head. "Allowing the families to mingle will lead to bloodshed."

Shin raised an eyebrow. "It seems that Lions are as territorial as any animal."

Minami frowned. "Not normally. But in this case, yes. There have been… complaints. Insinuations." She dismissed the servants with a gesture.

Shin perked up. "Meaning?" he asked after the servants had departed. He held up his fan. "No, wait, let me guess. The Seizuka and the Ichime."

"Yes, how did you know?"

"A guess, as I said. You mentioned their representatives were invited." Which wasn't unusual. The Crane often invited their vassals to family affairs. It was only polite, after all. Though he was a bit surprised that the Lion went in for such things. "What are they complaining about, specifically?"

"They… feel that there is some incongruity in Mosu's selection as groom."

Shin paused. "And how long have they felt this way?"

Minami took a deep breath. "Since the engagement was announced."

"There were other suitors under consideration?"

"Three, in total. One from each of the vassal families."

Shin tapped his lips with his fan, processing this new information. "Oh my. So, there are two disappointed suitors – not to mention families – and you've invited them to the wedding?"

"It is tradition," Minami said stiffly.

"And what do they think of Mosu's miraculous return?"

Her expression was answer enough. Shin sighed. "Well, I can see that keeping incipient hostilities from boiling over will require careful placement of each guest. I will study the charts today and come up with something." He glanced at the guest list. "Out of curiosity, how many guests?"

Minami grinned. "A hundred, at least."

"Ah."

"Will you be wanting to question them all?"

Shin mustered his resolve and gave a disdainful sniff. "I'm certain that won't be necessary." He paused. "I will want to speak to the representatives for each family, though. And the matchmaker, of course."

It was Minami's turn to look puzzled. "The matchmaker? Why?"

"Who better to ask about the arrangements?" Shin flicked open his fan. He recalled his last encounter with a matchmaker. They always made excellent conversationalists. "Who was the matchmaker, out of curiosity? An Akodo?"

"No. Shika Akari. She is staying here at River Keep."

"Ah, excellent," Shin said approvingly. "I shall speak with her today."

"I wish you luck. She's usually in the temple this time of day."

"Devout, then?"

"Perhaps." Minami paused. "She is always in the temple these days." Another pause. "Yoku... he is proving amenable?"

Shin heard the concern in her voice. Not for him, he thought – but for Yoku. He glanced at the bodyguard seated near the door, his fists braced on his thighs. "He is proving very helpful, yes. I trust you do not require him?"

"I am a general. I have an army. One man more or less is of no import." The way she said it gave lie to her words. He could tell that she missed having Yoku at her side.

"But some men are more important than others. He has served you for a long time, I think. Years, I would guess, though he doesn't look it."

"Since I was a girl," she said after a moment. "He… looked after Moriko and myself." She smiled slightly. "He was our… babysitter."

"A glorious duty," Shin murmured. Minami frowned.

"He did not think so, not at first. He was young. Eager for glory." She paused, her eyes straying to her bodyguard. "But he has been as a brother to me, regardless."

"And to Moriko?"

Minami's gaze hardened. "What of it?"

"Idle curiosity," Shin said, avoiding the question. Something about what Yoku had told him last night gnawed at him, but he couldn't say what that something was. He decided to change the subject until he could determine the nature of his uncertainty. "Any idea when the first guests should be arriving?"

"Tomorrow morning. Which means you have less than two days to get things ready. Do you think you can manage it?"

"Of course," Shin said, hoping he sounded more confident than he felt. "Now, what about Reo?"

Minami hesitated. "What about her?"

"She will be allowed to compete?" Shin asked, though it wasn't really a question. More a demand. Minami sighed.

"You will need to speak to the master of the Rich Frog Dojo. I was supposed to talk to him today after lunch, so I will introduce you."

"Excellent! I look forward to it." Shin eyed the guest list. "I suppose I should get started on that. But first – the bride and groom."

"What about them?"

"I should meet them, don't you think?"

Minami stared at him. "Why would you want to meet them?"

Shin raised an eyebrow. "Why would I not? I am overseeing the festivities, after all. Besides, you want me to determine the truth of things. That means I must at least meet them."

Minami looked away. "Fine. I shall send a servant–"

Shin stopped her. "No need. Let's be spontaneous." He rose and straightened his robes. "I find formality often gets in the way of a good introduction. Where are they?"

"They're breakfasting in the main gardens. Moriko likes to listen to the birds while she eats." Minami allowed herself a small smile. "Lady Ai tolerates it."

"And her husband-to-be?"

Minami hesitated. "Mosu is always with them. He doesn't eat in public, but… he seems content to sit and watch the others."

Shin nodded. If Mosu was disfigured in some way, eating in private would be the only way to maintain his dignity. Of course, it was also a convenient way of ensuring that no one saw him without his mask. He rubbed his hands together. "Excellent. All together then."

Minami sighed and rose slowly to her feet. "Let's get this over with. I have other matters to attend to today. I won't have my men found wanting when Lord Arasou arrives."

A few moments later, they were traversing the paper corridors of River Keep. Shin kept up both his end of the conversation and Minami's, even occasionally filling in a comment for Yoku, who trailed silently in their wake. Yoku, for his part, ignored Shin's attempt at banter. Minami might have cracked a smile, once or twice. But he could feel the tension radiating from both of them. He wondered if it was just the incipient arrival of the Akodo Daimyō, or something else.

He couldn't escape the feeling that there was more to this than Minami was saying. A Lion could be as petty as anyone, and concern for a beloved cousin had motivated more than one samurai into taking action. But even so, there was something about the situation that teased a certain… complexity.

Shin was still musing on this when they reached the main gardens. As Minami had said, the bride and groom were taking breakfast beneath the ornamental cherry blossom trees that stood sentinel over the garden. A carpet of pink petals had fallen over the garden; if it was an omen, Shin couldn't say what it foretold. Chaperones in the form of Akodo servants hovered at the edges of the gardens, waiting to be of service.

Lady Ai, the current head of Minami's branch of the family, was not in attendance, unfortunately. Or perhaps fortunately. Privately, Shin felt that particular confrontation was best saved for later. Lady Ai was infamous, in her way. Though Shin had never met her, he'd heard plenty. Besides which, her absence meant his full attention could be focused on Mosu.

Akodo Moriko proved to be a plump young woman with an easy smile and large, dark eyes. Her robes were of the highest quality and she wore them well, in contrast to Minami, who looked uncomfortable in anything that wasn't armor. She sat on a cushion and spoke gaily to her intended, who nodded but said little.

Itagawa Mosu towered over his intended, even seated. He was lean, but broad shouldered, with a thick mane of gray-streaked hair that tumbled down his neck in an untidy fashion. His robes were immaculate, but plain. But most striking was the golden mempo he wore over the lower half of his face. Wrought in the shape of a Lion's muzzle with its fangs bared, it combined with his hair to give him an unsettlingly wild appearance.

"I was expecting something a bit more put together," Shin murmured to Minami.

"His captivity changed him," Minami replied. She smiled as Moriko spotted them and rose lightly to her feet. "Good morning, cousin. You are looking well-rested."

"I sleep the sleep of the just," Moriko said, and laughed. Mosu rose as well, his hands clasped behind his back. Minami hesitated, and then nodded to him.

"Lord Mosu."

Mosu inclined his head. "Lady Minami. It gives me great pleasure to see you."

Shin paused. An awkward turn of phrase; a fine sentiment, but delivered clumsily. A sign of nerves, or something else? Mosu's eyes – dark, sharp – flicked to Shin, as if he'd noticed Shin's attentions. His eyes widened slightly; Shin wondered if Mosu recognized him. Unlikely, but not impossible.

Moriko noticed Shin for the first time. "Hello," she said brightly. "You must be Lord Shin." She paused, speculatively. "You are much better looking than Minami described. Not gawky at all. Though the white hair is a bit much."

Shin blinked. "Yes, well, one must keep up with the fashions." He glanced at Minami. "Gawky?" he asked, under his breath.

"You are very slight," Minami said without looking at him. Was she smiling? It was hard to tell. "Like a child."

"Bird bones," Moriko supplied, and giggled. There was a mischievous light in her eyes. She gestured. "Very thin and tiny." Minami guffawed.

Shin looked at them both, suddenly struck by how much

trouble they must have given the younger Yoku. He cleared his throat and bowed. "My bones are of normal proportions, I assure you both." Shin glanced at Mosu. "And this must be the happy groom – Lord Mosu."

"I am," Mosu said. There was no mischief in his eyes. There wasn't much of anything, really. Rather than windows, they were walls. "It is a pleasure to meet you," he continued. But there was hesitation there. Not a courtier's practiced pause, but something else. Worry, perhaps. Shin took him in, studying the way he stood, the set of his shoulders.

No, this one wasn't a courtier.

So what was he?

"I look forward to giving you both the wedding you deserve," Shin said, bowing again. Moriko frowned slightly, and Mosu visibly tensed.

"What does that mean?" Moriko asked bluntly.

Shin smiled at her. "Merely what I said."

"Forgive me, my lord, but I do not see why you are here." Moriko looked at Minami. "I'd hoped my cousin would see to the festivities."

Shin snapped open his fan and gave it a flutter. "Oh, never fear, she's in charge. I'm just... facilitating matters. Delegation is essential to any military operation."

"And what would you know of that?" Moriko asked, in an innocent tone. Shin gave her a sharp glance. He was certain the insult was not unintended. Moriko was trying to make him angry – why? To make him depart?

Minami seemed to sense it as well, for she cleared her throat. "Lord Shin has requested to see the shrine. I am taking him now and will return later." She gestured, and Shin followed her away from the others.

"I wasn't aware I'd asked to see the shrine," he murmured.

Minami sniffed. "What did you make of him?"

"At first glance, he seems personable enough. The mask is a bit off-putting, however." Shin considered what he'd seen in Mosu's eyes – alarm, worry, but quickly tamped down. He'd been surprised by Shin's arrival, but he'd hidden it well.

"But…?" Minami pressed.

"You're right. He is hiding something." He paused. "So is your cousin."

Minami stopped short, and he nearly collided with her. She turned. "What do you mean? Moriko is an innocent. Stay away from her."

"Nonetheless, she is hiding something." Shin shrugged. "It might have nothing to do with the wedding or her intended. But to know, I'll need to talk to her."

Minami stared at him for a moment, and then turned away. "I will consider it."

Shin stopped her with a light touch on her arm. She knew more than she was saying. "Consider it carefully."

She pulled away from him. "I said I would. And anyway, it's Mosu you should concern yourself with. That's why I brought you here."

Shin sighed. "You brought me here to find answers, Minami. To do so, I must talk to everyone. That includes your cousin." He snapped open his fan. "Whether either of you like it or not."

CHAPTER ELEVEN
Deer and Lion

The River Stone shrine was large; grand, even. It sat across the western bridge from River Keep, situated amidst a small grove of willow trees. Smaller river shrines, devoted to the spirits of the water and the willows, dotted the shore in the shadow of the trees. These older shrines resolutely faced away from the much larger, grander Akodo shrine, as if to dismiss the invader – or perhaps out of fear of their conqueror.

People came and went, visiting the shrine or going down to the river. Nearby merchants and businesses had opened up for the morning. Behind its high walls, an empty space, green with grass and the nubs of long-toppled willow trees, encircled the temple. "I thought the festivities would be held here, within the temple grounds. It affords privacy, and a defensive position."

"And why would we need one of those?" Shin asked idly.

Minami hesitated. "Just in case."

"In case what? The Unicorn launch an unprovoked attack, using the wedding as a distraction?"

Minami blinked. "Do you think they might?"

"No," Shin said, aghast. "That's ridiculous. No one is going to attack, and a hundred guests aren't going to fit in there. No. We'll block off the streets and set up entertainment for both the guests and the inevitable onlookers."

Minami frowned. "Onlookers?"

Shin sighed and opened his fan. "You are hosting the event of the season. A wedding such as this comes along only rarely. To have it here evokes a certain responsibility on your part. The people wish to celebrate with you. So, we will let them. Goodwill costs nothing."

"Except that it will inevitably cost something."

"Yes. Speaking of which, how are the Akodo coffers faring of late?"

Minami frowned. "Well enough to pay for this. Why?"

"No reason. I am merely considering all possibilities."

"I didn't bring you here to consider possibilities – I want to know whether Mosu is a fraud. Can you tell me that, or not?"

"Not yet. Soon."

"The wedding ceremony will take place in two days, Shin."

Shin waved his fan. "I am well aware of the time, Minami – never fear."

"You keep saying that. A lesser woman would take offense."

"Then I am very grateful you are not a lesser woman." Shin took in the temple as he spoke. A suspended roof rose over a tiled courtyard that spread out beyond the traditional torii arches. The tiles had been placed in concentric fashion around the single stone marker that gave the shrine its name. The tiles came in two colors – orange and yellow. The orange ones stretched from the entrance to within a few feet of the stone, where the yellow ones began.

Minami paused at the edge of the yellow tiles and Shin did

the same. The yellow tiles obviously marked the beginning of the main hall; only priests and shrine-keepers would be allowed past. A robed figure knelt before the stone, and rose as they stopped. Given the quality of his robes, Shin figured him for a priest.

"Lady Minami." The young man said as he turned to them. Shin was startled to see that his eyes were an unsettling golden hue. This, combined with the faint reddish tint to his thick mane of hair, made him resemble a lion. "Everything is progressing according to schedule, I hope," he said. His voice had a pleasing undercurrent to it, like the basso purr of the animal he resembled.

Intrigued, Shin gave his fan a flutter, attracting the priest's attention. A crinkle of confusion crossed the young man's face as he took in Shin's demeanor. "And who is this?"

"A friend," Minami began, hesitantly. "Daidoji Shin, might I introduce Kitsu Touma. He will be performing the ceremony. Lord Touma, Lord Shin will be organizing the accompanying ceremonies."

Touma cocked his head, furthering his resemblance to a curious feline. "A... Crane? How... interesting. Have you told anyone else?"

Minami rolled her eyes. "Yes, Touma."

"Are you certain?"

"Yes, Touma."

"Only he's still in one piece."

"*Yes*, Touma."

Shin observed this exchange with no little humor, and some small puzzlement. His experience with priests was limited, but they'd always struck him as rarified individuals. This Touma, on the other hand, seemed pleasantly frank. Personable, even.

There were stories about the Kitsu, of course. Eerie tales of prehuman ancestry that Shin paid little mind to. Children's stories and nothing more. But looking at Touma, he began to wonder if he was wrong. He'd come to realize of late that the world was far stranger than he'd assumed. Perhaps the Kitsu were part lion. Even as he began to wonder which parts, exactly, that might include, he sketched a simple bow and said, "I am pleased to meet you, Lord Touma. Your shrine is lovely. Simple, but there is an elegance in simplicity I find."

Touma eyed Shin's robes and said, "Do you?"

Shin smiled. It was rude but, he thought, not meant rudely, unlike Moriko's comments earlier. "Well, elegance takes many forms," he clarified. "It is equally in a zephyr's whisper, and the clean line of a well-maintained blade."

"Hida Chiyo," Touma said. "*A Year on the Wall.*"

Shin paused, startled. "You've read her work?"

"All of it. I prefer her later collection, *A Crab's Walk,* to *A Year on the Wall* if I'm being honest, but there's a definite power in the latter. A sort of… palm strike of poetry." He gestured emphatically, and Shin nodded.

"Yes, I quite agree. I was quite taken with the bluntness of her word choice. Do you find that there's a strange sort of subtlety in, well, unsubtle phrasing?"

Touma nodded. "Oh, yes. It's quite sneaky in its way. It lures you in and then – *strikes.*" He clapped his hands together, causing Shin to jump slightly. He fluttered his fan to hide this momentary lapse, but from the way her lips quirked, he suspected Minami had seen it. Touma smiled. "You are well-read, my lord."

"I am of the opinion that horizons exist solely to be expanded," Shin said.

Minami sighed and interjected, "Touma, have you seen Lady Akari this morning?"

Touma frowned. "Yes, why?"

"Lord Shin wishes to speak with her."

Touma glanced at Shin. "Something to do with the wedding?"

"In a sense. A wedding is about two souls coming together as one, and no one knows more about such things than a professional matchmaker." Shin resisted the urge to grimace even as he spouted the saccharine nonsense. From the look Minami gave him, he thought she wanted to hit him. He didn't blame her.

"What utter nonsense," she growled.

Shin linked his fingers. "Two souls, united in love."

Touma laughed. "You'll have to forgive her. Minami doesn't know much about such things. Too devoted to her duties as a general."

Minami turned her glare on the priest, and Touma retreated a few steps. "I meant it as a compliment," he added, hurriedly. "You are a very good general."

"Akari," Minami said flatly.

"Behind the temple, among the trees. She spends much of the day there. She says she prefers their company." Touma smiled gently. "I try not to take offense."

Shin left Minami with Touma and made his way behind the temple, trying to recall what he knew of the Shika family as he did so. While the imperial Otomo family were the premier neutral matchmakers in Rokugan, there were times when imperial influence was neither necessary nor desired.

The matchmakers of the Deer were renowned for their neutrality and their seeming ability to ensure matches that were emotionally strong, as well as politically. If the Akodo placed any value on the happiness of the couple to be wed, then a Shika matchmaker was a necessity. They were masters of the art of expectation; able to play off the desires of their clients, and ensure that the matches were strong, if sometimes unexpected.

Was that what had happened here? he wondered. Had Shika Akari somehow found Mosu to be acceptable, despite his many flaws? Was there some virtue mixed in among the wealth of vices? Regardless, he decided to be wary. The placid façade of the Deer was just that – a mask, worn by a family of professional manipulators. They made themselves seem harmless, an act which fooled more straightforward souls, but the Crane knew better.

He found Shika Akari standing among the willows. She was studying an ancient tree that stood sentry over the water. A maidservant knelt nearby, head bowed. The tree was scarred, gnarled and coiled in on itself, giving off an air of malign resentment. "Not the loveliest of trees, is it?" Shin said as he came to stand beside her. "I suspect it was used for sword practice at some point."

"There is more to beauty than aesthetic appeal," she replied, not looking at him. "You are the new wedding planner."

"Ah. My fame precedes me."

"No. I have no idea who you are." She turned. "Someone mentioned you had arrived, and since you are the only white-haired Crane staying at River Keep, I made an assumption." Akari was quite lovely, in a nondescript way. Her robes were dark, and she wore a necklace of alabaster gypsum. Combs of the same held her hair pinned up away from her face. "You are in uncertain territory, my lord."

"My footing is sure and my trail well-marked. Something I'm

told the Shika know a bit about." He paused. "I have heard that Aokami Forest is quite lovely – an untouched wilderness."

"Yes."

"I should like to see it someday."

She brushed this pleasantry aside with an impatient gesture. "Why did you wish to speak to me, my lord?"

"Call it curiosity. We are both outsiders here, after all."

"You more so than myself," she said. "The Lion and the Crane do not traditionally get along. Imperial peace notwithstanding."

He smiled thinly. "I like to think my presence here is a sign that relations are on the mend. Are you finding your stay pleasant?"

"I will be pleased when the ceremony is completed and I can return home."

"But surely being invited to the wedding is a great honor? Most matchmakers have little to do with things after – well – the match is made. That you are here shows how highly the Akodo value your contribution."

She looked back at the tree. "It is a balance; an honor on one hand, but a threat on the other. If things do not go well, it is the Shika who will bear the brunt of the Lion's wrath."

"And why would it not go well? Something to do with the complaints made by the other families, then?" he asked. A blunt question, but not a suspicious one, he thought. Akari looked startled by it nonetheless.

"What do you mean?"

"I mean, Mosu was assumed dead, yes? At least for a brief time. Was another match considered in that time? Someone... more suitable, perhaps?"

Akari studied him for a moment. "Why do you wish to know?"

"I have met matchmakers before. You had a list of potential candidates for the groom, I expect. One from every vassal family, at least. If not more. So, did any of them step up to replace Mosu?"

"And if they did?"

"Lady Moriko is a fine young woman, with an impeccable pedigree. A catch for any younger son – or daughter – under the right circumstances." Shin paused. "People have been known to… weight the dice, shall we say, when it comes to such matters…"

Akari turned away. "If you are accusing me of bribery, this conversation is over."

Shin tapped his lips with his fan. "I wasn't, but you raise a good point: were you offered some bonus for engendering such a mismatch?"

Akari whirled to face him. "How dare you question my honesty!" Fire – but measured. The anger of the wronged innocent. Yet something about it set his instincts a-quiver. She was too quick to assume such a pose, as if she'd been ready for such a question. But why would she expect her decision to be questioned?

Shin smiled. "It is a good thing to question and to test. In my opinion, a sword is only as sharp as its last stroke of the whetstone, and honesty is only as impeccable as the last time it was challenged."

Akari frowned. "What sort of wedding planner are you?"

"A very good one," Shin avowed. "I must know everything in order to plan for every eventuality – including potential disruptions to the festivities." His smile was as innocent as he could manage in the moment. Akari's frown deepened, but she didn't challenge his assertion. Instead, she sighed and looked away again.

"There were two possibilities besides Mosu. Ichime Asahi and Seizuka Omo. Both young, neither particularly suitable, but adequate."

"So Mosu was the best of a bad lot, is what you're saying."

Akari shook her head fiercely. "No, I am most assuredly not saying that. I am simply saying that as far as matches go, none of the three were particularly suitable. Differences in temperament aside, I judged that Asahi was too young, being nearly five years Moriko's junior, and that Omo was too... boisterous."

Shin peered at her. "Meaning?"

Akari snorted. "You'll see. He's invited, after all."

Shin leaned back slightly, giving her space. "I look forward to it. So, of the three Mosu was the best fit, then. How sad." He tapped his chin with his fan, as if thinking. "I'm told that there was a... financial component to the selection process."

Akari stiffened. "Who told you that?" Then, "You *are* accusing me of bribery!"

"Not you," Shin said swiftly. "I'm told the Akodo are under some slight financial strain at the moment. And that the Itagawa relieved them of it, in return for the match."

"You should not gossip," Akari said sternly.

"I know. My only vice," Shin said. He paused. "Besides all the others."

Akari snorted. "You think you are funny."

"I believe I have a substantial sense of humor, yes," Shin said. "Of course, not everyone shares my opinion." He paused again. "It is sad, when so many are so wrong."

Akari laughed at that, and Shin smiled. A bit of humor never went amiss. She looked at him, and then said, "I heard much the same. About the Akodo, I mean. But if such a thing occurred, it did so without my knowledge. I was given names and nothing more."

"So you weren't encouraged to find in favor of one over the others?"

Akari paused. "I didn't say that. Mosu was considered the favorite, early on. But I tried not to let it color my judgement."

Shin hesitated. "And might I inquire who asked you to consider him such?"

Akari smiled slightly. "You might."

Shin returned her smile. "Who was it?"

Akari leaned close, as if to whisper. "You shouldn't gossip," she murmured. Shin stepped back and couldn't help but laugh. He nodded in acknowledgment and smiled.

"You are quite right. As I said, it is my vice."

"The least of them, I expect," she said, giving him a pointed look. "It would be a true test of my abilities to find someone willing to take on such a challenge."

"I would not ask it of you," Shin said, too quickly. Akari heard the haste in his voice and her smile widened.

"Ah. One of those, are you?"

"I am content in my isolation," Shin said, looking down his nose at her.

"But marriage isn't about you, is it?" she countered. "It is about family."

Shin was about to reply – and stopped. "Yes," he said softly. "It is about family, isn't it?" He smacked his fan into his palm. "That is a good point. Thank you, Lady Akari. This has been a most enlightening conversation."

CHAPTER TWELVE
The Kitchens

Kitano Daichi lounged on the steps that separated the lower kitchens from the upper, deftly peeling an orange with the sharpened edge of the tip of his prosthetic finger. Traditionally, the lower kitchens were used for the storing and cleaning of ingredients. Here, it was also the station of the keep's taste-testers. They sampled each ingredient, each dish – even the water used for cooking – before it was served up to the keep's residents.

The tasters wore plain uniforms, marked with the mon of the Akodo. Each one performed their task with almost ridiculous gravity, nibbling at grains of rice. Kitano watched them with mild interest, wondering what it must be like to agree to die on behalf of someone else. It wasn't something you'd catch him doing. He sniffed the air, detecting the aroma of grilling fish and cooking millet cakes.

The actual cooking went on in the upper kitchens. Ingredients were prepared down below and then transported up for completion. Kitano had been sitting up near the hearth until he'd been chased out. He preferred the steps anyway. It was cooler down here. The lower kitchen had been carved out of the riverbank. It even had its own jetty for deliveries.

He flicked away a piece of peel and wiped his ivory finger on the front of his robes, his attentions on the other servants. Servants often knew more about the activities of their betters than anyone. It was one of the reasons they made such effective spies. The kitchens at River Keep were substantial, and filled with noise and movement. Deliveries of rice, fish and other fundamentals were constant, as was the preparation of said foodstuffs. And through it all, the servants talked. Gossiped, rather.

Kitano took it all in. The Lion servants mostly ignored him; he was used to that. Some of it was arrogance, some uncertainty. He wasn't part of the fabric here. That suited him just fine. An ignored servant was an invisible servant.

A ladle struck him on the head.

"Pick up that peel! Have you no decency?"

Kitano flinched. Then, with exaggerated slowness, he bent down to retrieve the bit of peel. When he'd done so, he looked up at his attacker. Eka was old; possibly the oldest person he'd seen on the island. Not withered, though; toughened, like an old nut. Her white hair was bound up messily, held in place with iron needles – used, he thought, for testing the consistency of cakes. She wore an apron and had a set of cooking knives sheathed on her hip. Kitano bobbed his head respectfully. "Good day, Mistress Eka," he said.

"Why are you lazing about, little bird? Don't you have something to do? Isn't your master wondering where you are?"

"He has little use for me," Kitano said, rising slowly to his feet. "I do my best to stay out of his way." The truth was, he'd been waiting for Eka. She was the daimyō of the kitchens – the ruler of the lower keep. The other servants, even those of higher status, deferred to her.

Kitano had quickly pinpointed her as the font of all acceptable gossip in the keep. If the servants knew it, Eka had probably told them, and warned them against sharing it. All of this meant that the easiest way to learn anything about anything in River Keep was to get Eka talking. That was the tricky bit. Eka didn't like him.

She glanced at him. "I can't imagine why such a fine, handsome lord like yours keeps such a disreputable sort like you in his employ."

"I'm told it's pity," Kitano murmured. He trailed after her, snatching some nuts from a nearby bowl as he went. He popped them in his mouth before she noticed.

Eka snorted. "Wouldn't catch a Lion feeling pity. Especially for a servant."

Kitano shrugged. "I suppose I'm lucky my master's a Crane."

She snorted again and made her way to the stove. It sat at the far end of the kitchen, close to the water. A small wooden table sat nearby, with a plate of fish ready for grilling. The fish were for the servants' lunches. Akodo servants ate well, Kitano noted. Better, in fact, than he'd expected. The Lion weren't renowned for their largesse, after all. Then, there were plenty of fish in the river. All they had to do was catch them.

Eka, he'd learned, insisted on cooking the servants' lunches herself. She watched out for the others. It was an admirable thing. Many would abuse such authority, if granted it. Eka seemed to regard it not as a privilege but as a responsibility. He leaned against the stone wall and watched her prepare the meal. After a moment, she glanced at him. "What?"

"What?" Kitano said innocently.

"Why are you lurking? Go do it somewhere else."

"But I wanted to take advantage of your wisdom."

"You wanted to take advantage of something, I bet." She deftly turned the skewers and peered at him. "You're not getting a free meal here. You're not one of us."

Kitano paused, as if to consider this. "I'm not the only stranger here, am I? Plenty of Itagawa servants running around. Do you treat them so poorly?"

"No. They are of the Lion."

"Ah. Well." Another pause. He'd learned from Lord Shin that pauses were like feints – they drew your opponent's attention wonderfully. Eka looked at him expectantly. "What do you make of him, then? This Lord Mosu?"

"What do you mean?"

"Well, I'd heard he was killed," he ventured.

The old woman's expression tightened. "And not a moment too soon." Then, as if realizing she'd said too much, she turned her attentions to her skewers. Kitano hid a smile. There it was. He scratched his cheek.

"Bad one, was he?"

"I'm not one to gossip."

"A bit of gossip is good for the soul – or so I hear."

That earned him a smile; one so quick, he almost missed it. "You don't give up, do you?" Eka murmured. "I've heard Cranes pay for that sort of thing."

Kitano grinned conspiratorially. "A little, if it's of interest." He tapped his robes. The small pouch of money Lord Shin had given him clinked softly. Eka's ears were keen though, and her eyes narrowed. Kitano went on. "Why not tell me, and I'll let you know if he'd be inclined to pay?"

Eka bared her teeth in a hard smile. "Why not pay me first,

and I'll tell you all I know? Or get out of my kitchen. Your choice, little bird."

Kitano chuckled. He'd expected nothing less. "Only if you promise to dole it out fairly among the others," he said. "A little goes a long way down here."

Eka's smile softened. "We take care of our own, little bird. Always have."

Kitano handed over the whole pouch. Anyone else, he'd have doled it out piecemeal. "Tell me about Lord Mosu."

"Disrespectful, is what he was." She continued turning the fish on the grill, and the smell of them and the sizzle made Kitano's mouth water. "He was a rude one. Gave himself airs, and him an Itagawa."

"What sort of airs?"

"Took liberties. With some of the more… impressionable girls." She glanced around, as if searching for eavesdroppers. "Some of the not so impressionable ones as well."

"Oh?"

She nodded, jaw set. "Had that manservant of his pay them off. Or so I heard."

Kitano frowned. "This manservant, what did you make of him?"

"A foul creature," she said flatly. "A killer and no mistake. Used to flaunt himself about, like his master. As if he were too good to speak to us." She sniffed. "Claimed his parents were samurai. If they were, they died of shame."

Kitano nodded. "I'm sure you are right. Those fish smell excellent, by the way. You have a deft touch with the skewer, Mistress Eka."

She smiled and went on. "The worst of it is, he used to be a student of the dojo here. Worked as a cleaner to earn his keep, if

you can believe it." She sniffed. "And him thinking he's too good for us."

"How'd he meet Lord Mosu?"

"No idea, but that was a match made in the hells, and no two ways about it." She paused. "Now that I think about it, they must have met at the dojo."

"Mosu was a student at the dojo?"

"All of them were. All the suitors. Lady Minami and Lady Moriko. The dojo here is acclaimed." She added the last bit proudly, as if it were her doing. "That Mosu was taught by the best teachers in all of the Lion lands. Not that he was much of a fighter."

"Maybe he learned from the pirates." Kitano eyed the fish longingly. "The way I hear it, being dead for a while improved his personality. Then, that might be wishful thinking."

Eka paused. "No. He's changed, some. More polite at least. Lost his face, but gained some compassion. Treats the girls better." She shook her head. "Doesn't mean I trust him." She gave him a sly glance. "The way I hear it, he's dead and the Itagawa replaced him."

"Why would they do that?"

"An important marriage, isn't it? Puts them one up on the Ichime and the Seizuka. That's what it's all about, in the end, with them above us. Status and saving face." She turned the skewers and lifted one, pointing it at him. "You mark me, he's not the real thing. And they all know it. But they go along with it because it'd make them out to be fools, otherwise." She sighed. "It's easier down here. Simpler."

"I agree with simpler. Maybe not with the easy part." His stomach rumbled noisily and he put his hand over it. Eka sniffed and handed him the skewer.

"I never could stand anyone going hungry. Eat, little bird."

Kitano hesitated, for form's sake, and then gratefully took the skewer. As he ate, he probed for more titbits of information. Names and places, encounters. Most of it fit with what he'd already learned. Mosu and Jiro had made few friends in the district; those they had made were of similar character. Kitano recognized a few of the names, including that of a ronin named Manabu, whose reputation was not the best.

Eka and the other servants seemed as surprised as anyone else that the match had been made. Lady Moriko was universally beloved; Mosu was universally loathed – or had been. Since his return, that loathing had softened to something like uneasiness. No one quite knew what to make of Mosu these days. He kept to himself, and neither gambled nor caroused.

That alone made Kitano suspect that Eka was right. A man could change, certainly, but to change that much? Something was going on, though he didn't know what. Luckily, he wasn't the one who had to figure it out.

After talking with Eka, Kitano made his way upstairs, finishing off the fish as he went. He paused as he spotted a flash of blue silk. Of course. It was only a matter of time before Lord Shin decided to pay a visit to the kitchens. Probably to try another of his 'recipes'. Kitano shivered. Lord Shin had many talents, but cooking wasn't one of them.

Shin was politely arguing with one of the cooks when he noticed Kitano. He ceased badgering the cook and made his way over to Kitano. "Enjoying yourself?" he asked, indicating the fish. Kitano finished and slid the skewer into his sleeve. One never knew when a sharp stick might come in handy. Also, there was still some fish on it.

"Not really. These Akodo are a snooty bunch."

"You should see the servants in a Crane castle. Permanent neck injuries from all the upturned noses. I assume you've kept your ears open."

"Yes, my lord." Kitano quickly filled Shin in on what Eka had told him. "Mosu was – is – a bad one. The servants hate him, or did."

"He was here that long then?"

"Didn't take that long, but yes. Months. Since before marriage was even discussed." Kitano scratched his cheek. "The Itagawa have a permanent berth at one of the wharfs. All the vassal families do. They don't use them much, but they all have a presence in the district. From what I heard, Mosu was sent here because they didn't know what else to do with him."

"They wanted to get rid of him."

Kitano nodded. "Seems like."

Shin grunted softly. "What else have you learned?"

Kitano leaned close. "Mosu wasn't coming to the city when the ship was attacked. He was leaving." He'd learned that early on, from one of the guards on the bridge. Soldiers talked too much, especially when they were losing at dice. He'd been saving it for last, because it seemed the most important. He couldn't say why, though. "Like he was running away from something."

Shin paused, frowning thoughtfully. "Yes, that is interesting." He smiled at Kitano. "Color me impressed, Kitano. You've done a good day's work, and quickly."

Kitano ducked his head. "Thank you, my lord."

"How much did it cost me?"

Kitano flinched. He tended to spend a bit more freely than was necessary, but it was all in a good cause. The money he'd given to Eka had been the last of his monthly stipend. "Not so much as all that, my lord." He paused. "Could use some more, though. Just in case I have to ask any more questions."

Shin smiled. "We'll see." He nudged the bowl toward Kitano again. "Have a rice ball. I made them myself."

Kitano looked at the bowl, and then at Shin. "I... ah, I ate already, my lord." He patted his stomach. "All full up."

Shin sighed. "Ah. Well. Your loss." He selected a rice ball and bit into it. He paused, as if disconcerted by a sudden sourness. He chewed slowly and swallowed reluctantly, careful not to let any sign of his discomfort show on his face, but Kitano could read it in his eyes. "Are you sure you don't want one?" he asked, coughing slightly.

Kitano shook his head, careful to give no sign that he'd noticed his master's discomfort. "No, thank you, my lord. As I said, I already ate."

CHAPTER THIRTEEN
Drowned Merchant River

The three-masted sloop made its way downriver, the blue sails billowing with the wind. The crew went about their business with a commendable efficiency; though she didn't care for the woman, Kasami had to admit that Lun knew how to command.

"It was a bad idea, bringing him," Arban said, studying Kenzō covertly. The auditor stood on the lower deck, watching the water. He might have been on a pleasure trip, for all the concern he showed. "He's up to something." The Ujik burped softly and thumped his chest with his fist. "I hate boats."

"You didn't have to come," Kasami said as she ran her polishing cloth along the curve of her sword. They sat on the upper deck, out of the way of the crew. Arban burped again. He was looking distinctly queasy. She smirked as he closed his eyes and took a deep breath. She liked Arban, in a way. He was rough around the edges, certainly. Irksome, even. But he was as loyal to Gota as she was to Shin. "Indeed, you'd have had an easier time of it."

"Gota told me to go with you, so I go with you," Arban wheezed. He grimaced. "We could have taken horses."

"Feel free to swim to shore and find one," Lun said, crouching down beside them. She had an apple in her hand and took a bite. "Easier to get where we're going by river, though."

"And where is that?" Arban asked.

"Willow Quay," Kasami said. She looked at Lun. "You think they'll be there?"

Lun took another bite of apple. "If not, someone will know where they've gone," she said around her mouthful. She peered up at the sky. "Should be there any time now. After that, it's just a matter of finding someone willing to talk." She glanced at Kasami. "Keeping your hand off your sword while we're there might be a good idea. They don't like samurai in Willow Quay, and they'd probably just as soon bury you in the shallows as talk."

"They can try," Arban said, grinning. Then his eyes widened and he scrambled for the rail, where he proceeded to be noisily sick. Lun chewed thoughtfully as she watched him, then glanced at Kasami.

"So," she said.

Kasami paused. "Is there something on your mind?"

"Always. What is he hoping to find exactly? It's not like river pirates keep records about who all they've killed, or not killed, as the case may be."

"He wants to know about a Lion vessel that was attacked a year ago. A sloop. There was a Lion courtier aboard and he was taken for ransom."

"A year is a long time to be a captive," Lun said, doubtful. "A long time not to get a ransom as well. Assuming they didn't pay it."

"Of course they didn't."

"Of course," Lun repeated, scratching her cheek. "Can't go around paying ransoms. People might get the wrong idea." She grunted. "If they didn't pay, he's dead."

"Probably. Only he's getting married in a few days."

Lun paused. "Is he now? How's that?"

"Lord Shin thinks he's a fraud. He wants me to find proof the man is dead." She hesitated. "Time is of the essence."

"So, we're not just looking for pirates, we're looking for a dead man." Lun gestured. "The river is littered with dead men. Graves are stacked three deep on these banks. It's like trying to find a grain of rice in a bushel."

Kasami grunted. "And yet, I intend to do so."

Lun rubbed her eyepatch. "Of course you do." She took another bite of her apple. "Won't be easy. Like I said, it's not like they keep records."

"How many ships have been taken for ransom since then?" Kasami asked.

Lun looked out over the water. "None, to my knowledge. The Lion were upset. They beheaded pirates for days – those they didn't nail to masts or bury in the shallows."

"Exactly," Kasami said. She flipped her sword over and began polishing the other side. "Pirates' memories might not be long, but I'd bet that someone remembers what happened, given the Lion's response."

Lun grunted. "The Crane must be rubbing off on you."

Kasami paused, wondering whether that was an insult or a compliment. She decided it was simply an observation and dismissed it. When no reply seemed forthcoming, Lun rose to her feet. "I need to see to the crew. Remind them we're here on business."

Kasami grunted in acknowledgment, but didn't look up from her sword. She found that such mundane activities gave her time to think. This time, however, her thoughts were interrupted by someone behind her, coughing to catch her attention.

"I still wish to speak to you," Kenzō said.

Kasami turned. The auditor stood behind her. She grunted and turned back to the water. She was still surprised that he'd actually accompanied them. "Speak then, if you must."

"Where are we going?"

"Willow Quay."

Kenzō grunted. "A haven for criminals. Why?"

"We are looking for criminals."

He frowned. "Why?"

"Because Lord Shin wishes them found."

Kenzō cocked his head, as if in puzzlement. "Ah. Another of his little puzzles. I will never understand why he wastes his time on such unimportant matters." He glanced at her. "Or on such wasteful extravagances as theaters. Speaking of which, I find his decision to purchase such a place to be a curious one."

Kasami kept her eyes on the water. "As you said, he is prone to extravagance."

"Or perhaps it has something to do with the actress."

Kasami paused. "Actress?"

"Okuni was her name, I believe." Kenzō smiled thinly. "Only she wasn't an actress – or, rather, not solely an actress. She was involved in what others have called the 'affair of the poison rice', was she not?"

Kasami turned away. "I do not recall."

"Are you lying?"

The question – so blunt – caught her off guard. Kenzō was

normally not so blunt. This was a new side to him. Or perhaps he was simply adept at wearing a mask. Auditors, she belatedly recalled, were also investigators. She looked at him – really looked at him, perhaps for the first time – and saw not the officious representative of authority, but someone much like Shin. She almost smiled, but didn't. She doubted either man would care for the observation.

"Well?" he demanded, impatient. There was the difference. Shin was only rarely impatient, but Kenzō? Always. A hound on a leash; a hunting hawk on a tether. A flaw in his technique. Then, according to Shin, impatience could be used as a blade, capable of cutting through diffidence and reticence.

"I was not lying. I did not recall her. I do now. She vanished not long after the affair was concluded. As far as I am concerned, it was not soon enough."

"You didn't trust her?"

"No."

"Why?"

Kasami paused again. The full truth of that affair had not come out, insofar as she knew. Too many people in the city had too much to lose if that particular tangle of events became common knowledge. "She was an actress," she said. "Lord Shin had a weakness for them."

Kenzō frowned. "Had."

"He has other things to occupy his attentions these days."

"Yes, so I have seen. Where is she now, this actress?"

"Vanished, as I said."

"Is he hoping she will return? Is that why he bought the theater?"

"No."

"Then why?"

Kasami sighed. "He promised her that he would take care of her troupe. He thought the most efficient way of doing so was to ensure that they had a steady venue. One that he could oversee and fund–"

"Funnel," Kenzō interjected. "He is funneling funds through the theater."

"To what end?" Kasami asked softly. Such an accusation was as dangerous as a naked blade, especially when it came to the Daidoji Trading Council. Kenzō paused.

"I do not know, yet. But I will find out."

"Why tell me?"

"Because you are a Hiramori. Loyal to the Daidoji." Kenzō leaned close. "Do you find his… hobbies concerning?"

"I did."

"But not now?"

"It is better than the alternative."

Kenzō paused, as if considering this. "He has benefited greatly from them. Both financially and socially. There is… concern that he is using his position to enrich himself. That he has been doing so for quite some time."

"Such accusations are not for my ears," she said sharply. "I am his bodyguard."

"But you are not guarding him. He has sent you away, while he… ingratiates himself with yet another clan. Do you not find that odd?"

Kasami didn't reply. What was he getting at?

Kenzō waited a few moments, then asked, "What do you know about the death of Lord Shin's predecessor?"

Kasami paused, puzzled by this sudden change of subject. The death of Shin's predecessor, Daidoji Aika, had been declared death by misadventure. She had gone out without her bodyguard and been waylaid by robbers. Her body had been hurled into the river. A tragedy. Or so it had been declared by the great and the good.

Shin had doubted that was the whole of the truth, though he had only rarely expressed such thoughts to her. Nor had he undertaken any steps to investigate the matter, as he had so many others. At least, not to her knowledge. She looked at the auditor. "What do you know about it?"

Kenzō sighed, as if talking to a child. "Daidoji Aika was murdered. It is clear to anyone with any sense whatsoever."

"By robbers."

"Is that what he told you?"

Kasami hesitated again. The insinuation was ridiculous, and Kenzō knew it. But it lay between them nonetheless. A challenge, then. Given what he'd said earlier, about her being a Hiramori, he was obviously attempting to determine her loyalty. But why in this fashion? "He told me nothing. I found out for myself."

"So you didn't trust him. Not fully." Kenzō tossed the words like caltrops, attempting to trip her up. "You did not wish to be his bodyguard. Your complaints were noted in the record of this assignment."

Kasami straightened. "I stand by my words then, and now."

Kenzō smirked. "Have you changed your mind, then?" Another jab. She recognized the tactic from her time with Shin. Courtiers wielded words the way samurai wielded blades. Attack and counterattack. He wanted her on the defensive. Wanted to control the flow of battle. But control was an illusion, especially when it came to battle. Every Hiramori learned that truth in the cradle.

"Yes," she said simply. Then, for good measure, "I was wrong."

Kenzō blinked, momentarily at a loss. He had not expected her to admit such a thing – a misreading of her character, one Shin would not have made. That was another difference between men like Kenzō and Shin. Kenzō saw only what he expected. Shin saw everything. "Well then–" he began, but she cut him off.

"What do you know of Daidoji Aika's death, Lord Kenzō?"

He took a step back. "Only what I have said."

She pursued him. "Because Lord Shin would be very interested to know. He has made investigations into such matters something of a hobby, as you yourself mentioned." She paused, as if considering the matter. "Or could it be that you know nothing at all and are simply speaking out of malice?"

Kenzō drew himself up. But instead of chiding her, he said simply, "You are a credit to the Hiramori. So loyal, and to one who does not deserve it."

"I am loyal," she said. "And that is why I will forgive you your impertinence and insults. Killing you, while eminently satisfying, would have consequences for my lord. So, you will live another day, thanks to him."

Kenzō stared at her in bewilderment which gradually slid into a look of sick apprehension. His earlier confidence evaporated. "You dare to threaten me? I am a representative of the Daidoji–"

"No," Lun said from behind them. "You are a man on a boat. My boat. And here, I am the sole authority." Kenzō and Kasami turned. Kenzō opened his mouth to protest, but Lun took a loud bite of her apple and chewed noisily. "And, as the sole authority, I could have you thrown into the river. I could have you nailed to the mast or weighted down and dragged behind my sloop as bait for the kappa."

She took a final bite and tossed the core to Kenzō. "You came aboard my boat freely and of your own will. If you'd like to leave it the same way, I'd watch what you say about the man who pays me." She looked past him, at Kasami. "We're coming up on Willow Quay now. Better get your sword sharp."

CHAPTER FOURTEEN
Lady Ai

Shin took his cushion with a minimum of pomp. He wore his most sedate robe with its subtle embroidery, suggestive of loose feathers. The receiving room was smaller than he'd expected, smaller than his own in the keep, in fact. Had they given him the largest room? Was it some subtle criticism of him on the part of his hosts? He dismissed the thoughts almost as soon as they occurred to him and focused his attentions on his hosts.

Lady Moriko sat near the windows, a satsuma-biwa held sideways across her chest. She played softly, and not with her fingers but with a bachi stick, in the traditional fashion. She didn't acknowledge Shin, seemingly too wrapped up in her music.

Across from him sat the mother of the bride, Akodo Ai. She was a willowy woman, so ethereal and fragile in appearance that Shin wondered how she moved without collapsing into pieces. But her eyes were sharp, and there was a haughty intelligence in them. A keen mind, then. He would have to be circumspect – or rather, foolish.

The Lion expected a Crane to be one of two things: a manipulator or a fool. Shin preferred to be regarded as a fool.

No one challenged a fool, save another fool. And he didn't think Ai was that. He considered his opening salvo carefully, waiting until a servant had finished pouring the tea. Shin wafted the scent of the pot toward himself. He raised an eyebrow in surprise. "Dark Sky?"

"You have an exquisite nose, Lord Shin," Ai said politely.

"Thank you. I have often been complimented on my profile." Shin put on an expression of modest embarrassment. "Oh, you meant my recognition of the tea... how silly of me. Yes, I have often smelled it on my occasional visits to a certain tea house in Toshi Ranbo. I understand they serve several obscure blends there, though I will admit that I have not had the courage to try many of them. I prefer Silver Needle myself."

"Yes, I had heard that," Ai replied, though whether with acknowledgment or condemnation, Shin couldn't say. "Still, I ask that you try it, if only for my benefit. I wish to know what a cultured palate thinks of it."

"I shall give it my utmost attention, my lady," Shin said as he picked up his cup. It smelled delightful, though a touch too subtle for his tastes. He said neither of these things, however. Instead, he gave her a slight nod of approval.

"Speaking of your attentions, my lord: how goes the preparations for the festivities?"

"Oh, very well. I have arranged for a number of delightful entertainments for the guests, and the banquet is well in hand. Everything will be satisfactory, I believe."

"Satisfactory," she repeated. "A tricky word. For what a Crane might deem satisfactory, a Lion might find lacking." An insult – not quite veiled – and a challenge, all in one and issued in the softest of tones besides. Moriko came by it honestly, he reflected.

Nonetheless, Shin was careful to appear as if the implication had flown over his head. Instead of replying directly, he said, "Have you looked over the seating chart, by chance? I am eager for any advice you might be willing to bestow in that regard. After all, I am but a Crane, as you point out, and a Lion might look for... different things in his dinner conversation."

She blinked. "I... have not, no." Of course she hadn't, and he knew it. He doubted she'd ever looked at a seating chart in her life. Or even considered the necessity of one. Such things were not the province of nobility – at least according to the Lion.

"Oh! Well, I'm sure it's satisfactory," he said, placing a slight emphasis on the last word. Just enough to tweak her, but not enough to let her know for certain that he'd done so. "What about my changes to the menu?"

"Changes?" Again, Ai paused. "What sort of changes?"

"I thought to celebrate the binding of two families by providing the traditional meals of both. Akodo first, of course, prior to the ceremony. And then Itagawa afterwards."

"Are there differences?"

Shin gave her a startled look. "Of course! Subtle, I grant you, but these things are important. One must start as one means to go on. A blending of two families is much like a... mélange of spices, don't you think? Or a blend of tea, even." He indicated the teapot. "A careful balancing act, this... too much of one and too little of the other, and the blend is ruined." He took a sip of tea.

Ai studied him. He wondered what she'd made of his little speech. It was banal nonsense, of course. A naïve homily. The Akodo wanted to subsume Mosu; to make him a part of their family. Marriage, in his understanding, was as much a conquest as compromise. Two identities became one. But why Mosu? Why ingest such a poison? There had to be a reason. Finally, she said, "Perhaps it is so, among the Crane."

Shin hid a smile. The implied insult was not so veiled this time. Her gaze had turned flinty. He decided to give her another tweak. "I am told that the Lion venerate their ancestors with unequalled vigor. That the records you keep in regards to them are second to none."

She frowned slightly. "What of it?"

"Might I see them?" The question was uncouth, but calculatedly so. "I wish to ensure that both Moriko and Mosu's ancestors are sufficiently honored during the festivities. I am aware that time is a factor, but I am confident I can peruse the records and give them suitable recognition."

Ai hesitated. "I do not believe that would be appropriate."

"Ah, well. Perhaps I will ask Lord Touma, then. He may have some insight which will allow me to best suitably propitiate your ancestors."

"Satisfactorily, even," she murmured. He caught the amused glint in her eye as she spoke and allowed himself a cheerful smile. Hoping that she was suitably off her guard, he sent his next arrow over the wall.

"Might I ask a delicate question?"

She nodded. "Of course. You have asked so many already. What is one more?"

"Was there some… urgency to the matter of Lady Moriko's nuptials?"

Moriko's bachi skidded inelegantly across the strings of her biwa. Shin cut his eyes toward her, but she was looking out the window. A less perceptive man would not have noticed the slight trembling in her arms, or the set line of her jaw. He felt a flicker of regret. But the question was necessary groundwork for the rest to come.

Ai was silent for several moments. Then, "I had heard that the Crane were incorrigible gossips, but you are bold as well."

"I am told the Lion respects boldness."

"In warriors. Not in wedding planners." Ai's expression was one of mingled disdain and anger. "Why do you wish to know such a thing? What rumors have you heard?"

"No rumors," Shin said quickly. "But I had heard that the Seizuka and the Ichime were... unhappy with the selection process. And unhappy guests make for eventful festivities, I have found."

Ai peered down her nose at him. She was no longer fragile, but at once regal and fierce. A lioness defending her pride. "Who told you this?" she demanded.

"It is something I heard," Shin persisted. "And it seems there is some truth in it. How unfortunate." He pressed his hand to his chest, the very picture of surprised pity. As he'd hoped, Ai's expression hardened. She was angry now, but trying not to show it. He decided to press further. "I must say, if the need for Moriko to be married was so urgent, why was nothing arranged after Mosu's... disappearance?"

He kept his tone respectful, and one eye on Moriko. She was watching them surreptitiously, her biwa forgotten in her hands. He made a note to get her alone at some point. She knew more than Minami suspected, he thought.

"It takes time to arrange a match," Ai said after several moments. She glanced at Moriko, whose head was now bowed. "And having made arrangements, and with no sure sign of his death, we decided to... wait."

We, as opposed to I. The Akodo took such things seriously.

Shin glanced again at Moriko. How much of her enthusiasm for the marriage was real, and how much merely the mask of duty? Did it even matter?

"You decided to wait," he repeated. "A good decision under the circumstances." Especially if the Itagawa had paid for the privilege of a marriage. If they had a financial hold on the Akodo, the Akodo looking for a new suitor might not have been well received.

"Yes," Ai said softly. "So it was." She straightened. "If you have no more questions, I believe it is best that you return to your duties, Lord Shin. There is much yet to be done."

Shin pushed himself gracefully. "Of course, my lady." He paused. "One final question, if I might…"

Ai's expression was masklike, and her eyes were fixed on her daughter. "If you must," she said. "But make it quick. I have more than just your curiosity to attend to."

Shin accepted the rebuke with a bow of his head. "Yes, well… why him?" Another rude question, and altogether too glib. But necessary.

Ai's jaw tightened. "It is none of your concern, Crane. Leave us, please." She gave a curt gesture of dismissal, and Shin retreated, seemingly chastened. But she'd told him more than he'd expected. There was more to this arrangement than simple matrimony. Why allow her daughter to marry such an unsuitable groom? Why wait for him to return from the dead?

He was aware that he was overstepping. Minami had wanted him to discover whether Mosu was a fraud or not; she had not asked him to investigate the circumstances of the match itself, nor would she be pleased when she found out. But the two things were connected; it was all part of the same tangle of thread. Pulling on one necessitated pulling on the other. Otherwise, the knot would only tighten.

Yoku was waiting for him in the corridor. "You are making a nuisance of yourself," he said as he fell in behind Shin. "Lady Ai is not a woman to be trifled with."

"I assure you, I was merely making small talk," Shin said.

"Regardless, I have received word that the Ichime will arrive with the evening tide. You will be expected to meet them."

"Oh good."

"And Lady Minami has requested your presence for the afternoon meal."

"Wonderful. My visit to the kitchens made me quite hungry." He glanced back at the bodyguard. "But first, answer a question for me – did Mosu have some... virtue I am not seeing?"

"None that I am aware of."

"Then why him? Why not another Itagawa? Surely there is no lack of unmarried sons in the family? So why Mosu?" He stopped and turned, forcing Yoku to stop or run into him. "Shika Akari had no answer for me. Lady Ai refused to say. So why?"

"I do not know," Yoku said, a trifle defensively.

"Why was Mosu sent here?"

Yoku frowned. "What do you mean?"

"He trained here, at the dojo. But I assume he went home, at some point. Why send him back here? To get him out of the way – or to get him into place?"

Yoku's frown deepened. "What are you accusing us of?"

"It's not an accusation. Just a question. Why was he here?"

"I do not know."

"But you must have an idea. An opinion. Share it with me, if you would." Shin sighed. The Lion were proving to be a closemouthed lot. "He was – is – your cousin. You know enough to have some opinion of the man. Some context for me."

Yoku was silent for long moments. Then, "Mosu chose himself."

"What do you mean?"

"He asked to be allowed to court Moriko. His family agreed. I cannot say why. Perhaps they wished to be rid of him. Perhaps..." He trailed off, a sour look on his face. "What is done is done. It does not matter."

Shin studied him for a moment before turning away. "Oh, I believe it does. I just cannot say why as yet."

CHAPTER FIFTEEN
Willow Quay

Willow Quay had sprouted like mold along the inner curve of a secluded cove on the Drowned Merchant River sometime during the last century. The cove itself provided a refuge of sorts from both the river's raging current and the occasional patrols from the City of the Rich Frog. The shanty docks and crumbling wharfs of the slum were a haven for smugglers and pirates. Not all the trade that passed through was illicit, just most of it.

Lun's sloop had taken anchor at one of the outermost jetties, and her first mate, Torun, was haggling with the owner of the wharf over the fees. From what Kasami could see, this mostly involved a lot of threats on both sides, and some theatrical gesticulation. She adjusted the hang of her armor and checked her swords. It felt as if she rarely wore her armor these days, though she knew that wasn't true.

It was not a subtle tactic; Shin would be disappointed, she knew. But she had no patience for investigation. Shin enjoyed the slow teasing of information out of reluctant parties, but she thought it nothing more than a waste of time. Better to announce oneself and force answers at the point of a sword. It saved time, in the end.

Kasami pushed the thought aside and concentrated on her surroundings, as she would any battlefield. She looked at Lun. "You know pirates. What is your opinion?"

Lun flipped up her eyepatch and rubbed the scarred socket. She pointed to one of the buildings. "Sake house."

"Why?"

"Too drunk to fight back."

Arban laughed. "That suits me." He gestured to the gangplank. "Shall we?"

"I will do this alone," Kasami said. Arban frowned.

"Lord Gota told me to stay with you."

"And I have no intention of letting you out of my sight," Kenzō said sharply. He pushed through Lun's crew with an expression of arrogant disdain. "Not until I learn what your master is up to."

Kasami grunted and turned away. "Fine. But if anyone gets in my way, I will not be responsible for what occurs." She marched down the gangplank and across the wharf. A crowd had gathered, but its interest wavered slightly as it caught sight of her. A fully armored samurai was not a common sight; it also promised potential unpleasantness in the near future. Samurai were a sign of authority, and Willow Quay was allergic to such.

"We're attracting a lot of attention," Arban murmured.

"Good," Kasami said. "Let them look. Let them worry."

"They might decide they don't like it."

"Again – let them." She glanced at him. "Subtlety is a courtier's weapon. I am not a courtier. I am a warrior. I will do this my way."

The sake house sat on the street corner facing the river. It was an ugly little structure, with mildewed timbers and a frayed banner outside – an old back-banner, bearing the marks of battle. The banner itself was burnt and the mon illegible. A half dozen guards loitered outside. The local militia, Kasami assumed. Even outlaw towns needed someone to keep order. These looked as if they were waiting for someone.

They saw the group heading for them and an immediate conversation took place – an argument, actually. Arban laughed. "Looks like they're trying to decide whether to run now, or tough it out for a few more moments." He glanced at Kenzō. "Care to wager on which they'll choose? I'll give you good odds."

"Stay here," Kasami interrupted. "Keep an eye on them. I will go inside."

"Alone?" Arban asked.

"Do not worry. I will be diplomatic."

"That's what I'm worried about," Arban said. He looked at the guards speculatively. "Still, if we stay out here, so will they. Might be for the best."

Kasami, already moving toward the entrance to the sake house, didn't reply. All conversation inside ceased as she entered. She paused, letting her eyes adjust to the dimly lit interior. It was crowded: smugglers, sailors, and pirates. They watched her warily as she moved into the center of the common room.

"I am Hiramori Kasami. I am here on the authority of Lord Daidoji Shin. I am looking for pirates."

Coarse laughter greeted this declaration. Most of it from a table near the door. She took note of its occupants; four men, all armed. Something about them reminded her of the guards outside, and she decided to keep one eye on them. She continued, "A Lion vessel. It was taken a year ago. There were captives – a courtier, perhaps others. I wish to know the whereabouts of the pirates involved."

"Is there a reward?" one of the men from the corner table shouted.

"There can be," she said, after a moment's hesitation.

More laughter greeted this. The speaker stood, his hands folded inside his robes. He was tall, tattooed, with long hair bound in a single braid. A ronin, perhaps. He had that look. "Somehow I don't believe you. Maybe you should leave."

"What you believe does not matter. A substantial reward is offered for information."

A murmur ran through the patrons. Kasami studied their faces, searching for something more than interest. She was looking for worry, fear. Someone who hoped no one would step forward. And she found it at a bench near the far wall. A man, in a group; his eyes darted around, as if looking for an escape route.

She studied him; he had the look of a sailor. Older, weathered. The others in his group didn't. They looked like merchants or townsmen. She pointed at him. "You."

Silence fell once more. She gestured imperiously. "Come here."

"Stay where you are, Rashi. You don't have to do what she says. Willow Quay doesn't belong to the Crane." The speaker in the far corner had come out from behind his table. His friends were still sitting. "It belongs to us. We're in charge here."

"And who are you?" Kenzō demanded as he stepped inside. "How dare you ignore the orders of a superior? You will tell us what we wish to know or the iron wing of the Daidoji will crush this pesthole and all within it."

Kasami stared at him in shock, unable to believe he'd done something so bewilderingly stupid. The ronin shrugged off the top of his robes, baring his chest and arms – and freeing himself to draw his swords. He did so, snatching his long blade free of its sheath and holding the edge beneath Kenzō's throat. The auditor looked less frightened than affronted. "Drop your swords, or your master loses his head." He sneered at her. "Come to slum it, then? You samurai think you can come out here and throw your weight around. Well, not today."

"I thought I told you to stay outside," Kasami said, ignoring the ronin.

"I was curious," Kenzō said. "Tell this ruffian to release me."

Kasami looked at the pirate she'd been about to question. The man's eyes flicked to the back. He tensed, ready to run the moment her attentions were elsewhere. She was tempted to let Kenzō suffer for his idiocy. Instead, she sighed and turned to face the ronin, her hand resting atop the hilt of her sword. "Let him go."

"I don't think you understand how this sort of thing works," the ronin said. His companions had gotten to their feet as well. They were all armed, but out of condition, unshaven and uncertain. They looked to him for orders. He'd send them first.

"It isn't me who lacks understanding." Her hand tightened about the hilt of her sword. "But I shall enlighten you, if that is your wish."

"Oh, I'd like nothing better. Rashi, go tell Souta that someone is asking about him. We'll hold her here for him."

Kasami heard the pirate spring to his feet and run. She made no move to stop him. She thought, perhaps, that she wished to talk to this Souta. Letting him come to her sounded more efficient than running around hunting for him. "You will lower your sword and let Lord Kenzō go."

"Or what?"

"Or I will not kill you."

The ronin snorted. "That doesn't seem like much of a threat."

Kasami smiled.

The leader stepped back, still holding his blade to Kenzō's throat. The other three came for her in a rush. She waited for them, allowing them to get close. Unlike their friend, they weren't ronin – just thugs with blades and not enough sense to know when they were outmatched. She drew her sword at the last instant.

Her blade was as light as air, and it danced in her hands. They died swiftly, expiring each in turn, with a minimum of effort on her part. When it was done, she angled the blade so that the blood ran off it and onto the floor. She looked at the ronin.

"I will not kill you," she said softly, "but I will make sure that you can never again wield a sword." She tilted her head. "A fate worse than death for a man such as yourself."

The ronin shoved Kenzō aside and charged toward her. His attack was furious, almost frenzied. She'd frightened him. A frightened warrior was a distracted warrior, and a distracted warrior was one who contributed to their own defeat. She avoided his first blow. He stumbled slightly, but recovered quickly. He recalled some of his training, at least.

The ronin slashed at her, moving more quickly than she'd expected, and she twisted aside, catching the blow on her shoulder guard. Off-balance, she staggered into the wall of the sake house. The back of her head connected with the timbers and she nearly fell to her knees. The world swam about her.

This would not be a good death.

Then... a scream. A body collapsed to the ground before her. She looked up, expecting to see Arban or Lun. Instead, Kenzō stood some distance away, hand extended and an unhappy expression on his face. She blinked and looked at the fallen ronin. The man was dead, a slim knife rising from the back of his neck. The blade had entered at the base of his skull, severing his spine. A neat throw, incredibly difficult. She looked back at Kenzō, who snarled, "Well, don't just crouch there, Hiramori.

Can't you hear that more of them are on the way? We must get back to the others."

She reached out and jerked the knife from the dead man's neck. "I didn't know you were armed." She gave the blade a quick once-over – it was a simple thing; straight, razor-sharp. There was no cross-piece to the hilt. Well-balanced, too. A throwing knife, such as an assassin might use. Or, apparently, an auditor. She tossed it back and Kenzō easily snatched it out of the air. The blade vanished an instant later. She wondered how many more of them he had hidden about his person.

"I did not wish you to know," he said simply. "We really must go. There are too many of them, and these cramped quarters will only hinder you." He looked back the way they'd come. The sound of rushing feet was louder now. "Though it appears our time has run out…" He retreated from the doorway at her curt gesture.

"Not ours," she said softly. Her head had cleared and the world felt stable beneath her feet once more. "Theirs. Stay behind me."

The first of the pirates rushed into the back room, waving a sword. He wore a suit of Ujik mail over his filthy robes and bore an ill-fitting helmet. The leader, she assumed, likely self-appointed. He looked as if he'd armored himself hastily. He slid to a stop as he saw what was waiting for him. Others followed, and soon a half dozen pirates crowded the doorway. They shifted nervously, eyeing her with obvious fear. "Surrender, samurai," the leader barked, somewhat hesitantly.

"No," Kasami said. She was getting tired of people telling her to surrender. It was irksome. "You are Souta?"

The man puffed up. "I see you know who I am."

"I don't. I know only that I need to ask you some questions. Surrender, and I will make it a painless interrogation."

This provoked some muttering, and Souta attempted to jostle some of his followers forward with curses and blows from the flat of his blade. They were reluctant to go, however. Kasami waited, saying nothing, her sword held low – invitingly.

Finally, tired of their indecision, she cleared her throat. "I only need one of you," she said simply. "The rest may go."

One of the pirates – a burly woman clad in brightly colored robes – shoved several others aside and raised a bow. "She's only one woman, cowards," she barked as she loosed an arrow. She had some skill, but it was child's play for Kasami to cut the arrow from the air. As the pieces fell, several of the pirates ran.

Kasami paused and said, "And now there are only three of you."

The woman in the colorful robes glanced at Souta in his makeshift armor. Then, as if in perfect harmony, they both shoved the third pirate – a scrawny youth in threadbare clothing, clutching a spear – toward her, like an offering.

Kasami accepted their gift, easily batting aside the spear-tip and disarming the pirate. She rammed the hilt of her sword into his belly, knocking him to his knees. "Stay down," she murmured to the wheezing youth. She looked up, but the other two pirates were already fleeing as the others had. She briefly considered pursuit, but decided against it. She wasn't here to kill pirates, just to question them.

She set her knee between her captive's shoulder blades and pinned him to the floor. "If you attempt to escape, I will remove one of your legs. If you wish to walk again, you will cease your squirming." The youth's struggles ceased immediately. She quickly tore a strip from his robes, pulled his hands behind his back, and knotted his wrists together. Then she looked at Kenzō. "You have my thanks."

He gave her a startled look. "For what?"

"Aiding me."

He sniffed. "Letting you die would have been a waste of assets." He looked down at the pirate. "You expect this one to know something?"

Kasami jerked the youth to his feet. "No. I expect him to know someone who might know something." Before she could continue, Arban entered the sake house, his sword wet with blood. He took in the bodies and shook his head.

"Looks like I missed the fun."

"Trouble?" Kasami asked.

"The ones outside got antsy."

"And now?"

"Not so antsy. But the whole quay has been alerted. We need to get back to the ship before someone decides to do something stupid. Or Lun decides to leave us."

"What about the others?" Kasami asked.

"Lun sent Torun and some of the others to back me up when the trouble started. They caught the ones who came after you before they got too far. The fools surrendered without much of a fight." He set his sword across his shoulder. "Looks like you put the fear of the Crane into them."

"Good. Three captives are better than one," Kasami said. She shoved her prisoner toward Arban. "Take him. I will question them when we are safely away."

CHAPTER SIXTEEN
Lady Kanna

"No, no, and no. Wedding banners must be joyous, not solemn or fearsome. These deep oranges evoke violence, not love…" Shin clucked his tongue in dismay. "We need something lighter. Do we have a peach hue, perhaps? Maybe a tasteful blue?"

"No blue," Minami said without looking up from her logbook. They were taking lunch in the receiving room of Shin's guest quarters. Minami had brought an armful of paperwork with her; Shin suspected it was a ploy to keep him from plying her with small talk.

Shin sighed noisily. "Blue is a soothing color."

"You heard her," Yoku grumbled from behind him. "No blue."

"It appears I am outnumbered. Peach, or softer. I will have no harsh colors at this wedding. It will be fraught enough as it is." Shin waved the cloth merchant away. He glanced at Kitano, who was kneeling nearby. "Where are we with the food?"

"The kitchen staff have taken your suggestions under advisement, my lord."

Shin frowned. "That doesn't sound promising. Perhaps I should pay them another visit."

"I don't think that's necessary, my lord," Kitano said quickly. "I'll... ah, encourage them to consider the matter more seriously."

"Do not arouse Eka's wrath," Minami said, setting down her logbook.

"I wouldn't dream of it. There's an old Crane saying: never annoy those who cook the rice." Shin sat back. "I will be seeing to the entertainment this afternoon. Any requests?"

"Nothing too expensive. Or too raucous."

"Of course. I shall hire the most subtle of jugglers, the most innocuous clowns."

She frowned at him, and he hid a smile behind his fan. "Are any of Mosu's family here?" he asked, changing the subject.

Minami nodded. "His mother. She was in charge of the delegation that brought him to the city. She has been... helping with the wedding preparations." Her expression said what she thought about that, and Shin smiled. "She is very eager to see her son married."

"As any mother would be."

"Stepmother," Yoku murmured. Shin glanced at him. Yoku grunted and went on, "She is his stepmother. Itagawa Naoki remarried after the death of his first wife – Mosu's mother. Some believe that is what precipitated his... behavior." He frowned. "I think that nothing more than an excuse, however."

"She was a hard bargainer, I recall," Minami said. "Wanted permission to sell Itagawa mempo to the Unicorn and the Dragonfly. Something which was forbidden."

"Until now," Shin said. Minami nodded.

"She is an unpleasant woman. Arrogant. But clever."

"Dangerous, then," Shin said.

"Supremely so," Minami said. "And I would rather you didn't antagonize her the way you antagonized my aunt. As it is, I've had to convince her not to have you killed."

Shin laughed, but the look on Minami's face caused the sound to die in his throat. He coughed and said, "Ah. I made a rare bad impression then."

She laughed. "Rare?"

"People like me," Shin protested. "I am very likeable."

"Evidence suggests otherwise," Minami said, grinning slightly. But her amused expression turned solemn. "You must remember that you are a Crane among Lions, Shin. Though I have learned to tolerate you, they have not. Besides which, you are not an investigator, you are a wedding planner. Act like it." She looked past him as the servants opened the door and rose to her feet. "In fact, start now. I invited Ikoma Kenko, master of the Rich Frog Dojo, to speak with you, as I promised." She rose and stepped around the table. "Master Kenko," she called out. "I am glad you could come. Might I introduce Lord Shin, our new wedding planner?"

Shin rose and turned. Kenko proved to be a stooped, older man, clad in dojo colors. His wizened features broke into a ready smile as he greeted Minami. "Ah, my child, my child. You are a vision of ferocity. If only we were graced with a good war to season you up some." He clapped her on the arms with paternal pride, and then turned a glittering eye on Shin. "And who is this river reed? Not your new suitor, I hope."

"Reed?" Shin murmured, glancing down at himself. Then, in alarm, "Suitor?"

"No," Minami said firmly. "As I said, Lord Shin is our new wedding planner. He graciously offered to help with the preparations, and I accepted."

"Shin," Kenko said slowly. "I know that name. I have heard it on the wind."

"I do hope the wind had good things to say about me," Shin replied.

Kenko frowned. "Some. Not all. Lord Azuma, at least, speaks highly of you." Shin blinked in surprise. Kaeru Azuma was the imperial governor's advisor, and he hoped, a friend. He wondered how Kenko knew Azuma. Kenko went on, "He says you are cleverer than the average courtier." He looked Shin up and down, paying particular attention to his hands. "He also says you're something of a swordsman. I thought the Daidoji preferred the spear."

Shin inclined his head. "I do have some small skill with a blade, but I prefer to wound with words – or a cutting glance – when necessary."

Kenko snorted. "Doesn't sound like any Daidoji I ever met."

"Met many then?" Shin asked, good-humoredly. Kenko snorted again, in dismissal this time, and looked at Minami. "He is not a wedding planner. He is a Crane. A merchant."

"Technically, I simply oversee merchants. But I am a Crane. And skilled at planning festivities such as this one. Speaking of which… I understand it is an Akodo tradition for there to be martial demonstrations during the celebrations."

Kenko nodded reluctantly. "What of it?"

"Well, as I am the organizer of this celebration, I'd like to know what you're planning." Shin paused. "And to make one small suggestion, if I might."

"Shin," Minami began, warningly.

Kenko rubbed his chin. "A few demonstration bouts. Swords, archery, wrestling. Guests will be allowed to participate, obviously. With permission."

"And who are the participants in the wrestling bouts?"

"My students, obviously. Some outsiders from other dojos in the city. They'll lose, of course. But that's the point. The wrestlers of the Lion are superior. Why?"

"I would like to suggest that you make an addition. I was accompanied here by a young woman – Fureheshu Reo. A niece of Ichiro Gota. I'm sure the latter name is familiar to you…" Shin trailed off, waiting for a reply.

Kenko grunted. "Perhaps. What is it to me?"

"She would like to participate."

Kenko glanced at Minami, who looked away. He looked back at Shin. "Why should I allow that?"

"Call it a favor."

"I'm not in the business of doing favors for Cranes. Especially Daidoji."

Shin paused. An idea occurred to him, and he gave a slow smile. "Tell me, have you or any of your students ever had the good fortune to match swords with a graduate of the Kakita Dueling Academy?"

Kenko frowned. "No. Why?"

"There is one in the city. My bodyguard, in fact. She would be glad to provide a demonstration of her skills at your dojo, in the event that you allow Lady Reo a chance to participate."

Kenko pondered this for a moment. Then, he gave a brusque nod. "Fine. I will give her a chance to prove herself. This afternoon, just before the evening meal. Come by the dojo, and we will see if she is worthy of this privilege." He bowed to Minami. "If there is nothing else, I have preparations to oversee." He departed without waiting for a reply. Shin glanced at Minami, but she seemed bemused by the slight show of disrespect.

"He's always been like that," she said. "Comes of having trained us all."

"Still, that was easy," Shin said, dusting his hands. He still had to convince Kasami, of course, but he was sure she'd prove amenable once he explained the situation. "For my next trick, I'd like to speak to Mosu himself. Get the groom's opinion on the festivities. They are partially in his honor, after all."

Minami frowned. "Mosu has been keeping to himself since his return. But he often takes lunch with his mother at this time of day. You might be able to find them in the gardens in the south wing – that's where the Itagawa are staying. But remember what I said: do not antagonize her. I have some authority over my aunt, but Itagawa Kanna is a law unto herself."

Shin bowed his head. "I shall be on my best behavior, I promise."

Minami snorted. "I know what your promises are worth, Shin. But carry on." She looked at Yoku. "Feel free to show him the way. If only to keep him from falling in the river." She paused. "Are you close? To knowing anything?"

Shin rose. "I believe so."

"The ceremony is in two days, Shin. We must know before then."

"And we will. One way or another." Shin looked at Yoku. "Shall we?"

Yoku led him to the southern wing of the keep. In a Crane castle, each wing of a keep would have had its own theme, its own story, told in colors and decoration. What was a castle, after all, but the culmination of many stories – those of the artisans, the servants, the soldiers and the nobles who would come to call it home. But the Lion preferred function to form. Each wing was much the same as the others, save for subtle differences – a painting, marking some victory; a statue in commemoration of a fallen Akodo hero.

As they followed the wooden walkway that spanned the defensive culvert that ran between each wing, Yoku said, "Lady Kanna is an honored guest of Lady Minami. You will not embarrass her."

"I have no intention of doing so," Shin said, looking at the bodyguard. "Yoku, I must ask – are you still convinced that this is some elaborate trick on my part?" Yoku said nothing. Shin sighed. "Very well. Tell me this: why would Mosu have been leaving the city the day he was captured?"

Yoku blinked. "What?"

"Mosu was leaving the city. I had been led to believe he was coming to the city when he was attacked. Or perhaps I simply assumed it. After all, why would a groom depart prior to his wedding – unless he had no intention of going through with it." Shin paused. "I am curious, what do you make of that, Yoku?"

"Does it matter?"

"Oh, it very much does. If Mosu was departing the city – fleeing, even – he must have had good reason. That reason might lead us to why his boat was attacked."

"It was attacked by pirates," Yoku said, as if explaining things to a child.

"Yes, but it's a bit of a coincidence, isn't it?" Shin held up a hand, preventing Yoku from replying. "I know, coincidences happen all the time. But even so, it is curious, don't you think?"

"No," Yoku said flatly.

"Kasami would find it interesting," Shin lied. Kasami would, in fact, have much the same reaction as her Lion counterpart.

Yoku grunted, but didn't reply. As they passed into the southern wing, Shin noted with some interest that the Itagawa had made themselves at home. Itagawa guards were stationed at all access points, and Itagawa courtiers murmured in the corridors. That was fairly usual, when it came to weddings. So why did they all look so worried? He was about to broach the question to Yoku, when they arrived at their destination.

Like the other wings of the keep, this one was built around a central garden. It served two purposes – beauty, and arable ground for the planting of crops should a siege erupt. Shin knew from his own nosing about that each wing was also equipped with its own kitchens – smaller versions of the one he'd visited earlier. In effect, each wing of River Keep could stand on its own in the event of an attack by enemy forces. If anyone attempted to take this place from the Lion, they would pay a heavy toll in blood.

The southern garden was much like the other he'd seen: willow trees and ornamental shrubbery. This one had a bamboo fountain in the corner, and a decorative runnel to carry water from one side of the garden to the other. The soft clop of the deer scarer was accompanied by birdsong.

Lady Kanna sat at the center of the garden, surrounded by courtiers and servants. At Shin and Yoku's arrival, she dismissed the entire flock with a sharp gesture and they hurriedly scattered to the four corners of the garden. "I wondered when I might be receiving guests," she said.

Yoku stopped and bowed low. "Hello, Lady Kanna."

She peered at him. "Is that Yoku I see before me? You look older than I recall. Running after the Akodo brat must be more stressful than I imagined." She sniffed disdainfully and turned her attention to Shin. "And who is this popinjay?" Despite the question, Shin suspected she already knew the answer.

"Daidoji Shin," Shin said, bowing low. "A pleasure to make

your acquaintance, Lady Kanna. I am to organize the festivities for the wedding."

"Are you now? A Crane? How unexpected." Kanna studied him, and he studied her in turn. She was older than Lady Ai, but not by much. The ghost of a beautiful woman haunted her face, but there was still something about her. Power, perhaps. Some people wore authority lightly; others draped it over themselves like armor. People like Kanna did not simply wear it – they took it into themselves and made it an inextricable part of who they were. "Will you take lunch with me?"

"Regrettably, I have already eaten." Shin made a show of looking about. He noted several bodyguards, standing unobtrusively at the edges of the garden. "I was informed your son would be here. I wished to speak with him if I might."

"Stepson," Kanna corrected stiffly. "His mother died young." She paused. "A tragedy, for her. Lucky for me."

Shin was momentarily taken aback by such blatant pragmatism. He wondered what path Kanna had followed to wind up where she was. A crooked one, he suspected. "Ah yes, so I was told."

"You hear much, for a newcomer."

"You know us Cranes – ever alert for morsels of gossip."

"Is that why you came seeking him? Perhaps you'd like to know what lies under his mask? Are you that sort, then?"

Shin, who wasn't quite sure what sort she meant, shook his head. "I assure you, I have no malicious intent. I merely wished to get to know him in order to better perform my function." He looked around. "I see he is not here, however."

"No. He had other business. Perhaps you will see him later."

"Perhaps I might talk with you instead, then." Shin waited for her to re-extend her offer to join her, and when she gestured with her fan, he sat.

"About what?"

"About him."

"And what do you wish to know?"

Shin pulled out his own fan and tapped his knee with it. "One hears so many stories about Itagawa Mosu. I merely wish to know which to believe."

"Believe any you like." Her expression was one of amusement. She could tell he was fishing for information, even if she didn't know why.

"They say he was quite… rambunctious."

"Perhaps," Kanna admitted. "But marriage calms even the wildest of us." Her cool gaze slid up and down Shin speculatively. "Are you married, Lord Shin? No. I expect not. You do not have the look of a married man."

"Defeated, you mean?" Shin asked.

"Stable," Kanna said. "You seem quite flighty to me. Then, you are a Crane."

"I'm inclined to take that as a compliment." Shin snapped open his fan and waved it gently. "How did he come to be the suitor of choice? A most curious arrangement, in my opinion. Not the sort a great family such as the Akodo might normally choose."

"The Fortunes smiled upon us," Kanna said smoothly. No protest, no complaint. Merely an elegant, if insubstantial reply.

He decided to press harder and see what, if anything, spilled out. "If so, only briefly. Else how do you explain his… disappearance?"

"Possibly. But he is here now, and that is the only thing that matters."

"Yes. Why did you wait so long, though? To tell his intended he was alive, I mean."

Kanna's smile turned cold. "I do not see how that is relevant."

"Were you uncertain? I can see how you might have been," Shin said lazily. Kanna's features tightened in annoyance.

"On whose behalf do you ask these questions?"

By her tone, she had someone in mind. He wondered who. "My own, I assure you."

"Then you are impertinent."

"And you are prevaricating. Could it be that you are embarrassed by your hesitation? How could a mother not know her own son?"

"Stepson," she reiterated. She smacked her own fan into her palm. "You are beginning to bore me, Lord Shin. I thought a Crane would be a more interesting conversationalist."

"And I thought courage the hallmark of the Lion. We are both mistaken, it seems." It was a dangerous gambit. Kanna's bodyguards tensed slightly, angered on behalf of their mistress. But she gave the first genuine smile Shin had seen on her face since they'd been introduced. She opened her fan and laughed softly.

"I forget, sometimes, that the Daidoji are made of iron and not feathers. Fine. It was neither embarrassment nor uncertainty that made us delay the revelation. We simply needed to ensure that the arrangement could proceed as originally agreed." She leaned toward him, fan raised. "He was badly injured, you know. It took months for him to recuperate. Even now, our doctors fear any undue strain might send him to an early grave. Luckily, he was stronger than anyone knew, else he would not have survived what those animals did to him." She looked away. "That is all I will say on the matter."

Shin nodded. "I thank you for satisfying my curiosity, however impertinent."

"If we are finished, I have some matters to attend to." She gestured and one of her servants brought forward a writing desk and utensils. "I look forward to seeing what you have made of the ceremony, Lord Shin. I am sure it will be a wondrous thing."

Shin, knowing a dismissal when he heard one, rose swiftly and exited the garden with the appropriate amount of haste. Kanna was a singularly ferocious old woman. Yoku fell into step with him. Shin glanced at him. "Minami is right – that is a dangerous woman. What's next on the docket, then?"

"You are to inspect the grounds where the festivities will take place before the first guests arrive. Lord Touma is awaiting you. He will oversee the preparation and sanctification once you are satisfied."

"Oh, Lord Touma will be there? How delightful. I've been meaning to speak to him again." Shin felt a flutter in his stomach as he considered the priest. Normally, he found mystics somewhat tedious, but there was something different about Touma.

"Let's be about it then, shall we?"

CHAPTER SEVENTEEN
Moriko

Shin was still ruminating on his conversation with Kanna as Yoku escorted him across the river to the shrine. The day was stretching on, and the shrine grounds were largely empty when they arrived. In contrast, the nearby streets were busy with deliveries, as decorations were set up and streets swept.

The local merchants were bolstering their stock for the expected influx of visitors. And there would be visitors. Not guests, per se – but the hangers on of hangers-on; every courtier invited to the festivities, if not the ceremony would be accompanied by servants and bodyguards, all of whom would need places to stay, food, gifts. A clan wedding was always a boon to the local economy.

The shrine had not been decorated, nor would it be until the last possible moment. For all that, there was a certain feeling of celebration within the air. Even the shrine attendants had a spring in their step. He proceeded into the shrine, Yoku trailing silently behind him, and found himself looking at the stone that occupied it.

It was quite large, a chunk of imposing solidity. He could feel nothing emanating from it. The air didn't hum with the breath of the kami. Then, perhaps it only did so for the Akodo. Even so, it was eerie, being alone in a shrine even in the middle of the afternoon. More than one ghost story started this way. Then, he quite liked ghost stories.

He looked up and paused. A spiderweb clung to the underside of the roof. Quite a big one. He was admiring its size and intricacy when Yoku cleared his throat, signaling someone's approach. Shin turned and nodded respectfully to Touma as the priest joined him. "You allow spiders to inhabit your shrine," Shin noted, gesturing to the arachnid with his fan. Touma followed his gesture and nodded.

"It is said they capture luck in their webs."

"I thought that was flies."

Touma smiled. "Those, too." He looked around. "I confess, I brought you here under a pretense. The shrine has already been reconsecrated for the ceremony."

"Oh?" Shin asked, feeling a flutter under his ribs.

"Someone wishes to talk to you."

"Oh." Shin did his best to hide his disappointment. "Dare I ask who?"

"Lady Moriko."

"Oh," Shin said, again. "How curious. Did she say why?"

"Not to me." Touma looked at the stone. "But I thought it best to give her privacy. I am here to facilitate, after all." He looked down. "She is waiting for my signal to enter."

"And will you give it?"

"That depends."

"On?"

"How you intend to approach her." Touma turned to face

him. "She is in a state of… disorder. Something has upset her. You, perhaps." His eyes flashed ever so briefly, and Shin felt a delicious shiver of unease.

"Any upset I have given has been unintentional."

Touma nodded. "I am sure you believe that is so." He paused. "This has been a trying time for them. A time of upheaval and uncertainty. And now, when the world seems to be all in order at last, there is… doubt. Hesitation."

"Mosu," Shin said softly.

Touma didn't look at him. "They wish to believe that this thing is so, and it would be better for all if it were. But some are determined to be obstreperous."

"I hope you are not referring to me," Shin said, with mock-injury. Touma smiled.

"No. Be gentle with her." He touched Shin on the shoulder, and then turned and left. Shin watched him go, then took a deep breath and said to Yoku, "Wait outside."

"But–" Yoku began. Shin held up two fingers.

"She clearly wishes to speak to me in private, and if she meant me harm, I doubt you'd be of much help. Wait outside, please." He didn't need to look at the other man to know he was frowning, but he didn't feel up to coddling Yoku's hurt feelings at the moment.

He waited in silence for several minutes, listening to the sounds of the river. It had a different quality here, in the shrine. Less a pervasive murmuration than an insistent whisper. It was almost hypnotic, though not quite as lovely as the rumble of the frogs.

"You came," Moriko said from behind him. "I was not certain you would."

"Of course. What sort of wedding planner would I be if I did not heed the bride's wishes? May I ask why you had Touma invite me here?"

"I wished to speak with you. Alone."

Shin gave a theatrical spin. "No one here now but myself and the spiders. Carry on."

"I know why you are here."

"Of course you do. To plan your wedding."

"No," Moriko said. "I know who you are, Lord Shin, even if my mother does not."

"I see." Shin paused. "I heard you playing the biwa earlier. I am something of a musician myself."

"Do not attempt to distract me." She paused. "You made my mother very angry, earlier today. She wanted you dead."

"I did not mean to offend her."

"I think you did." Moriko looked at the stone, and then at him. "I think you mean every impertinent question, every unpleasant insinuation. There is a saying among the Lion – a Crane's beak is only good for one thing... grubbing for worms."

"Crane eat fish, actually. Both the bird and the clan." Shin smiled. "Fish and small animals. The bird, not the clan."

"Quiet," Moriko snapped. "You are here to disrupt the wedding. I will not have it."

Shin looked at her. "And who told you that?"

"It does not matter. I can see it for myself. As I said, I know who you are."

Shin allowed himself a small laugh. "Despite what you might believe, I did not intend for my little ruse to hold up to scrutiny. It is more in the nature of plausible deniability." He tilted his head. "Why did you wish to speak to me?"

Moriko studied him for long moments, gauging him coolly. Shin, who'd been similarly studied by murderers, gamblers and samurai, felt somewhat ill at ease. There was a ferocity in her gaze that he didn't care for. Moriko was not a killer, he thought. But he was suddenly well aware that he'd been wrong about that sort of thing before. Finally, she said, "I want you to leave."

"Oh? And I just got here."

"Do not play games with me, Daidoji. You should not be here." She spoke accusingly, fiercely. A lioness protecting her territory. "You are endangering the reputation of the Akodo, and I will not allow it. Leave. Or I will inform my mother–"

"No, I do not think you will. If only for Minami's sake." Shin spoke sharply, and she jolted in surprise. She was either unused to being spoken to in such a manner, or hadn't expected it of him. "More, that you would make such a demand implies to me that Minami is correct and there is something untoward going on here." He pulled out his fan and snapped it open. "Perhaps you should save us all some time and tell me what it is?"

"How dare you speak to me in such a fashion," Moriko spluttered, her hands balling into fists. "I am a daughter of the Lion!"

"And I am a son of the Crane," Shin said. "Natural foes. Yet I am here on behalf of your cousin. She is worried for you."

"She should not be."

"And yet, she is. Why might that be, do you think?"

Moriko swallowed. "I do not know, and it does not matter. I am marrying Mosu."

"That isn't the question. The question is whether the Mosu you are marrying is, in fact, Mosu. The real one, I mean." Shin turned away, fanning himself. "Of course, there is a school of thought that asks whether such a thing even matters. But it does to Minami, so I am here. And I will not be leaving until she tells me otherwise."

"I will talk to her," Moriko began hesitantly. She hadn't planned for this, he could tell. She'd assumed he'd wilt at her first roar. How like a Lion. He felt something that might have been pity.

"Perhaps you should have already talked with her," he said softly.

"I will. And you will leave."

Shin looked at her. "I thought we'd already agreed I wasn't planning on it."

"I am done here." She turned away. "I will tell Yoku to escort you to the wharf. I am sure you can bribe someone to take you home."

"What did you feel when you learned about the attack? Given what I know about Mosu – the real one – I don't think it was sadness. Was it relief?" Shin extended his fan. "I bet it was relief, perhaps mingled with a bit of shame for feeling that way."

Moriko turned back. "How dare you!"

"You've already said that. And the answer is the same. I dare, because I am a Crane. More, I am Minami's friend. And there is very little I would not do for a friend."

"You cannot speak to me this way."

"And yet, here we are." Shin folded his fan and let it smack into his open palm. "We both have our steel drawn, our feet set. A fight will only end in our embarrassment – the embarrassment of Minami, of your family. Of the Itagawa."

Moriko stared at him, panting slightly. He knew that in that moment, if she'd had steel in her hands, he'd have been dead. Finally, she relaxed. "What do you suggest?"

"That we talk. Not as adversaries, but as... acquaintances. Tell me what you know, and I will do my best to help all involved."

"We do not need your help," she said flatly.

"You still have not sheathed your blade," Shin said, in a chiding tone. He extended his arms to either side, palms out. "Mine has been put away. Extend me the same courtesy."

Moriko glared at him for a moment more, and then sighed noisily. She looked away. "I felt sad," she said, after a pause.

"Sad?"

"When he… when I heard about the attack. I felt sad."

"Why?"

She peered at him. "Why do you think? My intended was dead."

"But now he is not."

"No. A great relief to all of us."

"I'm sure. I am told he is somewhat changed from the man he was. Understandable, perhaps, given what he has been through." Shin paused. "What did you make of him when you first met him?"

"Why does it matter?"

"I am curious."

Moriko looked at him. "It does not matter."

"Did you know he was leaving the city when he was attacked?"

Moriko frowned. "No."

"Do you have any idea as to why he might have been leaving?"

"No!"

Shin studied her. He felt she was telling the truth, at least in regards to this. She seemed surprised by the idea. Insulted, even. "Do you know why you were to be married?"

"What do you mean?"

"It's rumored that the Akodo have suffered some financial difficulty recently. That they offered a marriage in return for remuneration, in order to maintain solvency."

Moriko flushed. "You are wrong."

"Am I?" Shin held her gaze. "How so?"

"The Akodo are strong. We do not do these things because we must, but because it is our duty to our vassals. It is their right to request a dynastic marriage, and our responsibility to see that their rights are honored."

Shin almost applauded. It was said with such conviction that he almost believed her. But he trusted what Konomi had told him. Once Ito brought him the proof he needed, there would be no disputing it. Until then, however, he had to tread lightly. "Perhaps," he said simply. Then, "Who told you that I was here to ruin the wedding?"

She shook her head. "It does not matter."

"I dislike it intensely when people say that. Everything matters. Every bit of information is important, even if it is not immediately obvious why. I would not ask such questions otherwise. Honestly, you Lions are such – such – oh! So stubborn." He thwacked his palm with his fan, hard enough to sting.

"I should tell my mother. She must know of this."

Shin waved this aside. "Of course she must. You would be an ungrateful daughter otherwise. But that you haven't yet tells me that you are uncertain as to whether it is truly the wisest course of action."

Moriko growled softly. Shin could see the resemblance between her and Minami now. The same set to the jaw, the same bullheaded righteousness. "Trust a Crane to talk about wisdom at such a moment. There is no wise or foolish here, only right and wrong."

"Counterpoint: there is no right or wrong in this. Only wise actions and foolish ones. It hurts nothing to wait. Conversely, if you rush to inform the Lady Ai, then I will likely be forced to leave, and your cousin will be embarrassed. Perhaps so much so that she is relieved of her duties here." Shin looked away, as if weighing the odds of such an occurrence. "If that is what you wish to do, I will not stop you. After all, if it does not matter to you that you are possibly marrying a murderer, why should it matter to me?"

"A murderer?" Moriko said, clearly startled by the idea.

"Well, yes. If your betrothed is not Mosu – and we both know he is not – then he is likely connected in some fashion to the conspiracy that claimed Mosu's life. I intend to find out who he is and how he was involved."

She stared at him. "You don't think the attack was a coincidence," she said softly. "You think someone set Mosu up. Why?"

"I do not know. I have my suspicions, but they are, as yet, unfounded. I have no evidence, merely theory. That is why I am asking questions." Shin looked at her. "Your mother knows something. So does Lady Kanna. I believe you do as well, even if you are not aware of it." He gripped his fan in both hands. "This is about more than a simple case of stolen identity. And until I learn what that is, I will continue to ask questions." He fixed her with a steady eye. "Now, will you stop me – or help me?"

CHAPTER EIGHTEEN
Interrogation

Kasami looked down at the two pirates kneeling on the floor of the sloop's hold and considered her plan of attack carefully. Among the Hiramori, piracy had only one reward – death. Her first instinct had been to kill them both and question the youth. But Lun had asked to be the one to question the youngest of their captives, leaving Kasami to deal with the other two. Arban had joined her, though she hadn't asked him to do so.

They'd left Willow Quay with all due haste. Lun's crew had set fire to a few other vessels to cover their escape, though Kasami doubted that any pirate would have been stupid enough to follow them. But now they needed to know where to go from here.

Sighing, she drew her sword and sat down on a crate. She pulled a polishing rag from within her armor and ran it along the curve, following the angle of the blade to its tip before starting over. "What are your names?" she asked as she polished her blade. The weapon balanced across her knees was an open threat, and she intended it to be taken as such. The greater their fear, the less inclined they might be to dissemble.

The woman spat on the deck. Kasami didn't cease her polishing. She glanced at the man, Souta, who sniffled nervously. His stolen armor rattled as he shifted his weight. "Where did you get the armor?" she asked, almost gently. He looked away. She indicated Arban, standing quietly behind her. "My companion is Ujik. It is he who wishes to know. If you do not tell him, he may decide to question you himself."

The pirate swallowed convulsively and peered at Arban. She heard the Ujik step closer. "Among my people, we often find cause to question those who do not wish to talk," Arban said. His accent roughened to a barbarous edge; normally, he spoke Rokugani quite well. "We have developed many ways of dealing with this. The first is I take my knife and I make a small cut on your chest. Then, little by little, I will widen the cut and peel the skin away from the muscle, strip by strip, until… well."

He looked down at the two pirates, a flat, mirthless smile on his face. "I once knew a nomad who endured the loss of most of his skin before he finally managed to bite off his own tongue and drown himself in blood." He sighed. "A brave man, my cousin. I was very proud of him, even as I cut away at him." He drew his knife. "You, however… I do not think you will last as long as my cousin."

Souta stared at him, eyes wide. "I- I- I…"

The woman glared at them. "You will not allow this, samurai," she spat. "You won't let this Ujik kill two Rokugani. Even if we are pirates."

Kasami nodded. "You are right." She put her cloth away and stood, sword in hand. "I will not let him torture you. Instead, I will simply kill you both and question the boy. The sight of your heads will undoubtedly impress upon him the seriousness of this matter." She moved behind them and raised her sword. The woman twisted around, now in a panic.

"No! Wait! Please, my lady, we will tell you what you want to know!"

"Please, please," Souta wailed, collapsing onto his face.

Kasami met Arban's amused gaze. He nudged Souta with his foot. "So, can I start cutting on this one, or...?"

"Sheathe your knife, nomad. They are feeling talkative, I think." She sheathed her sword and crouched beside the woman. "A year ago, a Lion ship was sunk by pirates a few days from the city. Captives were taken. Were you a part of that crew?"

The woman shook her head in confusion. "No, my lady. I... a year ago? This is about something that happened a year ago?" From the look on her face, Kasami knew that she'd struck a nerve.

"Do you know anyone who was part of that crew?" Kasami asked. She caught the woman's chin in her hand and forced the pirate to look at her. She glanced meaningfully at Souta as she asked the question. The woman gave a brief, reluctant nod. Kasami wondered what the connection was between them. Friendship? Or something else? She pushed the thought aside and turned her attentions to Souta. "You were a member of this crew?"

Souta nodded jerkily, nearly banging his head against the deck. "Just a- a crewman. Not an officer. I was... I- I left, after the... after we took the ship. I had enough money to- to buy my own."

"There was that much loot to be had?" Arban asked.

"No," Souta said. "We- we were paid."

"Paid," Kasami repeated. "By whom?"

"I- I don't know." Souta didn't meet her gaze. "W- we were

paid to attack the boat. Afterwards, I- I left. The others decided to- to keep the captives for ransom. I wanted no part of that. I don't know anything else, I swear!"

"You abandoned your comrades?"

"They were fools, my lady," the woman said sharply. "Greedy fools. They knew better. The Lion don't treat with pirates, and they certainly don't pay ransoms. Souta was smart to leave." She glared at him. "Would have been even smarter to put the money into a sake house or find a few girls and start a brothel, but no – someone wanted to run his own ship."

Souta flinched, and Kasami got the distinct impression that this was an old argument. She snapped her fingers, catching the woman's attention. "Perhaps you can answer my questions, then. Do you know who paid Souta and the others?"

The woman grimaced. "No. If I did, we'd have gotten more money out of them, I can tell you that. With the stingy sum they paid Souta's old crew, he could barely afford a single-masted fishing boat. And even that had holes in it." She glanced at Souta again. "A fishing boat. Sometimes I wonder why I married you."

"That makes two of us," Arban said.

"U- Uska, no," Souta whimpered.

"Don't you Uska me," she snapped. She caught sight of Kasami's face and took a breath. "We don't know anything."

"What about the rest of his crew?"

Souta made a small sound in the back of his throat. Uska went pale. "Dead, my lady," she said. "All dead. All those who… took part in that foolishness are dead."

"The Lion?"

"No," Souta whispered. "A demon. A hungry ghost. It killed them all."

Kasami grunted. She'd been raised on tales of hungry ghosts

wandering the Uebe marshes. According to her grandmother, they led travelers astray and ate the eyes of those who became trapped in the mire, dooming the unfortunates to join their ghastly ranks. She shivered at the memory but pushed the feeling of trepidation aside forcefully. "Where did this happen?"

Souta shook his head and didn't reply. Uska said, "There's a concealed cove a day's sailing from here. That's where they took the captives."

"And no one has thought to use this cove since?"

Uska looked horrified by the thought. "It's haunted, my lady."

"Ghost or not, you will guide us to this cove. And we will see whether the dead man that haunts it is the one we are after." She looked down at the pirates. They didn't need both of them, and it was her right to execute them. But she had no taste for it. "After that, we will see what will become of you."

She and Arban left the hold. One of Lun's crew was on duty at the entrance, and at Kasami's gesture, went down to watch the captives. She found Lun on the upper deck, sitting on the rail. She was deftly peeling a piece of fruit with a small knife and tossing the scraps over the side. "Offering to the river," she said as Kasami joined her.

"The spirits like fruit, then?"

"I assume they'll eat most anything," Lun said. She stabbed her knife into the rail. "Well? Are they dead?"

"No."

Lun's eyebrow rose. "Really? I bet Torun you'd kill at least one of them."

"I offered," Arban said.

Lun snorted. "I expect you did. What did they say?"

"A concealed cove."

Lun frowned. "Lots of those on this stretch of river. Smuggler's paradise."

"It's haunted," Arban added helpfully.

Lun snorted. "Lots of those, too. There's a ghost for every bend in this river."

"They'll show us the way," Kasami said.

Lun nodded. "The other one didn't know anything. Some fisherman's son, looking for a life of adventure." She popped a piece of fruit into her mouth. "He's decided a change of career is in order. You have no problem with that, I trust?"

Kasami studied her. "He's a pirate."

"In his defense, he wasn't a very good one." Lun looked out over the water. "They mostly used him to fetch and carry. Before today he'd never even had a taste of combat."

Kasami paused, considering. She was inclined to argue, if only on principle, but Lun was no fool. Crude, yes. Disrespectful, very much so. But not a fool. "He is your responsibility," she said, finally. Lun nodded and finished her fruit. She wiped her hands on her clothes and sheathed her knife before hopping to her feet.

"Hopefully your friend won't make a fuss about it."

"Friend?" Kasami glanced at Arban.

"I think she means Kenzō," he said. He looked around. "Where is he, anyway?"

"Checking our manifest for discrepancies, last I saw," Lun said. "I left Torun to keep him out of trouble." She leaned over the rail and glanced at Kasami. "He really saved your life, then?"

"He did."

"I thought he was more dangerous than he looked." Lun rubbed her eyepatch. She lowered her voice. "You had much experience with auditors?"

"No," Kasami said.

"I have. They're a sneaky bunch. Good at ferreting out secrets – and then taking advantage of them. All in the name of the Daidoji Trading Council. I wouldn't turn your back on him. He's probably already figured out the best place to slide that knife of his, if it comes to it." Lun paused. "He could have an accident. Lots of accidents on the river."

"No," Kasami said after a brief moment of hesitation. She was somewhat surprised Lun had made the offer. It showed how truly loyal to Shin she was.

Lun smiled thinly. "It's not just our employer I'm worried about. The Daidoji favor a scorched earth policy when it comes to this kind of thing. They'll punish us all if they think Shin–"

"Lord Shin," Kasami corrected absently.

Lun grunted. "Lord Shin, then. We'll all pay the price if they suspect Lord Shin of some wrongdoing. Getting rid of him here and now might be for the best."

"Lord Shin has done nothing wrong."

Lun gave a bark of laughter. "You and I both know that doesn't mean a damn thing to the people pulling Kenzō's strings. They sent him to find something and that's what he'll do. Even if he has to invent it himself."

"And killing him would just give them what they want," Kasami said. She paused, hands clenched atop the rail. "He's bait. No, a feint. Designed to draw us out. I am certain of it now. He is a provocation, nothing more. And the longer he is here, the more frustrated his masters will become."

Lun scratched her chin. "That's a better plan how, exactly?"

Arban leaned back lazily against the rail, balancing on his elbows. "Simple. You turn their feint back on them. Old nomad trick. The longer you keep everyone chasing their tails, the more time you have to figure out where you should strike. Or whether you should strike at all." He leaned further back and looked up at the sky. "Sometimes it's more profitable to leave your enemies guessing. When you do the unexpected, you gain the advantage."

Kasami nodded, considering Arban's words. In truth, she'd considered dispatching Kenzō several times, but couldn't bring herself to think seriously on the matter. Especially after he'd saved her life. Some part of her wondered if his presence wasn't simply a twisted expression of concern on the part of Shin's grandfather. Perhaps he hoped that by shaming his grandson, he might somehow drag him back home where he would be safe.

Only Shin had no intention of going anywhere. And come to it, neither did she. She pushed back from the rail. "I am going to speak to Kenzō." Arban made as if to join her, but she stopped him with a look. "Alone."

"Not planning to do something stupid on my boat, I hope," Lun said.

"Time will tell," Kasami said.

She found Kenzō and Torun easily enough, and the latter was grateful to be relieved of his babysitting duties. Kenzō had Lun's logbooks spread across the deck in a circle and was studying them awkwardly, head bowed and his hands behind his back. "There are inconsistencies here," he said when he noticed her presence. "So many irregularities, but no pattern. Merely shoddy bookkeeping. Disappointing."

Kasami sketched a brief smile. "Captain Lun keeps a more accurate record in her head, I am told."

Kenzō paused. "And who told you this?"

"Lun."

He snorted. "Of course. I am certain she is lying. When I find out how, I will inform Lord Shin. I am certain he would wish to know."

"I doubt it."

Kenzō looked at her. "You wish to speak to me about something."

"Lord Shin…"

"What about him?"

She hesitated. Just for an instant. Then, she plunged on. "What have you learned?"

Kenzō frowned. "What do you mean?"

"You have been stalking him for some time, Lord Kenzō. You have spoken to his friends and enemies. To those who owe him money, and those who believe he owes them. You have questioned those who have done business with him, and even – once – his servants. But never me. And never him."

Kenzō's eyes narrowed in suspicion. "Because he avoids me."

"But I am here." She sat down cross legged on the deck, adjusting the angle of her sword as she did so. Some might see what she was about to do as a betrayal of her lord, but she knew it was anything but. "I cannot avoid you. Ask." She took a deep breath. There was no going back now. Only forward.

"Let us see if we can find this truth you are after together."

CHAPTER NINETEEN
Grappling

Reo rubbed her wrists nervously. "I hope I am ready for this," she whispered.

"I do as well," Shin said, giving his fan a flutter. It was warm here, but not stifling. The Akodo dojo was set back from the river and the district both. It was a simple affair, lacking in pretense. High, solid walls and sturdy outbuildings. The dojo itself was decorated with banners signaling its allegiances to the families of the Lion. The Akodo mon surmounted all others, of course.

The practice yard was well swept and neatly organized. The students, both sumai and otherwise, had been gathered about a circle outlined in straw bales. Torches had been lit, against the encroachment of evening. The students were excited; then, anything out of the ordinary excited students. Especially at a dojo. A few tossed curious glances Shin and Reo's way and Shin waved gaily, eliciting laughter.

Kenko joined them. He looked Reo up and down and gave a grunt of approval. "She gets one chance," he said to Shin, hands clasped behind his back. "Only one. She goes out of the circle, she leaves this dojo."

"And if she wins?" Shin asked.

"We will see."

"How many matches?"

"As many as I see fit." Kenko smiled. "Is that agreeable?"

Shin looked at Reo, who, after a moment's hesitation, nodded. He smiled and inclined his head to Kenko. "We find that agreeable."

Kenko gave a small smile. "Excellent. She has confidence at least." He indicated the practice circle. "Take your position, Lady Reo." He looked at Shin. "You may observe, if you have no other pressing duties."

"None at the moment. I wished to speak with you anyway, if I might."

Kenko put on a bored expression. "Oh? About what?"

"This and that."

Kenko grunted and surveyed his students. "I am not inclined to indulge in small talk."

Shin nodded, as if this was to be expected. "Tell me, what did you make of him? Mosu, I mean." He was curious as to what a man like Kenko might make of Mosu. Specifically, whether Mosu could have fought his way free of a band of pirates.

Kenko squinted and gestured to one of his students. The young man rose smoothly to his feet, despite his bulk, and entered the circle to the applause of his fellows. "A gambler. Not a good one, either." The old man glanced at Shin. "I heard you were one as well. Are you a good one?"

"I grant myself some skill at dice. Then, I have always had good luck to make up for my shortcomings." Shin smiled. "What about you?"

Kenko didn't reply. Shin decided to try a different tack. "Did he ever come here to gamble?" That got a reaction. Kenko glowered at him.

"What do you take us for? We do not allow that sort of thing here."

Shin almost believed him, but beneath the bluster was a hint of amusement. Every dojo had its own rules, its own way of doing things. And the Akodo, for all their unbending image, were as prone to bending those rules when it suited them as anyone else. The students set up a raucous stamping of their feet – the roaring of lions at the challenge.

In the circle, the match commenced. Reo didn't so much lunge at her opponent as interpose herself, matching her rival's charge and ending it before he gained much in the way of momentum. She planted her feet, dug her fingers into the meat of his shoulders, and pitched him over her hip. The Akodo wrestler went down with a thump, out of the circle.

Silence fell.

Shin smiled and glanced at Kenko. "The Badgers are rightfully considered masters of the sumai circle, I understand."

The old man frowned. "She's strong, I'll give her that. But Jokai was not the most skilled of our stable – barely a journeyman." He waved forward another wrestler. This one approached more respectfully. Reo glanced at Shin, and he nodded.

"And this one?"

"More experienced," Kenko grunted. He looked at Shin. "Why her?"

"Oh, you know. Friend of a friend, social obligations. Speaking of which, what do you make of it all? The groom rising from the dead and such?"

Kenko sniffed. "Not my business. The dojo keeps me too busy for gossip."

"I'm sure it does." He paused. "And his manservant used to be a student here, no? Or so I hear," he added quickly, as Kenko turned a glare on him.

"And where did you hear that?"

"Oh, around and about, you know. A Crane cannot help but collect gossip – it is both a strength and a weakness. I suppose there's no truth in it, then?"

Kenko grimaced. "Jiro was… a difficult one."

"His parents were samurai?"

"Ronin," Kenko said flatly. "They served the Akodo faithfully and well, and I took in their son out of respect for their memory. In time, he would have made a fine warrior."

"Yes, I'm told he was quite lethal, in his way."

Kenko frowned. "A decent swordsman. He had good instincts. A natural with a blade, but no discipline." His frown deepened as Reo tossed her second opponent out of the ring. The match had lasted a few moments longer than the first. "Not like that one. Whoever taught her knew what they were doing."

"Her uncle, Ichiro Gota. As I believe I mentioned."

Kenko blinked. "So you did. There's a name I haven't heard in years. He used to be quite something. Heard he retired to be a merchant or some nonsense like that." He waved a third wrestler into the circle – an older student, larger and heavier than the first two. "Damn shame."

"He seems happy."

Kenko grunted in apparent disbelief. Shin tried to steer the conversation back on course. "Tell me more about this Jiro – he seems an interesting fellow."

"That's one word for him," Kenko said. He gave Shin a

suspicious look. "Why do you want to know about him? According to Mosu, he's dead."

"Yes, killed by pirates. A sad end for a promising student."

"And a well-deserved one." Kenko paused. "Minami suspects Mosu is an impostor. Is that why you're here, Crane?"

Shin snapped open his fan and gave it a flutter. "I'm here to organize the wedding festivities, nothing more." He watched as Reo and her opponent circled one another. "What do you think? Will you allow her to participate?"

"I haven't decided yet."

Reo and her opponent came together. What followed was a more desperate affair than the first two, with lots of shoving and grunting. Maybe the third wrestler wasn't as arrogant as the first two; or, more likely, he'd observed her style and was now attempting to match it. He hoped Reo had a few more tricks up her sleeve.

Shin and Kenko watched the contest in silence. Shin could feel the dojo master mulling something over, and he had the sudden realization that they were engaged in an unspoken wager. Kenko was indeed a gambling man, apparently.

A tense few moments ensued. Reo strained against her opponent, barely holding him at bay. Or so it seemed. Then, with a curious motion that Shin barely noticed, she somehow broke free and swooped under the man's guard. A moment later, she'd somehow hefted him into the air. Her face was tight with strain as she turned toward Kenko – and flung her opponent bodily out of the circle with an explosive grunt.

Shin applauded loudly, causing Reo to flush in embarrassment. Kenko clucked his tongue and walked over to the fallen man. He nudged him with his foot and gestured for his student to get up. Then he looked at Reo, who stood panting in the center of the circle. "You are... acceptable. You will have a match at the festivities. You will be allowed to wear your clan dojo colors, should you wish. More than that, I cannot promise. But if you win – there will be potential patrons aplenty in attendance." He turned back to Shin. "Come. Walk with me."

Shin joined him and they strolled a short distance away from the students, who'd gathered around Reo to congratulate her, loudly and with all due enthusiasm. Fierce as the Lion were in battle, they were even fiercer when it came to celebrating the bravery of a worthy opponent. Shin was pleased for her.

"You asked me what I thought of Mosu," Kenko said.

"I did."

Kenko paused. "He trained here, you know."

"So I gathered."

Kenko nodded. "The sons and daughters of Akodo vassals are welcome in any Akodo dojo. It is only fitting that our servants be as well-trained as their masters."

"How considerate."

Kenko gave a crooked smile. "It is, yes." His smile faded. "Mosu had some promise. Not much, but some. But he allowed himself to be led by bad examples. He was arrogant and in need of humbling. But he never got it with Jiro around. Jiro would put himself between Mosu and anyone who challenged him."

"Jiro sounds less like a manservant and more like a bodyguard."

Kenko hesitated. "He might as well have been. That was what we were training him for. In time, he'd have made some noble a good guard dog. Another waste." He looked away. "When they join the dojo, every student is given a dojo partner."

"Yes, I am aware." Shin thought briefly of his own dojo partner, Iuchi Batu, and the mischief they'd gotten up to as young boys. Batu was happily married now, and overseeing law and order in one of the Unicorn's most lawless cities.

"No, you are not," Kenko said sternly. "Among the Akodo, such a partnership is a sacred thing – closer, sometimes, than blood kinship."

"Ah. And who was the unfortunate Akodo partnered with Mosu?"

"Not an Akodo. An orphan. The son of wave people."

Shin snapped his fan shut. "Jiro."

Kenko nodded. "I knew it was a mistake, even then. I hoped they would… temper one another. Instead, it only made both of them worse. And then Jiro left, and I thought Mosu would learn – but he left as well, when his mother died."

"Why did Jiro leave? Or was he kicked out?"

Kenko was silent for a moment. Then, "He killed another student. A duel. Not sanctioned, but a duel nonetheless. One of our brightest."

"Why?"

"Who knows why a wild beast does anything? We had no choice but to expel him. The dead boy's family demanded it. But when next I saw Mosu, there was Jiro, shadowing Mosu once again – this time as his servant, rather than his friend." Kenko sighed. "Fortunes alone know how he inveigled that. But he always was a cunning one." He looked at Shin. "And dangerous."

"What about Mosu?"

"Clever, but not especially so. He talked a better fight than he ever gave."

"Hence hiring Jiro."

"Smartest move the Itagawa ever made. And Jiro as well. The Itagawa were willing to protect him, where we wouldn't. So long as he kept Mosu alive, they returned the favor."

"Do you know that for a fact, or is it just supposition?"

Kenko smiled mirthlessly. "Tell me, Crane – what do you think?"

Shin hesitated. "If it is a guess, I suspect it's a good one." He paused. Shin frowned. "The student Jiro killed… Mosu instigated it, didn't he?"

Kenko turned away, but that was answer enough. Shin tapped his lips with his fan. More and more he was beginning to wonder if Mosu had been nothing more than a convenient mask for someone much more dangerous. It wouldn't have been the first time a servant with more intelligence than empathy had abused their master's trust in order to improve their own lot. And if that was the case, how had a fool like Mosu survived where someone as deadly as Jiro had not?

The simplest answer was – he hadn't. And that someone else was under the mempo.

Someone a good deal more deadly than a dissolute nobleman.

CHAPTER TWENTY
Mosu

"Well then," Shin said. "What have you found out?"

Ito looked around with surreptitious interest. "It is as you suspected, my lord." It was likely the first time he'd been across the river, let alone in River Keep. Lanterns had been lit on the balcony outside the receiving room, and servants lit smaller lanterns all around the room itself, providing plenty of light.

Reo was still out celebrating, as was to be expected. Shin had already written a letter for Ito to deliver to Gota, letting him know of her success. Shin poured the tea, and Ito picked up his cup and continued, "The Akodo have suffered somewhat reduced circumstances of late. Last year's harvest was poor, among other things. Their coffers are not dry, but nor are they as full as they might otherwise have been."

"Hence the marriage," Shin said, sipping his own tea. Ito's information confirmed what Konomi had told him. "What about more recently?"

"Better than last year, but not exceedingly so." Ito paused. "That is likely why they are so eager to see the arrangement consummated. It is not just a matter of honor, but also of necessity."

"If things were so desperate, why no marriage in the interim?"

Ito shook his head. "I can't say, my lord. You'd be better off asking them."

"Rest assured, I will." Shin paused, studying his guest. "What else?"

Ito hesitated, but only for an instant. "There are... definite irregularities where the Lion shipping has been concerned. Here and elsewhere, but mainly here."

"Define irregularity."

"Ships sunk or missing; cargoes afflicted with blight..."

"Poisoned shipments of rice," Shin said softly. Ito nodded.

"Several." He was silent for a moment. "If there is a pattern it is only in the frequency. All shipping on the river suffers from minor depredation; it is the cost of doing business. Indeed, the Daidoji Trading Council factors it into those costs. But it is minor and occasional. The Lion – the Akodo, specifically – have suffered repeated economic attacks over the last year. Not just pirates; smugglers, thieves... price increases, stock sold out from under Akodo-aligned merchants. Were I a suspicious man, I might see this not as bad luck, but as a campaign; one waged with precision, if not subtlety."

"And its aim?" Shin asked, but he thought he already knew.

"In the short term, or the long term?"

"Both."

"It is the same: to cripple the Akodo hold on the city, and possibly to provoke them to rash action." Ito folded his hands on his lap. "All I know for certain is that we are not involved."

"Well, that's a relief. My question is, who is?"

Ito shrugged. "I do not know. It is like attempting to locate a single strand in a knot. The harder you pull, the tighter the rest become."

"Could it have been Mosu, or someone in the Itagawa?" Shin realized how foolish the idea sounded even as he asked it, but he pressed on, determined to finish his thought. "Someone attempting to force the Akodo into a situation where a marriage would be... advisable?"

Ito shook his head. "It would take more resources than I believe the Itagawa possess to do so. They have money, but not the necessary contacts – though the Ichime or the Seizuka might." Ito paused, as if a sudden thought had occurred to him. Shin, who'd had the same thought, leaned forward.

"All three together might be able to humble their patron, albeit in oblique fashion," he said. "The reason is obvious – a dynastic marriage, closer ties to the Akodo and subsequent greater opportunities to improve the social and financial fortunes of the family. But it would be a tenuous alliance; one of convenience. When the deed was done, all bets would be off."

"Leading to an attempt on the life of the victor, you mean." Ito frowned slightly. "But why? What would they hope to gain?"

Shin held up three fingers. "Three potential suitors. One off the board leaves two. Which begs another question... if they allied once before, why not again?"

"Seizuka and Ichime, against Itagawa?" Ito ran a hand over his head. "I see no reason why they wouldn't. But they failed."

"Ah, but that means they might well try again. Indeed, they might have already done so." Shin pondered this, his mind racing along multiple varied routes of mischief. The kitchen in River Keep was an obvious point of weakness, as were the entourages of the guests. Was that why the Itagawa looked so nervous? Were they expecting trouble?

He made small talk with Ito until it was time for the other man to depart. When he was alone, he sat quietly, letting it mull over in his mind. He considered taking his suspicions to Minami, but only for a moment. There was no proof, only a theory. The Seizuka and the Ichime would deny it, or worse, use it as a club to further hammer home their supposed grievances with the selection process. Of course, if his theory was correct, those grievances suddenly made more sense.

No, best all round to question the Ichime and Seizuka when the opportunity came tomorrow. If he was correct, the more he learned, the clearer the picture would become. Only when it was fully realized would he take it to Minami.

Of course, it would be better for everyone if that happened before the ceremony took place. He still had a day before the day of the ceremony. A lot could happen in that time. And hopefully Kasami would find something more tangible in the interim. He stirred himself and looked at Yoku, still sitting beside the door. The bodyguard had been listening, of course. Shin wanted him to listen. If Yoku was going to be any use at all, he needed to know the facts. "Tell me, Yoku… did the Itagawa make public the loss of their son?"

Yoku frowned. "Of course."

"And what of Minami's suspicions? Were those too made public?" Shin waved Yoku's reply aside. "Perhaps public is the wrong word. Known, then."

"We do not gossip." Yoku sniffed.

"You may not. But what about the servants? The soldiers? Gossip, once spoken, spreads like fire. It is impossible to snuff out."

"What does it matter?"

"Perhaps it doesn't," Shin said. He wondered what lengths

Minami might have gone to in order to make Mosu leave. Had she threatened him? A possibility. He could feel the edges of it, now. A conspiracy, undone by greed or simple mischance. But who had instigated the undoing, and why? And what part did this false Mosu play in it? Was he merely an extension of the original scheme, a flawed attempt to fulfill obligations and snatch success from the jaws of failure? Or was there something else to it?

There were questions he needed to ask, but he didn't know what they were. Not yet.

A knock at the door interrupted his ruminations. Yoku answered it and stepped back inside. "He's here," he said. "As you anticipated."

"Ah. And more quickly than expected. No flies on him. Is he alone?"

Yoku nodded. "No guards, no servants. Just him."

Shin gestured. "Send him in. Wait in the corridor if you would. He's more likely to speak freely if we're alone."

"He's also more likely to attempt to kill you."

"I trust I will be able to hold my own for the few seconds it will take you to get back inside. Go, go." Shin shooed Yoku away and settled back to wait. He didn't have long. Mosu entered as soon as Yoku let him, and he prowled into the room warily.

"Well?" Mosu said after a few moments. His voice was oddly distorted. Some of that was due to the mask, Shin thought. But the rest, well. There was no telling what sort of injuries he'd received in his captivity. Or maybe he was attempting to mask his voice. "Why did you wish to speak to me?" Mosu continued, his words tinged with impatience.

"You were not there when I spoke to your mother earlier," Shin said lightly. "A disappointment. I'd hoped to speak with you."

"Moriko said as much." Mosu touched his mask, as if nervous.

"Ah. She did speak with you then. I hoped she would." Shin smiled. "I do feel it is important to get to know you."

"Why?"

"Call it professional pride." Shin opened his fan and stirred the air. He avoided staring at the mask, though it was a fine piece of craftsmanship. "The Itagawa are known as the finest mempo makers in the empire. Or so I'm told."

"Yes. I am told much the same."

Shin chuckled politely. "No interest in the family business, then?"

"These are not the hands of a craftsman," Mosu said, holding out his hands, as if for inspection. Shin took the opportunity to study them. Mosu's hands were large, and marked by scars. Calluses lined the fingers – the calluses of a swordsman. But Mosu was not a swordsman. Perhaps he had decided to learn, after his captivity.

Shin decided to test the waters. "Are they those of a gambler?"

Mosu paused. "Once."

"But not now?"

"Games of chance have lost their luster for me." Mosu's eyes narrowed. "Are you a gambler yourself, then? You have that look, if you will forgive my impertinence."

"Do I?" Shin looked down at himself, as if checking for some stain on his robes.

"It's in the eyes. In my experience, there are two types of gambler – the ones who lose, and the ones who win. The former are more numerous than the latter. But you can always identify the latter. They all have the same look in their eyes."

Bemused, Shin asked, "And what look is that?"

"One of constant calculation."

Shin hesitated, but quickly regrouped. "I have been dying to ask how you managed to escape from your captors. No one I spoke to seemed to know."

"Because I have told few people."

Shin fanned himself. "I cannot imagine not sharing such a story."

"No, I expect not." The jibe was to be expected – Shin had left himself open to it. But the comment was blunt. Delivered flatly. It was hard to read Mosu. The mask hid so much of his face that there was little to work with save his eyes. But it was enough. As he'd realized earlier, Mosu didn't have the eyes of a courtier. No, his gaze was flat and sharp – like the edge of a blade. He wondered if anyone else saw it; he couldn't imagine Lady Kanna not noticing the change in her stepson.

Shin smiled. "Well. Will you share it with me?"

Mosu hesitated. "I would rather not, thank you." He made as if to turn away. "I am sorry, I am not in the mood for company at the moment." He started walking.

Shin followed him. "Nerves, is it? I understand all grooms feel that way. Then you've had the pleasure of experiencing it twice now."

"Yes."

Shin stopped. "Something I still don't understand, though. Why were you leaving the city that night?" As he'd hoped, Mosu stopped as well, and turned.

"What do you mean?"

"You were leaving that night. Not coming to the city, as I'd first assumed." Shin closed his fan and tapped his chin. "Dangerous things, assumptions. I'd assumed, as with the Crane, that the groom absented himself from his intended for a time. A bit of a breather before the main event, as it were. But that is not how the Lion does things. No, the Lion – specifically, the Akodo – often keep the groom close to hand, especially in the case of dynastic marriages. The better to prevent any embarrassment." Shin gave Mosu a long look before adding, "Such as a reluctant groom attempting to escape his impending nuptials."

Mosu was silent. Shin smiled and pointed his fan at Mosu. "Why were you leaving, my lord? And in the dead of night? What could have prompted such foolishness?"

Mosu stared at him, his gaze cold and bright. Shin felt a flicker of unease that grew as that awful gaze remained on him. He'd felt fear before. Little fears, big fears – he was a stranger to neither. Fear was a wise adviser, whose counsel only a fool ignored. And right now, fear was telling him to take a few steps back.

So Shin took a step forward instead. "Well?" he asked softly.

Mosu blinked slowly, like some great cat puzzled to find a bird in its mouth. "That is none of your concern, wedding planner," he said finally. He turned away again and this time Shin let him go. He'd seen something beneath the cold fury; just a hint of another, stronger feeling.

Guilt.

It was unexpected, but not unwelcome. He'd known men and women who lacked the ability to feel guilt or remorse and they were, by far, the most dangerous individuals he'd ever come across. If Mosu had been one of those... well. But he wasn't. Angry, yes, but also guilty. And guilty men could often be convinced to unburden themselves.

The question was, how to do so?

CHAPTER TWENTY-ONE
Ichime

Yoku smiled mirthlessly as he watched the Ichime ferry-boat dock at the quay the next morning. "Ichime," he said. "Graspers and social climbers. They seek their own advantage in everything. Much like the Crane."

Shin smiled slightly. "And yet they arrive first. Eager for a seat at the table, or something else?" He twirled the parasol Kitano had located for him and relished the coolness of the shade against the heat of the morning. Kitano lurked behind him, endeavoring to enjoy some of the shade for himself.

Yoku grunted. "What do you mean?"

"Never mind." Shin had spent the evening in a fitful slumber. His head was full of theories, none of them particularly solid. He had too many questions and precious few answers. He was certain now that there was more going on here than Minami had admitted. Whether she knew about it or not, he couldn't yet say. But it was a tricky knot nonetheless, and one he was having great fun unpicking.

Shin watched as the newcomers disembarked. The Ichime delegation was substantial, but not enormous. Courtiers and samurai, followed by a flock of servants and bodyguards. According to Minami, the Ichime Daimyō had sent his uncle, Kazuya, to oversee their presence at the wedding.

Coincidentally, Kazuya was also the grandfather of the prospective Ichime groom, Asahi. Shin wondered if they'd brought the boy as well. Possibly. The politesse of such a thing was debatable, but he knew so little about the Ichime or their internal culture that it was all but impossible for him to say whether they might consider it a good idea. He glanced at Yoku. "Tell me about the Ichime."

"I thought I just did." Yoku grunted and scratched his chin. "They are a forge family. They make armor suitable for foot soldiers." He made it sound like an insult. Then, to a Lion, maybe it was.

"Of which the Akodo have many."

Yoku nodded. "It gives them airs. They imagine themselves to be more important than they are." He paused. "They weren't best pleased by the choice of groom. They complained to the daimyō."

Shin glanced at him. "Really? Which one?"

Yoku bared his teeth in a mirthless smile. "Theirs, ours and the Akodo. Anyone who would listen, really. Fools."

"Why fools?"

Yoku snorted. "Because it was mere playacting. They knew they had no chance. They offered up a mere boy, when anyone with sense would have sent a seasoned warrior. To throw a tantrum on behalf of a lost cause is a shameful waste of effort."

"And how were they to know they had no chance?" Shin held up a finger. "Hold that thought. Time to greet the new arrivals. Come along, Yoku. Try to keep your claws in their sheath, eh?" He started forward, a smile on his face and a spring in his step.

Ichime Kazuya proved to be a stern-faced man of indeterminate years, though Shin privately judged him to be quite old. He had his hand clamped tightly on the shoulder of a young boy, who looked simultaneously nervous and bored. "This is unacceptable," Kazuya barked when he caught sight of Shin. "Where is the commander of this garrison to greet us? I fear the hospitality of the Akodo is not what it was in my day." He paused, eyes narrowing. "You are not an Akodo. Who are you?"

"Daidoji Shin at your service, Lord Kazuya," Shin said, bowing floridly. "I have the honor of being the wedding planner for this momentous affair."

"Wedding planner? Daidoji? Can the Akodo not plan their own affairs?" Kazuya fired the questions like arrows. "Surely a Crane is not invited."

"To the ceremony? Alas, no. But as to the rest, I am the authority." Shin flung back his sleeves and pressed his hands together. He gave Kazuya a friendly smile. "Rest assured, you are in the safest of hands." He glanced at the boy. "And who is this impressive fellow?"

Kazuya's grip tightened almost imperceptibly on the boy's shoulder, causing the youth to wince slightly. "My grandson. Asahi."

"Ah. One of the unlucky suitors."

Kazuya grimaced. "Yes. That is one word for it."

"And is there another?"

Kazuya drew himself up. Shin read the sour satisfaction on his face, and pegged him as a man who nurtured grudges the way a mother cared for her children. "He was cheated. Were you not cheated, Asahi?"

Asahi made to speak, but Kazuya overrode him. "You see? He

was insulted. We were insulted. I intended to make a complaint to the Akodo Daimyō this evening. But now we are insulted further. A Crane – to greet us? We should leave immediately!"

Shin waited for him to finish, twirling his parasol. When Kazuya's splutters had died away, he said, "If you wish. Your affairs are your own, and you know your own mind. If you feel insulted, I encourage you to depart. Though I will point out that doing so might well be construed as a greater insult to your hosts, the Akodo."

Kazuya grunted. "And what is that to me?" But he hesitated as he said it.

"Again, as I said, you know your own mind. But surely you would not have the Seizuka and the Itagawa profit by your absence."

"Profit…?" Kazuya looked at him. "What do you mean?"

"Merely that your absence would be taken as an admission of defeat. A surrendering of the field to your opponents." Shin paused. "After all, if you are not here to make a complaint, will your voice be heard?" He smiled at Asahi. "The boy looks tired. Why not send him on to your rooms, while you and I discuss matters further?" He turned to Yoku. "Yoku will see the boy arrives safely. Won't you, Yoku?"

"He is an Itagawa," Kazuya said.

"Yes, but we try not to hold that against him. Off you go, Yoku." Shin gestured flippantly, and Yoku went, if grudgingly. Asahi seemed only too glad to get away from his grandfather. Shin didn't blame him. As the herd of Ichime hangers-on filed past, Shin stepped back and indicated for Kazuya to join him. After a moment's hesitation, the old man dismissed his bodyguards.

Together they went to the edge of the wharf and watched the

barges float past, heading for the warehouses farther downriver. Kazuya sighed. "I have always hated this city. A provincial backwater, important only because others wish to own it."

Shin fanned himself lazily. "I quite like it myself. As backwaters go, I have seen worse. Still, you are possibly used to grander surroundings. You have come from Ninkatoshi, I believe? In the… Kokoro province?"

Kazuya glanced at him. "You know of it?"

"Oh my, yes. My grandfather spoke of it often. He studied for a brief time at Feathered Claw Dojo. I myself have never visited, but I have often enjoyed the peach-infused sake which I'm told originates there." Shin smiled at the other man. "I do like a good drink now and then. What about yourself?"

He already knew the answer to his question. Minami had briefed him on Kazuya's propensity for covert tippling. The older man wasn't a drunk by any means, but he liked his rice wine, nonetheless. At Kazuya's hesitant nod, Shin waved forward Kitano, who came bearing a pair of black lacquered sake flasks decorated with the images of peaches and lions. Kitano produced cups as Shin gestured for Kazuya to choose first.

Kazuya sniffed his cup when it had been filled and looked at Shin. "What is this?"

"Sake," Shin assured him. "A bit early in the day, I know, but I thought you might be parched after such a long journey."

"No, Crane. This show of friendship. You do not know me. Why ply me with alcohol? What do you want?"

Shin smiled and took a sip. It was quite good. A bit more peach than he preferred, but one had to make allowances for creativity. "To talk, nothing more." He paused as Kazuya took a swallow and nodded in apparent satisfaction. "Truth be told, I'd heard there was some disagreement surrounding the circumstances of this joyous occasion, and I wanted to know more. I thought it best to ask you."

"Why do you care?" Kazuya asked, taking another sip.

"Because if there are hard feelings, they might boil over during the festivities. Accusations, arguments... duels. Why, it might ruin everything. As the person responsible for keeping things on an even keel, you can see why I might be... concerned." Shin handed his parasol to Kitano, who took up a position behind them.

Kazuya nodded slowly. "Yes, I suppose." He emptied his cup and peered at Kitano expectantly. Shin took the flask from his servant and refilled Kazuya's cup himself. Kazuya raised an eyebrow at this, but said, "Disagreement is too polite a word for the situation."

Shin said nothing, inviting Kazuya to continue with a twitch of his fan. The old man snorted. "Mosu was unsuitable. Is unsuitable. Everyone knew it. The Shika's conclusion was... flawed."

"How so?"

Kazuya sniffed. "Is it not obvious? Money changed hands."

"It is no small thing to accuse a Shika matchmaker of bribery."

Kazuya lifted his chin. "No, but for the good of my family, I must." He took a convulsive swallow of sake. "Someone must take a stand!"

"So you intend to complain to the Akodo Daimyō."

"Not just me." Kazuya's expression became sly. "The Seizuka intend to complain as well. An official complaint. Indeed, it is they who suggested it. Wise counsel, as it turned out. We will see how haughty the Itagawa are then."

"I am surprised no one attempted to rectify the situation... earlier," Shin said innocently. "Then, perhaps the pirates got to him first."

Kazuya eyed him. "Yes. We intended to complain, but there was no need after his disappearance. We pressed for a new suitor to be chosen, but the Akodo were stubborn. They refused – delayed matters. And then, well… he returned."

"A miracle, some might say."

"Some, perhaps." Kazuya leaned close. "I have heard rumors, however, that the miracle is not all that it seems."

"Oh?" Shin asked, refilling Kazuya's cup.

"Is that you, Kazuya, you old whiner?" a new voice interrupted.

Kazuya nearly choked on his sake. Shin turned to see Lady Kanna approaching, a servant with a parasol hurrying to keep up with the old woman. "I'd heard you'd arrived, dragging that poor child with you like a trophy. Why do you insist on embarrassing him?"

Kazuya grimaced. "What would you know of it, woman? You have never been embarrassed a day in your life." He said it as if it were an insult. Maybe it was, in his mind. Kanna laughed.

"And here I find you bending the Crane's ear with your malicious gossip."

"It is only gossip if it is untrue," Kazuya said, glaring at her. "Prove to me that Mosu is who he claims to be, and I will retract my accusation."

"Even if I did that, you would still complain, like a child who cannot have his own way." Kanna locked eyes with the Ichime representative, until Kazuya looked away.

"I do not have to stand here and listen to your lies. I am going to my rooms." He gave Shin a terse nod and stormed away. Shin turned back to find that Kanna's glare had now fixed on him.

"What do you think you know?" Kanna asked without preamble. "My stepson told me of your conversation last night.

And now I find you in conversation with Kazuya of all people. You have crossed the line, Daidoji. I will have your explanation as to why."

Shin nodded. "First, a question, if I might."

Kanna frowned. "Ask."

"Whose idea was it?"

"What are you talking about?"

"Who suggested such a course of action?" Shin didn't specify. He suspected he didn't have to. Her expression was masklike, as impossible to read as one of the mempo her family crafted. But there was something in her eyes – a fire. Anger? Or maybe worry.

She drew herself up. "Whatever you are implying, there is no truth to it. And I intend to lodge a formal protest with the Akodo Daimyō, upon his arrival this evening."

"That is what Kazuya said."

Kanna snorted. "Even a blind rat can find a grain of rice on occasion."

"Oh no, you misunderstand. You are the object of his ire, not me. Kazuya told me that the Seizuka intend to do the same."

Kanna's eyes narrowed to slits. "Did he now?"

"Oh yes. He was quite certain that the Akodo would heed whatever it is he has to say." Shin took the remaining flask of sake from Kitano and gave it a slosh. "Sake? It seems a shame to let it go to waste."

Kanna glanced at the flask, and then at him. She snorted. "You are flirting with me."

"Perhaps a little," Shin admitted.

Kanna looked out over the river. "I was quite the beauty in my youth."

"And intelligent, I imagine."

"Intelligence comes with age, to replace beauty, which can

only fade." She held out her hand and Shin quickly filled it with a cup. "Kazuya intends to make a formal complaint, then? That surprises me."

"Why?"

"A formal complaint draws attention to the circumstances of the arrangement."

"Ah. Something a wise man would not wish to do, I take it."

Kanna emptied her cup in a single gulp. She held it out and Shin refilled it. "No. A wise man would have accepted his loss and started a new game. But Kazuya has never been wise. It is why I refused to marry him when we were young."

Shin blinked. "Ah. Oh. That explains the animosity I sensed."

Kanna gave him a sidelong glance. "I expect it does," she said, smiling bitterly. "I will neither confirm nor deny the truthfulness of your insinuations, Daidoji. I will say merely that the Akodo brought it upon themselves by their refusal to heed common sense."

"Meaning?"

"I have said too much. It would be best for all concerned if the matter were left to lie. The matter is settled, whether Kazuya approves or not."

Shin considered this and decided to take a chance. "I do not believe he came up with the idea to complain on his own. He does not strike me as a man to take formal action without some... prodding from a third party." Like the Seizuka, for instance.

Kanna frowned. "You think Omo put him up to it."

Shin focused on her use of the man's name. She knew him, then. Well enough, at least, to think him capable of causing trouble. "I do not know. I have not, as yet, had the pleasure of meeting Lord Omo. The Seizuka are set to arrive this afternoon."

"I doubt he will come himself," Kanna said, with the implication that Omo knew better. "Then, he has surprised me before."

"And why would he miss this? It is going to be quite the party." Shin knocked back his cup and handed it to Kitano. How had Omo surprised her? he wondered. It seemed impossible that anyone could surprise such a fierce old woman. Regardless, he was surprised how open she was being. Then, she likely hoped he'd be the cat among the larks. Shin wasn't quite sure how, nor did he expect she'd tell him.

"True. And if there is a party, Omo is never far away." She paused. "I do not yet know what your game is, Daidoji, but be wary around him." Her smile was cold.

"Like yourself, Seizuka Omo is more than he appears."

CHAPTER TWENTY-TWO
Seizuka

The receiving room of River Keep grew hot as the day wore on. It was stifling, despite the open doors and windows. A servant waved a large fan, keeping the air in Shin's immediate vicinity moving.

It had been a long day. After seeing the Ichime settled into their rooms, and meeting with the merchants tasked with supplying the food for the wedding feast, he'd settled down to hire the entertainment. Minami, of course, had done little in this regard, leaving the bulk of the task up to him. It was just as well.

Shin closed his eyes for a moment. He could smell the river and the gardens, and the sweat of the unwashed bodies in the crowd before him. Said crowd was composed of the dozens of street performers that had arrived with the morning tide, or from within the Lion district itself. Conjurers, singers, dancers, puppet-men – most were itinerants, traveling from one town or village to the next. A wedding provided ample opportunity to ply their trades and earn enough coin to get them to their next port of call, or even beyond.

Shin had already booked a puppet show, a handful of musicians and a juggling act that employed a variety of sharp objects. The performers would be scattered about the grounds where the festivities would be taking place, in order to break up the flow of the guests and hopefully keep attention suitably diverted.

Beside him, Yoku grunted. "This is taking too long."

"Patience. We're almost finished." Shin opened his eyes and tapped his fan against the surface of the writing desk, cutting the performance before them short. The street performer paused and turned to face Shin full on. The young woman was ingeniously made up; her right side looked like an elderly townsman or farmer, and her left, a wandering ronin. The two characters had been engaged in a ridiculous argument, but Shin was impressed by her ability to maintain the rhythm of a real conversation. "Your repertoire," he began. "Is it strictly bucolic humor, or...?" He gestured airily.

"Oh no, my lord," she said quickly. "I can do stories of adventure and heroism as well. A few moments, and I can adjust my makeup–"

"That won't be necessary," Shin said. "Consider your services retained." He named a fee – grossly inflated, he knew – and continued, "That should be enough, yes?"

Her eyes widened and she bobbed her head, all but falling to her knees in her haste to bow. "Thank you, my lord. Oh, thank you!"

Shin dismissed her with a wave of his fan. "I look forward to your performance." He heard Yoku growl softly as the young performer hurried away and the next applicant readied themselves. Shin glanced at the bodyguard. "You have something you wish to share?"

"That is too much money."

"But it is my money, and I can spend it as I wish, no?"

"It is still too much money. They think you are a soft touch."

"There are worse things to be known as." Shin glanced at the map of the grounds he'd sketched and made a mark, indicating where the one-woman theater would set up. He studied the map, frowning. "One more should do it. What do you think? A singer?"

Yoku grunted. Shin looked at him. "Not a singer, then. Perhaps some form of folk dancer? No? Suggestions are welcome."

Yoku remained resolutely silent. Shin sighed. "Fine. I'll just use my best judgement, then, shall I?" He motioned the next applicant forward. The man was old, stooped, and his bare arms and chest bore a latticework of scars. A cloth wrapped bundle was secured to his back by a silk cord. A former soldier, perhaps – or something less legitimate. Shin pushed the observation aside and said, "And what do you do?"

The man gave a toothless smile and unwrapped his bundle. It proved to be a sword; a simple blade, showing signs of use and wear. Yoku tensed slightly. The old man took a deep breath, stretched, bent his head back, and slid the sword into his mouth and down his throat. Shin blinked. "My word, that is impressive." He glanced again at Yoku, whose eyes were wide in obvious startlement. The old man carefully withdrew the blade and wiped it down. He bowed without a word.

"You are hired," Shin said, clapping briefly. "A good sword swallowing is just what this wedding needs." He named a fee, and the old man bowed low in agreement. Shin sat back with a sigh. "Dismiss the rest, if you would."

Yoku smiled and stepped forward. He bellowed a dismissal

in his best battlefield voice and the guards stationed around the receiving room snapped into action. The crowd of disappointed street performers was quickly and efficiently dispersed. Some complained, of course, but not too loudly or for too long.

As the last few stragglers were seen out, Shin stretched, trying to work the kinks out of his shoulders and neck. He'd been seated too long, and he'd skipped his morning exercises. Kasami would be most disappointed if she found out. Thinking of that made him wonder where she was now, and whether she'd found anything. The rest of the guests, including the Akodo notables, were set to arrive in the evening. That didn't give him much time to untangle this matter. Kazuya would likely make his complaint as soon as possible, and if the Seizuka intended to do the same, there might not even be a ceremony.

Part of him wondered if it weren't simpler to just let things play out. But that would undoubtedly lead to embarrassment for Minami, if not everyone involved. And the truth was, he was curious now. He wanted to know what was at the heart of this little drama.

He looked at Yoku. "Well, that's done. What's next?"

Yoku rubbed his face. "The Seizuka will be arriving soon, if they are not already here." He didn't sound best pleased by the prospect. Shin studied him.

"And is Lord Omo with them?"

"Their messengers didn't say. But almost certainly."

"Lady Kanna seemed to think he wouldn't come."

Yoku frowned. "Omo has many flaws. Lack of courage isn't one of them."

"Tell me about him."

Yoku paused. "A good swordsman. One of the best in his family. No other skills worth noting, however. Unless you count making the wrong sort of friends as a skill." A muscle in Yoku's cheek jumped. "He will be troublesome. He and Mosu were... close, once."

Shin rose gracefully to his feet. "Were they, then? How close?"

"Friends," Yoku said tersely.

"Birds of a feather, then?"

Yoku snorted. "Trust a Crane to put it that way. Yes. They gambled together. Caused trouble together. At first."

"And then?"

Yoku was silent. Shin nodded, as if the other man had spoken. "A falling out, then. How interesting. Before or after the search for Moriko's groom?"

"I am not certain. Does it matter?"

"Possibly." Shin opened his fan. "It might matter a great deal. Have you ever heard of the Kitsuki investigative method, Yoku?"

"No."

Shin gestured dismissively. "No matter. Perception, awareness and intuition – these are the watchwords of Agasha Kitsuki's methodology. They rely on the gathering of evidence and details in order to winnow truth from falsehood. But my own method is somewhat more holistic; evidence, for instance, can be fabricated or interpreted wrongly. What matters is the people involved. Their hopes and desires, their failings – their motives. All crimes begin and end with people. Who thrust the knife and why is more important than the knife itself. Or such is my opinion."

Yoku stared at him for a moment, then snorted. "Rubbish. Words. Truth is for the clans to decide. All else is falsehood."

Shin sighed. "Yes, I figured you'd say something like that.

Anyway, tell me about the Seizuka. Not a forge family, I think."

"No. Cartographers. Mapmakers. Useful, but wise enough to understand that their use does not entitle them to anything more than the respect of their betters."

"Save when it comes to the prospect of a dynastic marriage."

Yoku frowned. "They earned the right."

"As did the others. Tell me, why did it take so long?"

Yoku looked startled. "What?"

"Lady Kanna implied that the Akodo had refused to allow the marriage until recently. Why would they do that?"

Yoku frowned. "I am sure I do not know."

"Take a guess. Venture an opinion. Share your thoughts. You are an Itagawa, Yoku. You serve the Akodo, but you are an Itagawa. You must have heard things. You must have your share of assumptions."

"I am not a gossip."

"No. Tell me this then, how did your family feel about it?"

Yoku looked uncomfortable. Finally, he said, "They were not pleased. Rather, I should say Lady Kanna was not pleased."

"Why?"

Yoku shook his head. Shin peered at him. "Was it someone in the Akodo who prevented it?" He watched Yoku's face as he spoke, reading the minute muscle twitches that played across his cheeks and between his eyes. He got his answer in the way Yoku's eyes slid away from his own, just for an instant.

"No," Yoku lied. "I do not wish to speak on this matter any further." He shifted impatiently. "We should greet the Seizuka. Or would you like to go and insult another of our guests first?"

"No, I can do that after, I suppose." Shin followed Yoku to the wharf – not the same one the Ichime had arrived at. Like them, the Seizuka delegation had made most of the trip overland, through Lion territory. They'd only moved to water when it came time to reach the keep. As he followed Yoku, Shin noted with some satisfaction that the decorations he'd chosen were being arranged.

Peach banners decorated every pole, and the floral arrangements he'd selected – despite Minami's egregious lack of interest – garlanded support beams and archways. Red lanterns were being hung where their light would be most useful. Windsocks, bearing the interlaced mons of the Akodo and the Itagawa – Shin's idea – were being hung from the highest appropriate points. Several hundred origami lions were also being crafted by the finest paper-workers in the city, to better decorate the feast tables.

It was all coming together nicely, if he did say so himself. Which he had to, because no one else around here was willing to. A thought occurred to him, and he said, "Gifts."

Yoku glanced at him. "What?"

"Gifts. It's a Crane tradition that the hosts of a wedding give the guests a little something to remember the occasion." Shin snapped his fingers. "We'll need a guestbook as well, so that Moriko and Mosu will have a record of the well-wishers."

Yoku shook his head. "Crane traditions have no place at an Akodo wedding."

"Crane traditions have a place at every wedding, Yoku. If there is one thing we Crane do better than everyone else, it's establishing social conventions. The wedding ceremony, the festivities, our idea. Decorations, our idea. Little paper decorations for the tables? That's ours as well. You are welcome, by the way."

Yoku turned away with a snort. "I misjudged Hiramori. I thought her a hotheaded fool. But clearly, she is a font of patience not to have removed your chattering tongue by now. I will apologize the next time I see her."

Shin frowned. "I'm sure she will be pleased."

The wharf, like the rest of the keep, was in the process of being decorated, though not to the same degree. As Yoku had feared, the Seizuka had already arrived, albeit in smaller numbers than the Ichime. Only one, in fact. A single representative, accompanied by a small escort of guards and servants. He was waiting patiently beside the boarding ramp for the vessel that had brought him when Shin and Yoku arrived.

The Seizuka representative was a slight man, with an academic's stoop. He bowed to Shin and gave Yoku a nod. "Yoku. I am glad to see you again."

"Hinata. I did not expect to see you. How did you come to have this duty?"

"Luck of the draw, I fear," Hinata said. He saw Shin's bemused expression and clarified. "I am a cartographer by trade. My duties normally take me to the hinterlands. Boundary disputes and such. But someone was needed to show the flag, as it were."

Shin nodded. "Of course, but I was under the impression that Lord Omo would be representing the Seizuka."

"He is. I'm here to – ah – keep an eye on him," Hinata said, puzzled. "He arrived a few days ago. He was impatient to leave and couldn't be bothered for me to be finished with my previous assignment. Is he not here?"

Shin paused, startled by his words. "A few days…?"

He glanced at Yoku, who shook his head and said, "We weren't aware of this."

"No, I expect you weren't." Shin looked at Hinata. "Why did he come here so early?"

"He said he had business in town. Omo has many contacts

among the merchant class." Hinata paused, and Shin heard the doubt in his voice. "I hope he arrived with no trouble. I'd hate to have to explain how I lost him..."

"He's here, I have no doubt," Yoku grunted. "He's off somewhere indulging his debauchery, most like. Even he would not dare to risk the wrath of the Akodo." He frowned. "I should send someone to find him, however. At least to let him know you've arrived..."

Shin held up a finger. "Don't worry about it. I have someone who is more than capable of finding a man like Omo, regardless of where he chooses to hide." He smiled. "Besides, I'd quite like to meet him. He sounds like a most interesting fellow."

CHAPTER TWENTY-THREE
Cove

Kasami leaned over the rail, lost in thought. Arban sidled up to her. "Lun is talking about hiring those two idiots we caught. Souta and… what was her name?"

"Uska," Kasami replied absently.

Arban snapped his fingers. "That's right. Uska. Apparently, Souta can cook. And Uska can make Souta cook." He turned and leaned over the rail. "I still hate being on the water, but I will admit there are worse ways to travel." He cut a glance at her. "So, what did you two talk about, then?"

Kasami pushed back from the rail. "That is none of your concern." Kenzō had done most of the talking. His initial questions had been simple ones, designed to put her at ease. The rest would come later. She could feel his intent; he was like a swordsman drawing a pattern with his blade. It didn't worry her. Indeed, it made her think better of him. They were engaged in a duel, and duels could be won. She looked at Arban. "Where is Kenzō?"

"Bothering Lun, last I saw," Arban said. "Why?"

"I wish to finish the duel." She went to the upper deck, where Lun stood behind the wheel, her good eye fixed on the river ahead. The sloop swayed as it navigated a bend and Kasami instinctively braced herself, locking her feet and letting the deck roll beneath her. Lun glanced at her and smiled.

"I knew you were a sailor the first time I saw you walk," she said cheerfully. "You've got the gait, and the instincts."

"The Hiramori learn to navigate the marshes before they can walk," Kenzō said. He stood behind Lun, with his back pressed to the upper mast. "Or so I am told." He inclined his head to Kasami – a mark of respect he had not previously shown her.

Lun saw her puzzled look and added, "We've been chatting. His lordship has many opinions on the way I run my boat."

"Your record-keeping is atrocious and you're paying your crew entirely too much," Kenzō said. "If you simply trimmed some costs and invested in a proper purse-keeper, your entire operation would see a marked increase in profitable intake."

"But it wouldn't be as fun, then," Lun said, giving the wheel an adjustment. The sloop bounced over a patch of rough water and Kenzō stumbled slightly. He touched the mast to steady himself and his face twisted up into a pinched expression.

"If you're going to vomit, do it over the side," Lun said without looking at him. She glanced again at Kasami. "Did you want something? Maybe you were looking for him?" she added hopefully.

Kasami nodded and looked at the auditor. "Since we have time, I would like to continue our conversation, if we might."

The auditor nodded. "Yes. We may as well."

"I'll let you know when we arrive," Lun said, tapping the wheel.

Kasami led Kenzō down to the lower deck and made her way

to the prow of the sloop, where they wouldn't be disturbed. Kenzō said, "You are to be commended for your directness, Lady Kasami. It is no bad thing to lack subtlety. If fewer people thought they possessed the gift of cunning, the world would be a better place."

Kasami paused, uncertain as to whether that was a backhanded compliment or a veiled insult. "Yes," she said, settling for ambivalent agreement. Kenzō nodded and clasped his hands behind his back. He said nothing for a moment, and she took the opportunity to observe him – clearly observe him.

Things she should have seen before were now obvious. Kenzō held himself close, but he moved quietly when he wished, and gracefully. The way he'd thrown the knife in Willow Quay had been smooth – practiced. He'd had training, but not the same sort she'd had.

Despite this, she thought she had the measure of him now. He wasn't an enemy, though neither was he a friend. He had his duty, even as she did. For that, she would accord him some courtesy at least for now.

"I am given to understand we are heading for some sort of cove now," he said after a moment. "One that we only know exists because several pirates claim it to be so."

"Yes," Kasami said simply.

"Pirates are not known for being truthful."

"They are when it's a matter of life and death."

"And what do you expect to find there?"

Kasami paused. "I do not know. Something. Anything that will help Lord Shin in his investigation. That is enough."

Kenzō nodded. "Let us hope." He fell silent again. Then finally, he said, "As fascinating as that is, however, it is not why I wished to speak to you."

"I was not under that impression," Kasami said.

Kenzō smiled; it was perhaps the first genuine smile she'd seen on his face. "I have pondered how best to approach this, but your willingness to answer my questions has convinced me that you are my best hope for seeing my duty through."

Kasami frowned, uncertain as to what he meant. Before she could ask, he went on. "I will be blunt – some in the Trading Council believe Lord Shin to be enriching himself off the back of the council's reputation. That his various investments and dalliances are done in order to make himself rich, at cost to his family." He held up a hand, forestalling her protest. "Despite my earlier insistence on the matter, I must admit that I have found no evidence of this. But that means little when it comes to matters such as this."

"And what sort of matter is this?"

"In the simplest terms, the Trading Council is afraid. Lord Shin has made several seemingly foolish investments of late – all of which have paid off but his insistence on these gambits is concerning. They believe he is endangering both their reputation and their finances, as well as the fiscal solvency of the Daidoji as a whole."

Kasami nodded slowly. "He believes largesse is to be enjoyed – and shared." It was less a protest than an explanation. She had never been comfortable with Shin's willingness to throw money away, seemingly at random.

"Yes, an admirable quality in a nobleman and terrible one for a merchant." Kenzō frowned. "Everything I have learned says that Lord Shin's vice is a love of games of chance. Only it appears he has traded dice for investment. His predecessor was much the same."

Kasami paused. "That is the second time you have mentioned

his predecessor." Her confidence in her earlier assumptions wavered. He was being uncharacteristically blunt. Why? Was this some new tactic on his part? If so, it seemed an odd one.

Kenzō frowned. "Yes, and with good reason. It would be unfortunate if Lord Shin suffered the same fate."

"Was that a threat?" Kasami asked, in a deceptively mild tone. She didn't think it was; the auditor wasn't one to threaten. So why bring it up?

"No," Kenzō said hastily. "Merely a fact. Daidoji Aika was also prone to iniquity – or so the official record states." He looked out over the water. "A fact which greatly troubles me, in regards to Lord Shin."

"Why tell me?"

"As I said, you are a Hiramori. Loyal to the Daidoji." He paused. "But also, I think, loyal to Lord Shin. Do you understand?"

She stared at him, trying to parse his words. Then realization struck like a thunderbolt. "You work for Shin's grandfather," she said softly. And in that moment, she suddenly understood Shin's disdain for the old man. They had sent him here as punishment, and he had made the best of it. And now he was to be punished again.

Whatever Kenzō had found – or thought he'd found – it was meant to be nothing more than arrows in the quiver of Shin's grandfather. She relaxed. Kenzō would make no reports to the Trading Council, or, rather, his reports would say what that fierce old man wanted them to say.

Kenzō smiled thinly. "I work for the Daidoji Trading Council," he said.

"He is the council."

Kenzō laughed. "In his own opinion, most assuredly. In

reality, he is but one voice. A loud one, perhaps – but even the loudest voice can be drowned out, if enough speak against him." His amusement faded. "Lord Shin stands accused and that is enough. A decision has already been made, somewhere. I was sent to find a justification for it after the fact. That is my duty, and I will continue to do it."

"Then why tell me?"

"Because I have spent these past months learning that Daidoji Shin is not Daidoji Aika, and I think… our investments would suffer for his loss. So, we must come up with a solution to the issue at hand. The council's fears must be assuaged, or Lord Shin will be removed from his position."

Kasami's hand fell to her sword. If he noticed, Kenzō gave no sign. "They fear he is… flighty. Spendthrift. Irresponsible."

"Yes," Kenzō said.

"We must show them he is none of those things." Kasami sighed. There was only one answer to a problem of reputation. She knew it, and Shin knew it as well, though he tried his best to pretend otherwise. "Lord Shin must be wed."

Kenzō nodded, his expression one of relief. "That is my conclusion as well. The problem is…"

"Shin is resistant to the concept of marriage."

"That is one way of putting it, yes."

"He views it as an existential threat," she added.

"That is a better way of putting it," Kenzō admitted. "I thought – hoped – that a solution would arise naturally. I had hopes for his relationship with Lady Konomi, but that seems to be nothing more than a dalliance." He stopped as a cry from one of the crew interrupted them. Kasami turned to see Lun and Arban hurrying toward them.

"What is it?" Kasami asked.

"We've spotted the cove," Lun said. "Looks like you're going to find your dead nobleman sooner rather than later."

CHAPTER TWENTY-FOUR
Lion Town

Kitano bit into the peach, relishing the taste. Fruit had been a rare treat before he'd come into the Crane's service. Now he could have it practically whenever he liked. He'd feared it would lose something for being so readily available, but so far it all tasted just as good. He leaned against the alley wall of the sake house and watched the suckers duck in and out of the gambling joint across the street. It was operating out of the back of a merchant's shop, and it was hard to tell the gamblers from the patrons.

The Lion district had its own red lantern area. The Lion had their vices, just like anyone else. Gambling was ostensibly illegal in Lion territory, so there were no established houses – only smalltime joints that moved from one backroom to another like steppe nomads.

That said, he still noted more than one familiar face. Degenerate gamblers most of them, drifting from one joint to the next. A few ronin, looking to sell their swords to the winners for protection, or to the losers for revenge. Or beggars, like Roku.

He smelled Roku before he saw her. She stank of the shallows and the rotten places beneath the wharfs. Wordlessly, he offered her the remainder of his peach. A grubby hand snatched it. At first glance, Roku was barely more than a child. It was only when you looked closer that you realized how old – ancient, in fact – she really was.

She was a wizened stump of a woman, wrapped in rags, her hair knotted into coarse and grimy locks. She scuttled, rather than walked. He'd seen her run once. It had been an unpleasant experience, like watching a spider race across a web. But there was little that went on in the red lantern areas that Roku didn't know.

How she learned what she knew, he couldn't say. Rumor had it she was on a first name basis with the kami of the rivers and the willow trees. Others claimed she was actually a Scorpion noblewoman playing at being a beggar.

All he really knew about her was that she'd been haunting the alleys of the city since before he'd been born. A few moments of gnawing and smacking followed the payment of the peach and then Roku said, "He's in there."

He didn't ask whether she was certain. Roku knew what she was about. Instead, he asked, "Bodyguards?"

"Not that I saw," Roku hissed.

"So he's alone. That's good." No bodyguards meant it would be easier to observe the man. Good bodyguards paid attention to people who were paying attention to their master. He glanced down at the beggar. "How long has he been here?"

"Few days. He was over the river for a bit, and then came here. Must have been kicked out of wherever he was staying."

"That happen a lot?"

"From what I hear, more often than you'd expect."

Kitano grunted and scratched his cheek. "So he got kicked out and came here without telling anyone. That's interesting." He looked down at Roku. "What else?"

"He was asking after someone – a Shika." Roku grinned, showing too many gaps and not enough teeth. "She's been at the dice some. That's who he's after."

Kitano frowned. The only Shika he knew of was the matchmaker. What was she doing here? "How do you know?"

"Because he was at another joint and doing well, until he heard she was here." Roku looked around. "Word is, they have old business."

Kitano nodded, rolling it over in his mind. He wondered whether Lord Shin already knew about it and whether he'd care. Safest way was to tell him regardless. "Anything else?"

Roku sniffed and wiped her nose. "I hear things."

"Like what?"

"Got another peach?"

Kitano shook his head. "No. Got some money, though. Then you could buy a couple for yourself."

Roku gave a wheezy laugh. "I can just steal them if I want them that bad. But give me the money anyway. I'll find some use for it." She held out a hand and Kitano deposited a small amount of koku. Roku counted it in a glance and cleared her throat. Kitano sighed.

"This is coming out of my pocket, you know."

"It's coming out of your master's pocket, you mean."

"It's all the same pocket." Kitano gave her a few more koku – and then a few extra. Lord Shin could afford it, and it never hurt to be generous. Roku cherished her grudges, but she cherished charity even more. "Tell me."

"He's got a bad reputation, that one. Him and another Lion

cub – an Itagawa, I think – used to run roughshod over the dice games in this district. They got in trouble a few times."

"What sort of trouble?"

"The sort that sees blood on the streets."

"Anyone die?"

"A few." Roku paused. "The Itagawa had a bodyguard. Word is, he sank a few bodies in the river on behalf of those two."

"Jiro," Kitano said softly.

"Maybe. I didn't bother to learn his name."

Kitano nodded. That was entirely sensible. The less you knew, the safer you were when it came to men like Jiro. "What else?"

Roku licked her lips. "The Itagawa – I asked around about him. Thought you might want to know more."

"Did you now?" Kitano asked, bemused. Roku scratched herself in an undignified manner and chuckled.

"I like to keep my ear to the ground. The Itagawa – the one getting married – he ran out of a gambling dive one night a year ago like his robes were on fire. Some Lion samurai came barging into the place looking for him, and there was a fight."

"What happened?"

"The samurai beat this Jiro, is what happened. The Itagawa ran – and Jiro limped after him. No one died, but folk were talking about it for weeks after."

"What was the samurai's name?"

Roku shrugged. "No one seemed to know. Or if they do know, they're not saying."

Kitano nodded. "Well, that's something." He looked down at her. "Anything else I should know?"

"Lots, probably. But nothing about the Seizuka." Roku patted him affectionately on the arm. "Nice doing business with you, Kitano."

"And you, Roku," he said, but she was gone before the words had left his lips. He shook his head, bemused. Then, with a grunt, he stepped into the street.

As he ambled toward the gambling joint, he was forced to sidestep to avoid a pair of Lion samurai bearing the Ichime mon. They were already inebriated, starting the celebrations early. The whole town showed signs of the impending festivities. Musicians and street performers held up traffic, while merchants marked up their prices for the influx of unwary visitors. Every common room was full and every inn booked to the rafters.

Kitano liked a good party as much as anyone else, but like any experienced grifter, he knew these celebrations were akin to fires looking for places to spread. Joy turned quickly to anger when you had this many strangers in one place, especially when one family had a grudge against another. But that wasn't his problem. His only concern was locating Seizuka Omo and reporting back to Lord Shin.

Ordinarily, he'd have simply taken Roku's information to his master and left it at that. But with this sort of crowd, it was best to make sure. And if he happened to make a few wagers himself, well, that was between him and the fortunes.

There weren't any guards. The place was too small to need them, or maybe whoever was running it was too cheap to hire them. Inside, it was crowded. A too small space crammed with too many bodies. The room stank of sake and sweat. A blind woman with a bandage wrapped around her eyes played a shamisen in the far corner. Dice were rolled, wagers called. The clack of cups was loud as they slammed down against betting tables. Pressed against the walls were low tables where those not playing could drink and watch and wait for an open seat to join a game.

As operations went, it seemed a profitable one, and mostly aimed at the lower classes. There weren't many samurai in here. Samurai were risky propositions as far as patrons went; if they were losing, they might just decide to declare themselves winners – or else they'd draw steel and threaten the other patrons. Better the crowd was merchants and sailors; they might get frisky, but they were less likely to challenge one another to duels.

Kitano made his way unobtrusively around the room, his eyes flicking over the games and the faces of the players. Omo was easy to spot. He'd gotten a description from one of the Seizuka servants, and he was one of a handful of bushi in the joint. Omo was big and broad; all fat and muscle, with his hair pulled back in an untidy bun, and a thick ruff of beard decorating his round face. He looked less like a samurai than a sumai wrestler gone to seed, but from what Kitano had learned, he was deadly with a blade. Not as good as Kasami, perhaps, but close. More lethal than anyone else in the joint.

The Seizuka samurai gave a loud laugh and gestured to a server to bring him a drink. He'd had a few from the look of him, but didn't seem particularly incapacitated. A group of cronies hung around his table, laughing at his jokes. Kitano studied them with the eye of a man who'd had his share of cronies, once upon a time.

They were the usual sort – gamblers and drunks, some of them armed, most of them not. Jackals all and Omo, the lion who ruled them. He played at being a generous lord, buying drinks and spotting them wagers, but Kitano saw through it. Omo was as selfish as any samurai, and his predator's gaze was fixed on his prey.

Kitano followed Omo's gaze to a far game, where a woman

tossed the dice. Her fellow players gave out a communal groan as she won again and again. She had some skill, but her luck was fraying and her nerve with it.

He recognized her as the Shika matchmaker Lord Shin had spoken to. So Roku had been right about that. She looked focused – frightened, but elated as well. He knew that look. Habitual gamblers often had it. Some could make one wager and walk away, but others kept going until their purse was empty. They couldn't help themselves. If that was the sort she was, it added a new wrinkle to things. He wondered what Lord Shin would make of it.

One of the servers wandered over to her and whispered something. She jerked erect, eyes wide and seeking. She found Seizuka Omo in the corner and stared at him in obvious horror. Then she fled without collecting her winnings. Kitano watched her go and rubbed his nose, thinking. Omo was frowning. He hadn't intended for her to run. What had he wanted? To talk? About what? Too many questions. Best to let Lord Shin answer them.

Kitano ran his hand over his head and grunted.

Time to go. Lord Shin would be waiting.

CHAPTER TWENTY-FIVE
Grave Goods

The cove was a secluded gouge in the side of the river, hidden between a pincer of narrow rock, encrusted with trees. Someone had tried to indicate the entrance at some point, and a half rotted wooden post jutted from the water like a forgotten grave marker. Birds rose from the trees as the sloop dropped anchor. To Kasami, their cries sounded like those of dying men. She shook the thought aside, annoyed with herself for indulging in such ridiculous fancies.

"This is the place," Lun said, half seated on the rail. "Nasty looking little inlet from what I can see – too many rocks, too much sand. No way I'm taking this scow in there; she'd get bogged down as soon as we entered. You'll need to take a skiff. We can lower it over the side."

"You're not coming with us?" Arban asked.

"And leave my boat here? No. Besides, I'm a captain, not a gravedigger. I'll be here when you get back."

Kasami peered at her. "You're scared of the ghost, aren't you?"

Lun scratched beneath her patch. "Aren't you?"

"No. It is the living that worry me, not the dead." She looked at Arban. "What about you? Are you scared as well?"

"Ujiks do not fear spirits. We do, however, have a healthy respect for them." He grinned. "But I told Gota I would see you back to the Crane in one piece, and so I shall brave the wrath of the dead in order to protect you."

Kasami gave him a flat stare. "If there is a hungry ghost waiting for us, I intend to see that it eats you first."

"It would be my honor," Arban said, with a mocking bow.

Kasami turned away from him with a grunt of annoyance. As much as she'd come to like the Ujik, he still got under her skin at times. He had a worse sense of humor than Shin. Her eyes briefly met those of Kenzō and the auditor inclined his head. He'd already made clear he had no interest in accompanying them. Privately, Kasami was relieved. Her most recent talk with the man had left her uncharacteristically uncertain. She needed time to consider his words.

She looked at Lun. "Any sign of our pursuers?"

Lun shook her head. "Not so far. But they might have decided to drop anchor upriver somewhere and follow us on foot. We can keep an eye out for them if it's worrying you."

Kasami grunted. "Fine. Ready the skiff. I'll need Souta as well. If he used this place, as he claims, he'll be able to show us where we need to go."

Souta proved to be resistant to the idea of going ashore. He'd been shucked from his ill-fitting armor, and seemed the happier for it, but as soon as he was brought before Kasami he fell to his knees, weeping. "Don't make me go back there," he wailed.

Kasami looked down at him in consternation. Souta banged his head on the deck in his paroxysms and she felt the eyes of the crew on her. Not on him. Souta, they understood. He was a coward and that was all there was to it. But she was the one who was going to force the coward to do something he was incapable of doing.

It made her angry. She had her duty, didn't she? Who were they to judge her for doing as her lord had asked? She looked around, meeting their gazes, forcing them to look away. Only Lun didn't blink. Lun knew, she thought. Lun had sent fearful men into the jaws of storms, or tipped them into the river.

Uska, who'd followed Souta onto the deck, said, "I'll go with you." She looked down at her husband, not in judgement but in sad resignation. She touched him gently. "I will go, Souta. You wait here." Souta blubbered and said nothing intelligible. Uska looked at Kasami. "Is that acceptable, my lady? I've heard all his stories, and some of them twice. I can help you just as well as he could."

"Better, from the looks of it," Arban said.

Kasami waved him to silence and nodded. "Very well. But be warned, I will suffer no treachery. The sentence for piracy is death and I will execute that sentence if you try anything foolish." She looked at Lun. "We will need a shovel and some candles, if you have them. And someone to pilot the skiff."

"I'll do it," Torun said, with a glance at Lun. Lun nodded.

"Fine. We'll keep an eye out for whoever has been shadowing us. You go find this dead man of yours."

The skiff was a small, flatbottomed craft that Lun used to carry cargo to and from the sloop when there was no wharf handy. The crew lowered it over the side quickly and Torun leapt down onto it, carrying a pole in one hand and a shovel in the other. Kasami and the others followed more carefully.

The skiff moved smoothly into the cove. The rushing waters of the river eddied here, and the current had no strength. Torun skillfully navigated around the rocks and toward the far end of the cove, and the elbow of rock rose up over the river.

"Souta claimed there was a cleft in the rockface," Uska said as they neared the rock. "That was the entrance to the cave."

"I don't see any cleft," Arban said.

"They hid it behind a curtain. They painted it to look like rock, but he said you could spot it if you watched the water… there!" Uska lurched up slightly, rocking the skiff, and pointed. "Look there!"

Kasami followed her gesture and saw that there was a curious undulation where the rockface met the water. She indicated for Torun to approach it. As they drew near, she saw that Uska was telling the truth; a slash of cloth, painted in hues of gray and brown, had been draped over the rocks. "Clever," Arban said.

"Not that clever," Kasami said. "Any passing fisherman might have spotted it."

"But they didn't," Arban pointed out. Kasami deigned not to answer. When they were close enough, she brushed the ragged fold of cloth back, revealing the entrance to the cave. Arban lit a candle and set it into an iron blackout lantern. The orange glow revealed a waterlogged cave. The river waters swirled in and out, making the skiff rock unpleasantly. She glanced at Torun and nodded. The sailor poled the skiff forward, into the cave.

Once inside, Kasami saw that it was smaller than she had first assumed – less a cave than a culvert. But despite the low ceiling and cramped walls, it wound back and down into the shoreline a fair way. Torun grunted. "There'll be a smuggler's tunnel somewhere, leading inland. No pirate worth his rice would forget to make an escape route."

"The voice of experience, eh?" Arban mused. Torun grinned, but didn't reply.

Kasami ignored them both. By the light of Arban's blackout lantern, she could make out a small wharf constructed at the lip of a natural ledge in the cave wall. There was another smaller aperture beyond that, marked by a sagging reed door. "There," she said, her voice echoing loudly in the confined space. Bats skittered through the air above them, fleeing toward the sunlight.

Torun guided them to the wharf, which had seen better decades. The wood was soft with rot and flexing in an unsettling fashion when Kasami climbed off the skiff. She paused for a moment, one hand on her sword, listening. All she heard was the splash of water and the squeaking of bats. Then – a thin whistle of air, and the soft rattle of reeds. There was a draft coming from behind the door. She headed for it as Arban and the others climbed onto the wharf. The door was secured with a moldy rope looped over an iron hook. She lifted the rope and the door swung inwards, clattering as it struck the wall of the tunnel beyond.

Arban joined her a moment later and let the candlelight play across the interior of the tunnel. "How far back do you think it goes?" he murmured. Kasami glanced at Uska.

The pirate frowned and said, "Souta insists this part of the river is a honeycomb of caves. He claims they used them to hide stolen cargo until they could find a buyer."

"It wouldn't surprise me," Torun murmured, rubbing his head. "Caves make good hiding places. Warm in the winter, cool in the summer. Lots of ways in and out, easily defensible." He caught Kasami's eye and shrugged somewhat sheepishly. "Or so I hear."

She snorted and entered the tunnel. The air was wet and cool, but not as damp as the cave itself. The floor was uneven, worn flat by use and time rather than shaped by a craftsman. Torun grunted. "This cave has been used for a long time."

"Smuggling isn't a new profession. Neither is piracy," Kasami said. She looked at Arban, and he nodded and stepped into the tunnel. He moved warily, and they followed. The tunnel branched out into a tiny warren of low caves. Most were full of forgotten cargo – bales of silk and cotton, now degrading; moldy casks of vinegar and rice. There were pallets as well, and a table. But no sign that any of it had been used in months.

Kasami looked at Uska. "Where would they have kept prisoners?"

Uska gnawed her lower lip, clearly trying to recall Souta's tales. "Back there somewhere." She indicated the rear of the warren, where the tunnel continued on. "He said there was a... a pit. Not a deep one, but deep enough. It flooded when it rained."

"A pit?" Kasami repeated, disapprovingly. Uska looked away.

"I had no part in that. And neither did Souta. They never took a prisoner, save the last one." She hunched forward, as if waiting for punishment. Kasami looked away.

"Keep moving," she said.

They hadn't gone far when they found the first of the bodies. The tunnel was filled with them. Half a dozen, maybe more, but it was hard to tell. "He never mentioned this," Uska breathed, her eyes wide with horror.

"By his own words, he'd already left by the time this happened. No doubt there were survivors, though. That would be how the stories got started." Kasami picked her way through the carnage. The bodies were largely decayed, and animals had been at them. What was left was neither pleasant to look at nor smell. Weapons lay scattered where they'd fallen and she could see telltale marks on the tunnel walls, indicating wild strokes.

Arban had already reached the far end of the tunnel. "One man," he said.

"What?"

"One man did this. One person," he amended. He indicated the floor of the tunnel. "All the bodies are positioned as if they were coming this way when they were killed. As if they met a headlong charge." He glanced toward a small aperture with a rusted grill hanging open. It was clearly the pit Uska had mentioned. "Maybe they were trying to stop someone from escaping."

"And the prisoner killed them?" Kasami asked doubtfully.

"Or whoever came to rescue him."

Kasami shook her head slowly, trying to picture it in her mind. She'd fought in worse places, but the idea of such a close-quarters slaughter was far from a pleasant one. She traced a gouge in the wall and saw the originating stroke in her mind's eye. The mark of fear. When had the panic set in? After the first death, or the second? It had been quick. Some of the dead had the look of crushed leaves on a forest floor – trampled, rather than cut down.

"A hungry ghost," she murmured softly.

Arban looked at her, his face pale in the light of the lantern. "I thought you didn't believe in ghosts."

"I believe. But I did not think this was the work of one."

"And now?"

"No. Look – there. What does that look like to you?" She pointed to the floor behind him, where a dark stain marred the worn rock. Arban lifted the lantern and cursed.

"A blood trail. Something – someone – was dragged down this tunnel."

"Maybe it leads to the surface," Torun said, his voice a croak. He looked frightened, but his nerve was holding firm so far. "Fresh air would do me good about now."

Arban set off at a trot, leading the way. The tunnel sloped upward and eventually came to a natural opening, covered now by willow fronds and populated by grass. The grass had grown since anyone had last passed through the opening, and as Arban swept the fronds aside, a blaze of sunlight fell across the entrance.

Willow trees clustered on all sides of the entrance, effectively hiding it from sight. A quick look around was all Kasami needed to identify their location, downriver from the cove. "I knew they'd have a way out," Torun muttered.

Kasami ignored him, her eyes sweeping the ground. She spotted the grave almost immediately. It wasn't hidden; even if she hadn't been looking for it, the broken sword jutting from the mound of grassy earth would have alerted her. She gestured to Arban and they stood over it, looking down. "Someone's under there," he said.

"Yes, but who?" Kasami said.

"Let's find out." Arban took off his sword and shucked the top half of his robes. He took the shovel from Torun and began to dig without waiting for anyone else to offer. Kasami had to give the Ujik credit – unlike a Rokugani, he had no ingrained distaste for handling the dead. It took less time than she'd expected to open up the grave. Then, perhaps whoever had dug it had been in no condition to do so either deeply or well.

Finally, he stepped back and jabbed the shovel into the pile of earth he'd made. "Found him, or what's left of him."

Kasami stepped to the edge of the grave and looked down. The body was a pitiful sight; for all intents and purposes, it –

he – had been hacked to pieces. What was left of it was wrapped in filthy robes that had once been fine.

"Is this who you were looking for?" Arban asked, softly.

Kasami shook her head. "I do not know. But whoever it is, they are coming with us."

CHAPTER TWENTY-SIX
Omo

Shin looked up at the gambling establishment and clucked his tongue. "Such a dowdy place. Not even a banner. How will they attract business?" Kitano had been swift in locating Seizuka Omo and had found out much more besides. Shin was still pondering the information his manservant had brought him and what it all might mean. The tangled threads of this matter seemed to grow ever more tangled the longer he pulled at them.

"Is this wise?" Yoku muttered. He cast a suspicious look about their surroundings. "With the wedding in a few days, these streets are full of rowdy samurai. They might take offense to your presence, you being a Crane."

"Then you will just have to defend me," Shin said blithely. "Besides, I'm not carrying a weapon. They'd have to be very drunk – or very foolish – to think they're getting a fight out of me."

"It might not matter to them." Yoku grimaced. "Or to Omo. He's a brute and a fool. If he takes offense at your jibes…"

"I will keep my claws sheathed, have no fear," Shin said. "Wait out here for me. I'm not the only one he might take offense to."

He stepped inside and waved aside a server as she hurried to intercept him. "I see my party, thank you."

His voice and his bearing attracted some attention. A few patrons did a double take when they noted the color of his hair and of his robes. Whispers flew ahead of him like startled birds, and he welcomed it. When he reached the corner where Omo was holding court, the Seizuka was already alert to his presence. He dismissed his cronies with a terse gesture and they slunk away, growling in irritation. Shin ignored them, and fixing his attention on Omo. "Come to drink with me, Crane?" the other man said. "Or maybe you'd like to make a wager. I've heard you're a gambling man."

"Thank you, no. I merely came to speak with you." Shin seated himself without waiting for an invitation. Omo raised an eyebrow.

"About what?"

"First, you do not seem surprised to see me. Yet as far as I am aware, we have never been introduced."

"Oh, the whole district has been aflutter with word of the Crane Lady Minami brought in to oversee the festivities. Half the town are wagering on whether it's an elaborate prank, while the other half think you are to wed Minami in a surprise ceremony."

Shin coughed. "I am not planning to get married anytime soon, I assure you."

Omo shrugged. "I don't see why not. She's a handsome woman. Bit too thin for my taste, but who am I to judge, hey?" He leaned forward. "For myself, I think you are here for some other reason. You've been flitting about, poking your beak into matters that do not concern you." He grinned. "It's Mosu, isn't it?"

"What makes you say that?"

"Well, he's a fraud, obviously. The real Mosu is dead. Everyone knows it. The Akodo are trying to save face, and the Itagawa are taking advantage of the situation." He took a noisy gulp of sake and added, "Not that I blame them, of course."

"No?" Shin tilted his head, as if puzzled.

Omo snorted. "Given how much the Akodo resisted even discussing the possibility of a marriage, I'm not surprised Kanna is doing everything she can to keep hold of it."

Shin paused, and then said, "Lord Kazuya mentioned that both the Ichime and the Seizuka intended to make formal complaints as to the matter upon the arrival of the Akodo aimyo."

Omo stared at him for a moment and then gave out with a loud laugh. "He fell for it! Ah, the old fool." He slapped his knee and chortled for several moments. "I knew he wouldn't let me down."

Shin frowned. "I take it the Seizuka have no intention of making a complaint."

"No. Well, maybe. Not to my knowledge, though." Omo shook his head and looked at Shin. "Good joke, eh?"

"Yes," Shin murmured. He was starting to think Omo wasn't the most pleasant sort. "What reason did the Akodo have for refusing the marriage? Surely your families were allowed such a request."

"Why not ask the mother of the bride?"

Shin blinked. "You mean it was Lady Ai who protested the idea of the marriage."

Omo nodded, smiling. "Oh yes. She was very unhappy with the idea of her precious daughter marrying someone... unworthy." He laughed and slapped his belly. "Not that I blame her, mind. Look at what was on offer. Mosu, a stripling, and..."

"You," Shin said softly. Omo grinned.

"Yes, me. A drunk, a gambler – but a warrior. Just not the right kind of warrior, I suppose. Not a general, not even a captain." His smile faded. "Unworthy of the touch of an Akodo. They talk a lot, the Akodo; about the strength of the group, of loyalty and the needs of the many. Old Kenko hammered it into us at the dojo – that our path is not chosen by us, but by others. I never cared for that, myself."

"No. I would feel much the same, I expect," Shin said absently. Or such was the impression he hoped to give. In reality, he was thinking that Omo had been at the dojo with Mosu. Had he been the bad influence Kenko had mentioned?

"That's why I liked Mosu, I think. He and I were alike in that regard. Neither one of us had much use for the Akodo way. We both saw the hypocrisy of it. For all their talk of the many and the few, the Akodo always make sure that their needs are met first, that their decisions are the ones that guide us. Why our families put up with it, I can't say."

"I have heard similar talk before," Shin said carefully.

Omo leaned forward. "There are more of us who think that way than not." He knocked on the table. "Not that there's anything you or I can do about it."

"Except conspire to force them into agreeing to a marriage," Shin said smoothly. He wanted to see how Omo would react to such an accusation.

Omo stared at him for a moment, and then chuckled. "Well, I suppose someone was going to figure it out eventually. Never thought it would be a Crane, but... congratulations." Omo took a long swallow and signaled for another bottle.

"You don't seem bothered."

"As I said, it was bound to come out. Kazuya was going to spill the tea sooner or later, if only in a foolish attempt to prove his nephew was the better choice." Omo gave him a considering look. "It was all Lady Kanna's idea, if you're curious. That witch was eaten hollow with ambition long ago."

"Lady Kanna?"

Omo nodded. "You've spoken to her already, I expect."

"I have."

"Let me guess, she told you I wasn't to be trusted."

"Are you?"

Omo laughed. "I can be trusted as much as any man."

Shin smiled. A carefully made statement, worthy of any courtier. "But you went along with it," he said. Omo struck him as being loose with the truth. He was too relaxed; too rehearsed. He'd been waiting for someone to figure it out, and came up with an explanation that handily absolved him. Kanna wasn't popular with the Akodo for obvious reasons. Throwing her to the lions was the easiest way to satiate them if the worst happened and they learned of the conspiracy.

"Of course. An opportunity like that doesn't come along with every tide. I'd have been a fool not to agree when my family brought the matter up. It was Mosu who told me, you know," he added slyly. "About what she was up to, and how we might profit by it."

"Because you were friends, you mean."

"Yes. Were being the operative word."

Shin perked up. "Not now?"

Omo laughed, as if Shin had said something funny. "No," he said, pointing his finger at Shin. "He's a cheat and a coward."

"A cheat? Did you lose a wager to him?"

Omo smirked. "Something like that. He took money from me, and more than that. If there was any justice in this world, he'd have agreed to my challenge and he'd be dead."

"Why didn't he?"

Omo paused. "I told you, he's a coward."

"Did anyone offer to fight on his behalf? His servant, perhaps."

Omo frowned. "Jiro, you mean." He sat back and a look of unease passed across his face, as if the memory were unpleasant. "That... creature was Mosu's weapon, not his servant. Not an ounce of warm blood in that man."

"But he offered to meet your challenge on his master's behalf."

Omo swallowed. "He did."

"Why didn't you fight him? I'm told you are a fine swordsman. One of the finest in your family, as a matter of fact." Shin watched Omo's face carefully. The subtle twitch of muscle, the look in the eyes. Omo was frightened, even now. Even at a distance. Even with Jiro supposedly dead.

"He would have killed me," Omo said finally. Bluntly. He stretched his arms and laced his fingers behind his head. "The moment I looked in that monster's eyes, I knew he'd have killed me. Even if I killed him first, he'd have made sure I wasn't long behind him."

"You were afraid," Shin said. Not an accusation, simply a statement.

Omo, to his credit, didn't look in the least embarrassed. "I was."

"A samurai isn't supposed to fear death."

Omo laughed loudly. "A samurai isn't supposed to drink or gamble or cavort with women, but plenty of them do that." He grinned. "Mosu was a coward, but in the end, I suppose I was, too. Of course, I'll deny I ever said that if you decide to mention it to anyone. Maybe I'll challenge you for good measure."

Shin chuckled. "I'd prefer insults to steel, if it comes to that."

Omo took a drink and peered at him. "Why are you asking these questions, anyway?"

"Call it curiosity. Mosu fled the city before his untimely encounter with the pirates. He was running away."

Omo nodded. "I'm aware. Some samurai decided to teach him a lesson, is what I heard. He finally insulted someone who wasn't afraid of that wild dog of his."

Shin fanned himself, thinking. "What was the samurai's name?"

Omo shrugged. "All I know is that he came to me for money. I said no."

"He needed money?"

Omo snorted. "Always. He'd lost heavily at dice and needed funds to pay for travel." He paused and gave Shin a considering look. "This isn't just about the wedding, is it?"

Shin snapped his fan closed. "Thank you for speaking with me, Lord Omo. Our conversation was quite enlightening. I shall look forward to seeing you at the celebrations tomorrow." He rose and turned away, then paused. "One last thing, if I might... Shika Akari. Is she known to you?"

"The matchmaker the Akodo hired? No. Why?"

Shin smiled. A lie. A very blatant lie. Interesting. "No reason." He felt Omo's eyes on him as he departed. Yoku was waiting right where Shin had left him, trading glares with several local rowdies. They evaporated at the sight of Shin, melting into the afternoon crowd. Yoku looked at him.

"Well?"

"I was right. There was – is – a conspiracy, and Mosu is at the heart of it." Shin felt only a little satisfaction about it. He looked at Yoku. "More and more, I am getting the impression that Minami did not ask me here solely to solve the matter of

Mosu's true identity. But if that was the case, why not simply tell me?"

Yoku said nothing. His face might as well have been stone. Shin sighed. "Fine, be that way." He rubbed the space between his eyes, trying to ease the incipient headache he could feel coming on. "Mosu went to someone for money before he departed," he said after a moment. "Not his family, I think." He tapped his lips with his fan and watched a bird swoop over the buildings. The sun was low in the sky, painting the clouds in Akodo colors. An omen, though whether good or bad, he couldn't say.

Yoku grunted and looked back at the gambling house. "Perhaps Omo. They were friends, after all."

Shin tapped the air with his fan. "No, not Omo, I think. He denied it, in any event. But who else would gain from his departure? The Ichime, certainly. But Kazuya doesn't strike me as a man to give when he can take. Why help Mosu when killing him is cheaper, not to mention safer?"

"A lure? To draw him into the open?"

"You're thinking like a soldier. As if this is a game of feint and counter-feint. Courtiers do not think like soldiers. We pride ourselves on our subtlety, but in truth we are far more pragmatic. Mosu was a problem; the easiest way to deal with a problematic individual is to remove them. Paying Mosu only solves the problem temporarily. Killing him solves it permanently. Mosu would have known this. He would have avoided the other potential conspirators. Especially his stepmother."

Yoku looked vaguely perturbed by the thought. "Then who?"

"Someone not involved in the original plot, but who would have much to gain by Mosu's disappearance." Shin paused, opening and closing his fan repeatedly as he followed the thread to its end. "Ah. How stupid of me. Of course. It was right in front of my face the entire time. She practically told me when we spoke."

Yoku frowned. "Who?"

Shin turned and pointed his fan at Yoku, a wide smile on his face. "Why, the person with the most to lose by such a disastrous marriage, of course."

CHAPTER TWENTY-SEVEN
Akari, Again

"I feel I must remind you that the Akodo Daimyō will be here on the evening tide," Yoku said as they approached the shrine. "Minami wishes you to join her when she greets his party. I argued against it, of course."

"Of course." Shin looked at him. "You are very protective of her, even for a bodyguard. It is rare to see such loyalty." The words were carefully chosen. A theory had been brewing in the back of his mind since he'd spoken to Kitano. Omo had only confirmed its possibility. He needed to know if his suspicions were correct.

"What are you implying?" Yoku demanded, stopping short of the shrine gates. "Speak plainly, Crane, or not at all."

"I am thinking about family," Shin said, careful to keep his tone even. Yoku was already angry. It was best not to provoke him into foolishness. "You are Itagawa. Mosu was your cousin."

Yoku frowned. "As I told you earlier, I barely knew him."

"But what you knew, you didn't like." Shin waved aside Yoku's reply and pressed on. "How old are you, Yoku? Forty, if you're a day. How long have you been Minami's bodyguard?"

"What does that matter?"

Shin turned. "Shall I ask Lady Minami, then?"

Yoku half-reached for him, but stopped short of actually touching him. "No! Wait."

Shin turned back. Yoku grimaced. "Twenty years."

"Lady Minami is only in her mid-twenties. As she said, you've been guarding her longer than she's been a samurai – or a general, for that matter. Almost all her life. You know her well, don't you?"

Yoku took a deep breath and drew himself up. "What of it?"

"Must you always answer a question with a question? It's very tedious. Lady Minami and Lady Moriko are close in years, and affection. Minami regards herself as her cousin's guardian. Does that go for you as well?"

Yoku hesitated. Then nodded. Shin sighed in satisfaction. "Kitano learned that the night Mosu departed, there was an altercation at a house of ill repute. Mosu's manservant, Jiro, clashed with a samurai and came off the worst. Mosu fled afterward. He fled because he was threatened, and to a man like Mosu, his own life took precedence over everything – even the honor of his family. But in his haste, he ran afoul of pirates... and the rest we know."

Yoku looked at him. "What does this have to do with me?" he said slowly.

"I think you know."

Yoku glared, but Shin had endured worse. He waited, as patient as the sea. It was a guess, nothing more, but there was only one man he could imagine besting the phantom beast known as Jiro. Everyone else seemed frightened of him, even now. Except Yoku.

Yoku's glare faltered against the sheer, cool imperturbability of Shin's patience and he looked away, his hands knotting into fists. "It could not be borne," he said finally.

Shin said nothing. "It could not be borne," Yoku said again, more softly this time. "Do you know what he did, that worm?" He went on without waiting for a reply. "The scandal he caused, with his infidelity and his tricks?"

Shin felt something within him flinch back from the venom in Yoku's voice. Yoku continued, "The pain he caused, and without care! Indeed, it seemed to amuse him!" His voice was growing louder, like the warning growl of a lion. "I heard her weep, Crane. A samurai should not hear such a thing – but if he does, he must seek to correct whatever has caused such sadness."

Shin wondered who Yoku meant, Minami or Moriko; perhaps it didn't matter. "You challenged him. And he sent Jiro to fight on his behalf."

Yoku nodded. "Yes. Jiro." Again, his hands clenched. "That cur. He was more skilled than I expected. Our duel lasted longer than it should have."

"Long enough for Mosu to escape," Shin said.

Again, Yoku nodded. "The cur and his master fled." He hesitated. "When I... regained my composure, I realized what I had done. What people might say..."

"You feared they would accuse Minami of attempting to sabotage the wedding," Shin said. He could see Yoku's predicament clearly. "So, you said nothing of it."

"Yes," the bodyguard said. He made as if to explain, but Shin waved him to silence. His mind was already elsewhere, connecting the disparate facts into something approaching a cohesive whole. He spotted Touma standing near the entrance to the shrine. The priest waved him over, and Shin turned to Yoku.

"We will speak more on this later, rest assured." He went to meet Touma without waiting for a reply. He'd sent Kitano to deliver his request to the priest after leaving Omo. It had taken most of the afternoon for Touma to get back to him and Shin was beginning to feel impatient. "Is she inside?"

"Yes."

"The attendants?"

"I have given them other duties. Are you certain…?" Touma hesitated. "Only she was in quite a state when I spoke with her this afternoon."

"When was that? Shin asked quickly. Touma looked perplexed, but replied.

"An hour or two ago. Why?"

"No reason," Shin said. That meant Akari had come straight to the temple after Kitano had seen her flee the gambling house. A guilty conscience, perhaps. So much the better. "I will make this brief, I promise. I know you have much still to do before the ceremony tomorrow."

"And will there be a ceremony?" Touma inquired, one eyebrow arched in a way that Shin found somewhat distracting.

"That is not up to me, sadly," Shin said. Touma looked as if he wanted to argue, but merely shook his head and moved out of the way. Shin moved past him and stepped inside.

Shika Akari was waiting for him in the temple. She did not look at Shin as he entered. "You are not a wedding planner," she said, in a soft, accusing tone.

"Not professionally, but I do consider it a talent."

"You should reconsider," she said.

Shin snorted. "I'll take that under advisement." He let his impatience show, slightly. The ceremony was due to take place tomorrow afternoon. He needed the truth, and he needed it now. "I will come straight to the point. Itagawa Mosu planned to abandon his bride-to-be and flee the city. While this would be disgraceful, it would be as nothing compared to how badly an unsuccessful marriage would reflect on everyone involved. Especially you."

Akari closed her eyes. "Oh?"

"Yes. You arranged the marriage, after all. Regardless of why you chose Mosu – and I firmly believe that you did so against your better judgement – it was still your suggestion that sealed the compact. The Akodo and Itagawa would not have admitted blame themselves when Mosu's scandals inevitably disgraced his new family; you would have been the obvious scapegoat. Or so you deduced."

"Did I?" But she swallowed as she said it, and Shin knew he had her.

"Yes, you did. Because you are clever and observant. You told me so yourself. You knew that something was afoot, and that the entire arrangement was precarious. And Mosu knew it as well. He was a gambler, if a poor one. Gamblers are nothing if not observant. When he came to you for money, I have no doubt you were surprised. I also have no doubt that you reacted with commendable swiftness to provide him said funds."

Akari was silent for long moments. Then, "I could not give him all he asked for. He was not happy, but he was in a hurry. He didn't argue." She turned, her face a picture of misery. "I didn't either. I wanted him gone."

Shin paused. Something she'd said had struck a false note, but he wasn't sure what. There was more to it than what she'd claimed, he could tell that much. "I'm sure. But what happened after?"

She looked at him in confusion. "What do you mean?"

"You paid Mosu and he departed. Where?"

"I don't know. I didn't care."

Shin studied her. She wasn't lying, and he hadn't expected her to know. But it was disappointing nonetheless. He snapped open his fan and gave it a flutter. "Did you recommend that a new suitor be chosen?"

"Yes, of course."

"Which one?"

"Neither. I recommended an entirely new search, with new candidates."

"Why?"

"You know why. I told you last time, none of them were suitable." Akari frowned. "But... my suggestion was disregarded. I was told to pick between the remaining candidates."

"And did you?"

She hesitated. "No."

Shin paused. "No?"

"I was... asked not to."

Shin frowned. "By whom?"

From behind them came the sound of someone clearing their throat. Shin turned to see Touma standing a short distance away, his hands folded. The priest smiled and inclined his head in Akari's direction. "Lady Ai would like to see you, Lady Akari. She asked me to tell you that she is waiting in the gardens."

Akari bobbed her head and hurried away, leaving Shin somewhat at a loss. He'd had more questions, but Touma had outmaneuvered him. The question was, why? He turned away, irked. The priest joined him. "She looked practically in tears," Touma observed.

"Not my doing, I assure you."

"You are not a wedding planner, are you?"

"Why do people keep saying that? I am doing my best!"

Touma chuckled. "It was not a criticism, merely an observation." He looked at Shin. "Lady Ai doesn't care for you."

"No? Pity. I thought I was quite charming."

"I'm sure you were." Touma smiled gently. "Unfortunately, charm is often lost on Kitsu women. They prefer directness."

"She is Kitsu?" Shin raised an eyebrow in surprise.

"Yes." Touma sighed. "You are here because of Minami, aren't you?"

Shin peered at him. "Why do you say that?"

"I have been in this city long enough to know your name. To know of your... hobbies." Touma looked at the ground, a sly smile on his face. "As soon as we met, I knew you were here because of Minami's suspicions."

Shin decided to be direct. "In that case, what do you make of them?"

Touma paused. "What do you mean?"

"When we spoke earlier, you mentioned that Mosu was a surprising choice. What did you mean by that?"

"I told you his reputation was not the best..."

"Yes, but what did you really mean?"

Touma looked at him. "I am Lady Ai's cousin, you know. I told her who you were. That is probably why she took against you."

"That isn't what I asked," Shin said.

"No." Touma gnawed his lip for a moment. Then, "Mosu was not the original Itagawa suitor. Or so the rumor was."

Shin blinked. "Ah. Then why..."

Touma shook his head. "I don't know, but given what we know of him, I'm sure you can make a guess."

Shin stared into space for a moment, lining it all up in his mind. It was obvious why Mosu would inveigle himself into such a position. And if that were the case, it might explain Omo's sudden hostility to him. Omo must have thought the marriage a sure thing, until his old friend Mosu had slithered in under the threshold. Had Omo bragged about the conspiracy to Mosu in an unguarded moment? Obviously Mosu had seen the opportunity for what it was. If so, there was a sort of poetry in it. One conspiracy falling prey to another.

"You've figured something out, haven't you?"

Touma's words startled him. Shin glanced at the priest and saw that he was smiling cheerfully. "It's just, you have a peculiar look on your face," Touma went on. "Like a child who's won a prize."

Shin ignored that image and said, "Was it Lady Ai who asked Akari to delay choosing between the remaining candidates?"

Touma frowned. "What does it matter now?"

"I'll take that as a yes, or at least a maybe. If she did, why?"

"Why do you think?" Touma looked at him. "Lady Ai is unhappy with the arrangement, as any mother would be. Her daughter – her only child – given a choice between a boy, a brute and Mosu. So, she did what she could to delay matters, hoping that someone would see sense. Unfortunately, sense is in short supply these days."

Shin tapped his cheek with his fan. Lady Ai's unhappiness added a new layer to his theory. He'd assumed that the pirate attack had come as a result of the Ichime or the Seizuka, but what if Lady Ai had been involved? That would complicate things in a decidedly unpleasant manner, especially if Mosu knew.

But if he knew, why risk coming back?

Questions upon questions, and no answers to be had. He

hoped Kasami would return soon. More, he hoped that she'd found something – anything – to help him untangle this knot. He started as a bell began to ring. "What is that? An alarm?"

"Of sorts," Touma said. He looked at Shin. "The Akodo Daimyō has arrived. And I fear you are almost out of time, my friend."

CHAPTER TWENTY-EIGHT
Great and Good

Shin hurried toward the wharf, Yoku at his heels. The bodyguard was practically shoving him forward at times. Around them, lanterns were being lit and shops were closing as night fell. There would be a curfew tonight, Shin knew. The arrival of the Akodo Daimyō would shut down the entire district. "Faster, Crane, walk faster," Yoku urged.

Shin turned and swatted Yoku's hands away with his fan. "I am walking at a perfectly adequate speed, Yoku. What is worse, a few moments tardiness or me arriving lathered like a horse that's been ridden all night?"

"Tardiness!" Yoku snarled.

Shin stopped, refusing to move. "I disagree. A Crane might fly, or glide, or, in extreme circumstances, slide, but he does not run. Now stop bullying me."

Yoku snorted and took a step back. "We will be late."

"Then we will be late."

"Lady Minami will be embarrassed."

"Only if we make a scene – which we certainly will, if you

continue to shove me about like a recalcitrant child." Shin straightened the hang of his robes and continued to the wharf at a statelier pace. He could make out a high-masted sloop, far larger than the one he'd purchased for Lun, bearing the Akodo sigil on its sails. It sat alongside the wharf, with multiple boarding ramps already lowered. There were Akodo soldiers at the rails, watching the crowd below with cool wariness.

A crowd of worthies and their hangers-on had already gathered in an orderly mob along the wharf, waiting for the passengers to disembark. He saw Lady Kanna, with Mosu looming by her side. Lord Kazuya and his nephew stood a polite distance back and away. Kazuya's glare must have been burning a hole in the back of Kanna's head, but she didn't seem to notice. Lord Hinata stood a safe distance from the other two, looking nervous. There was no sign of Omo.

Shin made his way to Hinata's side, Yoku grumbling in his wake. "I see you are alone again," he murmured, fanning himself. Hinata looked at him and attempted a smile.

"Yes. Lord Omo has decided to absent himself."

"If he's not careful, the Akodo might see it as an insult."

Hinata sighed. "I do not think he cares."

"It must be a burden, to be associated with such a man."

Hinata glanced at him. "He is my cousin."

"Double the burden, then," Shin said, fanning himself. He studied the crowd, and found Minami standing at the forefront, with Lady Ai and Moriko. "I'd heard that Lord Omo thought himself a shoo-in for Moriko's hand. It must have been quite the disappointment to him to have them choose Lord Mosu instead."

"That's putting it mildly. He went on a bender afterward." Hinata glanced at Yoku. "Yoku can attest to that. He had to go drag Omo and Mosu out of more than one sake house in the weeks after the announcement."

Shin glanced at Yoku, who nodded. "Really? I'd heard he and Mosu had had a falling out over the matter."

Hinata frowned. "Who told you that?"

"Omo."

Hinata shook his head. "You could have fooled me."

Shin nodded, considering this. Had Omo lied to him, then? If so, why? Before he could ask another question, however, Yoku nudged him. "Lady Minami is signaling for us to join her. We must go."

Shin gave in and, after a polite goodbye to Hinata, allowed Yoku to hustle him up to the front of the crowd. Lady Ai ignored him utterly, as did Moriko. Minami leaned close. "You are late," she hissed.

Shin waved his fan at Yoku. "Blame Yoku. He is very slow." Behind him, Yoku made a strangled sound. Shin ignored him and continued, "Besides, they haven't even disembarked yet. Will I be expected to bow?"

"Yes, obviously."

"Well, I was just asking. You Lion do things so oddly." Shin gave her a sidelong glance. "Reo will be having her match tomorrow. Are you going to go?"

"I will be busy," Minami said after a moment's hesitation.

"No, you won't. I've blocked you off a parcel of time so that you can go."

She gave him an incredulous look. "You did what?"

"You're welcome."

She stared at him, but before she could say anything a sudden drumroll filled the air. A martial melody drowned out all whispered conversation. Shin hid a smile. Trust the Lion to turn even the simplest affair into an excuse for a display of military might.

Soldiers came first. A procession of spearmen, marching down the gangplanks with all due pomp and circumstance. They marched and wheeled with drilled precision into a formation resembling the walls and gatehouse of a keep. Those at the front stepped back after a moment, retreating until they had formed a corridor from the base of the gangplank to the edge of the crowd. Privately, Shin could not help but be impressed. He knew Minami kept her soldiers well-drilled, but this was something else entirely.

"The elite guard," Minami murmured. "They are always positioned on the third line of battle. Their discipline is extraordinary." Her tone held not a little envy, though whether for the thought of commanding such a force, or simply the thought of being in battle, Shin wasn't certain.

"Indeed," Shin said. He fell silent as a pair of figures appeared at the top of the gangplank. They paused for a moment; officers surveying the field of battle. Then, as one, they descended. Shin recognized them, if only from the descriptions he'd heard.

Akodo Arasou, the Akodo Daimyō, was a tall man, broadly built if not particularly handsome as the Crane judged such things. He was of an age with Minami, and moved with the callous indifference of a man used to rugged conditions. His betrothed, Matsu Tsuko, was nearly of equal height and, like Arasou, fully armored. Her movements spoke to an easy grace that put him in mind of Kasami when she was in one of her moods.

Despite the martial display, their entrance didn't strike him as particularly grandiose. He thought his grandfather would approve. The Daidoji were not much given to ostentation themselves. "I'm told he's the youngest son," Shin murmured as the daimyō and his betrothed made their descent. "Is that true?"

Minami frowned. "Lord Toturi has chosen a different path. Now hush, Shin – and be polite. Try not to embarrass me."

The daimyō and his intended were followed down the gangplank by a gaggle of courtiers and samurai, representing Arasou's court. Instinctively, Shin took note of certain faces. It was always useful to know who was in favor this season and who was not. He paused in his study when Minami stepped forward to greet the daimyō and his entourage. Lady Ai and Moriko joined her after a while, and the group exchanged pleasantries that Shin paid little attention to, until he realized that Lady Tsuko was staring at him.

"Why is there a Crane here?" she asked bluntly. Imperiously. "This is an occasion of great joy. We do not require the services of a bird of ill omen."

Shin blinked. But before he could speak up, Minami said, "He is my guest, Lady Tsuko. Lord Shin is… helping me with the festivities. I have no head for such matters." She smiled thinly. "I am a general, not a courtier."

"Are there not Lion courtiers in this city?" Arasou rumbled. "Why seek the help of a Crane? Especially a Daidoji?" He examined Shin the way a man might inspect his sandal after having trodden in something foul. "He is not welcome here."

"No, definitely not," a new voice interjected. "Especially this Daidoji of all Daidoji!"

All eyes turned to one of the courtiers on the gangplank. He was a short, sturdy man dressed in fine robes, with a biwa slung across his back. "What are you doing here, Shin?" Ikoma Ikehata bellowed, as he thrust his way to the fore and faced Shin.

"I came for that money you owe me, Ikehata," Shin said, with a laugh. Relief flooded him at the sight of the Lion courtier. Ikehata was an old acquaintance and, even better, one he was still on good terms with.

Ikehata drew back, a hand on his chest. "Me, owe you money? I've never heard such a ludicrous story. If anyone owes money here, it's you." He looked at Minami. "Arrest him."

Minami blinked. "What?"

Shin laughed again and flicked his fan at Ikehata. "No, arrest him. He is a wastrel."

"Takes one to know one. I insist you arrest this man," Ikehata said, poking Minami in the arm. "It is outrageous that a criminal like this is allowed to walk free."

"He's the criminal," Shin protested. He looked around. "Have you heard his singing?"

Ikehata staggered playfully. "You were the one accompanying me on the biwa. I hope you've learned more than one chord since then."

"Two, at least," Shin said primly.

"Try not to mangle them as well." Ikehata looked at Minami. "Well? Are you going to arrest him? He's broken the laws of good taste more than once."

"Says the man who appeared in public dressed like that," Shin said, waggling his fan at Ikehata. "Who dressed you? A child?" A muted flutter of laughter greeted his comment. The crowd was relaxing now.

Ikehata smoothed the front of his robes. "I'll have you know these robes are the epitome of style in Toshi Ranbo."

"Oh? Which century?"

Ikehata grinned and looked Shin up and down. "Still wearing blue, I see. Who needs originality when conformity serves just as well, eh?" More laughter. Lady Tsuko's expression had not altered, but Lord Arasou was clearly fighting the urge to smile.

"You look like a peach that fell off the back of a cart," Shin said.

"You look like a child's drawing of a sad bird," Ikehata fired back. He gestured to Shin's head. "Tell me, are you still dying your hair, or has it gone white from shame?"

"At least I have hair. Your wig could use some adjustment, by the way."

Ikehata patted his topknot. "This is natural, thank you."

"Yes, natural horsehair."

"That tears it," Ikehata said as he reached for the biwa slung across his back. "Let's have it out, here and now." Someone in the crowd hooted and there was scattered applause.

"I'm unarmed," Shin laughed, spreading his hands.

"Given how badly you play, that can only be an advantage."

Shin turned to Minami, a look of mock sadness on his face. "You hear how he insults your guest? Arrest him."

"No one is being arrested," Minami snapped. She looked back and forth between them. "What is this foolishness?"

"I beat him at a game of go five years ago, and the initial wager and accrued interest means he owes me... oh, quite a bit. He refuses to pay, of course." Shin smiled at Ikehata and the other courtier clapped him on the shoulders.

"Only because you owe me for sneaking you out of the House of Morning Dew that time. If Lord Ujiaki had caught you with his favorite girl, none of your pretty words would have saved you."

"How was I to know she was his mistress?" Shin protested.

Ikehata laughed. "True. Never knew old Ujiaki had it in him." He turned to Arasou and Tsuko, sketching a quick bow. "Even the Crane are capable of producing the occasional acceptable member of polite society, and Lord Shin here is... most definitely not one of them, but he is a most entertaining fellow regardless. If he's the one in charge of the festivities, they will be most enjoyable indeed." Hand still on Shin's shoulder, Ikehata turned and said, "Did you get my last letter?"

"The one that smelled like you'd dropped it in the street?"

"That's the one! I thought you'd enjoy that. It reminded me of the last time I smelled your cooking. Did you read *A Year on the Wall*, as I suggested?"

"I did, yes. Fantastic work."

"Excellent. No one on the boat has read it." He cast an accusing eye at the Akodo dignitaries. "Uncultured, the lot of them. I look forward to discussing it with you during the festivities tomorrow." He leaned close and muttered, "You always did enjoy a bit of risk, didn't you? Lucky thing for you I was here."

"Remind me to thank you later," Shin replied, sotto voice. "Tomorrow morning."

Ikehata squeezed his shoulder. "I accept payment in strong drink and good conversation." He turned to Minami. "I am starving. Tell me Eka is still in charge of the kitchens. That woman can grill a fish like no one else."

Shin quickly stepped back, relieved to no longer be the focus of the newcomers' attentions. He watched the crowd, taking note of who appeared pleased and who didn't. Most of the Akodo looked happy enough, save Ai.

Seizuka Hinata greeted Arasou in a polite, restrained fashion, clearly hoping the daimyō wouldn't notice Omo's absence. Kanna was less reserved, more triumphal, but not obviously so, save to a courtier's keen eye. That left–

"My lord!"

Shin turned. Kazuya was forcing his way through the crowd now, his bodyguards clearing him a path. "My lord," he called out. "Lord Arasou, I must speak with you!" Minami tensed. So did Lady Ai. The crowd quivered, some eager to see what happened, others appalled by the sheer effrontery displayed by the Ichime.

"Move them along before the daimyō notices," Shin hissed to Minami, as he snapped his fan shut and smoothly stepped into Kazuya's path. Yoku quickly squared off with the other bodyguards, who hesitated at the sight of him.

Kazuya hesitated, taken aback by this sudden interruption. "What? Get out of my way." He tried to sidestep Shin, but Shin easily blocked him.

"Oh, am I in your way? I do apologize." Shin glanced behind him and noted with relief that Minami was doing her best to hustle Arasou and Tsuko toward the keep. Ikehata, sensing trouble, was keeping the daimyō distracted with a rapid-fire discussion on the merits of plum wine. He caught Shin's eye and winked. Shin turned back to Kazuya.

"As you can see, the daimyō is clearly tired from his journey, and likely wishes nothing more than to have a bite to eat and perhaps a bath. I'm sure whatever this is can wait until tomorrow. Indeed, I would like to hear what you have to say, myself."

"I said, step aside," Kazuya snapped. Shin opened his fan and stirred the air.

"In a moment. Come by in the morning, if you would, and I might be able to procure a few more bottles of that delightful sake for you." Shin smiled politely into the teeth of Kazuya's growing fury. "We can continue our conversation from yesterday."

As he spoke, he sensed the crowd beginning to disperse. The other courtiers knew the excitement was at an end – or perhaps it was the sudden arrival of Minami's guards, who formed an inconspicuous line between the departing Akodo Daimyō and the Ichime contingent. Kazuya saw this as well and hesitated. His eyes flicked to Shin.

"Very well," he said. "Tomorrow."

Shin stepped back and the Ichime joined the mass exodus. With the Akodo Daimyō in residence, things would be quiet for the rest of the night. He turned to Minami. "Once again, you are welcome. The daimyō?"

"Lady Ai is escorting him and Tsuko to their quarters. Lord Ikehata was invaluable in keeping them distracted." She paused. "I was not aware that you and he knew one another."

Shin smiled. "There's a lot you don't know about me, Minami." He tapped his palm with his fan. "We Crane are full of surprises."

Minami turned away. "Let us hope you are lucky as well. The wedding ceremony is tomorrow, Shin. If you are going to find the answers we seek, you had best do so quickly." She departed, leaving Shin to watch the lights of the district dance on the river. Somewhere out there, he knew, Kasami was making her way back to the city. He could countenance no other possibility. She would not fail him. She never had.

"But if you could do it just a little faster, I would appreciate it," he murmured.

CHAPTER TWENTY-NINE
Kazuya

When Yoku showed Kazuya into the receiving room in the early hours of the next morning, the Ichime representative looked around and sniffed. "Your quarters are nicer than ours. How insulting."

"You strike me as a man to find insult in the turning of the seasons," Shin said jovially. He indicated the sake bottles lined up on the table like attentive soldiers. Kazuya studied them for a moment before taking his seat opposite Shin.

"A man must be attentive to his status, else he will lose it."

"I have found the opposite to be true," Shin said, in a mild tone. He gestured, and Kitano opened the first bottle. "It is a trifle early, but it is a day of celebration."

"Another insult," Kazuya said, but he didn't refuse the cup.

"No. The insult was your little stunt last night. The Akodo were most put out."

"If you hadn't stopped me—" Kazuya began.

"Things would have been much worse," Shin finished for him. "You are welcome, by the way. Least I could do for a man who has been so badly used by his fellow conspirators."

Kazuya hesitated. "What are you talking about?"

"You know exactly what I am referring to. Let us not insult one another by pretending otherwise," Shin said smoothly. A non-answer, but Kazuya seemed satisfied.

"You are not a wedding planner. I suspected from the first. The Akodo would never let a Crane in without some ulterior motive." Kazuya sat back. "Well? What are you then?"

"A friend of a friend," Shin said blithely.

"I should leave."

"You may, if you wish." When Kazuya made no move to go, Shin smiled and said, "It may be that I am the only person who can help you out of this web you've found yourself in."

Kazuya studied him for a moment, and then grunted in annoyance. "It wasn't my idea, I'll tell you that much."

"Lord Omo implied it was Lady Kanna who came up with the scheme," Shin said. Kazuya paused with his cup halfway to his lips.

"Did he? How curious."

"Why?"

"Because she told me it was his." Kazuya set his cup down, untouched. "She told me as well that he had surprised her with his cunning. She'd always disliked him. He was one of Mosu's boyhood friends, you know."

"So I've been told. Why did she dislike him?"

Kazuya looked at the bottles, as if trying to judge their contents. "I know only what I have heard from others. Omo was an instigator, even as a boy. He liked to cause trouble, start fights... Mosu idolized him. Copied him."

"Did Omo send Mosu to convince Lady Kanna to take part?"

Kazuya smiled sourly. "Yes." He chuckled. "You should have

seen the look on his face when he learned she decided to put forward Mosu as a candidate – like a cat who's caught a bird. I knew then they wouldn't hold by the terms of our agreement."

"And what was the agreement?"

Kazuya hesitated. "Nothing untoward. A fair opportunity for each."

"Is that why you agreed to participate in such a dangerous endeavor?"

Kazuya didn't reply. Instead, he tapped one of the bottles and said, "We had schemed to get only so far, but no farther. Let fortune decide."

Shin nodded. "And then Lady Kanna decided to take fortune in hand."

"I believe so. Omo told me that she had discovered the matchmaker's vices and played upon them. Knowing her as I did, I could believe it."

"Was this when Omo convinced you to make your complaint?"

Kazuya nodded. "He told me that Mosu was dead, and that Kanna had delivered a fraud in order to save face. He believed that if we acted jointly, we could force the Akodo to break the engagement and choose another suitor."

"And you believed him?"

Kazuya chortled. "No! But I knew he had some scheme in mind, and I thought better it was directed at Kanna than me."

"I think it was directed at both of you, actually." Shin leaned forward. "I spoke with Omo last night. He implied that he had no intention of lodging a complaint. A joke, he called it. I fail to see the humor in it myself, however."

Kazuya grunted. "I suspected as much when there was no sign of him. I sent messengers to the Seizuka quarters, but they had no idea where he was." He looked at Shin. "Why tell me this?"

"To see your reaction," Shin replied. He was satisfied that Kazuya was a dupe, if an aggressive one. He'd been aimed like an arrow and loosed to do his work. "As I said earlier, something is going on here. I know that you three – and Mosu – are a part of it. But I do not yet have proof."

Kazuya gave a bark of laughter. "Nor will you get it from me!"

Shin smiled. "No. I did not expect to. Even so, you have told me enough." He paused. "If I were you, Lord Kazuya, I would refrain from making your complaint publicly. Wait until a more optimal time."

"After the ceremony, you mean?"

"If you like. But think on this – Omo claims to have proof Mosu is a fraud, and he set you up to embarrass yourself. He is clearing the board of opposing pieces. Maybe he always intended to do so, or maybe he is simply opportunistic. If I were you, I would keep my distance from him. I have sent a messenger to Lady Kanna counseling the same."

Kazuya studied him for a moment. "Are you trying to implicate us – or protect us?"

Shin shrugged. "At the moment, I do not really know." He smiled and fanned himself. "But I will be sure to let you know when I figure it out."

Kazuya sniffed and picked up one of the bottles, weighed it and said, "I will take this for my trouble, and bid you good morning." He rose to his feet and looked down at Shin. "You asked why I took part. Family," he said. "Kanna is ambitious and a marriage for her stepson assures her status in the Itagawa is unassailable. Omo needs a good marriage to give him any prospect of advancement. But my nephew... he is just a boy.

There is no telling what sort of man he will be. Chances are, I will be dead before he figures it out. But with him married, the future of the Ichime as favored vassals of the Akodo is set. I took part not for myself, but for the Ichime."

Then he was gone. Shin looked at Yoku. "Well? What do you make of that?"

"He was telling the truth."

"Yes. It all fits together quite neatly, doesn't it? And that's the problem. No one will ever admit to this. We need proof." He looked at Yoku. "I might have some idea as to how we can get it as well…"

Before he could elaborate, Kitano hurried into the room, followed by Minami. "Shin!" she snarled. "I need to talk to you. Now!"

"Would you care for a snack?" Shin asked, ignoring her impatient expression. "I'm told Eka's millet cakes are a wonder."

She looked down at the sake bottles on the table and grimaced. "I am not hungry. Was that Kazuya I saw leaving?"

"It was. He wished to thank me for last night."

"Speaking of which," Minami began, glaring at him. "What have you learned?"

"You need to eat. Today will be very hectic. Who knows when you'll have time for a meal? I'll send Kitano to the kitchens." Shin gestured and Kitano slunk out of the room. Shin waited until he'd gone and then added, "As to what I have learned, well, that's a bit trickier."

"I am not in the mood for your games, Shin. You were lucky last night. But the Ichime and the Seizuka will put forward their complaints today, regardless of what we do. We are out of time. What do you have for me?"

"First, I doubt either will put forward a complaint today. That was Omo's little jest – an attempt to discredit the Ichime and clear the path for whatever he's up to. But since I told Kazuya that Omo had no intention of making a complaint, he's decided to restrain himself as well. So, on that front, the battle is stalled, if not won."

Shin tapped the rim of his sake cup, still untouched. It seemed a waste, but drinking so early was sure to upset his digestion. "Secondly, what I have at the moment is a profusion of loose threads; to make any sense of them, I must weave them together." Shin took a deep breath and went on before she could reply. "The question of identity is moot. We know that Mosu is not who he says he is. But why is that the case?"

"What do you mean?" Minami asked.

"What led to the deception? How did the pirates happen to attack his boat?"

"Bad luck," Yoku said.

Shin shook his head. "No. I do not think it was blind chance. And when Kasami returns, I expect that theory to be borne out."

"If she returns," Minami said.

"She will," Shin said, with a confidence he was having to work exceedingly hard at. "Regardless, I am sure my theory is correct. The pirates were told to attack Mosu's vessel. Someone told them there was a ransom worth having on that boat. But who might have done so? Perhaps a jealous rival – Seizuka Omo, for instance. He feels he was cheated and is not shy about saying so."

"Omo is a drunkard," Yoku protested.

"Omo is far more dangerous than he appears. Then, what about Ichime Kazuya? He might have believed that with Mosu out of the way, his grandson's pledge might be reconsidered. It's obvious that he didn't consider Omo a potential rival to Asahi."

He paused. "But again, one wonders – why the charade with the pirates? Why not simply kill Mosu by some more reliable method? He had no answers for me."

"Perhaps they tried and failed," Yoku said. He sounded interested despite himself. "Jiro was a warrior of no small capability. I can attest to that. And we know he killed others who threatened Mosu."

Shin nodded absently. "Perhaps. Still, how did the pirates know to attack that ship? Someone must have told them, but who? At first, I thought it might have been Jiro himself, but the more I've learned of him, the less likely it seems."

"What do you mean?" Minami asked. "He was a thug and a killer."

"He was the son of ronin, trained at the Rich Frog Dojo to be a bodyguard for the Akodo. Instead, he became one for Mosu. And by all accounts, he was loyal. Vicious, but loyal. Initially, I suspected he was using Mosu – and maybe he was – but he stayed beside him even when things became untenable."

"You think someone else set the pirates on them?" Yoku said.

"Yes." Shin sat back. "More to the point, how did Mosu come to be in that situation in the first place? The Akodo clearly didn't want this marriage, or at least Lady Ai didn't. So how did we get from no marriage to a marriage? What changed?"

"You know what changed," Minami said slowly.

"Yes, and isn't it funny that as soon as the request was denied, circumstances requiring its allowance arose? Almost as if a concentrated effort were made to ensure the Akodo had no choice. There are sharks circling, Minami. One of them got a taste and now the others are upset. It's the nature of sharks, I suppose…"

"What does it matter?" Minami asked. "If you are right, we

know that Mosu is dead, and that the man who will marry my cousin tonight is a fraud. That is enough."

"Is it?"

Minami looked at him. "Of course!"

Shin shook his head slowly. "Without hard proof, we have nothing. I doubt either the Akodo or the Itagawa will accept my findings as fact just because we ask them to." Shin folded back his sleeves and picked up his biwa. "No. There is only one option open to us in this instance, though it is not one I prefer."

"And what is this option?" Minami asked.

He was about to elaborate when Kitano suddenly rushed into the room. Shin stared at him in surprise. "She's back, my lord," Kitano burst out. "Kasami. She's back!"

Shin shook off his surprise and looked at Minami. He smiled serenely.

"I told you so."

CHAPTER THIRTY
Witness

Kasami cleared her throat and concluded her tale. She knelt before Shin and Minami, her hands folded on her knees. She still wore her armor, smelling of the river and her travels. "And then we returned here at all possible speed," she finished. Conscious of Minami's presence, she bent double, bowing as low as possible.

Shin flicked his fan, gesturing for her to straighten up. He hated when she bowed like that. It made him all too aware of the distance still between them, though he fancied it was less than it once had been. "And just in time, too," he said, with a glance at Minami. "Wouldn't you agree?"

Minami ignored him. "You brought the body here?"

Kasami nodded. "I did, my lady. I thought the family would wish to give him a proper burial, if nothing else."

"They won't," Shin said, fanning himself. It was nearly midday, and the festivities had begun. The ceremony wasn't taking place until dusk, which gave them some time, but not much. "I'd wager that if we announced the discovery of the body, our masked groom would simply declare it the body of his slain servant."

Kasami blinked and Minami nodded grudgingly. "Lady

Kanna is no fool. She will loudly declare that the body could belong to anyone, and my family will agree, just to put the matter to rest. We need actual proof."

"And how do you intend to get it?"

"Simple: I will elicit a confession from our fraudulent groom. One that can be confirmed by an unimpeachable third party." He'd come up with the plan the night before. A witnessed confession was binding under Rokugani law. The question of who the third party would be had been a trickier proposition. He'd initially considered Yoku, but decided against it for obvious reasons. No, someone else was required. Someone of impeccable character, who had no stake in the matter whatsoever. Even better, someone who owed him a favor.

Minami shook her head in puzzlement. "A confession? How do you intend to get that? And who is this witness of yours?"

There was a rap at the door. Shin smiled. "That might be him now. And far earlier than I expected."

It was not who he'd expected, however. "What is the meaning of this?" Lady Ai growled, as she stormed into the receiving room unannounced. Moriko and Touma followed more slowly, neither looking happy to be there. Shin paused, then indicated the seat opposite him. Kasami stood and quickly took a seat near Yoku.

"If you would like to sit, I would be happy to explain," Shin said. From outside, he could hear that the festivities were now well underway. Music and laughter painted the air in colors of joy. He wished he were outside enjoying it for himself. But needs must.

Lady Ai and Moriko sat, and Shin took the opportunity to glance at Kasami. She seemed unusually taciturn, even for her. He'd gathered there'd been some violence; Omo had sent someone looking for Mosu as well. Was it just bad luck that they'd followed Kasami's trail, or was it indicative of something more sinister? There was no way to know at the moment, short of questioning the groom – either the living one or the dead one.

At the thought, he found his eye drawn to Touma. The priest looked uncomfortable. "Well?" Ai demanded, snatching his attentions back to her.

"We have found a body," Shin began, with as much gentleness as he could muster. "Rather, my bodyguard, Kasami, found a body. We believe it to be–"

"Mosu," Ai interrupted. "You believe it to be Mosu. That is the only reason you would interrupt this day of all days." She raised her chin and looked at Minami accusingly. "This is your doing. I warned you, Minami…"

Minami, stone-faced, bowed her head. "I was doing what I thought best."

"You will embarrass us," Ai hissed. "Embarrass your cousin!" She indicated Moriko, who stood nearby, head bent and silent as the grave. She'd seemed willing enough to help him, but had avoided him most of yesterday. Shin wondered if that was on the advice of her mother – or Mosu.

Shin snapped open his fan. "No one will suffer embarrassment due to my investigation, I promise you."

Ai glared at him. "Your… investigation? No one asked you to investigate anything. You are not even supposed to be here. This is Lion business, and you are not a Lion."

"As people keep reminding me," Shin said, fluttering his fan. "Yet I am here, and I am investigating. If you wish me to go, you will have to ask Minami." Minami shot him a look and he felt a brief flicker of regret, but it seemed the best way to head off Ai's anger, if only for a moment. "But I do not think you will," he added. "I think you will hear me out, because you are just as worried as Minami. Else you would not have attempted to stop the wedding in the first place."

Ai bared her teeth at him. "That is not your concern. We do not need the help of a Crane. The matter is settled."

"It is not," Minami said, her voice as sharp as a blade. She glowered at her aunt, and Lady Ai glowered right back. Moriko seemed to shrink beneath the weight of their confrontation, and Shin felt a moment's pity for the younger woman. All the fire she'd shown in their previous confrontation seemed to have been snuffed.

He let Minami and her aunt glare at one another for a few moments before finally snapping his fan closed and tapping it on his table. They both looked at him and he felt an instant's panic. Then his poise reasserted itself and he said, "If you're finished, I believe I have something to add."

"Talk, Shin," Minami said.

"As I was saying, we found a body. More, we found the location where Mosu was likely held captive by the pirates who took him. And I believe, with a bit of luck, that I can learn how he came to be a captive in the first place."

"What does that matter?" Ai said.

"It matters because the man you have pledged Moriko to is not Itagawa Mosu," Minami said. "But you suspected that, didn't you?"

Ai looked at her niece in shock. "What are you accusing me of?"

"You knew that what the Itagawa were claiming was impossible. But you allowed it to happen regardless. He is not Mosu – we do not even know who he is!"

Shin cleared his throat. "I believe I do."

All eyes turned toward him. He hesitated. "Rather, I have a theory. One that I intend to test out as soon as possible."

Ai tensed. "You wish to question my prospective son-in-law? Is that it?"

"Him or the corpse," Shin said, with tactical bluntness. As he'd hoped, it rocked Ai back a few steps. Before she could respond, he looked at Touma. "I understand that the Kitsu are known as the 'speakers of the dead'. That some of their priests possess the ability to act as mediums – that they can contact the spirits of the dead."

Touma hesitated. "Yes. But I do not, however."

"You are a priest," Shin said.

"Not that kind," Touma insisted. Shin held his gaze for a moment, then nodded.

"Ah, well. Then it's Mosu we must talk to."

"No," Ai snapped. "Enough of this foolishness. The ceremony will be this evening. Moriko will be married. That is the end of it!"

Shin leveled his fan at her like a sword. "You seem very insistent for a woman who tried to prevent this from ever even being a possibility."

Ai looked at him as if he'd slapped her. "How dare you–?" she began.

"Do you deny it? You were against the very idea of a marriage, and only agreed when you were ordered to do so by the daimyō. Indeed, when Mosu was feared lost, you stalled rather than seek a new suitor because you hoped the matter would be forgotten. Or do I do you an injustice?"

Ai opened her mouth, then closed it. She took a deep breath. "You tread dangerous ground, Crane," she said finally. "I could have you killed."

"Yes," Shin said softly.

Her eyes flashed. "Perhaps I should. For the benefit of all…"

"Mother – be silent, before you say something that cannot be forgotten," Moriko said suddenly. Ai looked at her, made as if to protest and then looked away without saying anything. Shin blinked, startled. He wondered if Moriko's previous silence had been at anyone's behest, or whether she'd simply been waiting in the tall grass with the patience of a lioness. "You too, cousin. You have both made your opinions very clear. But since this concerns my future, I shall be making my own decisions." She looked at Shin. "I would speak with you in private, Lord Shin."

Bemused, Shin indicated the balcony. "Shall we adjourn to the balcony? A spot of fresh air might do us both good."

"Yes." Moriko stepped past him and he followed her out onto the balcony. When Shin had closed the doors behind him, she turned and said, "Mosu is dead."

"I fear so."

"Good. He would have made a worthless husband."

Shin paused. "You said you felt sad when you thought he was dead."

"I did. But I am not sorry that he is dead." She looked out over the river, toward the township. "Mosu was a coward and a fool. Omo a drunk. And Asahi, just a boy. I was sad because I was left with two bad options."

"Is that why your mother stalled, rather than allowing for a new suitor?"

Moriko nodded. "She was trying to protect me. She has always sought to protect me. And Minami as well."

"I do not think you need protection," Shin said.

She glanced at him. "No. I do not." She dimpled. "Still, it is nice to have."

"How do you feel now? About Mosu – whoever he might really be?"

She paused. "He is... not worthless. Strange. Absent. But not a fool. Not a coward. Kind and considerate, though quieter than I prefer. Whoever he is, he is... suitable. Mother does not agree."

"Neither does Minami."

"What do you think of him?" she asked.

The question surprised him and he hesitated. Finally he said, "I think he is in pain. Physical and otherwise. He is broken. Damaged."

She nodded. "Yes. But not irreparably so."

Shin smiled slightly. "You believe you can fix him."

She laughed softly. "No. I believe I can help him fix himself. But there are some things that cannot be repaired. Do you think he killed Mosu?"

Shin paused. "I do not know. I have my suspicions, but... I need to speak with him."

"He will never agree to that. You... frightened him last time, I think. Or at least put him on his guard. He will not speak with you willingly."

"We must convince him. I think the successful conclusion to this matter rests with him. The truth is in him, and we must draw it out."

"But how?"

Shin was about to reply when there was another interruption. He opened the balcony doors as Kitano showed Lord Ikehata in. The Ikoma courtier had his biwa on his back and a bottle in his hand. When he saw the sake still on Shin's table, he raised an eyebrow. "Starting the celebrations early, are we? I thought you'd least wait for me before you began."

"Something like that," Shin said. "I need a favor."

"You haven't even asked me how I slept," Ikehata protested. He looked at Minami and the others and his eyebrow rose further. It was an impressive feat. "Is this a conspiracy, Shin? Are we conspiring?" He sounded amused by the prospect.

"Not quite. More like unraveling a conspiracy." He looked back at Moriko. "I have a plan. But I require your help."

"What do you want me to do?"

"As you did before, tell Mosu I wish to meet. And that I intend to blackmail him."

Moriko and Minami stared at him. "What are you talking about?" Ai burst out. "What madness are you planning, Crane?"

Shin looked at her. "I should think that was obvious. I will reveal your son-in-law-to-be's true identity to the world if he does not meet me alone. One of the lower wharfs, I think. Some place we won't be seen."

"You can't be serious," Ai said, eyes wide.

"Oh, but I am." Shin paused, taking in their expressions with great glee. While Minami and the others looked horrified, Ikehata was smiling widely. "I'm not actually going to blackmail the man. But if he thinks I am, he will almost certainly show up alone."

"And if he doesn't?" Minami demanded.

Shin gestured to Ikehata. "That is where my friend Ikehata comes in."

"Me?" Ikehata said, his smile fading into a puzzled frown.

"Him?" Minami asked.

"Yes," Shin said. His smile was as sharp as a crane's beak.

CHAPTER THIRTY-ONE
Confession

"This is perhaps the most ridiculous scheme you have ever concocted," Ikehata murmured, strumming his biwa idly as he spoke. "I'm supposed to just sit here, then? Listen to you – what? Blather on to some masked fraudster instead of, I don't know, enjoying myself at the delightful festivities you arranged?" He paused. "The sword-swallower was a nice touch, by the way. Arasou was very impressed."

Shin tapped his palm with his fan. They stood a short distance from the wharf, in the lee of a stack of empty rice barrels waiting to go out on the next tide. "Oh good. What did you think of the color scheme? Too subtle?"

"No, no. Peach was the right choice. Calming." Ikehata stilled his strings. The sound of music drifted over the wharf. A river barge, festooned with flowers and decorative lanterns, drifted past. The locals had joined the celebrations, indulging in drink and song. Merchants had set up stalls on the bridges leading to the keep, as had a number of street performers. Shin had made certain the guards would allow it.

"Normally these affairs are so staid," Ikehata continued. "The

Akodo rarely allow themselves the luxury of a good party." He gave Shin a keen look. "However did you convince them to let you set all this up?"

"It didn't take much convincing." Shin paused. "Minami needed my help."

"And, of course, you raced to the rescue. Oh Shin, you never could resist someone in armor, could you?" Ikehata plucked the strings of his biwa. "What was the name of that Kitsuki? The one who taught you all that useless rubbish about motives and such?"

Shin frowned. "I don't recall," he lied. He did recall. Kitsuki Ko had been a serious-minded young woman, with a keen grasp of the investigative method and an almost nonexistent sense of humor. Getting her to laugh had been an ordeal worthy of song.

"Quite adept at Sadane, if I remember right." Ikehata looked at him. "And, as I recall, she thought you were going to propose to her."

"Don't be ridiculous," Shin said quickly. "She never thought any such thing."

"She was quite angry when you scampered off to the City of Lies."

Shin sighed. "She was angry before that. Hence the scampering." He looked at Ikehata. "I trust you remember the plan? No ad-libbing, this time."

"My ad-libbing kept those Ujiks from cutting your throat," Ikehata protested. Seeing Shin's expression, he sighed. "Yes, Shin. I will sit here and be inconspicuous and unobtrusive. Painful as such a thing might be for a man of my sensibilities." Ikehata paused. "I cannot promise I will get to you in time if he decides to do something... rash."

"Yoku and Kasami are nearby. If our groom-to-be decides to be troublesome, I will squawk and bring them running."

"Even so, if he is who you think he is, you might not get the chance."

Shin frowned. Ikehata had insisted on knowing everything in return for helping Shin, and he was already regretting having told the other courtier the abridged version of the story. He trusted Ikehata to keep it to himself, at least for the moment. "I do not think that will be an issue. He wants to talk."

"Are you willing to stake your life on that?"

"Yes. Yours, too."

"Mine?"

"I assumed you'd swoop in to rescue me, like that time with the Ujiks."

Ikehata snorted. "We'll see how I'm feeling when it comes to it, eh? Might be more entertaining to watch him chase you around."

Shin sniffed. "I have never been chased anywhere."

Ikehata grinned. "Oh? What about that time with the–"

Shin silenced him with a gesture. "He's here."

Mosu was striding purposefully across the wharf, his hands at his sides. He wasn't armed, at least not visibly so. Nor was he yet dressed for the ceremony. From what Moriko had told him, Lady Kanna had all but had her stepson under guard since his last encounter with Shin. It was probably for the best that Shin had found no reason to talk to Mosu until now. While he doubted that Ai, fierce as she was, would actually go through with her threats, he had no doubt at all that Kanna wouldn't hesitate to make him vanish.

He watched Mosu walk and noted again that it was not the

walk of a courtier. It was not the polished glide of a nobleman, but the prowling saunter of one who has stepped over his share of bodies. Not Mosu, then.

Jiro.

It had to be Jiro. It had been obvious from the first. Two men vanished, one man returned. The man who could fight his way out of a den of pirates. So why pretend to be the other man? Why, why, why? That was the question Shin desired to know the answer to. It was the key to the whole thing, he thought. If he could just find the answer, it would all come untangled in his hands.

As Mosu – Jiro – reached the edge of the wharf, Shin went to meet him. Jiro gave no sign that he noticed Shin's approach, though Shin was positive he had. He stopped a safe distance away and waited.

And waited.

Shin gave a discreet cough. Jiro didn't turn. "You slipped your guards," Shin said. "Lady Kanna will be furious."

"Yes," Jiro said, without turning. "I expect so."

"What do you think of the festivities so far?" Shin asked. "Satisfactory?"

"Moriko seems pleased," Jiro said, his eyes on the water. "That is all that matters to me. Her happiness is the important thing."

"An admirable sentiment."

They stood in silence for a time, watching the water. Shin looked at him. "Why did you agree to meet me?" The question came unbidden to Shin's lips. He thought he knew the answer already, but he was interested in hearing the other man's reasons.

Instead, Jiro sighed and said, "I was born on this river, you know."

"On a boat, one hopes," Shin said as he joined the other man at the edge of the wharf. Jiro laughed softly.

"A small boat."

"And your parents?"

"Wave people, appropriately enough. Mendicant ronin, both of them. They had been in service to the Akodo. Then, I expect you already know that."

Shin nodded. "Why did they leave service?"

Jiro shrugged. "Who can say? There are as many possible reasons as there are stars in the sky and fish in the river."

"You never asked?"

Jiro looked at him. The golden tracery on his mempo glinted in the light of the setting sun. "I was a child. I had many questions. That, however, wasn't one of them."

"And when you grew older?"

"They were dead and no longer capable of answering my questions."

Shin hesitated. "Ah. Forgive me."

"Why? You did not kill them." Jiro chuckled wetly before the sound turned into a wracking cough. "My apologies. The humidity is not good for my lungs these days. Too long in a damp hole, I expect." He thumped on his chest, as if trying to dislodge a blockage. "I always expected this city would be the death of me."

"You could leave."

"And go where?" Jiro gestured as if to encompass the surrounding district. "Jiro is dead; Mosu is to be wed."

"But you are not Mosu."

"Am I not?" Jiro inclined his head. "The others seem convinced."

"They do, yes," Shin admitted. He turned to look at the

river. "I did not bring you here to blackmail you. I merely want answers."

"And do I have them?"

"I think so. I think I know what this is all about, but I have no proof. Only theory. A guess, really. Would you like to hear it?"

Jiro motioned for Shin to continue. Shin smiled. "Excellent. You are Jiro, former manservant to Itagawa Mosu. Mosu is dead and was, until recently, rotting in an unmarked grave somewhere in the forests on the western bank of the river."

Jiro hesitated. "You... found him?"

"We did, yes." Shin recalled Kasami's description of the grave. "You buried him."

"Yes. He did not deserve to be left to rot."

Shin noted this, and continued, "He was killed by pirates after the pair of you were captured during your ill-fated attempt to escape the city. I believe he was killed prior to your escape, likely as a result of injuries sustained during your capture. How am I doing so far?"

Jiro was silent for a moment. "He died during the escape."

Shin paused. "So, you admit it."

Jiro shrugged again. "I see no reason to deny it. It is your word against mine, and both the Itagawa and the Akodo would prefer that I be who I say I am." He hesitated, and reached for the clasps that held his mempo in place. He removed the mask slowly, and Shin took an instinctive step back as he caught sight of the ruined countenance beneath. There wasn't much left of Jiro's face below his eyes. Just a ravaged expanse of raw, red flesh, a crumbled ridge of a nose and an awful grin of exposed teeth.

Shin mustered every iota of politesse available to him and

resisted the urge to avert his gaze. Instead, he said, "Does it hurt?" A silly question, but the only one he could think of in the moment.

Jiro gave another phlegmy chuckle. "Quite a bit," he wheezed. Shin winced. It wasn't pleasant, watching a man with no face try to talk. "But pain and I are old friends." He looked down at his mempo. "And, too, it serves as a reminder. It ensures that I cannot forget what I survived – and why."

"And what was that?" Shin asked. "I am told that Mosu's body, decayed though it was, showed no signs of similar... mutilation."

"No. Well, that would have been foolish," Jiro said. He re-donned his mempo, obscuring his disfigurement once more. Relief and guilt warred briefly in Shin's mind. He pushed them aside and concentrated on the matter at hand.

"They wanted him for ransom."

"They wanted the money he owed them."

Shin paused. "What do you mean?"

Jiro sighed again. "Mosu was... too clever for his own good. Good at getting into trouble, but not very good at getting out of it. That's what he had me for. Only there were some things I couldn't fix." He paused, looking down at his hands. "What gave me away? I saw it in your eyes the first time we met."

"Your hands. They're scarred, the way they would be from sword practice. My bodyguard's hands look much the same. But according to, well, everyone, Mosu wasn't interested in swordplay, much less practice. But you were telling me about the pirates."

"He was scared. That bodyguard of Minami's frightened him. Made him realize for the first time how precarious his – our – position really was. A quick death on one hand, or a slow death on the other. Just running wouldn't be good enough; his stepmother would drag him back, in chains if necessary. So, he needed to vanish."

"The pirates. He was going to fake his death," Shin said, in realization. A child's idea of a good plan, or one conceived by a fool.

Jiro nodded. "Yes. He – we – thought that our winnings might enable us to set up our own gambling establishment in some backwater town. That's all he really wanted, you know... the freedom and money to indulge his vices at his leisure."

"And what did you want?" Shin asked quietly.

Jiro looked at him. "I wanted to help my friend."

Shin frowned. "You thought of him as a... friend?"

"Why else would I do all that I did?" Jiro asked softly. He looked away. "I stole for him, I killed for him. He lied for me and kept coin in my pocket. We kept each other safe from the repercussions of... our respective foolishness. We were closer than brothers. We... loved one another." His hands knotted into fists. "That's what killed him, in the end."

"Tell me," Shin said.

"For months, we supplemented our takings from the gambling houses by selling shipping information to the local riffraff. Pirates, smugglers – even a few spies. Mosu had gotten close enough to the Akodo that he was able to get and sell the information relating to their shipments especially..."

"No doubt contributing to their financial hardship," Shin interjected. He thought he knew who had given Mosu that idea. It was all snapping into focus now. An ugly picture.

Jiro grunted. "I had not considered that, but yes. Most likely. It was not his idea, though. He got it from someone else."

"You?"

Jiro gave a croaking chuckle. "No. I knew better. It's a dangerous game, selling information. Mosu got the idea from his other friend – Seizuka Omo."

CHAPTER THIRTY-TWO
Revelations

Shin felt no surprise, only elation. This, along with what Kasami had brought him, gave him the shape of the thing. The picture was becoming clearer by the moment. He looked at Jiro. "Omo was selling information."

"For years. Ever since his family sent him to the dojo here. It was how he kept money in his pocket. Later, it was how he and Mosu kept off the creditors who weren't intimidated by my blade."

Shin allowed himself a smile. "I can't imagine there were many of them."

"A few. A reputation is only as good as its latest test. And there are plenty of desperate knifemen in this city."

"Is that why a dynastic marriage seemed such a tantalizing prospect to them?"

Jiro grunted. "Mosu wasn't interested in marriage. He saw it as a trap. He spent his life rattling the bars of the cage his stepmother placed around him."

Shin felt a sudden uncomfortable sympathy for the dead man. "Lady Kanna is ambitious. She saw Mosu as a piece on her board, then?"

Jiro nodded. "Everyone is a piece on her board. But Mosu was a pawn, at best."

"Until the prospect of the marriage came up."

"No. Not at first."

"What changed?"

"The previous suitor… changed his mind." The way Jiro said it made Shin smile.

"Mosu decided to deal himself into the game, then. Why?"

"Omo needed someone to make him look good," Jiro said. "He told Mosu that once he'd secured the marriage, he could pay Mosu's way forever. Mosu believed him."

"Because Omo was his friend."

Jiro sighed and looked away. "Mosu was a poor judge of character."

"He is not alone in that. How did he come to be chosen, then?" Shin waved aside Jiro's answer. "Never mind. I expect Kanna saw an opportunity and seized it. Omo is cunning, but he was outplayed. It must have galled him to realize he'd engineered the circumstances of his own humiliation."

Jiro chuckled. "Oh yes. According to Mosu – who heard it from Omo – Omo was behind it all. The brains to the Itagawa and Ichime's money. The attacks, the marriage. He proposed the idea to Lady Kanna, through Mosu. And then he convinced Mosu to put himself forward as a potential suitor."

Shin nodded. "Yes. He knew that the Ichime's intended suitor was a boy – unacceptable to the Akodo. It would come down to Omo and whoever the Itagawa put up. So he made certain that it was someone whose reputation would work in his favor."

Jiro grunted. "A reputation that Omo helped him build."

Shin waved this aside. "Let us not credit him with that much foresight."

"Perhaps we should. Omo was trouble from the day he entered the dojo. But he was never caught. He always left Mosu to take the blame." Jiro's hands clenched and relaxed. "I could never make Mosu see the truth of it."

"Instead, you did what you could to protect him."

"Someone had to," Jiro said. "I wish... no. It does not matter. I was not strong enough, in the end. I failed him."

Shin waited a few moments, allowing the other man to compose himself. Jiro was clearly struggling to maintain his equilibrium. Shin could only imagine the stress he was under. Then, gently, "Tell me about the pirates."

"Another suggestion from Omo." Jiro sighed. "Mosu made no friends here. He cheated at every turn. He used people with abandon. And eventually his creditors came calling as they always did." He paused. "I was trying to keep Mosu out of trouble, get him as far away from the keep as possible until the wedding, but..."

"Yoku found you."

"Yes. We fought, and I lost. After Yoku... nearly killed me, Mosu was in a panic. I'd never seen him so frightened."

"Yes. Yoku is quite intimidating."

"He wasn't frightened of Yoku." Jiro bent his head. "He was worried about me." He laughed harshly. "I don't think he ever conceived of me being beaten. He'd spent years assuming I was the most lethal killer in creation, and to see me humbled... broke his nerve. I told him it wasn't important. I could deal with Yoku later, if necessary, but he got it into his head that Yoku was going to murder me."

"Murder you – not himself?"

"No. Even Mosu wasn't that stupid. He knew Yoku wouldn't touch him. But I had no such protection. He feared that Yoku would complain to Kanna and that she would dismiss me, or worse. I wasn't worried, but he demanded that we flee."

"Because you were his friend," Shin said.

"It's funny, isn't it?" Jiro said, looking up at the clear sky above. "That friendship would mean so much to men like us." He looked at Shin. "My first day at that cursed dojo, I had no food. I had to earn my meals, you see." He paused. "Mosu fed me. I think he felt sorry for me. And like a stray dog, I was at his side from then on." He looked down. "He was a kind boy before he met Omo. But he looked up to Omo, and so he did as Omo did."

Shin nodded, saying nothing. Jiro went on. "When he realized we needed to get away, he went to the one person who'd always helped him... Omo. Omo suggested he pay some of those pirates we knew to carry him to an undisclosed location. They would get the boat, the cargo and a substantial payment once we'd been safely dropped off."

"Only the payment didn't arrive."

Jiro shook his head and gave a harsh chuckle. "No."

"Omo was in charge of the payment, wasn't he?"

"Yes."

"Mosu trusted him even after he'd upended Omo's scheme?" Shin asked, somewhat incredulous at the depths of Mosu's foolishness.

Jiro chuckled again. "As I said, Mosu had a blind spot. And he was convinced that Omo didn't blame him. It wasn't his fault that Lady Kanna had upped her bribe, after all. She wanted rid of him worse than anyone, including Omo, realized."

Shin laughed softly. "What happened then? I assume the pirates were angry."

Jiro nodded. "Very. We were captives by then, rather than

guests. If Mosu hadn't been there, I might have been able to bluff my way out. They were as frightened of me as anyone else. But Mosu begged me not to resist. He was so certain that Omo had just been delayed." He touched his mempo. "He realized the truth when they began to cut pieces off me. By then, I'd been in that hole of theirs for nearly two weeks with barely any food and only the runoff from the river to drink."

Shin winced. Kasami had described the pirate hideout to him in detail, including the pit where they'd kept Jiro. It didn't sound at all pleasant. Jiro was made of sterner stuff than most if he managed to come out of that relatively intact.

"I didn't trust Omo, but even I was surprised by such blatant treachery," Jiro went on. "I expected him to pay for Mosu's freedom, at least."

"He wanted them to kill you both," Shin said.

Jiro shook his head. "I doubt he thought about it at all, beyond the need of the moment. Omo is... a scrambler; quick to react but slow to think. It's one of the reasons he was never put in charge of anything larger than a toll house. I never thought his callousness would extend to Mosu, however."

Shin hesitated. The next question would be the most difficult. "How did he die?"

Jiro was silent for several moments. Then, "They let him go so that he might secure the money they felt they were owed," he said. "I was to be collateral."

"And they thought he would come back, driven by an excess of sentimentality?"

Jiro laughed hoarsely. "I didn't say they were smart. Mosu was good at talking, when he had to be. After all, he convinced Lady Kanna to back Omo's scheme." His laughter trailed off into a creaky wheeze. "But as it turned out, they were correct. Mosu...

came back. But not with the money. Instead, he returned in the night. With my knife."

"To rescue you," Shin said, in sudden understanding. Jiro nodded slowly.

"We were friends," he said simply. "But he had never been one for that sort of thing. He'd found his courage, but... not the skill to go with it." His fists relaxed and he looked at the water. "I don't know how he got back into the hideout, but he did. He managed to get me out – what was left of me – but they caught us." Jiro looked up at the sky, watching as a flock of river birds cut elegant loops through the warm air. "I told him to run. Begged him. But he wouldn't." Something wet shimmered at the corners of his eyes, but it was gone almost as soon as Shin noticed it. "He never listened to me." Jiro sagged slightly. "Not once."

"They killed him."

"Cut him down before my eyes," Jiro said, not looking at Shin. He turned suddenly, and his gaze was hot; something of the old Jiro yet remained, Shin thought. "So I returned the favor. I managed to get my hand on a sword. I thought I would die with him. But I didn't." The fire in his eyes dimmed. "I wasn't quite ready to die after all, I suppose. I owed Mosu a debt and death would not pay it."

Shin waited for him to continue. Jiro took a shaky breath. "I made him an oath as I buried him. And I returned to see it fulfilled. You know the rest. We were close enough in size that fooling the Itagawa was no difficulty – at least until I was brought before Lady Kanna. I thought for sure she would see through me..."

"I am certain she did," Shin said. "She is as observant as I. But she was also aware that you could be of use to her as Mosu. No doubt she went along with your deception in order to maintain her hold on the marriage. And as for the Akodo, well, they don't care. One Itagawa is as good as another to them. Except for Minami, of course."

Jiro nodded. "Except for Minami." He looked past Shin. "She knew the instant she laid eyes on me, just like you. Then, she always hated Mosu."

"For good reason."

Jiro nodded again. "Yes."

"Why pretend to be him at all? What does it profit you to step into a dead man's sandals?" Shin snapped open his fan. "Especially that man. The money? There's precious little of that. The Itagawa are the ones paying. The prestige? Mosu's reputation is hardly the best... so why?"

Jiro was silent for a moment. Then, "He died for me. The least I could do was live for him." He touched his mempo. "I told you I owed him a debt. Jiro was nothing. A wastrel and a cur. But Mosu could be something better, if he had the chance. A true son of his clan. A husband... a father, perhaps. His reputation is poor, but reputations can be mended. Past sins forgiven. Mosu will be remembered as a good man, and Jiro... Jiro will not be remembered at all. It is better that way."

"And Moriko?"

Jiro bowed his head. "She is a strong woman. Stronger than Mosu knew, or Omo. I will serve her as faithfully as I did Mosu, for as long as I can."

Shin studied the masked man over the top of his fan. It was hard to read a man who had no face. But the eyes were still there, and the eyes held everything a man was. He'd expected Jiro's eyes to be flat – empty. But the eyes that met his were full to overflowing. Jiro was weeping silently, and his gaze was a ragged thing, exhausted by the strain of being something he wasn't. Shin tried to imagine what sort of toll that might take on a person's mind, especially someone who'd already endured what Jiro had.

With a start, he realized Jiro was still protecting Mosu, even if the other man was dead. His reputation, his name, his place in the world. Jiro was sacrificing himself, his very existence, in order to keep his master – his friend – alive. It was heroic, in its way. Insane by any definition, but... heroic. The stuff of kabuki.

Shin stood silent for long moments, pondering his next move. Jiro, he knew, had confessed not out of arrogance but out of a need to be himself, if only for one last time. Finally, he said, "How did Omo raise the money?"

Jiro hesitated. "What do you mean?"

"Where did he get the money to pay for Mosu's departure? Money changed hands to pay for the boat. And more money to pay the pirates. Where did it come from?" Shin looked at him. "Not Omo, I think. Not his own money, certainly. Mosu visited Shika Akari before he fled, didn't he?"

"Why do I feel as if you already know that?"

"Because I know everything. Almost everything. Mosu wasn't alone when he visited her, was he?"

"No. Omo was with him. It was–"

"His idea," Shin interjected. "Yes, I gathered. Ikehata, come out now." Jiro jolted as Ikehata stepped into the open from behind the barrels. Jiro twitched, but made no move to run. Shin wondered if he'd expected treachery. "Did you hear?"

"Did I hear? I'm already composing a ballad." Ikehata eyed Jiro. "I'm tempted to write a damn play. This is the stuff of melodrama."

"Yes. Of course, we're missing the happy ending," Shin said. "But I think we can find one if we look hard enough." He looked at Jiro. "I will need your help, though. Can I count on you?"

Jiro hesitated, then nodded. "What would you have of me?"

Shin snapped open his fan. "Call it one last service for your friend, if you like."

CHAPTER THIRTY-THREE
Guilty Conscience

Shin hurried down to the willows, Touma in tow. "I should never have let you talk to her, before," the priest said. "She is under great stress." Shin could hear the concern in the other man's voice and wondered at its origin. Simple empathy, or something more? He pushed the thought aside.

As soon as he'd finished with Jiro, he'd sought out Shika Akari for one last conversation. One last puzzle piece to slot into place. But when he'd arrived at the shrine, he'd found Touma in a state, fending off a pack of Akodo and Itagawa courtiers with nothing more than a fierce glower. They'd scattered like frightened birds at the sight of Yoku and Kasami, however, allowing Shin and Touma to go in search of the matchmaker.

"Why did she refuse to meet with Lady Kanna? Did she say?" Shin asked. According to Touma, Akari had ignored a summons to attend the Itagawa representative. She'd also ignored a similar summons from Lady Ai earlier in the day. And had refused to meet with Kazuya when he'd shown up at the temple unannounced.

"No. I think she intends to do something rash," Touma

growled. "This whole affair has driven her to the brink of madness, I fear. She is a fragile creature." He glanced at Shin. "I blame you."

"Me? What did I do?"

"You started all of this."

"This all began well before I got here, and you know it. All I'm doing is trying to get to the truth before it's too late."

"Truth is but the shadow of a lie," Touma quoted.

"And a lie can be the shield of truth," Shin fired back. "Yes, we've both read Hida Chiyo, remember?" He stopped and turned, forcing Touma to stop as well. "How long have you known of her bad habits, Touma? I've been wondering how it is that no one else has brought up the fact that the Akodo's chosen matchmaker has the gambler's sickness. Oh, I'm sure she's good at hiding it, but no one is that good. Unless she's had help."

Touma stared at him, his yellow eyes smoldering with some ill-concealed emotion. Shin went on, "I wondered why she chose the temple as her refuge."

Touma's eyes narrowed. "Are you trying to imply something?"

"I wouldn't dare," Shin said lightly. He let his cheerful mask drop a moment later. "If you'd simply told me about this earlier – either of you – I might have been able to help. As it is, the truth must come out."

"Why?" Touma said, and the question was so plaintive that it took Shin aback. He wondered, not for the first time, what was between the priest and the matchmaker. He groped for an answer for a few moments before saying simply, "Because a man is dead. And someone must answer for it."

Touma looked away, and Shin turned and continued out to where he knew Akari would be hiding. He found her there, down by the water among the willows. She was seated on the roots, looking more disheveled than he recalled. It was clear to him that she hadn't been sleeping. Bad dreams – or a guilty conscience?

He paused, studying her for a moment. Then, loudly, "Did you come down here to drown yourself? Touma seems to think so."

She started, and then laughed sourly. "And yet you are the one here." She watched him as he joined her by the water.

"Only because I insisted. I imagine he was going to come bundle you up and carry you away. Very forceful, the Kitsu. Even more so than the Akodo."

She smiled and looked down. Her hair, unbound, fell into her face. "He is… naïve."

"Yes. The best ones always are."

She snorted. "He does have a certain something, doesn't he?"

"It's the eyes."

She nodded and was silent for several moments. Shin decided to loose his first volley. "I told Touma just now that I'd wondered why you'd made this place your refuge. Then, it struck me – Touma."

"Yes," Akari said, with a hint of pride in her voice. "He is… protective."

"And handsome." Shin paused. "Fierce. I meant to say fierce."

"That, too." She pushed a lock of hair out of her face and said, "You do not have to fear. I am not going to kill myself."

"No. I didn't think you were." Shin looked up at the trees. "But then, it's hard to tell with you Shika. A very canny bunch."

"High praise from a Crane." She sighed and scooped up a handful of water from the inlets made by the willow roots. "I had considered it, though. When all the paths in the forest are bad, which one do you take?"

"The least bad," Shin said. Then, softly, "Tell me."

Akari let the water slide through her fingers. "What is there to tell? Do you know what it is like to be a Shika matchmaker? We are the face of our clan. Our words carry a heavy weight." She looked at him. "My childhood was spent in memorization tests and logic puzzles. I could recite the names of every unmarried samurai in the Winter Court by the time I was six years old. Our words carry weight – and so do we. The weight of responsibility, of expectation."

Shin, knowing full well the weight of which she was speaking, said nothing. Akari looked up at the cracks of sky visible between the willow branches. "I am so tired," she said softly. "I was so tired. I needed... a moment. Just a moment where I could not see the pattern of it all. So, I took up a hobby. Based on chance."

"Where no one would know who you were or have any expectations. Yes, I understand." Shin sat down beside her. "Better than you can ever know."

Akari looked at him, and for the first time, he thought she was doing so without her mask in place. "Yes, I believe you do," she said after several moments. "I do not know how they recognized me. But they did. They told me that unless I did as I was told, they would reveal my shame to the Akodo."

"And your reward for going along was the money to pay your debts. Paid, no doubt, by all three families. Only one of them paid you more than the others, didn't they?"

Akari took a shaky breath and nodded. "The Itagawa. Lady Kanna summoned me; told me that Mosu had admitted everything to her. She implied that she would reveal my failings, unless I found in favor of Mosu."

"As opposed to whom?" Shin asked. He already knew the answer, but additional confirmation was one more arrow in the quiver. When hunting a lion, it was good practice to have more than one shaft at hand.

She hesitated. "He will kill me." There was real fear in her eyes and her voice. Shin wondered if she saw something in Omo that he had not, some dark malice that made him more frightening than the callous fool Shin had met. Maybe so. Maybe it was simply a matter of context – predator and prey. Or maybe, as Lady Kanna had warned, there was more to Seizuka Omo than met the eye.

"No. As of now, you are under my protection. But I must know his name."

"Seizuka Omo," she said, in a shaky tone. "He saw me in the gambling house, confronted me... he bought my debt to the house. All of my debts. Claimed he owned me."

Shin grunted. "That sounds like him. A most unpleasant fellow."

She gave a thin smile. "Yes. All the more gratifying when I could not do as he wished. You should have seen the look on his face when Mosu was announced as the accepted candidate. I think he would have murdered me then and there if it had not been in public."

"And then?"

"He threatened me, but when I told him what had happened – he retreated. I think he realized that there was nothing either of us could do about it."

Shin smiled thinly. That had probably been the only sensible course from Omo's perspective. Withdraw and live to scheme another day. Lady Kanna was not the sort of enemy one went after on a whim. "And you've made sure to stay out of his way since."

She nodded – and paused. "He got his own back, anyway."

"He blackmailed you a second time."

She looked at him in surprise. "You know?"

"I know more than you might guess. Continue, please."

She paused. Then, "I was told that Mosu had changed his mind. That he wanted to flee the city, but that he needed money to do it."

"The money Lady Kanna had paid you," Shin said. "The money you said you had given to Mosu, so that his failure as a husband would not reflect on you."

She nodded, but didn't meet his eyes. "You claimed that, not me. I merely agreed."

"Flummery," Shin said. "Regardless, you gave him the money."

"What I had not gambled away, yes." She frowned. "But I did not give it to Mosu."

Shin looked at the water, recalling what Jiro had told him. "You gave it to Omo."

She closed her eyes. "Omo demanded it in return for forgetting the whole matter and forgiving my debts."

"Mosu's flight would not have reflected well on you."

"No. But it would have been a simple enough matter to blame it on his weakness rather than mine." She sighed and looked across the river, toward the keep. "When he... died, and the Akodo hushed the whole matter up, I thought that was the end of it." A bitter chuckle escaped her. "I thought I had escaped."

"But...?"

"But they would not let me go."

"The Ichime and Seizuka."

She nodded. "They demanded another match be made. The Akodo agreed. And when I returned, both Lady Kanna and Omo were waiting."

"Omo wanted you to make a new match – him, obviously – and Kanna wanted you to stall until a new Itagawa suitor could be found, I'm guessing."

Akari nodded jerkily. "I had no choice. I isolated myself. Took to spending my days at the shrine. Kept them guessing as I tried to think of a way out."

"Only no way out presented itself. And then… Mosu came back." Shin looked up at the gnarled old tree and wondered if it was listening, and if so, what it made of all of this. "The Itagawa had their suitor back, the Akodo were more than happy to have the problem solved. That left you in the bind. And Omo as well. Is that why he was trying to speak to you in the gambling house yesterday?"

Akari bowed her head. "I had been so careful until then. I had not made a wager in weeks – months – but with the wedding so close and you asking questions, I- I needed a release. Just a moment, left to chance."

"Your bad luck that he was there. Or maybe he was waiting for you. Men like Omo are predators; they stalk the well-trodden trails of their prey, noses to the wind. What did he want? It is too late for blackmail to have any effect on the outcome."

Akari looked at him. "He claims that Mosu will not be a problem. I do not wish to know what he means. I do not wish for anything except to go home." She looked up at the trees. "I think he will kill me if I do not help him with whatever he has planned."

"Will you swear to that?"

She looked down. "If I do, I am finished. My family – my clan – will be tarnished by my failure. That is worse than death."

"Failure can be forgiven or forgotten. Death, on the other hand, is distressingly permanent." Shin looked out over the water. "I cannot promise you will come out of this unscathed, Lady Akari. I will do my best, but there are too many tangles in this thread to work them loose in the conventional fashion." He tapped his fan into his palm. "I am forced to use other methods."

"What will you do?"

Shin fanned himself. "Cut the thread, of course."

CHAPTER THIRTY-FOUR
Celebration

Minami looked at Shin, her face a mask of tension. "Are you sure about this, Shin? The ceremony is to be held at dusk and it's already late afternoon. We don't have time for theatrics, and in the shrine, no less." She gesticulated, indicating their surroundings. The shrine had been decorated for the ceremony, but was otherwise quiet. Touma had sent the attendants to enjoy themselves, ostensibly while he completed the last of the preparations.

"There's always time for theatrics," Shin said, tapping his fan into his palm. "And yes, it's necessary. The only way to permanently untangle this thread is to do so in the open. That means somewhere public, and somewhere where that the temptation to spill blood will be curbed. The shrine is the best place, trust me."

"I agree with Shin," Touma said from where he stood beside the huddled form of Akari. The matchmaker looked wan and ill; frightened, Shin thought. But Touma was providing moral support. "Much as I hate to admit it, he's right," the priest went on. "I don't think the spirits here will mind, given the circumstances. And the shrine is the one place in this district where no one will risk drawing a blade."

"Or so you hope," Minami said bluntly.

Shin indicated Yoku and Kasami standing nearby. "That's what we have them for, remember?" He sniffed. "But if you'd rather just take them all into custody now, and risk the wrath of your aunt, the daimyō and all the guests, feel free." Outside, all was joy. The music, the food, the entertainment. Everything as he'd planned it. Or so he hoped. He hadn't yet been able to enjoy any of it, unlike some. Ikehata had melted into the crowd as soon as he'd heard Jiro's confession. Shin trusted him not to gossip about what he'd heard, else he might have felt some concern.

Minami glowered at him resentfully, but said nothing. Shin nodded in satisfaction, patting her arm. "Do not fear, my friend. This will soon be at an end, as I promised. Once your soldiers round everyone up… ah! There we are, and right on schedule."

It was a surly group that was ushered into the shrine by Minami's people. Lady Ai, Moriko and Mosu. Kanna. Kazuya. And finally, last but not least, Omo himself. "What is the meaning of this?" Ai asked as soon as she caught sight of Shin.

"A good question, my lady," Omo said. "Because these men interrupted my drinking, and I don't appreciate that." He looked around, and Shin thought he saw a faint crease of puzzlement on the other man's face. Or was that concern? He hoped so. He hoped that Omo felt something of what Akari and Mosu and even Jiro had felt, as the traps he laid for them inexorably closed about them.

Minami gestured for her men to wait outside and turned to Shin. "Lord Shin has some questions for all of you before the ceremony." There was a murmur at this, and he saw several gazes sharpen and accusatory looks flash between the conspirators.

Kanna looked at Shin. "So, you've found something, have you? Or maybe you just think you've found something."

Shin gave her a winsome smile. "Well, we'll see, won't we?"

"Yes, let's," Omo barked. "Get on with it."

Shin gestured to Kasami. "A few days ago, I sent my bodyguard to look for the pirates who supposedly attacked Mosu's vessel last year. She was able to track down the cove where he was held and locate a grave where someone was buried."

Kazuya frowned. "Someone?"

"Mosu," Omo said, with a mirthless smile.

"Perhaps," Shin said. He waved his fan. "But we'll get to that in a moment. First, I'd like to tell you all a story. A story about family and duty."

Omo laughed. "I do like stories. I should have brought a drink."

Shin ignored him and continued. "It begins with three vassal families, each unique in their own way – save one. They have the right to marry into their patron family. So, one by one, they ask for this right to be honored. It doesn't matter who asked first, or why. Merely that they did." Shin turned to Minami. "And what was the Akodo response to this innocuous request? A request, mind, that any vassal family has a right to make."

Minami glanced at Lady Ai. "The Akodo refused."

Shin tapped the air with his fan. "The Akodo... refused." He made a theatrical turn. "Which, of course, is well within their rights as one of the great families. They don't have to acquiesce – it's simply considered good manners. But, well, the Lion and manners are not often on speaking terms." He looked at his audience. "And this, then, was the unfortunate situation the vassal families with an interest in dynastic marriage found themselves. A right owed them – denied. The question became how to... circumvent this denial."

"Get to the point, Crane," Omo said.

Shin smiled. "Oh, I am." He paused. "Where was I? Ah yes. Circumnavigation." He tucked his hands behind his back and faced the representatives of the vassal families. "One of you hit upon an idea – show the Akodo how much they needed you. But to do that, you needed to wound them first. It was a simple matter to attack the Akodo where they were vulnerable – their money. Financial pressure is among the keenest of blades – the victim can bleed out before they even realize they've been injured." Shin began to pace. "You were relentless: pirates, bribes, sabotage. A steady barrage of small misfortunes aimed at your patrons. A suicidally courageous assault. Then, courage is the hallmark of the Lion."

"An interesting tale," Kanna began. Shin silenced her with a gesture.

"One I am not yet finished with. This barrage had one goal: weaken the Akodo enough to force them to acknowledge your right to a dynastic marriage. Which it did. It was an ingenious ploy, worthy of the Scorpion or, dare I say it, the Crane."

"Get on with it, Shin," Minami said.

Shin waved his fan in acknowledgment. "This is where the problems arise. Only one suitor will be accepted. Initially, all three families agree to abide by certain rules of engagement, but that doesn't last long."

Omo snorted. "That's one way of putting it."

"Silence!" Kazuya snapped. Omo made an obscene gesture and the other man spluttered in useless fury.

"But there's a speck in the powder. One of the courageous

conspirators has an edge." Shin looked at Akari, who refused to meet his gaze. "More, he has insured that his only real rival in this game of courtship has no interest in being married off." Shin's gaze turned to Mosu, and then back to the others. "He thinks himself victorious." He aimed his fan at Omo. "Didn't you, Omo?"

To his credit, Omo didn't flinch from the accusation. Instead, he looked at Minami. "You had to bring him here, didn't you?" he said softly. "Had to interfere. Couldn't leave well enough alone. And now it's all gone wrong. Damn Akodo paranoia."

"Justified paranoia, in this case," Shin said. "You engineered this whole cunning little plot to catapult yourself into a dynastic marriage. You knew that Asahi would be considered too young for a proper match, whatever the Ichime told themselves. And you knew Mosu would be rejected out of hand, once you insured that he was the suitor, rather than someone more suitable."

"Only he wasn't," Omo said, tossing a venomous glare at Kanna. She returned his look with one of serene disdain. "The little weasel somehow managed to prove himself acceptable to our mighty patrons."

"Careful of your tone, Seizuka," Yoku murmured. Omo glanced at him, but only briefly. He didn't seem chastened at all. Indeed, there was a light in his eyes that Shin didn't care for. A wildness that possibly spoke to future foolhardiness. Hands still folded, he twitched two fingers in Kasami's direction and she gave a terse nod.

Omo went on. "It was bribery of course. The Deer needed money."

Shin spoke out. "Which you and Mosu knew, because you'd watched her at the gambling houses. Tell me, was it just good fortune that put her in your path, or premeditation?"

Omo looked at him. "Do I strike you as the sort of man to plan things out?"

"You strike me as a man who's a good deal smarter than he wishes people to know. Especially people in a position to do him a good turn."

Omo snorted. "And is that wrong?" He looked around, as if daring anyone to disagree. "No, Crane. It wasn't planned. I thought the fortunes were smiling on me when I spotted Akari losing all her money at dice."

Akari flinched as he spoke. Head bowed, she turned away from the group. Shin felt a moment's pity for her. In a moment of desperation, she had thrown away her reputation and potentially damaged that of her family. "And what did Mosu think?"

"Ask him yourself. He's right there." Omo's grin widened into something unpleasant. "Only he isn't, is he? I knew Mosu. That man isn't him."

"You have no proof," Kanna said sharply.

"Proof?" Omo laughed. "What do I need proof for, when the merest whisper of impropriety will be more than enough to make our hosts reconsider?" He looked at Minami and her aunt. "Isn't that right, Lady Ai?"

Ai didn't answer. But that was reply enough for some.

"I knew it," Kazuya said, with a hiss of pleasure. He'd finally caught up with what was going on. "Mosu is an impostor. The marriage contract is void. A new suitor must be chosen. I put forth my grandson as the worthiest of the original candidates."

"A stripling," Omo said, with a grin. He spread his arms. "Why choose a mouthful of rice when she can have an entire bowl?" He looked at Mosu – or, rather, Jiro. "Besides, I'm a sight handsomer than this one, whoever he is."

"I should have killed you that night on the dock," Jiro said softly. Moriko caught his arm, stilling him. Her expression was set, eyes flat. Shin wondered how much of this she'd already known, or at least suspected. Had Lady Ai seen the truth of it and told her daughter? Or was Moriko simply more observant than anyone gave her credit for?

Omo paused, eyes narrowing. Then, they widened. "Jiro…" he breathed. His hand fell to the hilt of his sword. While he'd known Mosu was a fraud, it was clear he hadn't realized just who was under the mask. "But you are dead. I told them to kill you."

"They tried." Jiro tilted his head. "Perhaps they succeeded."

"No. No." Omo took a step back. "Why would you…? Madness."

"Keep your hand off your blade," Yoku said harshly. Omo glanced at him and then at Kanna, his expression one of disgust. "Did you know what you allowed into your fold, woman? That… thing might as well be a ghost. It's certainly not a man. Not anymore, if it ever truly was."

Shin allowed himself a bark of laughter, which drew a furious look from Omo. "You're one to talk, Omo. Jiro was a monster, yes. No one denies that. But he was a simple monster. His crimes were simple crimes – bloody, but small. And all committed out of misplaced loyalty. Yours, on the other hand…" Shin snapped open his fan. "You organized a conspiracy against the Akodo, cost them no small amount of money, blackmailed them into a marriage… and then attempted to kill the man chosen to marry Akodo Moriko."

Moriko made a soft sound in the back of her throat, a wordless growl like that of a lioness denied. Omo looked at her, as if seeing her for the first time.

Shin kept talking. "Mosu came to you when he decided to

flee his impending nuptials. His friend, his confidant – did you make the arrangements for him?" He glanced at Jiro. "Is that why you met them at the docks that night?"

Omo tore his gaze from Moriko and swallowed. "What does it matter now?"

Shin ignored him and went on. "You intended for them to kill Jiro, for obvious reasons. Did you intend for them to kill Mosu as well? Or was there to be a split of the ransom?" Shin snapped his fan shut before Omo could reply. "No, you're quite right. It doesn't really matter, I suppose. You wanted him gone, and gone he was. Until he wasn't. Until he came back like a ghost risen from the grave."

Omo growled wordlessly and flexed his hand. It wasn't on his sword, but he clearly wished it to be. He pointed at Jiro. "Whatever the Crane's accusations, that man is an impostor. And if it becomes known – if any of this becomes known – the Akodo's reputation will suffer…"

Minami stepped forward. "The Akodo's reputation is not your concern. Not anymore." She gestured to Yoku. "I have heard enough. Take him into custody."

Omo's sword sprang into his hand with impressive speed. He was already pivoting as Yoku reached for his own blade a half-second too slow. Omo's blade slashed across Yoku's chest and the bodyguard staggered back, reaching for the wound. As Yoku toppled, Omo was moving toward Jiro and Moriko, his teeth bared.

CHAPTER THIRTY-FIVE
Pursuit

Even as he moved to intercept Omo, Shin wondered what was going through the Seizuka's head. Did he want revenge, or was the act driven by simple spite? A need to destroy what he couldn't have. Either way, Shin intended to prevent it. His fan snapped up and out. Omo's sword came down, slicing through paper and connecting with the steel tines of the fan. Shin snapped the fan closed, trapping the blade and twisting it away and down. Omo cursed and drove his fist into Shin's stomach.

Shin stumbled back, trying ineffectually to suck in a breath. Omo snarled and raised his sword. Shin's life – mostly mistakes, he thought with some annoyance – flashed before his eyes. But before Omo could strike, Kasami was there. Her blade intercepted his. She glanced down at Shin. "Idiot," she said. "Get out of the way."

She shoved Omo back and Shin scrambled out of the way, wheezing. Omo retreated with his sword extended before him. His eyes darted around, looking for a way out.

"How dare you draw steel in this shrine," Touma began. The

air smelled of copper and Shin felt a sudden weight on his other senses as the priest gathered his power. Omo glanced at him, eyes widening.

Jiro roared and leapt. So startled was Omo that he barely had time to swing his sword out. The blade struck Jiro's mempo, tearing it from his face, exposing his ravaged features. Omo flinched back, but not in time to avoid the knife that Jiro sank into his side. He howled and sprinted for the river with one hand clutched to his injured side.

Kasami needed no prompting to give chase. Touma made as if to pursue as well, but Akari stopped him. Minami looked at Shin. "We need to catch Omo before he gets off the island." She glanced at Yoku, who was sitting up with some help from Moriko. The bodyguard was bleeding freely, his face pale, but he was still alive. Shin saw concern in her eyes nonetheless.

"Stay here," Shin said. "Kasami will catch him."

Minami shook her head. "No. It is my responsibility. This has all been my responsibility. I should not have brought you here." She looked at Yoku. "Yoku, I–"

"Never mind, my lady," Yoku said through clenched teeth. "Do what needs doing." Minami nodded and paused.

"May I have the use of your sword, Yoku?"

The injured samurai nodded and awkwardly proffered the weapon's hilt. Minami took it, and – after a moment's hesitation – drew her own and offered it to Shin. "Since you seem to have forgotten yours."

Shin took her blade gingerly, with respect. "Every time I carry one, people expect me to use it," he protested.

Minami smiled. "Well, let's see if you remember how to use it. Come, Crane. It is time you see how a Lion hunts." She led him out of the shrine. Touma was waiting for them with Kanna and Kazuya. Outside, the two men Minami had left on guard were both dead. Shin felt a hollow gnawing of guilt in his belly.

"He ran toward the town center," the priest said. "He's probably hoping to hide among the crowds watching the demonstrations by the dojo students."

"Let's hope," Shin said, recalling that he'd marked the common area near the shrine for the sumai demonstrations. He'd wanted Reo to have the best audience possible. "Given his state of mind, he might be inclined to attempt something more desperate. See to the others, just in case he comes back. And send someone to inform Lord Arasou that there is trouble." He glanced at Kazuya and Kanna, neither of whom looked happy. "If I were you two, I wouldn't go anywhere. Not just yet."

He turned and saw Minami was already hurrying along the street that led away from the shrine. Outside the shrine, the wedding festivities were in full swing. There were people everywhere, and the air throbbed with noise.

Omo bulled through the crowd that filled the street, shoving startled passersby out of the way as he headed for the common area where the sumai circle had been set up. His sword flashed, thankfully unbloodied as yet. Shin flinched inwardly even so, cursing himself for his foolish need to show off. If he'd been smarter – quicker – Omo wouldn't have made it out of the shrine. Wouldn't have killed those men. But he had, and now it was likely that some other innocent would pay the price.

The crowd heaved back from the danger in their midst, dispersing and knotting up like a shoal of startled fish. The bales of straw that marked the sumai ring were knocked over, and the wrestlers scrambled back as Omo staggered into the ring, searching wildly for something – anything – that might save him. His eyes widened and a triumphant snarl stretched across his pale features.

Shin spied Seizuka Hinata standing at the edge of the crowd, a startled look on his face. Samurai in Seizuka livery were nearby. "Hinata – cousin," Omo howled. "Assassins – treachery – help me!"

Hinata, to his credit, did not react immediately. His attendants were not so cautious. Several of them took a step forward, hands on their swords. The crowd was in a surge now, yelling, shouting. Ichime and Itagawa courtiers arguing with Seizuka and each other. Akodo soldiers trying to calm things down; others reacting to one side or another.

Kasami vaulted the straw bales, sword in hand. Omo spun, barely parrying a blow that would have otherwise removed his arm. He retreated, still bellowing for help. His side was stained red, but he wasn't slowed much by the injury. Seizuka samurai moved to aid him, if somewhat hesitantly. They were confused, but it would only last a few moments, Shin knew. He looked at Minami. "We have to calm this crowd! This is going to turn into a riot otherwise!"

She nodded grimly and set about trying to pull together the scattered Akodo soldiers. Shin hurried toward Kasami and Omo. Their duel had devolved into a circle chase, with Omo trying to break away and Kasami cutting him off at every attempt.

But the Seizuka were closing in, though fighting their way through the crowd. When they reached the circle, all bets were off. Omo was one of their own and Kasami a stranger – not even a Lion. They'd try and cut her down without a thought, and she'd return the favor. Shin had to intervene before things turned bloody.

Omo saw him coming and bared his teeth. "You! Stay back,

Crane." He shoved bales aside, trying to make room for himself. Shin spotted several wrestlers loitering nearby, including Reo. They backed away as Omo stumbled toward them, his sword waving in a threatening manner. "Help," he cried. "Itagawa assassins! We are betrayed!"

That did it. A Seizuka samurai darted through the press, hand on his sword. Kasami intercepted him before he could reach Shin. More of them arrived, pushing through the crowd. Kasami glanced at Shin. "Go! Catch him, I will hold them off."

Shin didn't hesitate. If Omo escaped, they would never find him. Worse, he was exactly the sort of fool to hold a grudge. Shin didn't fancy looking over his shoulder for the rest of his life. He shouted, trying to disperse the crowd. No sense giving Omo access to any more potential hostages.

Omo staggered down a side street, heading away from the crowd. Shin followed. Omo was slowing down now, leaving a trail of red in the dust of the street. He made his way toward one of the small wharfs that dotted the inlets of the district, where merchants unloaded their wares from the small barges that glided through the great gates at the entrance to the Lion-held portion of the city.

Most of the shops here were closed and the few people in evidence scattered as the sword-wielding apparition limped toward them. Omo slumped against a wall, scant feet from the wharf. He was breathing heavily. Shin slowed, hoping all the fight had drained from his quarry. "Omo…" he said softly.

Omo spun and lunged, quick as a cat. His sword carved the air as it descended toward Shin's head. Shin managed to interpose his own blade at the last moment. He retreated, taking a tighter grip on the hilt. "There is nowhere to run, Omo. Even if you do get out of the city, you won't get far bleeding like that."

Omo gave a wheezy laugh and licked his lips. "He was always good with a knife. I should have killed him myself. But I couldn't be bothered. Out of sight, out of mind." He shook his head. "That'll teach me to ignore my instincts."

"I suspect it was your instincts that got you into trouble in the first place," Shin said. Omo took a step toward him, more surefooted now than he had been a moment ago. A ploy, Shin realized belatedly. Omo had drawn him in, away from Kasami – why? To kill him? Shin retreated another step.

"Maybe," Omo grunted. He studied Shin with a bleary gaze and said, "I lied, earlier."

"You'll have to be more specific," Shin said.

"About the Shika dropping into my lap. I didn't know who she was. Just another loser at the dice." His expression became sly. "Until someone whispered her name in my ear."

Shin tensed. "What do you mean?"

Omo's smile was savage. "I'm not the head of the snake, Crane. I'm just one more bit of wriggling tail. Like Kazuya and Kanna." He bared his teeth. "Like others... some in this city. It took me a while to figure it out, but I did. They were just using us to hurt the Lion, the same way they'd used others." He laughed hoarsely and took another step toward Shin. His blade dipped. "They set it all in motion. I'm the victim here. Funny, isn't it? Mosu thought I was his friend, and I thought they were mine..."

"Who are they?" Shin asked, his attention riveted on the other man's face.

"It doesn't matter. They'll be dead when I get hold of them." Omo's sword flicked up, slicing through Shin's sleeve and nicking his arm. Only Shin's speed saved him from a debilitating wound and he cried out in alarm. He ducked away from Omo's next blow and let his borrowed sword glide in a riposte across

Omo's midsection. Omo cried out and nearly fell, but he was made of sterner stuff than that.

Berserk now, Omo hacked at Shin. All finesse, all skill lost, buried beneath brute frenzy. He was bigger, stronger; skill wouldn't be enough. Shin defended himself as best he could, but Omo was determined to kill him – even if he himself died in the process.

The raw fury of his attack forced Shin back until Shin's foot slipped on something – Omo's blood, he thought – and he fell back against the side of a building. Omo roared in triumph and lunged, sword up–

"Lord Shin! Get down!"

Shin dropped prone as a straw bale hurtled through the air, striking Omo in the side of the head. There was a sickening crack and Omo spun in a lazy circle, his sword dropping from nerveless fingers as he toppled onto his face with a thump of finality. His heavy form twitched gracelessly for a few moments before going still. Shin stared at the body, regret mingling with relief, and then turned to see Reo standing at the end of the street, panting.

"I- I saw you chasing him, and I thought I should help," she said. She had a sickly expression on her face as she straightened. "I didn't mean to… is he… is he dead?"

Shin looked at the body and nodded slowly. "Yes. And no doubt about it."

CHAPTER THIRTY-SIX
Explanations

In the aftermath, the arguments started. Kazuya against Kanna, Kanna against Akari; each side accusing the other of having been in cahoots with Omo. It only became worse when Lord Arasou summoned everyone to the main receiving room of River Keep, where he insisted on hearing the whole story from Minami, as well as a statement from Ikehata. The subject of Jiro wasn't brought up, until Kazuya decided to roll the dice one final time. Shin couldn't fault the old man's courage, whatever else.

Kazuya drew himself up to his full height and faced his lord with an expression of dignified expectation. "My lord, it is obvious to me that this man is an impostor. Whatever else has occurred, that fact is surely undeniable. I ask that you strip the Itagawa of any claim to this marriage and bestow it upon the remaining, worthy contributor – my nephew, Asahi."

At this, Kanna made a rude noise – hardly ladylike or what one might expect in the presence of a daimyō. Kazuya rounded on her. But before he could say anything, Shin cleared his throat.

Then once again. The burgeoning argument stilled and all eyes turned to him. The Crane in a cave full of Lions. He smiled and made to speak.

"No," Arasou said quietly. Shin closed his mouth. The Akodo Daimyō studied him for a moment and then turned to Tsuko. She smiled, and Arasou sighed and turned at last to Moriko. "Well?"

"I say he is Mosu," she said, her chin lifted. Tsuko clapped her hands, as if in encouragement, or perhaps support.

"Then he is Mosu. This, at least, is settled to my satisfaction." Kazuya looked as if he might argue, but a single glance from Arasou was enough to stifle any protest he intended to make. Arasou turned back to Shin. "As to the rest of it… come, Crane. I would speak with you in private."

Shin bowed his head and followed Arasou outside, into the gardens. The daimyō stared at nothing in particular for several moments before saying, "There was a conspiracy, then?" He didn't look at Shin as he said it, and the fact made Shin somewhat nervous.

"Several, actually," Shin said.

"They conspired against us."

Shin hesitated. One wrong word here, and he might well be responsible for the deaths of several people. "I believe so, yes. But there is no proof, save the word of a dead man. I could well be wrong, and it is nothing more than coincidence."

"Are you wrong?"

Shin took a breath. "I do not know, my lord."

Arasou grunted and turned. "It is a simple question."

"Forgive me, my lord, but it isn't. I believe that you have been the victim of a conspiracy. But as to whether these are the conspirators, well… there it becomes rather murky. It could be that they, too, are victims, in a sense. That this was done for reasons other than simply acquiring an Akodo bride and that your vassals only acted to seize the opportunity fate seemingly provided."

Arasou was silent for several moments. "I have never had a head for strategy," he said finally. "That has always been my brother's skill. He looks at a battlefield and sees a pattern. I look at a battlefield and see only opportunities for glory." He peered at Shin. "I think you would like him. Like you, he has too many thoughts in his head."

Shin said nothing, and wondered if Arasou was attempting to compliment him, or insult him. Arasou sighed and turned back to the garden. "Right or wrong, there is little to be done. The battle is over, for better or worse. Moriko has made her choice, and I am not strong enough to deny her. Tell me this, though – is he a good man, whoever he is?"

Shin hesitated. "I believe he is trying to be." A gamble, but he'd always had luck on his side when it came to dice. He believed that Jiro – or Mosu – wanted to be better than he had been. To be a good man, worthy of the name. Redemption was not measured in a single great act, but a hundred small ones. Time would tell whether he was correct in his assessment of the man behind the mempo.

Arasou relaxed. "Then nothing more needs to be said. You are dismissed. Send my cousin out, if you would. Minami and I have much to discuss."

Shin bowed his head and retreated, relieved. He stepped back inside and gestured for Minami to go out. She nodded to him as she swept past, head high. Shin paused, watching as the servants closed the doors, sealing away the conversation between daimyō and general. He stared at the door, trying to see through it. Trying to imagine what Arasou might be saying to Minami. Was he chastising her? Complimenting her?

"She will be fine, Shin," Ikehata said from behind him, startling him. "Which is more than I can say for Kazuya and Kanna." Shin turned and the Ikoma handed him a cup of tea. "Arasou might not punish them, but they're known now. The daimyō is aware of them in a way he wasn't before. They might regret that before too long. It's never worth the effort required to attract a lion's attentions – or so I've found."

"What do you think will happen to them?" Shin asked. Despite everything, he hadn't disliked either Kazuya or Kanna. Both had merely been doing what courtiers did – scheming to improve their fortunes and that of their families. He found it hard to blame them for that.

"You know as well as I that the Akodo will keep them close, but never again allow them the sort of privilege they once enjoyed. Their families will isolate them and ignore them, if only to prove our merry conspirators were acting to their own benefit. Kazuya's nephew will never attain a high rank. Kanna's influence will dwindle to nothing. And the Seizuka, well... who knows?" He looked at Shin. "Drink your tea."

Shin drank his tea. "I told Arasou that Mosu was an acceptable choice."

Ikehata frowned. "Except he's not Mosu."

"You and I both know that doesn't matter. He's Mosu if Arasou and Moriko say he's Mosu."

"They'll keep an eye on him regardless," Ikehata said doubtfully. He tugged on an earlobe. "I'm told that the Shika is being sent home after the ceremony. Not in disgrace, but..."

"In disgrace," Shin said, sipping his tea. "Touma will be accompanying her."

Ikehata raised an eyebrow. "You heard that?"

Shin sighed. "No. I just guessed. But that's a problem for someone else." To the best of his knowledge, the Shika didn't allow their matchmakers to form relationships outside the clan. Whatever was going on between Touma and Akari, it wasn't destined to have a happy ending. Then, was anyone ever guaranteed such a thing?

The doors opened and everyone turned as Arasou stepped inside, followed by Minami. "After speaking with my cousin, I have decided to let the rest of this matter lie in the grave that has been dug for it." He paused, studying each person in the room in turn. "That does not mean it is forgotten, or forgiven. But it will not be spoken of, and no punishment will be meted out. As far as the public record will show, the conspiracy began and ended with Seizuka Omo, and him alone. With his death, the matter is laid to rest. The wedding ceremony will proceed as planned."

A palpable quiver of relief went through most of the people in the room. Minami caught Shin's eye and smiled thinly. Arasou wasn't finished, however. He extended a hand to Shin. "But before we move on to happier things, I wish to acknowledge the efforts of Lord Shin in helping us with this matter. You have done us a good turn, Lord Shin. Crane or not, the Akodo owe you a boon. Name it and it shall be yours."

"May I attend the wedding ceremony?" Shin asked hopefully. He hadn't gotten to enjoy the festivities, but being one of the few Cranes ever allowed to attend a Lion ceremony would be quite the social achievement. He wondered what his grandfather would say.

"Except that," Arasou said, with a slight smile. The Akodo Daimyō thought he was funny. Polite laughter at Shin's expense filled the room.

Shin sighed. "Never mind, then. No boon necessary. A good deed is its own reward." He bowed low as the daimyō turned away. Arasou and Tsuko departed, followed by the others until only Ikehata and Minami were left.

"Cheer up," Ikehata said. "Now you're free to answer my challenge from yesterday."

"Your what?"

Ikehata hefted his biwa. "I believe I challenged you to a duel of musical skill, Shin. I took the liberty of sending a servant to fetch your biwa." He flicked the strings playfully. "Wedding ceremonies are tedious anyway."

Shin laughed and nodded. "Very well. Though I must warn you, I have improved some since the last time we matched strings."

"I should hope so. Last time you made our audience's ears bleed." Ikehata slapped Shin on his injured arm, provoking a wince, and strode out. Minami shook her head.

"If what I've heard of your playing is anything to go by, you haven't improved that much," she said, not looking at him.

"Perhaps you simply have no appreciation for music," Shin said defensively. He paused. "How is Yoku?"

"He will recover," she said. "I should not have brought you here." She glanced at him. "I am sorry, Shin. I endangered you, and for no reason at all."

"Hardly no reason," Shin chided. "And a little danger never hurt anyone." His arm gave a twinge and he rubbed it. "Reo was quite impressive in her matches, I'm told. Everyone is talking about her."

"Everyone is talking about her because she broke a man's neck with a thrown straw bale," Minami said pointedly. "It's not something people forget quickly." She paused. "Still, she saved your life. I owe her something for that."

Shin nodded. "True. I told her you would have tea with her tomorrow after the festivities are concluded. She is looking forward to it."

Minami made as if to protest, then smiled and shook her head. "Fine."

They stood in awkward silence for a moment. Then, Shin said, "You knew about the conspiracy. That is the real reason you asked me to involve myself in this."

Minami shook her head. "I suspected, nothing more. I needed someone to tell me I wasn't being an overprotective fool." She looked up at the sky. "You aren't a child, Shin. Neither am I. We both know how these things work. But I thought – no, I knew – that something foul was going on. I thought, at first, whoever had sent that poison rice to us last year was up to their old tricks. I do not know whether to be relieved or concerned that it is a different party."

"Yes. Well, about that…" Shin began hesitantly. It was only a suspicion, after all. But something told him that Minami, at least, ought to know. She looked at him.

"Omo… said something that made me uneasy."

"Omo said a lot of things."

"Yes, but he mentioned getting the idea from someone else." Shin paused. "The… individual behind the poison rice conspiracy may have also been influenced by another. The same individual, perhaps, who encouraged Omo." He looked her square in the eye. "An unseen hand moving unknowing pieces on a board."

Minami looked at him intently. "Who else have you mentioned this to?" she asked after several moments.

"No one." Shin forced a smile. "I have no evidence. Merely the word of murderers and conspirators, and both know those are worth less than dust. But it is more than coincidence, I think."

Minami nodded slowly. "Yes." She paused. "I feel I should mention that if there is a strategy at work, you have upended it twice now."

"Yes, I had thought of that." Shin felt a flicker of unease. He gave himself a slight shake. "Still, a problem for another day." He smiled at her. "You should be celebrating with the others. Mosu will be a most worthy member of the Akodo, I have no doubt." He snapped open his fan. "And if not, well… I'm sure Yoku will have a suggestion or two."

CHAPTER THIRTY-SEVEN
Kenzō

Three days after the wedding, Shin was putting the finishing touches on a letter to Gota, thanking him for his aid, when Kasami entered his room and said, "We must talk."

Shin set his brush down. "About what?" He'd felt her circling him since the end of the wedding. He'd known something was bothering her, but had been confident she would tell him what it was soon enough. He'd had other things to occupy him in the interim.

As soon as he'd returned from the Lion district, he'd put Ito on the trail of Seizuka Omo's acquaintances and business associates. Ito hadn't asked why, but Shin suspected that the merchant already knew what Shin was looking for. If there was some connection, however tenuous, between the affair of the poison rice and this one, Ito would find it.

There had also been a funeral at River Keep after the wedding – a quiet affair, attended by only a few people. Shin had been among them, though he hadn't known Mosu. Jiro had been in attendance as well, head bowed. He remained at the grave long after the others had left, or so Shin had heard.

Then, of course, there had been the matter of Kasami's duel with Kenkō. A close-run thing, he thought, though he admitted he was no judge of such things. Kasami had won, of course. But it had taken some effort, and to say she hadn't been happy about it was an understatement.

"Kenzō."

Shin stiffened. "What about him?" He'd been surprised to hear that Kenzō had accompanied Kasami on her outing. The thought of the auditor on a boat, any boat – especially *Lun's* boat – was an amusing one. Less amusing had been Kasami's admission that Kenzō had saved her life, displaying previously unknown capabilities.

"I… talked with him. While he was traveling with us."

Shin's gaze sharpened as he studied her face. Normally, Kasami was incredibly hard to read. She was good at hiding her emotions. But now he could see everything – and what he saw, he didn't care for. "I can't imagine why you would've tortured yourself in that fashion, but go on. What did he have to say for himself?"

She hesitated. Then, "We spoke of your future."

"My… ah. Oh." Shin felt as if he'd taken a punch to the stomach. "So. The day has come, has it?" He glanced around, unconsciously – instinctively – searching for the nearest exit. "Took them longer than I expected." He felt short of breath and forced himself to calm down. "But even so, it seems a trifle… soon, don't you think?"

"Not soon enough, to hear him tell it."

Shin pinched the bridge of his nose. His heart was hammering and there was a pressure in his head that hadn't been there a few moments ago. "Damn it. Konomi was right. I should have dealt with him from the first. Stamped out this foolishness before it got out of hand."

Kasami was silent for a moment. Then, "It is the duty of every Daidoji to marry and further the interests of the clan."

"Yes, but you're overlooking one very important thing…"

"Which is?"

"I don't want to." Shin tapped his fingers on his writing desk. The initial panic had receded and his mind was functioning once more. "If they'd already made a decision, I would have been informed – and not by a mere auditor. They'd have sent one of my innumerable cousins. One of the ones I don't like."

"Do you like any of them?"

Shin paused. "I'm rather fond of the ones who haven't learned to talk yet."

Kasami snorted. "So, if they haven't made a decision, why are you worried?"

"Because what I suspect is that Kenzō will be making a recommendation that I be entangled in matrimony." Shin frowned. From the look on her face, he could tell his suspicions were correct. "Let me guess, he wanted you to convince me this was the wisest course of action."

"I believe he is correct." She paused, and he could see that there was something she wasn't saying. "I believe it is what you must do."

Shin frowned. This was a complication he could have done without. But there was little he could do. Even avoiding Kenzō would only delay the matter a short time. He was barely listening as Kasami continued.

"You… endanger yourself with your antics. You amuse yourself at the expense of your reputation. If the Trading Council decides that you are… unsuitable, they might…" She trailed off, hesitating again. It was very unlike her, and it brought him back to himself.

"What? Dispatch me the way they did my predecessor?" He smiled mirthlessly at her expression. "Did you not think that had occurred to me as well? I have never ceased my investigation into that matter, nor do I intend to until I know for certain what happened to Lady Aika. Whether her death was truly misadventure, or... something else."

"Then you must know that the possibility exists," Kasami began. Shin cut her off.

"If it does, it is of no importance to me. I have chosen my life. It has not chosen me. That is how it shall remain, whatever my family insists." He took a deep breath. "Fine. You have made your sally and I have rebuffed it. Kenzō need never know. We shall take a trip. Yes, a trip. Somewhere fun. Perhaps we shall pay a visit to Batu and his new bride, or – yes, Lady Konomi offered me the use of her country estate. That will be perfect. He will never find us there. By the time he realizes we've ducked him, it'll be too late." He paused. She had an odd look on her face. "What?"

"He is coming here today. I told him you would be here."

Shin stared at her. "What?"

"In fact, he should be here any moment now," she continued.

"What?"

Kitano slid open the door and stepped into the room. "My lord, a visitor..."

Shin whipped around to look at Kitano. "What?" he said again. His faculties had deserted him, leaving him adrift in a morass of confusion.

"It's Lord Kenzō," Kitano continued.

Shin snapped back to himself and looked at Kasami. "Treachery," he said, in an empty voice. He'd never imagined that she might do this to him.

She didn't flinch. "I am here to protect you. Even from yourself." She pushed herself to her feet and looked down at him. Her expression softened. "Would it be so bad?"

Shin didn't immediately reply. "We've had this conversation before, as I recall."

"Yes, and you had no good answer then either."

Shin rose, the picture of injured dignity. "We will discuss this later."

"Just hear him out." She hesitated. "For my sake, if no other reason."

Shin sighed. "I never imagined you for a dirty fighter, Kasami."

She forced a smile. "I am a Hiramori. It is what we do."

Shin chuckled. "Very well. I will hear him out. But I make no promises." He gestured to Kitano. "Show him in, Kitano. Let's get this farce over with."

Kenzō was already downstairs when Shin and Kasami arrived. He sat promptly when Shin indicated the mat across from his own. "I am told the Akodo wedding went well, my lord. No doubt due to your efforts, I am sure."

Once again, Shin could not help but marvel at how Kenzō could say something flattering and make it sound insulting at the same time. "Yes, well, let us hope," Shin said. "Kasami tells me you were of great help in her efforts." He cast a quick glare at Kasami, who was seated in the corner of the room. "I must say I am somewhat surprised to hear it."

Kitano carefully laid out tea and then hastily departed. Kenzō eyed it warily. "I'm surprised she mentioned it."

"Why?"

Kenzō flicked a finger dismissively. "It was of no import. I did nothing, merely observed Lady Kasami at her duties."

"Why did you feel the need to do so?" Shin poured the tea,

serving Kenzō before himself. A moderate show of respect, and one that seemed to surprise his guest. Kenzō shot a glance at Kasami, as if wondering whether she was responsible for this change of attitude.

"Curiosity." Kenzō sipped his tea.

"I assume that curiosity is now assuaged and you will be returning home."

"Yes. In a few weeks."

"A few weeks?" Shin asked, suddenly alert. Another glance at Kasami, but she looked as puzzled as he felt. What was left for Kenzō to do?

"I must talk with a few more people." Kenzō paused. "But I can say that I have all but made my conclusions."

"And might I ask what those conclusions are?"

Kenzō paused again. "You are a... risk, my lord. A financial and social disaster waiting to happen. You lack tempering."

Shin sat back, feeling somewhat insulted. "Tempering," he repeated. Familiar words. Painfully familiar. He wondered, not for the first time, if Kenzō was working with his grandfather. That boded ill for his chances of squirming out of this particular predicament.

Kenzō nodded. "The best way to accomplish this is also the easiest. I will be recommending to my superiors – and yours – that you be married. As soon as possible."

"Married," Shin said. There it was. Despite expecting it, he still felt as if a hollow pit had opened beneath him. It was as if every evil portent he'd feared had come true. He cleared his throat. "Any idea as to whom?"

Kenzō set his tea down. "I am sure I do not know. I assume your family will make the arrangements. No doubt a worthy candidate will be found." He hesitated. "A husband or a wife will do you good, my lord. Matrimony has a settling effect on even the wildest spirit, I'm told, ensuring that your risky behavior is moderated." He smiled. "Let me be the first to extend my congratulations."

"Thank you," Shin said, his voice cracking despite his best efforts. He swallowed, or tried to. It felt as if there was a lump of lead in his stomach.

Married.

Daidoji Shin, married. Inconceivable. Impossible.

Imminent.

He forced a weak smile and sipped his tea.

"How exciting."

CAST LIST

CRANE

Daidoji Shin – *nobleman and amateur detective*
Hiramori Kasami – *bodyguard in service to Daidoji Shin*
Junichi Kenzō – *nobleman and auditor for
the Daidoji Trading Council*
Kitano Daichi – *gambler and manservant to Daidoji Shin*

LION

Akodo Minami – *noblewoman and
garrison commander; client*
Itagawa Yoku – *bodyguard in service to Akodo Minami*
Itagawa Kanna – *noblewoman; step-mother of Mosu*
Itagawa Mosu – *long-lost nobleman; samurai and survivor*
Jiro – *servant of Mosu; thought to be dead*
Ichime Kazuya – *nobleman; grandfather to Asahi*
Ichime Asahi – *nobleman; suitor to Moriko*
Seizuka Omo – *nobleman; suitor to Moriko*
Akodo Moriko – *noblewoman & younger
cousin of Akodo Minami*
Akodo Ai – *noblewoman; mother of Moriko*
Kitsu Touma – *priest tasked with performing the marriage*

OTHER

Iuchi Konomi – *Unicorn noblewoman and patron of the arts*
Shika Akari – *Deer Clan matchmaker; suspect*
Ito – *merchant and spy*
Lun – *captain and former pirate*

ABOUT THE AUTHOR

JOSH REYNOLDS is a writer, editor and semi-professional monster movie enthusiast. He has been a professional author since 2007, writing over thirty novels and numerous short stories, including *Arkham Horror, Warhammer: Age of Sigmar, Warhammer 40,000,* and the occasional audio script. He grew up in South Carolina and now lives in Sheffield, UK.

joshuamreynolds.co.uk
twitter.com/jmreynolds

Adventures in Rokugan

EXPERIENCE THRILLING ADVENTURES IN ROKUGAN LIKE NEVER BEFORE!

Adventures in Rokugan brings the famous setting of *Legend of the Five Rings* to the ever-popular ruleset of the 5th Edition SRD.

Alongside a new focus on vanquishing monsters, undertaking quests, and fighting for love or survival, *Adventures in Rokugan* promises to provide something for all fans of Rokugan.

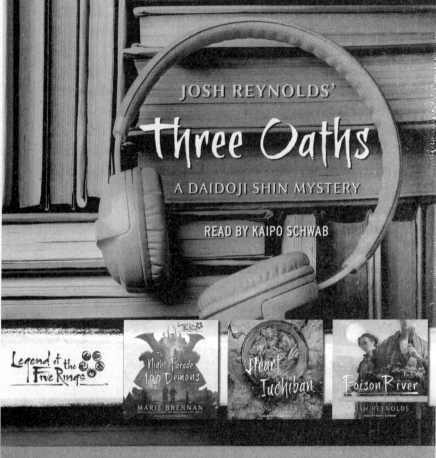